The Winged Child

Jessie Kimball

PublishAmerica
Baltimore

ISBN: 1-4241-5713-7
PUBLISHED BY PUBLISHAMERICA, LLLP
www.publishamerica.com
Baltimore

Printed in the United States of America

I would like to dedicate my book to David and Angela,
my angels in Heaven.

To Cooper & Irene

Janie Kimball

INTRODUCTION

How dear to our hearts are the tales of the "Gay Nineties."
The elite dined on plover, champagne, and fresh terrapin.
Everything was gilded from a saucepan to a soul. The wealthy lived in castles with gable and turret. Those days of romance were unequaled in France, so we are told. A prince of a fellow decked out his princess in Empress jewels as a sign of his wealth and success.

Fathers built ballrooms for their daughters to capture princes and dukes.

An invitation to one of "Diamond Jim" Brady's dinners was for the crème de la crème; seventeen courses in all. The prodigal Lillian was copied by women, as fast as they dared. Although the railroads were fraudulent and Wall Street in crash, toasts were drunk with champagne and everyone laughed. "Panic, begone!"

My heroine, Joanna, is born into this environment. She is the youngest daughter of Andrew Holan, a powerful, arrogant attorney and investor. Joanna finds life full of a darker truth under the dazzling splendor of this era...a woman could only live through a man! She experiences great wealth, great grief and great poverty. She is swept from the elite society of New York to the harsh environments of the West.

My story evokes a grand passion for living as the characters contend with the reality of true love and the vanishing innocence of the Fabulous Nineties. Historical events are interwoven with the prejudices of that time. Joanna defies social convention as she becomes a woman of fierce independence. It is a time we can only imagine...when a woman was pedestaled in some circles and stepped on in others.

PROLOGUE

First, we drink;
Then we eat
If we're still upon our feet.
—"Uncle Billy" Fitzhugh.

The Gay Nineties 1890-1900...

This was an age of fabulous years, so we are told! The waltz was divine and they danced til dawn after dining on plover, terrapin, and champagne. Everything was gilded from saucepans to ladies. Seventeen course dinners were served on platters of gold; black pearls in oysters, diamonds given as dinner mementos and cigarettes were rolled in *thousand grand* bills.

Though the Market would go bust and recover; the joys were in excess. They laughed. "Panic Begone!"

"Ah, Fate!" we say, "to have lived in those grand days!"

The American girl of the 1890s was idealized by sketches of Charles Dana Gibson. Women were referred to as *American Beauties* or *Gibson Girls* and then pedestaled from worshiping men. Unchaste women were referred to as airy and fairy. Divorce was déclassé. It was whispering disgrace!

Dwellings were castles with gables and turrets. Beauties rode on bicycles with golden wheels studded with diamonds.

Financial crisis brought foreclosure of mortgages, destitution for many farmers, fall of wages and strikes in 1893. Some were affected and some not at all.

My story relates about the pomp, as well as the poverty. Beauteous Joanna Holan experienced both. She was born into upper crust society with a background of platinum assets. The struggle within her family trailed a cloud of scandal when the market crashed and railroads went fraudulent. She was overcome by a great sense of shock and bewilderment when her family became socially unacceptable. Joanna's search for knowledge was not to be repressed. Her warmth, beauty, and brilliance will keep you spellbound as she travels the unknown.

An American Toast circa 1893/1894
I'll toast America's daughters—
let's all fill their glasses-
Whose beauty and virtue
The whole world surpasses;
May blessings attend them,
Go where they will,
And foul fall the man
That should offer them ill.

BOOK ONE

CHAPTER ONE

Joanna was experiencing an awakening deep within her. What an exciting discovery to realize that she was pretty and had a charm that made people very attentive to her. She turned slowly and flirted with her image in the ornate cheval mirror. She hesitated and peered intently into the silvered glass. A tall beautifully formed girl stared back with a mass of burnished curls framing her face and dazzling eyes the color of amethysts.

She sighed. She would never become the beauty her sister was. Sometimes it hurt to look at Elyce, so elegantly graceful, that lovely oval face with its deep blue eyes and that glistening silvery blond hair carefully parted in the middle. Elyce was so wonderfully put together everyone was in awe of her.

Perhaps, Joanna thought, *I will meet someone at Elyce's coming out.* Lately she dreamed often of meeting her one true love. An unexpected knock at the chamber door startled her.

"Yes," she called, "come."

Her maid peered around the door. "Miss Joanna, Madame wishes to see you in her sitting room."

"Thank you, Annie. Please tell her I will be there in a moment."

Stepping into delicate leather slippers, she brushed her hair and smoothed her skirts, Mama never wanted to see her looking anything less than a lady. She kicked the train of her skirt aside and walked briskly down the long carpeted hall.

The dressmaker was adding the last touches to her sister's dress as she entered. The gown was a masterpiece with layers of embroidered white lace sparked with pearls and crystal.

"Oh, it is perfection. Slip it off, Elyce," said Caroline Holan as she hovered over the dress, fluffing out the enormous skirting, "I am well-pleased with the results of your alterations, Mrs. Hoffman. It would have been disastrous had the gown not fit. Imagine, having a Worth and not being able to wear it. Even worse," she sniffed, "Elyce not having a Haute Couture costume to wear at her debut!"

Then with obvious relief she sat down and poured herself a cup of tea. Caroline had made a recent journey with her dear friend, Lady Griffin, to Europe. She had been in utter despair when both daughters had become ill with influenza just days before sailing. Having been assured by the doctor they were out of danger and in good hands, she made the crossing without them. Measurements in hand, she had spent three consecutive weeks shopping in Paris and had gowns made for the girls and herself at the houses of Doucet and Charles Worth.

"Elyce, darling, it is unfortunate that your illness caused you to lose weight and especially at a time like this! Ah well, you will still be my beautiful girl," stated Caroline.

She then turned to Joanna. "Dear, slip on your gown for alterations." She watched Joanna's dress being lowered over her head and was taken aback by the beautiful young woman before her. She had been so involved with her many engagements and the plans for the ball she failed to notice her baby blossoming into a swan. The champagne chiffon gown was accordion pleated with satin inserts and a wide satin sash. The color brought out the auburn fire in Joanna's hair and made her violet eyes glow.

"Why, Joanna, you have become a young lady overnight. Stars, you will bear more watching than Elyce!"

Joanna stared at the carpet with cheeks burning. "Oh, Mama, don't take on so. I am so excited for Elyce, I only want her ball to be a huge success."

"It will be. Papa will see to it every lady's dance program is filled and I have invited two gentlemen for every lady. That will certainly make everything go off well," laughed Caroline, "Even the oldest Dames will dance the night away!"

"Oh, Mama," laughed Elyce, "You are a caution!"

"Saints preserve us! The ball is less than two weeks away. There are not enough hours in the day with the planning plus luncheons and dinners; I am forever changing costumes and rushing thither and yon." She rose and opened double doors into her large wardrobe. "Mignon, I need you for a moment."

Caroline Holan's wardrobe was so extensive her Dresser kept an inventory of both her attire and of her magnificent jewels encased in commodes with drawers lined in velvet.

"Yes, Madame," answered the comely little French woman, coming in from the large room.

"I will need some jewelry, preferably pearls for this costume Joanna is wearing." Mignon carefully laid out two drawers of pearl necklaces in various colors of pink, cream, grey and black. Caroline picked one strand of perfect lustrous cream pearls.

"There, dear, these will do nicely with ear drops," she stated as she fastened the necklace about Joanna's throat.

"Thank you, Mama, they glow like small moons!" exclaimed a delighted Joanna.

"Yes, they are exquisite, but then, only the best in Holan House!"

Caroline Anna Holan had few saintly qualities, she was what her world was; its morals hypocritical and as fake as the wasp waist and bustle. She was born to her role, a perfect hostess and a woman of charm and energy. She had a dazzling smile and large luminous eyes fashionably enhanced by belladonna.

Holan House was a showcase rather than a home and Caroline felt blessed she had two lovely daughters to grace the impressive mansion. She and her husband entertained frequently and held many social functions in the six-story masonry located in fashionable Madison Square in New York City. The Holan social standing was of the utmost importance. Elyce's coming out ball was to be held in the massive ballroom on the first floor and it was being flawlessly planned. It must be absolutely perfect.

The mansion was a blur of activity, the servants were well instructed in their duties and expected to carry them out faultlessly. Florists and caterers conferred with Caroline on a daily basis while the servants were polishing and cleaning each and every object in sight.

Andrew Holan, the master of the house, spent many hours at one or another of the prestigious men's clubs in Manhattan. It was said more business deals were finalized over a good glass of sherry at the club than in the office. He was an attorney, art collector and speculator who made and lost millions.

Caroline was becoming harried as the weekend drew to a close and suggested over dinner that Andrew take his daughters for an outing.

"Splendid, we will attend a match of baseball tomorrow," was his reply.

"Oh, thank you, Papa. It has been ever so long since we have gone with you," exclaimed Joanna, her eyes sparkling.

"Oh, Andrew, you know I find the game vulgar and unbecoming a lady. Really, it is just a passing fancy and it will never become popular," sniffed Caroline. "Why not a day at the park with the girls?"

"Oh, Mama, it is such fun to watch. We will conduct ourselves in proper fashion, I promise you!" Elyce excitedly retorted.

"Humph, how can one be proper sitting in the dust? Take gloves and your parasols and do not let one ray of sun touch your complexions," Caroline admonished.

Turning to Andrew she pleaded, "Dear, please don't allow them to shout like barbarians, either."

"Caroline, they will be my perfect girls. Stop fussing; we are Holans. Whatever we do, people mimic, thinking it is the latest fashion."

"Nevertheless, our social standing must always be uppermost in our minds. Our daughters must wed well."

"Fiddlesticks, look at our beauties, they can have their pick here and abroad!"

"So you say."

Andrew had a hawk nose prominent over an impressive moustache and at present that moustache was twitching with annoyance. His blue eyes that generally glittered with a fierce zest for living, were narrowed like steel slits. "Must we find fault with everything that is not in a Tiffany setting, Caroline?"

"Good Lord, Andrew, my daughters are as precious as any jewels!"

Joanna was becoming uneasy. Papa was not home that often and he and Mama were always at odds lately. "May I be excused?" she asked and headed up to her room.

Elyce came up shortly after and they sat and talked of the situation between their parents.

"Whatever is the matter with them, they are barely civil to each other?" asked Joanna.

"Darling, they have little in common," answered Elyce. "You know that Papa's passions are women, horse racing, and the theater."

"Don't say such things about Papa. He adores Mama!"

"I sometimes wonder as he finances careers of so many artists and singers…being especially generous if they are female and comely."

"Elyce, Papa is just kindly, he likes to help the disadvantaged and I think that is commendable. I find it embarrassing to hear you talk of such things."

Elyce stood and walked to a window seemingly in deep thought. She turned and crossed the room to sit in a cushioned chair opposite Joanna. She stared intently at Joanna and took one of her hands in hers. "You read the gossip columns as I do so you must see Papa's name mentioned often with women. That is why we must heed Mama's words of advice so we shall never find our names mentioned there."

"Oh, how boring! One must never allow any intimacies such as kisses or embraces and one must keep herself 'pure' before marriage for gentlemen do not marry common girls!" aped Joanna in her mother's voice.

"For shame, Joanna, unwanted babies are a fate worse than death and Mama says babies are implicit with intimacies!" scolded Elyce, her blue eyes flashing.

"Hmm, did she elaborate on what these intimacies are? Do you know?" Joanna's tone was deliberately mocking.

"No, I only know that most men are predatory and prey on un-chaperoned girls. That is why we can never, ever venture outside without Mama, Papa, or our governess."

Joanna shrugged. "I want to be kissed and embraced; I so want to enjoy being a woman and finding my true love!"

Elyce grimaced. "You must never let a man offend your maidenly sensibilities in such a crude fashion."

"Oh, Elyce, please, how about your Mr. Marshall Davenport? You seem to be so gone on him. Wouldn't you like to kiss him?"

Elyce smothered a smile and blushed prettily. "I must admit I dream about it."

Joanna laughed aloud and did a little jig, "There, you see, it is a natural thing to want to do if you care for someone. I cannot see how one little kiss can make one common."

"It is not just one kiss, Joanna. It is given as a token of deepest love when you are spoken for."

"Pooh," said Joanna, changing the subject, "let's decide on what we will wear to the baseball match tomorrow. I just adore watching the players, they are so handsome and muscular! I so wish I could find someone to sweep me off my feet."

"Joanna, Papa would not be impressed to hear you talk like that. He would never allow us to attend again. These young men are not of our social class."

"You must admit, it is exciting."

"Yes, it is."

The next day the girls sat demurely in afternoon frocks of poplin with matching parasols covering their faces. They had an excellent view from their father's private box.

The teams of the National League were matched against the American Association of Baseball. Their father had told them a man named Abner Doubleday was credited with inventing the game at Cooperstown, New York. Although it was a gentleman's game with no commercialism, there were wagers made against each team. The players were very colorful, dressed in striped caps, colored suspenders, large bow ties under chins, and bibs emblazoned with large letters depicting the teams. Their stockings were distinctive; all white for the Chicago White Stockings and red striped for the Cincinnati Red Stockings. The muscular players were warming up, swinging their bats and strutting up and down before the boxes. Women could be heard murmuring as they flirted coyly with the players.

Then the exciting call, "Striker to the line!" and a player strode from the Mule Bench to the plate. The crowd was hushed during the pitches and when the ball was struck, there were hurrahs and shouts of, "Well struck!" followed by calls of, "Leg it, leg it, leg it!" as the player rounded the bases. When the striker made a score there was a loud ringing of the bell on the scorer's table.

It was an exciting game and the White Stockings won, much to Andrew's delight. He had wagered large bets on the team.

"My, I have never seen such strutting except at a horse race. These players are magnificent, really!" Joanna said as she gazed with interest at the winning team.

"I did enjoy the match and I know Papa did. He was off in a hurry to collect his winnings," laughed Elyce.

A player suddenly leaned over the box and twitched a magnificent mustache at them. He then lifted his striped cap and smiled broadly, "My ladies, did you enjoy the match?"

"Ever so much!" answered Joanna with a smile.

"Are you unescorted? Would you like to have dinner with me at the Club House?" he inquired.

"Oh, gracious, no. Our father is with us and we are leaving shortly," answered Elyce nervously.

"Thank you for asking, that was very kind of you, sir," added Joanna, still smiling prettily.

The player laughed and winked at Joanna then walked cockily away.

"Joanna, how could you encourage him?" asked Elyce crossly.

"Pshaw! I never encouraged him, he was rather handsome."

"Thank heavens, here comes Papa," uttered a relieved Elyce.

"Did my pets enjoy the match?" asked Andrew, his blue eyes twinkling happily.

"Yes, thank you, Papa. It was wonderful!" exclaimed Joanna, sighing.

"It was exciting," Elyce added as they exited the box.

CHAPTER TWO

The day before the ball was a blur of activity. In the afternoon both girls were to nap, but Joanna was too excited. Finally the hour came to dress. Joanna with the help of her maid was struggling into an elaborate corset. Annie pulled the laces to achieve the wasp waist, arched back figure so desired.

"*Eeee*, not so tight, Annie, I cannot breathe and it is crushing my ribs!" panted Joanna as she clung to a chair back. Annie eyed her mistress with sympathy and released the laces a bit. Once Joanna's breath had returned, Annie knelt to slip satin slippers on the long legs encased in white silk hose. Joanna's dress flowed over her leaving her elegant shoulders and neck gleaming above her well defined bust. The tight lacing caused an artificial enlargement of the bust which created the extreme decolletage so fashionable. The finishing touches included having the hairdresser arrange her hair and Annie clasping the necklace of pearls around her neck. Joanna picked up her kid gloves and fan, "I believe I am ready."

"Oh, Miss Joanna, you will be the envy of every woman at the ball," Annie said admiringly.

At that moment the chamber door opened and Elyce rustled in, a vision in white and silver.

"Oh, darling, you look like a princess!" Joanna exclaimed.

Elyce was in rapture, also. "See what dear Papa and Mama gave me for this night," she said, putting a hand to her throat where sparkled a necklace of diamonds and pearls.

"It is exquisite, and perfect with your costume."

"Oh, Elyce, just think, after tonight you will have no more governesses, no more rigid rules about bedtime, the world is your oyster. All doors will be open to romance and adventure! Oh, I can hardly wait until my time comes!" sighed Joanna.

"Oh, do compose yourself, dear. I feel like one of Papa's prized mares being put on display," laughed Elyce, her blue eyes sparkling. "I just hope Mr. Davenport will make his intentions known soon."

"You really care for him, don't you?" asked Joanna with a sinking heart. Elyce sighed. "I adore him, and he is the moon and stars to me."

Joanna's face clouded for just a moment. She loathed Marshall Davenport and secretly hoped her dearest sister would find someone more suitable.

They joined their parents in the ballroom. The event was everything Joanna had hoped for. Elyce, Caroline, Joanna and two of Elyce's closest friends received in the gold and white ballroom against a wall of gardenias and roses. Enormous crystal chandeliers glittered in the reflected light of a hundred flickering candles. The parquet ballroom floor was waxed to perfection and dusted with a fine layer of French chalk. Huge ferns and vases of flowers graced corners and garlands of roses and gardenias were looped along walls and marble pillars. Musicians played in a cluster of palms on the balcony. In alcoves buffet tables adorned with carved ice dolphins and swans groaned under cornucopias filled with black caviar. Silver platters held seafood meats, salads, croquettes, and soufflés. Compotes were heaped with ices, cheese straws, eclairs, russets, bonbons nuts, meringues and cakes. A six foot champagne fountain danced like a cascade of gold, and dozens of white gloved waiters lined the wall ready to serve.

The parents and chaperones were being seated in cushioned chairs and settees scattered about the perimeter of the dance floor. The air crackled with excitement and jewels and gowns sparkled in the candlelight. The Page held up the first dance program and the ball began.

Elyce, being the debutante, danced every dance, returning to receive during the intervals. The first hour, Joanna and the two friends helped welcome guests. Caroline, as hostess, would remain for another half hour to receive any late arrivals. She was resplendent in a pink and gold brocaded satin gown with drapes of pearls caught to a stomacher of diamonds. A tiara of diamonds spiked with pearls sat on her perfectly coifed head.

Joanna was excused from receiving and went to rest her feet. She sat conversing with a much bejeweled dowager when Marshall Davenport approached. He was the son of a wealthy railroad baron, tall, blue eyed; a trifle ferret faced with an enormous flared moustache waxed to needlepoint tips. He was a braggart and a charmer. Old and young ladies fell under his spell and his name appeared on every hostess's list. Joanna shuddered. Caroline adored him and Joanna loathed him.

Bowing to both women, he asked Joanna if her dance program was filled. To her chagrin she answered no and wrote his name in it with the tiny pencil attached.

"There," she said rudely, "it is for the next waltz."

His eyes raked over her lingering on her well defined bust. She opened her fan and turned back to the dowager.

"Until later, then, Miss Holan," said Marshall and, with a stiff bow to the dowager, turned away.

What a serpent, Joanna thought to herself and her shoulders shivered under her draped gown.

The music began and Joanna looked for her father and she saw him approaching, this was his dance. *My, he looks especially dashing,* Joanna mused.

Andrew was resplendent in his full dress coat and stiff linen all immaculately white. A bouquet of flowers attached to a lapel and delicate gray gloves completed the outfit.

"Oh, Papa, how handsome you are," exclaimed Joanna, her eyes gleaming as largely as the diamond in his bosomed shirt.

"Thank you, Puss. I must say, you look quite grown up this evening. Where did my little girl disappear to?" he asked, leading her to the dance floor.

"Oh, Papa, you tease, I am still Jo just dressed in all kinds of frills."

"You make my heart hurt to realize how old I am becoming; having such a beautiful young lady in my arms and knowing it is my baby rather rattles me." Andrew smiled fondly as he whirled her to the music.

The dance ended and as they moved off the floor, Joanna's heart stopped for a beat. Her eyes widened as a tall, handsome man watched them approach. He was blond, bronzed, clean shaven, nose long and straight; a smooth, firm chin and eyes a blending of gray and blue. Her father boomed, "Timber! How good to see you!"

The stranger answered, "And I you!"

Then, turning to Joanna, Andrew said, "Allow me to introduce my other daughter. Joanna, this is Timber Alexander, an old friend of Uncle John's and mine."

Joanna extended her gloved hand and breathlessly said, "I am delighted to make your acquaintance, Mr. Alexander."

The stranger bowed and raised her hand to his lips murmuring, "The pleasure is all mine, Miss Holan."

Oh, my, what a mouth and dimples, thought Joanna, her heart in her throat. Her father's voice brought her back to reality.

"Timber is a surveyor working out West. He has done a lot of work for John when he is not working for one of the rail companies."

Mr. Alexander asked to be added to her dance program and then, acknowledging the dowager and bowing to Joanna, both men moved off.

Joanna was immensely grateful for her fan and used it to cool her pink cheeks. Her knees felt like water. That Mr. Alexander had had an enormous effect on her!

The page was holding up the dance card number. She then saw Marshall threading his way through the throng to her. "I've come to claim my dance, lovely lady."

He guided her across the floor to the tune of an Austrian Waltz. The hand encircling her waist was gripping her very closely making it most uncomfortable. His hooded eyes were devouring her and he pressed her even closer which put her in an ungainly position, pushing her bosom tight against his chest.

She protested, "Sir, you are too bold!"

He immediately released her and whispered, "Ah, my dear Joanna, your charms are too much. I am besotted, I want to ravish you," then kissed her ear breathlessly.

Her back stiffened, her eyes sparked with fury. "Take me off the floor, sir, our dance is finished!"

He hesitated, and then glided her to the edge of the ballroom floor. "You have not seen the last of me," he said brusquely, his face dark.

She left him with cool dignity, oblivious of the tall young man coming toward her. Tears pricked her eyes as she bumped into a massive chest.

"Miss Holan, are you in distress?" asked a deep voice above her. It was Mr. Alexander.

"Oh, I am sorry," Joanna answered and retreated, then looked away in embarrassment.

"Can I be of assistance?" he asked.

Here seemed strength, power and concern and Joanna felt calmness settle over her. She turned, lifted her eyes and put a gloved hand on his arm. "It is nothing; you are very good, indeed, to be concerned. I'm afraid someone thought his excessive charm would encourage impropriety."

Timber Alexander smiled. "Well done, young lady. Would you care for a glass of punch to settle your nerves?"

"Indeed I would, thank you," replied Joanna as they made their way to one of the refreshment tables. She sipped her punch and once again thanked Mr. Alexander for his thoughtfulness.

"I was watching the dancers and I noticed that your partner's demeanor was not pleasing you. I was about to intervene when you left the floor," explained Timber.

"Dear me, I did not know it was so obvious. Mr. Davenport is a cad. I loathe him!" snapped Joanna, peering up at him through thick, dark lashes. "This is my first dance. Usually I am in the balcony with my grandmother or a chaperone. He's ruined my evening." Her voice quavered and her eyes sparkled with unshed tears.

Timber smiled despite himself. This lovely young girl had no inkling what a picture she made, her lovely pouting mouth looking as if it ached to be kissed and her fair face framed by a cascade of curls was indeed tempting. As she grew older she would be a stunner. He attempted to make her feel better by saying, "The evening is yet young. You'll have a capital time. Look over there." He nodded his head. "Now that unfortunate lady does have a problem!"

Joanna looked at whom he was referring to; Plump Margaret Howard was attempting to follow a little man who was hopping like a toad. It was pathetic and funny at the same time. She laughed outright and turned away. That put her at ease and she smiled when she saw Timber's gray eyes shining with delight.

He stated, "Miss Holan, my next dance is with your sister so I must take your leave. Promise me you will behave in my absence."

"Please, my name is Joanna and of course you are excused," answered Joanna, her eyes twinkling.

"And I, likewise, would appreciate your calling me Timber." Smiling, he took her hand. "I will look forward to my dance later."

Joanna watched his retreating figure and felt a glow from head to toe. He was just the handsomest man!

She enjoyed her other dance partners; they were rather witty and admiring. Joanna radiated charm and the gentlemen found her fascinating.

Timber Alexander finally returned and took her in his arms; it was a most animated dance. He commented how lovely Elyce was. Joanna nodded in agreement and breathlessly said, "I worry dreadfully about her, though, she imagines herself in love with Marshall Davenport."

"What?" Timber said and stopped dancing momentarily. "That ill-bred rake! Surely your parents disapprove?"

"My mother believes him to be a most eligible catch as he comes from a fashionable old family. Papa and his father belong to the same clubs so he is allowed to call on Elyce. I find him loathsome and his behavior offensive, but dear Elyce thinks him a romantic dashing figure. Oh, my, I shouldn't be discussing this," added Joanna, alarmed.

"I will not repeat a word," answered Timber thoughtfully.

It was breaking dawn when *Goodnight Ladies* played and the ball ended with the refrain *After the Ball Is Over*.

As the sun rose, Joanna, exhausted and delirious with happiness, fell into bed. She dreamt of the gallant gentleman who had come to her rescue.

The Holan family slept until afternoon and then had trays brought to their respective rooms. Elyce joined Joanna and they tittered and giggled over the ball until evening. Papa was not at dinner and their mother seemed distressed.

"Mama, is something wrong?" asked Elyce between courses.

"No, darlings," she answered, picking at her food. "I am just exhausted and had hoped your father would be here for dinner."

"He must have a business appointment," stated Joanna in defense of her father.

Caroline sighed. "But of course."

Joanna found herself yawning and then giggled as she saw Elyce doing the same behind her palm. Joanna was relieved when she could be excused and retire.

She was being shaken gently. "Miss Joanna, it is Annie. Please wake up."

"Is there a problem, Annie?"

"Your mother has summoned you and Miss Elyce to the Morning Room, Miss Joanna."

"Blast, I am barely awake. Is Elyce awake?"

"Yes, ma'am. She will be coming to your chamber when she is dressed."

Joanna rose groggily and with Annie's help did her toilette and dressed. Elyce knocked and entered the room. "Good morning, Jo, I wonder what this is about and at such an ungodly hour of the morning! It is barely past dawn."

"It must be important for Mama to be up so early," yawned Joanna. "She is never up before nine at the earliest."

Elyce sat down on a chaise and smoothed her hair. "I hope Mama is well. She seems dreadfully sad lately and I saw her weeping one day last week."

"Hmmm, well, Papa has been away on business or staying at the Club a lot. She probably is consumed with loneliness."

"Possibly…"

The girls left the room and walked the hallway. Before they reached the lower stairs, Joanna whispered, "I hope it is not something we have done to upset her."

Elyce whispered back, "It is probably Papa; he is having another flagrant affair. The magazines and the gossip sheets are brimming with Papa and that singer, Lottie Royal!"

"Really and truly?"

Continuing, Elyce whispered even more loudly, "The other evening, after leaving Delmonico's, he unhitched her horses, stepped in harness and drew her carriage down the avenue…the shame of it all!"

Joanna giggled, the notoriety and adventure made her father seem a most romantic figure. "Mercy, Elyce, he always makes grand gestures. He loves life, Mama used to be high spirited, too, but she never does anything dashing now."

"Pshaw, Jo, you are such a child!" snorted Elyce, then, shrugging her shoulders and holding her head high, she entered the Morning Room with Joanna at her heels.

Caroline was having breakfast at a wicker table that overlooked the terrace and gardens. The sisters took seats opposite her and waited with hands folded neatly in their laps. Caroline rang for the maid, then turned to the girls. Her eyes, usually so luminous, were very dull and her face had an unnatural paleness.

"Good morning, darlings." She smiled. "Flora, bring the girls whatever they wish for breakfast," she said to the maid.

Then her eyebrows went up and widening her eyes in astonishment, she said, "Heavens, Elyce, whatever have you done to your hair?"

Elyce patted her frizzed bangs and answered, "Lizette is going to oil the curl out, Mama. She got the new iron too hot."

Joanna, understanding at once how distressed her mother was, began to apologize for being late for their summons.

Caroline sighed. "I cannot keep a proper household anymore. My dears, I am angry and disturbed, but not at either of you. I have been so absorbed in my own affairs I have not been very considerate towards either of you. I do, however, have good news. We have received an invitation to Queensgate for Grandmother Kate's birthday celebration. Countess Dorothy Roberts is hosting a grand dinner and dance for her. It will be held next month on the evening of her natal day and we will travel by rail to Rochester. Now, we must make some arrangements for alterations on the other new gowns I purchased."

"Mama, will Papa be going with us?" asked Joanna.

"Heavens, I should hope so, this is being held in honor of his mother. She would never forgive him if he did otherwise," retorted Caroline peevishly.

JESSIE KIMBALL

The balance of the morning was spent over breakfast and planning wardrobes. By mid-afternoon Caroline and the girls were in the drawing room doing needlework when Andrew Holan entered the front portal. The girls ran into the reception hall to greet their father. They stood quietly while the butler helped him remove his outerwear and umbrella.

"What a picture you make, sweethearts," he said, beaming. The light flickering from the chandeliers made an aura about them. The wood lining the hall gleamed with a patina of age and set off a gathering of family portraits that frowned and smiled down at the lovely young women. He gathered them to him in a monstrous bear hug; he did so adore his daughters. "Let us go into the parlor. Where is Mama?"

"Waiting for you, Papa, as we all were," answered Elyce.

After dutifully kissing Caroline on the cheek, Andrew went to stand before the blazing fire. "It is cold for June, must be all the rain we are having," he remarked as he stared into the hearth, his expression a bit troubled. Elyce and Joanna sat on a sofa opposite him, their faces glowing. He turned and smiled and that smile transformed him into their handsome wonderful father. His blue eyes crinkled and his white teeth shone under his mustache.

"Well, sugars, I have something for you. It has been an especially good week for your papa so I can let you enjoy some of my good fortune." He slipped his hand beneath his vest coat and pulled out two blue velvet cases handing one to each daughter.

Joanna opened hers first and, with a happy shriek, rose and ran to her father. "Oh, Papa, how lovely. Thank you!"

Elyce did likewise. Nestled in the boxes were exquisite diamond hair clips.

Joanna's was star shaped and Elyce's in the shape of a crescent.

He laughed. "Never forget, you are the moon and the stars to me."

Seeing Caroline's disappointed look, he crossed to her and commented, "I haven't forgotten you, my dear. I will give it to you later." He kissed her on the tip of her nose and she turned away from him.

"We can wear these when we go to Gram's soiree, Papa, how perfect!" Joanna said.

"Grandmother's soiree? When is this, and why have I not been told?" he asked in an agitated voice.

"Mama just told us, Papa, you will have to ask her for the details," responded Joanna.

Andrew, his face set, turned to Caroline. "Well, what is this about, Caroline? When were you going to inform me!"

24

Caroline felt her throat constrict. Her hand tightened around the embroidery hoop she was holding. Andrew was a bear when he was agitated and the way his moustache was twitching was a bad sign. "Really, Andrew, I just got the invitation yesterday and you were not here. I did not feel it would be improper to tell the girls."

"I do not wish to learn of details like this from my daughters. You should have discussed this with me first. It is an issue of family principle. Am I not the head of this household?"

Trying to calm the situation, Caroline answered in a quiet voice, "Of course you are, Andrew. I assumed because this was being given in your mother's honor, we, of course, would attend. The girls must have gowns fitted and I must make proper arrangements for the journey."

"When is the date, how long must we be gone?" he asked abruptly.

On learning the details, he poured a brandy and pensively sipped it. "I do not know that I can get away then."

"Oh, Andrew, you must! Your mother would be devastated, not to mention it would shame her if you were not in attendance." Tears were shining in Caroline's eyes and she furiously blinked to keep them from falling.

Andrew answered firmly, "You can be quite certain, my dear, I will decide what is best. I have to consult my calendar and find if it is feasible. There is no reason why you and the girls cannot attend. Meanwhile I will make arrangements for our rail car to be at your disposal."

Setting down his goblet, he handed Caroline a large oblong velvet case. "I had intended to give you this at a happier occasion, but you will have use for it at Rochester." He then strode quickly out of the room.

Caroline gasped as she opened the case. An opulent *colliers de chien* of diamonds, sapphires and pearls lay glittering on the black velvet. She held the elaborate cascading collar to her throat as she beheld her image in one of the oblong mirrors. She smiled with delight; the collar emphasized her statuesque elegance. Andrew's attitude, at times was crushing, but his lavish gifts could certainly made one forget his small ways.

"Oh, Mama, it is a stunner! You will be the envy of everyone and it must have cost a fortune!" gushed Elyce. "I can hardly wait to become a hostess and have fine things."

"It looks heavy, but you wear it well, Mama," added Joanna.

"We must carry on our planning, best to retire to our rooms and I will send for the dressmaker."

Caroline's thoughts turned to herself and her role in upper class society. Her major concern now was clothes for Queensgate and making proper appearances for herself and her daughters.

CHAPTER THREE

Andrew, meanwhile, was pacing in his chamber. Another crash and the bottom had fallen out of the stock market. He was not completely ruined as he had invested in real estate and still had some gold and railroad stock. He had enough to keep him going, but on a much smaller scale. He had purchased the jewelry on a whim hoping it would bring luck. If not, it was an investment. He never discussed financial affairs with Caroline, as she had no mind for it. He was torn. He had bought a huge house for his paramour, Lottie, and must now tell her he could no longer afford it or her upkeep. She was one of the loveliest women he had ever known. He would miss her charms and that definitely made for a foul mood!

But Holan House was his first concern! He had all the latest conveniences installed; shower baths with solid marble tubs and gold taps, two lifts and electricity powered by a huge dynamo in the basement. He smiled as he thought of Caroline; she refused to use the lifts as she felt them unsafe. He had never refused her anything, even her great extravagance in decorating, and she had done so with a good eye. The mansion was a showcase with rosewood, marqueterie, ebony, ormolu, Tiffany windows and lamps, carved marble fireplaces, Brussels carpets and walls hung with masters throughout. He had made a wise decision when asking Caroline to be his wife. She ran a flawless house, the servants were well instructed in their duties and expected to carry them out faultlessly. She insisted that they be scrupulously honest as they were exposed daily to priceless temptations. She had taught the girls at an early age they were not to confide or discuss family affairs with any of the servants. There was a definite barrier between servant and superior in Holan House. It made Andrew uncomfortable, but he was always courteous and considerate while Caroline at times was haughty and arrogant. In this, Andrew insisted that his daughters follow his example; he disliked vain and unkind children.

Oh, how he adored his daughters! Elyce, his cool beauty and Joanna, his fiery baby...no, no longer a babe! Joanna was almost seventeen and

27

blossoming into a great beauty, also. She would be making her debut next year.

He began to pace again. His investments must begin to turn around or he could find himself in a drastic state financially.

The following weeks were busy ones for Joanna and Elyce. Joanna looked forward to visiting her beloved Grandmother. Joanna could confide in her and knew she was caring and sensible. Mostly, she wanted to tell her Grandmother about Marshall Davenport and hoped that she could instill some sense into Elyce. Each time Joanna tried to discourage Elyce about him she would become hostile. Marshall had been calling regularly bringing flowers and extravagant gifts.

One afternoon when the girls were in the drawing room, the butler announced Marshall and gave Elyce his calling card on a small silver tray.

"Oh, do show him in," Elyce said, rising excitedly patting her dress and her hair.

Joanna rose as he entered the room.

He carried a nosegay and a box for Elyce. He leaned over her and whispered into her ear. Joanna saw her flush and purse her lips together as she accepted his gifts. He turned to Joanna and bowed, "Miss Joanna."

Joanna nodded, but said nothing. She sat down and began to read a book. She so wished she could leave the room, but it would be rude and improper to leave Elyce alone with him. They talked in low voices, and then she overheard Marshall, "Don't be so thorny."

"Oh, where are you going?" Elyce cried as he rose.

"To the devil if you persist!" he answered angrily.

Elyce burst into tears and fled the room.

Joanna rose and said coldly, "I will see you to the door, sir."

"You do that," came the answer and Joanna's heart stood still as he swung around facing her. As he walked over to her, he leaned his face down close to hers, "I will taste your secrets someday, my sweet, I promise!"

"You are despicable, take your leave, sir, or I will call for help," she snapped.

She stood trembling as the front portal slammed. Then Cecil, the butler, came into the room. "Are you all right, Miss Joanna?"

"Yes, thanks, Cecil," she answered. Composing herself, she hurried upstairs to Elyce. She was lying face down on the bed and sobs shook her shoulders. Joanna sat down beside her. "Dearest sister, I am here."

Elyce sat up and tears streamed down her lovely face. She held out her hand to Joanna who asked, "Tell me what has happened to upset you so, if that scoundrel has hurt you."

"Oh, Jo, I love him desperately!" and down went Elyce's face into a handkerchief and now she cried despairingly.

Joanna hugged her sister to her. "I don't believe he is right for you, Elyce. There are so many others that care for you, good sensible gentlemen."

"I don't care; I cannot love anyone else, ever!"

"What has he done to upset you so?"

"He teases me by not proposing; he wants to keep company, but says he is not ready to commit himself." There was quiver in Elyce's voice and she wiped her red nose. "What's to become of me? I would die for him; I shall never marry anyone else!"

For a moment Joanna thought of telling Elyce what her true feelings were about Marshall, but decided to go to Caroline instead.

"Dry your eyes. They are all puffy. Tomorrow is Sunday and you will see Marshall at church. Perk up, I must go, I have some things I must attend to."

"I am better, Jo. Truly I am. Go, now I am being childish."

Joanna kissed Elyce's cheek and left the room. She was full of sympathy for her sister, but secretly hoped something would change her feelings for that rogue. Somehow, she resolved, she must get Elyce out of harm's way.

Joanna hurried to her mother's suite and knocked on the door. A maid answered. Joanna asked to speak with her mother. She was ushered in. Caroline was seated at her dressing table. "I was just finishing my toilette, sit down, dear. What can I help you with?"

"Mama, I am concerned about Elyce. She is so in love with Marshall and he is making her miserable."

"Why?" asked Caroline, turning from her dressing table to face Joanna. "Has Elyce done something to upset Marshall?"

"Mama! She is desperately in love with him! He is dreadful, he is a cad and he flirts with everyone."

"Joanna, watch your tongue! Pray tell what he has done to you to carry on so?"

"He held me fast tight at the ball and he whispered things to me."

Caroline's face paled and her eyes went wide with astonishment. "Oh, do cease, I will hear no more! Marshall is third generation Davenport. He is considered the most eligible of bachelors. He may have his faults, but you must learn to overlook them, remember your own. I know he is a fiery young man, highly romantic and impulsive. Has he not been extravagant to Elyce?

I am certain his intentions are honorable. You are still young, Joanna. One must never forget that how important it is to marry well. One must find a gentleman socially acceptable and well endowed financially to provide all the necessities in life.

"If a gentleman is indiscreet, a wife must ignore it for there might be extenuating circumstances. If Marshall flirts with you, be certain you do nothing to encourage it."

"Horses, Mother, horses!" cried Joanna.

"What did you say?" screamed Caroline.

"I said horses! Grandmother says horses! If you think I would ever encourage such an ass as Marshall Davenport…oh, perish the thought! You are impossible!"

"Well, I never…"

Joanna slammed out of the chamber her skirts swirling. She would never understand Mama who cared for material things so much more than her own daughters.

Dinner that evening was a quiet affair. It was a simple menu of six courses: broiled oysters, lamb chops, omelet soufflé with Virginia ham, fish mayonnaise in cases, plover, celery salad, Charlotte Russe, ices, cheese, and crackers.

Andrew and Caroline made polite conversation.

"Elyce, you have hardly touched a morsel, are you not feeling well?" asked Caroline.

"I am fine, Mama, just a bit tired," answered Elyce, keeping her eyes downcast.

"Are you having a caller this evening?"

"No, Mama, Marshall and I had a misunderstanding this afternoon."

"Oh, dear, well, watch yourself, darling. Guard against the little piques, be the first to ask pardon if there are hasty words."

Joanna snorted, "This is so trying, I would never be the first to say forgive me, especially if a person had been cruel to me!"

"Andrew, I want you to speak to Joanna. She has been insulting and used profanity to me today. I will not tolerate it!" retorted Caroline loudly.

"Well, young lady, I will see you in my study after dinner. We will try to clear up this misunderstanding," answered Andrew soberly.

He could not imagine Joanna behaving that badly. He looked at her intently, her violet eyes were sparkling with angry unshed tears and her lower lip was quivering. He ached to comfort her, knowing full well that Caroline was incapable of being a loving parent.

Dinner was agonizing for Joanna. Her mother was such a disappointment to her. Her attitude was that of other matrons, but Joanna knew she had more than feathers for brains and intended to use them. It was not her desire in life to sit and languish in beautiful clothing and jewels.

When she was summoned to the study she felt like the most misunderstood person in the world. Perhaps Papa would listen and care.

"Sit, Joanna. Now tell me what has happened and why you used profanity to your mother. I will first tell you this; under no circumstances will I allow you to be disrespectful to your mother, understood?" her father gruffly said.

Joanna explained her feelings about Marshall and Elyce. She told him of her visit with her mother and what she had said.

Her father was shocked into silence for a few minutes and stared at the ceiling. He looked at Joanna and asked where she had heard the profanity.

"Papa, Gram uses it often. I did not realize it was such an awful expression. I will apologize to Mama, but I strongly disagree with her attitude," answered Joanna.

Her father stood up and turned his back to her. Joanna then noticed his shoulders were shaking and he guffawed out loudly. After a few seconds, he asked, "Anything more you have to tell me?"

"No, Papa."

Andrew then turned around, still chuckling, and sat down. "My dearest child, you must understand a woman's lot in life is hard. That is one reason your mother and I want you girls to marry wisely. It is most important for you to have stability and security."

"But, Papa, to compromise oneself to marry a wealthy person of low moral character, is that wise?"

"You told me Elyce loves him. How would she be compromising herself? I do not feel love necessarily makes a good marriage, but it makes it easier to go down if there is feeling for each other. I do believe that parents should make decisions for their children's marriages as it will be in their best interest."

"Oh, Papa, I shall never marry if I do not love the person."

"I hope, Puss, for your sake you will find your Prince Charming. Now we must let matters take their course with Elyce. We shall pray that she will find happiness with or without Marshall."

"Yes, Papa, I will not interfere again."

Andrew came to Joanna and held her close. "Now you must apologize to your mother. I shall have a little talk with my mother about her use of words around my children. Please choose your expletives more carefully in the future, dear Jo."

"Thank you, Papa, for listening. It is frightening to grow up and make decisions. Being a child was such a secure world, now it is painful to become an adult," Joanna said very seriously.

Andrew kissed her on top of her nose saying, "You are excused. Go to your mama and all will be well with the world."

"I love you, Papa."

"And I you, dearest daughter."

CHAPTER FOUR

"Are you ready?" Elyce asked, cracking open the door to Joanna's chamber. Joanna checked her appearance in her gilt framed mirror. "I guess it will have to do," she was remarking on a pert straw perched on her head.

"Oh, you look remarkably well put together. Hurry, now, you know how Papa hates to be kept waiting."

The girls dashed down the stairs and out to the front lawn where Andrew stood beside an open carriage door. He handed them up and then drove off in the double team carriage. Caroline looked splendid in dahlia colored cashmere ornamented with Kensington embroidery; her stylish hat had a puffed crown with gold plumes curling over her chignon. Elyce was wearing a periwinkle blue faille and percale suit. A tri-corn blue straw with ribboned flowers perched smartly on her silvery blond hair.

Joanna, still in a misses costume, felt like a brown wren. She was attired in brown lightweight suiting with piping of white. Her ecru Tuscan straw was trimmed in brown velvet and feather pompons.

Sundays were quite like a fashion parade. The cream of the social elite belonged to the Anglican Church. Fathers aired the families in carriages and then grandly escorted them up the church steps and down the long aisle to the family pews.

Andrew was well pleased with how handsome his wife and daughters were. He felt remorse that his girls were becoming young women and he would lose them to another household in the near future. As he sat beside Joanna, he smiled; the girlish simplicity of her costume seemed to only enhance the maturing figure beneath it. She might become the real beauty of the family, but she would remain his *baby* forever. She turned and winked at him. He winked back his mustache twitching in delight. She was so like him in many ways. They shared strong wills, capricious moods, wit and vivacity. This formed a strong bond between father and daughter which Caroline and Elyce found unsettling.

Joanna was at her happiest seated with her family in this lovely Anglican Church. The ritual and the sacraments always moved her. An aroma told her

Papa was well perfumed with cloves, which meant he had been tippling before they left home. He often did this before church and Joanna worried if had a problem confronting the Lord.

Following the service, Andrew and Caroline engaged in conversation with the minister and members of the congregation. Marshall and his parents were in the crowd and approached.

Marshall tipped his hat then turned to Elyce. "Miss Holan, may I call this evening?"

Elyce grinned. "But of course you may, Mr. Davenport."

Joanna glared at him and a cold smile crossed his lips.

He whispered in Elyce's ear and she demurely smiled. As he turned away, Elyce said, "He wants to start anew and mend our differences."

Joanna bit her lip to keep from making a comment, but she thought to herself what an odious snob he was. That evening, the world tipped for Joanna.

Elyce burst into her room. "Jo, he has asked me! He is now speaking with Papa to plead his suit!"

Joanna gasped, "You mean he has proposed to you?"

"Oh, yes, my fondest wish has come true," responded Elyce, doing a little dance and hugging herself."

"You cannot be serious!"

"Oh, Jo, be happy for me, I love him and he loves me."

Despair washed over Joanna, she was losing her best friend, her dearest sister to that despicable man. She realized now Elyce would never give him up. Once the marriage contracts were arranged satisfactorily, their engagement would be announced.

"El, you know how I feel, I will not say another word about him," Joanna said solemnly. "Life will never be the same without you," she continued, with a little quiver in her voice.

"No one can come between us. I will love you always," responded Elyce.

"You are certain of his feeling for you?"

"Ah, he declared his love over and over." Color fused Elyce's cheeks and with a look of mingled joy and pride. "He tells me what an accomplished girl I am and that I will make a fine mistress for his home."

Then a tap on the door and a joyous Caroline swirled into the room. Grasping Elyce to her bosom she cried, "My darling, what wonderful news, how utterly divine this match is! A Davenport, so well established and a gentleman!"

"Oh, Mama, I forgot my beautiful ring!" exclaimed Elyce. She held up her left hand and a huge pigeon blood ruby encircled by diamonds flashed in the light.

"My stars, it is exquisite! Papa will contact our attorney tomorrow to draw up the contracts and terms of your dowry. We must also contact the church so the bans can be posted. I cannot imagine anything pleasing me more!"

"Oh, Mama, do you think the negotiations will take long?"

"No, darling, with both families approving the contracts, it should be settled quickly."

Caroline put a hand to her forehead and rolled her eyes. "Mercy, as soon as we return from Rochester, I must make arrangements for the announcement. We must make a crossing for your trousseau. Joanna, you will join us, I do not wish to leave you here alone."

Joanna's face sparked interest. She thought to herself, *Perhaps Elyce would meet someone new and give up that rake!*

The following weeks Andrew's presence was limited. He stayed at the Club more nights than home. Joanna missed her father and worried about him. He seemed not his old self lately.

CHAPTER FIVE

The morning of departure to Queensgate dawned early. The trunks, valises and other baggage were stacked in the hall. Andrew's private rail car had been added to the train. They were to leave Penn Station mid-morning. The three women were dressed in stylish traveling costumes; each carried a parasol and a small piece of hand luggage. A baggage coach followed their coach. Andrew was waiting at the Station; his handsome figure standing out amid the bustling crowd. He had decided only the week previous to travel with them for the celebration. Caroline had fretted for weeks and had been miserable; she had tried all her persuasive powers to make him commit to going with them.

One evening, he snapped at her, "Don't be wheedlesome, Caroline. I will have no more of it!" and slammed out the door.

Caroline had burst into tears and then secluded herself in her suite for days. When Andrew returned a few days later coldness settled over the house. There were more angry scenes between him and Caroline. Despite the wide rift in their marriage they tried to keep the situation submerged, especially from their daughters, who really were well aware of the situation.

More of Andrew's philandering had reached print. Elyce called Joanna's attention to an article in one of the papers that read: *MAN ABOUT TOWN Andrew Holan has been seen frequently at the Races, but it seems it isn't the racehorses he is taken with but a new little filly on his arm.*

Now as they approached, he dazzled them with his beautiful smile and held out gloved hands to embrace them. They followed him and settled into the plush rail car. The housemaid and butler began immediately arranging everything for their comfort.

Joanna removed her hat and jacket and leaned her head against the window as the train pulled away from the station. Once the billowing smoke began to clear she enjoyed the passing sights of the city. There were no problems of transportation; horse cars just needed some hay and a whip. She saw the new electric, a genuine sensation. One Sunday Papa had taken the family on this trolley car trip for a diversion. The trolley had garlands of lights, a band played in the rear, everyone sang songs; it had been a grand day. As the train slowly exited New York City, bicycles passed as did Victoria surreys, hansom cabs and riders on horseback. Ladies and gentlemen strolled the avenues arm in arm. As much as Joanna liked the city, she truly loved the green fields, tall trees and silvery streams and rivers they now began traveling through.

She thought of her beloved Grandmother Kate, who was really the model mother figure in Joanna and Elyce's lives. Summers were always a delight, whether spent at Queensgate or at the family seaside villa at Newport, as Kate was always in attendance. In a pretentious world where everything was gilded from saucepan to chamber pot, she taught them about the reality of life. She believed that fresh air, milk and vigorous baths made strong women. While Caroline believed that jewels made the woman, Kate would often remark, "Jewels cannot compare with white teeth, finely kept nails, clean scalp and well brushed hair." She taught the girls to play croquet, Roque, and lawn tennis. Last summer she had engaged a fencing instructor for them. Fencing had become a fad for the gentler sex to stimulate the circulation and Kate believed in exercise. They were quick to learn the foil positions of the sword, hand and body. In fact, both girls did so well, their French instructor entered them into "The Ladies Class" at the New York Fencer's Club. They became remarkably expert in the execution of thrusts, parries, and feints. Sadly, Caroline came to watch an exhibition and immediately made them discontinue. She was appalled at the stature of the women and declared it most unladylike. Often, when Caroline was busy elsewhere, Joanna and Elyce would grab closed umbrellas and go through the motions of fencing, giggling the whole time.

"Miss, would you like some refreshment?" asked the maid.

"If you would be so kind, a cup of tea," answered Joanna, still thinking of her Grandmother. Caroline had complained to Andrew after the fencing incident that Kate was turning the girls into tom boys.

"Curses, she is only making them aware of caring for their bodies, not filling their minds with silk and feathers!" was his reply.

Joanna felt her Grandmother was a bit of a health fanatic due to the sickly daughter in law, Daphne and her son, Wilfred, who lived at Queensgate. *Poor Uncle John*, thought Joanna. John Holan resembled his brother, Andrew, although a walrus mustache compensated for a more aquiline nose. John, being the eldest, had inherited the family fortune and estates. Queensgate, the family estate, was located on the outskirts of fashionable Rochester. The main house was a large Post Colonial with facades of Greek revival; it had thirty five rooms, twelve baths and nine fireplaces. Mother Katherine (Kate) Holan still lived on the estate surrounded by her Hepplewhite, Sheraton and American Empire furniture. The walls were hung with canvases of Rembrandt, Gainsborough, Tintaretto and other masters. Family portraits of Holans past looked down from walls throughout the massive house.

Living with Kate were John, Daphne and their twin children, Wilfred George and Winifred Avery. Daphne had a prolonged labor in birthing the twins. The first twin, Winifred was delivered eighteen hours before Wilfred, a breech birth. Daphne never fully recovered from her labor and endured a very languorous existence. Servants attended her every need. She was a small pale woman with a comely face. Kate ran Queensgate with a firm hand and oversaw the development and education of the twins. Wilfred, suffering from his difficult birth, never succeeded catching up with his sister in either stature or intelligence. It broke John Holan's heart and he turned his affections to Winifred indulging her every whim. Now, at fourteen, she was a pretty girl with flashing green eyes and much schooled having had four governesses. Her father bragged she was all fire and fury. She detested her sickly brother and mother and avoided them whenever possible.

Both Joanna and Elyce disliked their cousin, Winifred, who was always preoccupied making a great impression, pouting her lips, swirling her skirts and showing no passion but vanity. Joanna was not looking forward to being civil to her.

The trip was pleasant and on arrival in Rochester they transferred to carriages and made the short drive to Queensgate. The first glimpse of the big house made Joanna's eyes tear. Here so many pleasant memories had been made and she realized her childhood was now behind her, lost forever. As she alighted from the carriage, her beloved Grandmother was standing at the top of the landing smiling. She was a remarkable looking woman, soon to be sixty five. Her snow white hair was piled high on her head; her great wild eyes were still luminous and sparkling. Her dazzling smile, which Andrew had inherited, was illuminating a face nearly free of wrinkles.

"Oh, Gram," cried Joanna as she picked up her skirts and ran up the steps.

"Oh, my darlings, welcome welcome!" Kate said as she held Joanna tight in an embrace. "Are you fatigued from traveling? Oh, I have looked forward to your visit!" She turned to Caroline and Elyce and embraced them. Andrew then lifted her off her feet in a bear hug. "Put me down, you scoundrel!" she lovingly laughed. "Come, your rooms are ready. The maids will show you up."

Upon entering the foyer, they were greeted by Wilfred and Winifred. Wilfred was small, slightly built with a head too large for his body. His voice was guttural and he spoke as if his tongue was too large for his mouth. There were wisps of pink hair around his ears and his pallor was the color of flour. He had lovely expressive Cornish blue eyes that twinkled happily. Winifred, taller by two heads over her twin, was elegantly dressed for one so young. Wilfred laughed and clapped his hands in excitement. Winifred, on the other hand, clearly accustomed to her father's admiration, stood like a queen in state. Her glittering eyes showed no emotion, they were almost menacing. "Ah, you have finally arrived, did you have a good journey, Aunt Caroline?" she asked, ignoring the sisters. She did not smile and there was no welcome in her face.

"Quite good," answered Caroline.

Joanna stepped forward, "Winnie, how kind of you to greet us." Then turning to Wilfred she embraced him and kissed him on his head.

The young man grinned. "Oh, ooh, J-J-Jo and Elyce, happy!" he stuttered.

Andrew boomed admiringly, "Well, talk about a little beauty! Our Winnie is growing into a rose!"

Winifred with no passion but vanity now laughed and preened like a little bird. "Oh, Uncle, you are a charmer! You all must need your rest. I will see you at dinner." And with a little pirouette she was gone.

A maid showed Joanna and Elyce to their room. The Dresser was unpacking their trunks in the luxurious room. The bed was set upon a dais and the steps leading up to it were carpeted in deep royal blue. There were heavy brocade drapes that could be drawn to enclose the bed. The painted ceiling was decorated with clouds and nymphs. Elyce put on a silk wrapper and stretched out on a chaise lounge. Joanna sat opposite her in an overstuffed brocade chair after donning a wrap of blue China silk with Michelin lace.

"What an absolute horror Winnie is! All airy and strange, so impressed with herself...and she is only fourteen!" exclaimed Joanna.

"Oh, fiddle, she is just spoiled, she will outgrow her affectations," answered Elyce, stretching her arms over her head.

"Pooh, she has always been wicked; look at the mean things she did to Willie as a child. She depresses me dreadfully."

"Well, darling, I think we should just enjoy ourselves and ignore her. I say we do all sorts of wonderful things like we did as children. We will go for walks and get out the canoe, ride and relax."

Opening her eyes wide and yawning, Joanna said, "Sounds wonderful, but I need a little nap to refresh me."

"Likewise..." And they crawled onto the huge bed and laid their weary bodies down.

CHAPTER SIX

The evening for the Dinner Ball was upon them. Joanna and Elyce had spent three days relaxing and enjoying the large mansion and grounds.

Despite the obvious tension in their marriage, Andrew and Caroline maintained a civil and proper front. Andrew enjoyed visits with his mother, rides with his brother in the woods and fields of his boyhood home.

Joanna, dressed only in her elaborate corset and French open drawers, watched her sister being dressed for the occasion. *How beautiful she is*, thought Joanna, admiring Elyce in her blue damask gown with layers of embroidered lace and tulle. Garlands of pearls and crystal were draped about her waist and hips. Her hair was wrapped high on her head with pearls woven through it and the diamond star was clasped to one side. About her throat lay the diamond and pearl necklace given to her for the debut. *How could she ever be happy with the likes of Marshall Davenport? He doesn't deserve her*, mused Joanna.

Caroline had told Kate the marriage contracts were settled and an announcement ball was forthcoming, in fact, the invitations were in the post.

Kate had questioned Elyce if she were certain Marshall would make her happy and Elyce had answered, "Oh, yes, he is rich, well educated and powerful, I just adore him."

"You should only marry for love, dear one. Sometimes love of substance can be deadly."

Elyce had laughed and retorted, "Oh, I am going to have a wonderful life. Gram, he is wonderful."

"Miss Joanna, may I dress you?" asked the maid as she handed Elyce her kid gloves. Joanna lifted her arms and pale champagne watered taffeta settled about her. A sash of turquoise satin emphasized her nineteen inch waist. Her mantle was of gold gauze; Caroline insisted that it be worn to cover her shoulders and the extreme decollete. Joanna's hair was rolled around rats creating a soft Gibson girl do and her diamond crescent twinkled high above her brow. After fastening a gold lavaliere of seed pearls and diamonds about her throat, the girls donned their cloaks and joined the others in the main foyer. The coaches were lined up in the driveway for the drive to Lady Roberts.

Torches blazed and footman scurried as carriages arrived at Winterhall. The splendor, the formality, and the hugeness of the manor overwhelmed Joanna. They entered the immense hall with its domed ceiling. After handing off their wraps, each lady was given a card and a dinner table number. Each gentleman was given an envelope bearing the name of the lady or ladies he was to escort into the dining area hall. Lady Dorothy greeted her guest of honor and led Kate into the drawing room where maids were circulating flutes of champagne among the guests.

Later after a nod from Lady Dorothy, the butler announced dinner. John escorted Lady Dorothy and Kate into the massive dining room to the head table.

Joanna was seated across from her father and as yet had an empty seat to her right. The tables were almost a vulgar display of silver. Huge ormolu candelabras illumined the silver place settings and barracat crystal. Candied fruit spilled from Epergnes and small bouquets were at each lady's seating.

Joanna was conscious of a gentleman being seated to her right and turning was astonished as she gazed into familiar blue gray eyes. "By my word," she gasped, "I thought you had gone west."

"Business detained me, your Uncle and I have been reviewing maps to determine if a rail spur is feasible close to his holdings in Wyoming," answered Timber Alexander with a smile.

"Oh, please, tell me more about the Western Frontier and its great expansion. How I admire those pioneers that made the move west, hardy souls."

Timber's eyebrows rose with mild shock. Most women were hardly intellectual and seldom brilliant, but finding Joanna to be both, he began an animated conversation as the multiple courses began.

Joanna glanced at the menu and hoped she would not get heady from the wines. She was overjoyed when the tiered birthday cake ablaze with candles was rolled in. She was a bit giddy; she was giggling too much and beginning to prattle. Following dinner the women retired to the powder rooms to repair their toilette.

Arrival of other guests after ten signaled the beginning of the Ball. Uncle John led the dancing off with his mother. Joanna watched her Grandmother glide through a waltz. Kate was still a striking woman in pearls and gray satin.

As more couples began dancing she singled out her mother and father. Her father was dashing in black tails, black tie, and boots of patent leather and gray gloves. Caroline looked elegant in green panne velvet. A collar of emeralds and diamonds encircled her neck and a diamond tiara sat on her elaborately coifed head. She had a very melancholy look about her, not her usual regal air due to Andrew's flagrant infidelity. This time it had shattered much of her self esteem. In good society, sinning in private was no impropriety. Had he been more discreet she could have turned a blind eye, but now she seemed faced with a compromised marriage. To leave him was unthinkable, for scandal would damage the family's image and the cream of the social elite would avoid any contact with them. Divorce was déclassé. (Whispering disgrace!) Andrew also realized, for the importance of respectability and business, he was under pressure to keep his marriage intact.

Timber felt like he had a feather in his arms. Elyce was light on her feet and followed his every move. Silvery curls were slipping from the coils on her head framing her lovely face. Her heavily lashed blue eyes were shining with happiness. He marveled anew at how beautiful she was.

"You seem particularly happy this evening, Miss Elyce," he said, smiling down at her.

"Oh, indeed I am!" she laughed exposing perfect white teeth. A dimple played at the side of her mouth.

Timber wanted to cover that sweet mouth with his own. He wanted to pull her close, take her in his arms and softly caress her. His heart pounded and his body ached. Oh, sweet Elyce, how he wanted her for his own.

"Actually," he heard her continue through a daze, "I am not to breathe a word of this until it's announced, but because you are a dear family friend, I'll tell you. I am betrothed to Marshall Davenport."

Timber's heart felt ripped in half. *My poor darling*, he thought to himself. "Fancy that," he replied, "are the contracts settled?"

"Oh, yes, Mama has already made plans for the announcement ball. I love him with all my heart and I know nothing like this will ever be so exciting again."

When the music ended Timber escorted her off the floor with a heavy heart. Thanking her, he kissed her gloved hand and left the ballroom.

Joanna danced, never lacking a partner. She kept looking for Timber and when she saw him, some of the joy left her face. He was dancing with Elyce and was totally absorbed. The admiration he felt for Elyce showed on his handsome face. Her sister was laughing and her beautiful upturned face was glowing.

"Oh my, I must sit, I feel a bit faint," she said to her partner and he escorted her off the floor.

"May I get you some punch, Miss Holan?," he asked with concern.

"Thank you, no," she answered, fanning herself vigorously. She chewed her lower lip nervously. She didn't want Elyce to marry Alexander, but she could not bear it if Elyce married Timber. She excused herself and went out into the foyer. Seating herself she gazed about her. The immense hall was lined with chairs, lounges and huge pedestals of flowers. Crystal chandeliers hung from a domed ceiling and a gilt wood console holding lit tapers sat beside her. Joanna felt as cold as the marbled onyx floor.

"Mind if I join you, Joanna?" She started at Timber's voice.

"Not at all, I felt the need of some air," she stammered.

"I had been hoping, eventually, to dance with the other beauty of the family," he said, smiling. When Joanna didn't answer, he continued, "I was shocked to learn Elyce had become affianced to that dandy."

"Oh, Timber," Joanna gasped, turning to him, "She adores that despicable person and Mama does, too! I cannot believe my smart lovely sister can be so blind!"

A sharp caustic voice made them both start; "I declare, whatever are you doing out here without a chaperone, Joanna?" Winifred stood tossing her curls in disdain, her eyes flashing green ice.

Timber rose and bowed to her and her chaperone, "Why, little Winifred, how nice you look, so nice to have you inquire about Miss Joanna's welfare."

"My, Mr. Alexander, you do carry on! Humph! Come, Gwen," she retorted as she flounced away with her chaperone.

"Oh, kittens, she will bust her bustle hurrying to Mama. What a horrid minx!"

Timber burst out laughing.

Joanna's violet eyes sparked fire and her cheeks flushed. "She is really horrid, you know. Has been all her life," exclaimed Joanna angrily as she turned to face him.

"Do you realize what a resemblance your cousin has to you?"

Joanna tossed her head disdainfully, "From childhood we have been told we looked somewhat alike. Perhaps that is why she dislikes me so. My hair is darker and hers is like flame and I am taller. She has extreme self confidence, which I lack, and she has a cold demeanor."

"Yes," said Timber, "she has a haughty bearing for one so young."

"Sometimes I think she is deficient in emotions. I cannot bring to mind ever seeing her cry, even as a child. Is not that strange?"

"Most unusual. Yes, you are similar in looks, happily the comparison ends there as you radiate warmth," he commented. "Let us put all this behind us, would you care to dance?"

"Yes, kind sir," Joanna answered with a flutter in her voice, he affected her deeply. They entered the stately gold and white ballroom; Timber bowed and took her in his arms. Her pulse leaped in her throat, his closeness unnerved her and she missed a step. Timber laughed and held her closer. Then she tripped! He tried to catch her, but she landed on the floor in an undignified heap. It took her a moment to realize she was sitting quite in the middle of the dance floor, shirt askew, her ankles and legs exposed, all dignity gone! Timber was leaning over her holding out his arms. She tried getting to her feet, but found she could not bend at the waist, her stays were too tight. Timber's eyes twinkled with merriment as he put his hands about her waist and lifted her quickly to her feet. "Are you all right, my dear?"

She was trembling in his hold. "How awkward of me, I am mortified!"

"Shhhh, just dance, it will all pass in a moment," and he expertly led her through the remainder of the dance.

On the return home Joanna told Elyse of her embarrassing fall. "I did not notice, did you Mama?"

Caroline was resting her head against the back of the seat, her eyes closed. "Umm, did I notice what?"

"Jo falling on her diererré," answered Elyce, her eyes sparkling in the carriage light.

Caroline snapped to attention, her eyes wide. "What! Not on the ballroom floor?"

"Oh, Mama, I tripped, and Mr. Alexander picked me up," Joanna answered quietly.

"Gracious, I am happy I did not witness that indignity! I hope your skirts stayed in tact, Joanna!"

"Well, truthfully, my ankles and legs were exposed, but for just a second!"

"Oh My Stars!" exclaimed Caroline and uttered a groan.

"Bless my buttons, Caroline," a spirited burst came from Kate, "don't carry on so. It is not the first time a man has witnessed a well turned ankle nor will it be the last! Land sakes, Timber didn't feel it was a spectacle, he has accepted my invitation for dinner tomorrow evening."

Joanna felt on the verge of crying when she caught Elyce's eye; the comical side of the happening suddenly struck them both and they began to laugh. Suffering from exhaustion they laughed until tears ran down their cheeks, even Caroline joined in. The unfortunate incident caused the evening to end gaily and the sisters were still giggling when they fell into bed.

The following morning they lay luxuriously in bed waiting for a maid to bring breakfast. Staring at the ceiling Joanna thought of Timber and imagined being in his arms. Elyce's voice brought her back to reality with a start.

"Two more days, well, closer to four counting the return trip home, and I will see Marshall. It seems like an eternity," she sighed.

"Oh, Elyce, I can relate a bit to your feelings, I think I am falling in love, too!"

"Tell, tell !" exclaimed Elyce sitting up and then looking down at Joanna.

"Timber Alexander, he is just divine!" answered Joanna with a smile, "and a gentleman, I might add."

"Oh, indeed he is splendid, has he showed any interest, Jo?"

Joanna shook her head and in a small voice answered, "Not really, I despair at our limited acquaintance. He is leaving for the west. I probably will never see him again.."

Elyce spoke seriously, "Joanna, dearest, you are so beautiful and so talented, you can have your choice of just about anyone you pick. Timber has yet to make his fortune and if he does, time will tell. We can never predict the future, but don't feel he is the only man in the world."

Joanna sat up, shrugged her shoulders and answered, "I am merely laboring under the delusion that he could care for me, and anyway, he is more taken with you than me."

"Mercy, please don't say that. You know I love Marshall," answered Elyce, frowning. "I have never encouraged Timber Alexander in any way."

Joanna smiled, mollified, "Dear Elyce, you do not have to encourage anyone, you need only to focus your cornflowerblue eyes on a man and he is in a state of rapture."

A rap on the door, "Oh, here is the maid, put on your wrap and we will have breakfast. I can't dwell on this one second longer."

Dinner that evening would prove to be unforgettable. Lady Adelaide Hungerford, a wealthy Boston widow, was one of the guests. Joanna marveled at her looks. She paraded an ample bosom, had painted her face and rouged her lips all to good advantage. She was witty, outspoken and dazzled everyone with her accounts. She had hovered over Timber before dinner and

Joanna began to wonder if this passionate older woman was having a liaison with him. He was very attentive to her. Joanna had pulled Elyce aside and behind her opened fan whispered to Elyce of her thoughts.

"Silly, that is Timber's mother! His father died some years ago and she remarried, then she had the misfortune to lose Lord Hungerford also."

Joanna felt great relief and looking closely she could see a family resemblance.

Uncle John escorted Daphne into the drawing room. She resembled a little wren; her hair pulled severely from her face in a chignon. There were violet shadows under her eyes and her complexion had a ghostly pallor. When Joanna and Elyce paid their respects to her, it was obvious she was very ill.

Joanna was seated between her father and Timber at dinner. Elyce was at Timber's left and directly across from Joanna was Winifred. Tonight it was a bit like looking at a reflection of oneself. Winifred's flaming hair was pulled back into a cluster of curls and her emerald eyes were enhanced by a gown of green watered silk. Joanna thought how mature she looked. Winifred glared at Joanna with disdain and turned to her father with a dazzling smile.

As if reading Joanna's thoughts Timber said, "She could be your twin, remarkable resemblance."

Joanna smiled at him and through gritted teeth said, "I hope I never have such a disposition as she displays."

"You know perfectly well that will never happen," retorted Timber.

The table was glowing with candles; low arrangements of flowers were scattered throughout, a large crystal chandelier glimmered overhead and a glass harp tinkled faintly in the background. As the dinner commend, Joanna would sneak glances under her long lashes at Timber' s profile, thinking he was almost perfection.

Timber, meanwhile, glancing at Elyce's beauteous face thought sadly, *My dearest, you were lost to me before I found you, but I shall love no other.*

Through dinner with its many courses, John, Andrew and Timber had an animated discourse about the wonders of the West and the railroads. Joanna learned historical facts while enjoying the closeness of Timber leaning over her when speaking with her father. Timber spoke of the many early surveyors who had carried their lives in their hands, of the pick and shovel men who followed. The work had to be done behind the protection of the rifle and revolver. He continued of how hard the Indians fought against these men with the flags, plumbs, and levels. He said, "They were the precursors of the greater army following. An army that laid a path for the iron feet of the "horse" that would outstrip the mustang in speed and the buffalo in strength. Thirsting for blood, the Indian awaited the opportunity to add one more item to the cruel record of the quarrel between red man and white." He sipped wine from his goblet and gravely added, "Truly the early railways were parts laid in blood, marked by the lonely graves of victims of arrow and tomahawk. Many Indian braves lost their lives fighting against that mighty, snorting Iron Horse that destroyed the beauty and grandeur of their land." He sadly recounted how rail coaches filled with wealthy thrill seekers shot everything in sight, especially the buffalo by the thousands. "This," he continued, "had triggered greater hostility of the Indians and made them even more dangerous. Even after the meeting of the Central and Union Pacific at Promontory Point twenty-five years ago in Utah, military guards are still posted at some of the rails."

"Why?" asked Joanna.

"There are still renegades and robbers causing trouble. Many 'narvies' still die struggling with ties and rails on the new spurs. In the past the railroad hired seven thousand Chinese to be platelayers followed by bridge gangs and tracklayers. We are using many of their descendants for the new spurs. As more railroad beds are laid, the hunting ground of the Indian and the home of the buffalo will soon be gone forever."

"Never. That land is so wild and so vast there will always be plenty for all, white and red man!" exclaimed Andrew, shaking a finger in the air.

John shook his head negatively, "I agree with Timber. I also feel the white man will bring untold disaster to this land." John went on to speak of the Great Plains, the splendor and grandeur of the Rocky Mountains, and of the Yellowstone River and falls. He described the mighty red trees on the Pacific coast, so tall their tops could not be seen for the clouds, and of other mammoth trees, bigger around than a building that grew in groves by the Merced River in California. "The sad reality is, these mighty trees are old and we are cutting them down by the hundreds. Tell me again, Andrew, that the white man is not destructive!"

"Remember, John, we need the rail for prosperity, we need the stock to keep the country solvent. America must be fed and railroads are transporting cattle to market at a far faster rate than the horse could! We are shipping materials all over the country, the railroads are now the mighty backbone of America," answered Andrew. "We also need the timber to build with and with growth comes change."

"At a great cost, perhaps at too great a cost," stated John.

Intoxicated by these stories, Joanna knew she would one day travel west. Early in John's marriage he had headed west, a tall assured sportsman, he spent time in Montana and Colorado driving cattle and traveled the buffalo trails. His soul was sick over his ill wife and son, but he found his heart in that wild beautiful country. He bought land and now a great lodge in Wyoming was in the process of being finished. John planned to take Wilfred with him on his return hoping the pristine area would improve his son's health. He spoke of a number of Europeans, mostly Englishmen, who had invested heavily in American cattle and land in Wyoming Territory. Two English syndicates had bought seven million acres in Texas. Two Dukes each owned over 500,000 acres in Wyoming. Other titled men were buying in Colorado and Montana. John's acquisition was small in comparison; he was running 30,000 cattle and 500 head of horses but doing well. The big attraction for the English was hunting game, especially the American bear and buffalo. While John was an avid hunter, but his main interest was in his ranch.

After dinner the women retired to the drawing room. Elyce and Joanna conversed with Lady Adelaide.

Daphne began a terrible bout of coughing; she withdrew and left the room.

The continued conversation was about Timber, his love of the West, and of Lady Adelaide's worry during his long absences. Kate joined them and Joanna gave her a quick hug. "Oh, Gram, it is so delightful to be here again, this house is a testament to all your love and caring through the years. Each time I return, I appreciate more what Queensgate means to me. How right it is for all of us, a true haven."

"Oh, really!" sneered Winifred upon overhearing Joanna. Her face was flushed with red spots of anger. "This is my father's house. This is where I was born, where I belong, not you cousins!"

"Winnie, what ever has overcome you, child? This is my home; all my grandchildren are welcome here as you are." exclaimed Kate, her voice shaking.

"It is not your home! Grandfather left it to Father. You should be in the Dower House!" Winifred screeched, unmindful of the other guests.

Kate's face went white, she suddenly felt old and shriveled inside, but she stood tall and never blinked.

Joanna put her arms protectively around her Grandmother. She felt Kate's bleakness in herself. She turned her head and hissed at Winifred, "You have overstepped your authority, you will regret this!"

Winifred stood defiantly, and her eyes glittered. Her voice was filled with venom as she answered, "I loathe all of you!" Then she lifted her skirt, turned and ran from the room.

Elyce, with a look of shock on her face asked, "Mercy, whatever is wrong with her? What have we done to upset her so?"

Kate shook her head, "It is nothing you have done for she is too old for her years. She is trying to step into my shoes. John now must take a firm hand or all will be lost for her." Kate lifted her chin, fanned herself and smiled at Lady Adelaide, who nodded in sympathy and said, "Now, where were we, it was a most interesting conversation, was it not about my dear Timber?"

Later the women joined the men in the music room. Joanna and Elyce entertained their Grand mother's guests. Joanna played the pianoforte and Elyce sang in her sweet soprano.

At the conclusion of the evening Kate told John she must speak with him first thing in the morning, it was most important. John, noting how upset his mother was, took her by her arm and questioned her. "I cannot discuss it this evening, I must retire." She then went upstairs.

Back in their chambers, a concerned Andrew questioned Caroline about his mother's behavior. As he slipped into a smoking jacket, Caroline explained Winifred's remarks. Caroline began to undress behind a screen and she asked about the Dower House.

Andrew lit a meerschaum pipe then answered, "The Dower House was built by my Grandfather when Queensgate was built. My Grandmother was thirty four years younger than he and Grandfather wanted her to have security when he died. I am certain you are aware that upon a father's death the oldest male, or if no males, the eldest female heir inherits the estate. He deeded the Dower House, which we refer to as the guesthouse, to her with five acres and monetary provisions. In his native England, the larger estates had Dowager Houses and he felt it was a good tradition to carry on. Had Daphne been in better health, I am certain Mother would have turned Queensgate over to her and moved into the Dower. Poor John, what would he have done without Mama? She has overseen the nursing and care of Willie and Daphne and helped raise Winifred."

Caroline, now in a wrapper, seated herself at the dressing table and began to brush her hair. "How sad for everyone concerned. Things can never be the same at Queensgate."

"John does have a situation on his hands. Daphne was in mortal pain this evening and now this." Andrew closed his eyes wearily and the smoke from his pipe curled about his head. Things for all of us will never be the same were his thoughts.

Joanna and Elyce lay quietly talking in bed. They were both heartsick that their cousin had shamed their beloved Grandmother.

"I wonder what Uncle John will do with Winifred? Maybe he will send her to Europe to a finishing school," mused Elyce. "Uncle John has so catered to her she is now a product of that indulgence."

"He ought to horsewhip her and put her in the basement for good measure!" said Joanna.

"Oh, that would be cruel, Jo. I just do not understand why she dislikes us so, 'tis a puzzle. She really has never had a mother; perhaps she is rebellious about that. But, then again, Gram has always been here for her. She could be afraid that she might become ill also."

Yawning loudly, Joanna said, "Who knows, not I? Are you sleepy?"

"That I am, sweet dreams, dear."

Joanna rose early the next morning, quietly dressed not wanting to disturb Elyce. She tiptoed to the door, then hurried down the hall and descended the stairs. The sun was beginning to cast a rosy glow through the leaded glass windows in the morning room. She slipped her mantle over her shoulders and went out on the terrace. Inhaling the morning air, she embraced the day. She could hear voices coming from the garden; an earnest and steady conversation floated up to her. *Oh, dear, should I return inside or ignore the voices*, she asked herself. She paused and then turned toward the house. "Joanna, Joanna darling, good morning, please come join us!"

Kate and John were now in full view walking up a path. Joanna went slowly down to them.

John asked, "Do you enjoy the gardens, too? Mother likes to have an hour of sun each morning to keep her heath."

"We are going to have breakfast on the terrace, please join us, dear," said Kate, kissing Joanna on the cheek.

"I don't want to interrupt you," answered Joanna.

"We have concluded our conversation, come, we will enjoy this beautiful morning and have breakfast. I need a robust cup of coffee," said Kate.

During their breakfast Joanna spoke of how worried she was about the relationship between Elyce and Marshall. She said, "I do not feel he will offer the stability Elyce needs and she is far too caring for a man like him."

Kate thoughtfully retorted, "He has quite a reputation as a ladies man and I would have thought you a careless sister, indeed, were you to think otherwise. Still, I am not inclined to admit that she is doing a foolish thing. She adores him and he can offer her security. Marriage may strengthen his character, it does most men."

John added, "A girl endowed with Elyce's beauty and intelligence will not be treated with indifference. Put your fears to rest, Joanna."

"I pray you are correct, Uncle John, I can only hope for her happiness."

Turning to Kate, John said, "Then it is agreed that Winifred will be traveling west with Will and I as soon as the house and lodge are completed. Actually, the house should be done by the time we arrive."

"I worry about her social life, her debut. Have you considered that, John?"

"Dearest Mother, she is not yet fifteen, she has two years before being introduced into society. She cannot continue here with such an attitude. I will not allow her to berate you again."

Kate lay her hand on her son's arm. "I am so sorry, John, truly I am."

"She cannot dominate our lives; we have Daphne and Will to consider. I am to blame if anyone is. I have spoiled her terribly to compensate for Daphne's illness."

"I hate to have her leave feeling as she does."

John rose and kissed his mother. "If I may be excused, I must talk to Winifred and find Andrew. He and I have some business contracts to sign." Bowing to Joanna he withdrew.

"Ah, Gram, how depressing life can be. Winifred has become a perfect nuisance, I am losing my dear Elyce and I am smitten with Timber. He didn't even say goodbye."

"Stars, child, he is so taken with his job he has no time for fancy. Fate awaits you, do not get impatient. If I have learned one thing in life, it is the mystery and wonder of not knowing what the future holds. The ending is the only thing we are certain of."

"Oh, Gram, I don't want to think about death, your brilliance and warmth have always been my rock!"

"Dear, death is a fact of life as well as aging. Enjoy your beauty, even the bitter sweetness it sometimes brings."

"You do not seem old, you think young, you relate to all of us."

"I repeat myself, enjoy your youth. It flashes by in a twinkle; suddenly you find your soul encased in a worn out body. There is no joy in aging. One has to be strong and not resentful."

"Oh, Gram, you are beautiful inside and out. You have such honesty and candor; you have always been my idol and strength."

"Darling, you will grow into strength, it comes with experiences, good and bad. I do have one regret, I have failed Winifred miserably." Kate said sadly.

"I disagree. She is a willful, naughty girl who insists on having her own way. She has a streak of wildness that I doubt anyone can tame. Sometimes I wonder if she is brain afflicted."

"Good Lord. I hope not, Joanna!"

Andrew came through the French doors and cheerfully called out, "Good morning, how is my Mama? Where is everybody?"

Kate retorted, "Good morning, darling. Evidently everyone is abed. No, not really, John was here earlier and he has gone to find Winifred."

"As well he should, I understand she made a dreadful scene last evening," Andrew said, pouring a cup of coffee.

Kate spoke so low he had to strain to hear her, "She wounded me deeply, he is taking her west and I feel responsible."

Andrew's face was very sober and there was a sound of repressed anger as he answered. "You have been a caring mother and grandmother. You nursed Daphne and Wilford and ran Queensgate for John. Evidently Winifred has no remorse over her feelings and I know John must be in state of despair."

Joanna, piped up, trying to change the course of the conversation, "Papa, I want to go west one day. Listening to Uncle John and Timber last evening was so exciting."

Andrew sighed, "Puss, it is a long journey, dangerous at times and no comforts as you know them. I would not want you exposed to the elements, so to speak."

"Oh, Papa," said Joanna, knitting her eyebrows, "that's just it; I want to be exposed to life, the good and the bad. I want to live, not spend my days shut up in a big house worrying about the latest modes and dinner parties, it is all so shallow!"

"I do not agree with you, Joanna, it is the way of the world. We men have been taught to carefully pedestal and protect our women folk I would never allow you to be exposed to any danger. It is nothing I wish to discuss further."

Joanna knew the subject was closed and she kept silent.

"Ah, me, I had such hopes for Winifred. I do despair," said Kate, gazing into space.

Andrew leaned toward her and placed his hand over hers and gravely said, "Mama, you must stop carrying on so. Life is a game, we play to win, but many times we lose. We climb that ladder to be at the top, and then once we are there, we must work to stay there. Our life style changes, we want more and more. Sadly, when we look down that ladder we have climbed, only then do we realize how much we have lost along the way, (friends that did not have our ambition or values; and a simple way of living?) I find now I am miserable, wasted time and money and disappointed my loved ones." Then seeing Kate and Joanna's looks of astonishment and concern, he laughed, "Sorry, I got carried away."

"Papa, you have always loved life so, I am shocked to hear you so morose," Joanna said softly.

"I am a bit tired of terrapin, champagne and plover. I fear my age is catching up with me. I have one daughter wanting to go west, my wife wants plates of gold, and my other daughter is to marry a rich dandy with no scruples."

Joanna had never heard her father talk so despondently. He was always so chipper and gay. As if he had read her mind, he gave her a smile that went straight to her heart.

"Not to worry your pretty little head. What a splendid morning, I believe I am ready for breakfast. Kippered herring and scrambled eggs with brains sounds filling."

"I will ring for you, dear, anything you want, you order," smiled Kate lovingly.

The New York homecoming was different from all others. There was a certain amount of ceremony and sadness about it. Elyce was giddy over being reunited with her betrothed. Caroline and Andrew were immersed in their thoughts with little to say to each other. Joanna felt as if she had a heavy weight in her heart knowing Elyce was lost to Marshall. She could not shake the ominous feeling she had about their relationship. She was dealing with the overwhelming passion she felt for Timber knowing that he only felt brotherly affection towards her.

The weeks passed quickly and the announcement ball was upon them. It was elegant and well planned. Elyce was in ecstasy and looked particularly beautiful; a devoted and adoring Marshall never left her side. The press described the brilliant feté in full detail.

Caroline, now relieved to have the announcement soiree behind her, turned full attention to the trip to Europe for Elyce's trousseau. She booked aboard the stylish Transat French liner, the Touraine. Preparations got underway for the time aboard. The daughters had not been abroad since youngsters and were so very excited.

Andrew was preoccupied, as usual, with affairs and still spending overnights at the Club. He did, however, come with Marshall to the ship to see his family off. He waited aboard until the gangway was to be withdrawn and then he hugged Elyce and Joanna and said with a sigh, "I shall miss you, have fun, and take care of your mother."

"We will." They chorused in unison as he began descending the gangway. Marshall hugged Elyce and followed Andrew.

As the sleek ship sailed, Andrew and Marshall watched from shore. The girls waved handkerchiefs until they no longer could see land. Caroline had long since retired to their suite pleading fatigue.

The girls decided to explore the first class decks and conveniences. The Touraine was definitely Parisian, lavish in decor. Her gilded paneling and electric lighting made her considerably brighter and more charming than the dark wood and leather habits of the English liners or, the German liners which struggled to emulate Wagnerian castles.

The grand salon took their breathe away. The combination of dazzling vistas of mirrors, marble, polished brass, intricately laid tile and plush carpeting was an overkill of grandeur. Even more astounding was the grand staircase, all sweep and grand descent. Its mirrored backdrop of three tiers of cascading exuberance allowed the first class passengers to majestically descend the carpeted marble steps to dinner. It made for a smashing entrance.

After becoming lost on two occasions, the girls decided to retire to their sumptuous private quarters. The *cabines de grand luxe* could accommodate as many as six members of one family. The suite had an Empire style dining room for lunch, if one did not feel social or, for dinner if one wished to entertain. There were three bedchambers and a maid's quarters. Two maids were busily unpacking trunks so the girls rested before dressing for dinner.

The crew and officers were as much a part of the ambiance as was the cuisine and decor. The pursers were very attentive, especially to the pretty young Mademoiselles.

Their dining table assignments were with highly placed officers and very chic and distinguished passengers. The Touraine, being one of the first liners to have refrigeration, was able to serve an exquisite cuisine of several courses washed down with Chambertin, the noble French Burgundy.

At the first formal dinner, Joanna was seated next to the charming son of a wealthy cotton broker. He was Pierre de Beoudean from New Orleans.

As the crossing progressed, Joanna came to enjoy Pierre's company. They strolled the decks, watched sunsets and danced after dinners. For her, however, none of the fairytale quality existed that had surrounded Timber. She appreciated Pierre's intelligence and Southern eloquence while he was quite taken with her beauty and warmth. Their friendship became particularly significant for Pierre. He told her of his childhood in the new South after the Civil War. His tales horrified her. She had never known the pangs of hunger, of not having clothes or shoes, nor of a home only warmed by huddled bodies for lack of fuel. He painted pictures of the South, which after almost three decades, was still struggling to rebuild what could never be again. It drew her outside herself and this view of the still torn states shocked her. She was enchanted, though, when he told her of the beauty of New Orleans. He extended an invitation to her and her family to visit the family plantation on the outskirts of the city.

When embarking at Le Havre, Pierre was given permission to call on Joanna. Caroline was most impressed with the well bred young gentleman.

They arrived in Paris and settled into their elegant apartment in one of the most fashionable sections. On the second day Caroline took the girls to the most influential and distinguished dress designers of France, Jean and Gaston Worth. The Worths and assistants studied the young women like artists, outlined dresses and ordered special fabrics in particular colors for both. Elyce's wedding gown was the last and most detailed to be decided upon. Repeated fittings would follow for a number of weeks. They also were fitted for gowns at Jacques Doucet, then Creeds for sportswear and tailored suits. Learning of a new designer of splendid lingerie, a Madame Pacquin, Caroline visited her house of fashion. She was thrilled with the beautiful work and made purchases for the three of them. Most of the custom designed creations would not be ready for several weeks. In the meanwhile, Pierre was happy to take Joanna and Elyce sightseeing.

Many evenings Pierre escorted them to the Opera, other evenings they spent enjoying the youthful gaieties of the rich.

When the fittings were behind them, Caroline had one last obligation before making plans to leave Paris. She asked Pierre to accompany her. Andrew's only request for a souvenir from Europe was a billiards table. Billiards has deep roots among the French, having been a favorite of French Royalty. One afternoon they happened upon a small shop that commissioned tables for the wealthy nobles. The owner showed them a magnificent table crafted of rosewood and beautifully inlaid with exotic woods. It had finely chiseled Dore bronze mounts and scrolled feet. It had been built for a gentleman who unfortunately met his demise under the wheels of a carriage. Caroline paid a princely sum for it and made arrangements for shipment to the states.

Caroline had made plans for other excursions through Europe. Once the costumes were finished, she hoped the girls would enjoy the travel.

Pierre was leaving for Strasbourg to visit relatives. He had been a most entertaining companion and they regretted his departure. Joanna would especially miss their lunches at quaint cafés and the delightful hours they spent sightseeing. Before he left, he brought her a nosegay in a bracelet holder.

"How thoughtful you are, dear Pierre!" she exclaimed happily, "I shall keep this until I can come to New Orleans and dance with you!" She snapped the gold bracelet on her wrist and held the bouquet to her nose inhaling the fragrance.

"Just think of me once in a while, Mademoiselle, I shall miss you terribly," Pierre said sadly. He had fallen in love with this exquisite creature and hoped, one day, to court her. "You will answer my letters?"

"Of, course, Pierre, we have become such close friends!" she answered, smiling.

Pierre grimaced at the words, he had hoped she would be distraught at his leaving. She was young; he would give her time. He gave Caroline and Elyce elaborate tin boxes of Maison Chocolates and told them farewell. Joanna walked him to the door. As he opened it, he looked down at her and then kissed her lightly on the cheek. "Until we meet again, dear Joanna, do correspond," he said and left through the portal.

A few days later they left by rail for Baden Baden to take the baths at a fashionable hotel. They toured Goethe's house in Frankfurt, had a fascinating time in Heidleberg wandering the ruins of the Elector's Castle and Gardens. As they enjoyed the view of the Nectar River from the great terrace Joanna commented, "What a jewel box of history Europe is. History just dances through the castles, cathedrals and cities. It is a rapture to be here, everything new to us is ancient and haunting. So many tales, so many ghosts. I can understand the envy the Americans have for the Europeans and the immolation. Americans are awash in wealth and twice as comfortable, but their heritage is lost. We can buy titles or marry titles, but true blue blood stays in Europe."

"Oh, kitten's mittens, who wants a lord or baron, not I! I am tired of travel, I want to go home," retorted Elyce. "I miss Marshall and we can always return."

The Alps were a fairyland. The high green meadows were dotted with Swiss cattle and goats. Some of the cattle had coronets of flowers about their horns while others had bells around their necks. "What splendid animals!"commented Joanna as they traveled the countryside.

"Umm, I suppose so," murmured Elyce for her heart was heavy and she looked more wistful each day. She had asked her mother to shorten their stay in Europe and return home. Although Caroline had plans to tour Italy and go to her favorite city, Prague, she was concerned about Elyce. Elyce's heavy eyes, loss of appetite and wan face decided her to cut the tour short and go directly to London. Elyce's homesick heart rejoiced at the news and immediately wrote to her beloved Marshall of the change of plans. Joanna was disappointed, but bore it well. She had desperately wanted to go to Rome and Florence. However, she was troubled at how downhearted Elyce had become and missed her sister's usual exuberance. Once in England, counting the days until the return to America cheered Elyce.

The trip through the countryside was one lovely landscape following another. The huge baronial estates were like paintings by the masters. Every shade of green imaginable surrounded the homes. Many had cattle belly deep in clover while others had flocks of sheep that looked like fluffy cotton on carpets of green and yellow.

It rained the first few days after arriving in London, nothing to be seen but black umbrellas and fog. The rain, which had been a steady splattering curtain, now turned to a fine mist with sun glowing through it like a pearl. Days were spent shopping and then sightseeing, places of interest such as the Tower of London, Westminster Abby, Kensington Museum, and the London Bridge. Late afternoons found them at Hyde Park to watch the social parade. Heavy antique coaches showed off their varnished wood and brass exteriors, fat jeweled dowagers rolled about in gold and red coaches with pestilions of red livery in front and powdered footmen in gold livery in back. It was all very spectacular. One evening, a majestic coach clattered down the street. Powdered lackeys and meticulously uniformed blue coats attended the coach. To the girls delight it was the beautiful Alexander, Princess of Wales, who waved and nodded right and left. Men raised their hats and ladies curtseyed. Joanna and Elyce curtseyed and Joanna marveled at the affection shown the Princess.

Some evenings Caroline would hire a hansom cab and take them to the *Route de Roi* (Avenue of Kings). Men, women and children rode magnificent steeds, the women in fancy habits and high hats trailing long veils. Everyone trotted solemnly up and down for the most part, however, several young people flirted by exchanging floral boutaineers.

Caroline's London relatives accompanied them to the opera, concerts at Albert Hall and the ballet. It was quite exhausting as well as delightful and they were looking forward to relaxing on the cruise home.

They arrived in New York invigorated and refreshed. They had calm seas on the crossing which was most unusual.

Andrew was there to greet them, the old warm, laughing, vibrant father and husband. Joanna was delighted and joyously hugged her father. Elyce was in a state of ecstacy when Marshall arrived, his arms loaded with roses.

The days following their homecoming were happy ones shared by all. Caroline was busy once again in the social atmosphere about her. Elyce's wedding was scheduled for the following year in June. Caroline resolved to have Joanna's debut in October as she had celebrated her seventeenth birthday. The country was once again in an upswing. William McKinley and William Jennings Bryan were campaigning for the presidential election. The Holan family attended many campaign high teas and balls. At one ball alone, dignitaries Admiral George Dewey, Police Commissioner of New York, Theodore Roosevelt, Colonel Wood and Rear Admiral W.T. Sampson were in attendance.

Joanna lapsed into her own little world. She was moody, irritable, and pensive by turns. She lost her appetite and neglected her appearance. On the opposite hand, Elyce was in high spirits. She was with Marshall most evenings, attending balls, soirees, ballets and the like. The sisters had been so close, now Joanna felt broken. Elyce was in a world she could not share and Joanna faced her debut, which oppressed her. She felt guilt over her feelings of resentment.

Caroline was full of reproach, but eventually began to be anxious over her moodiness. She questioned, "What is making you so unhappy, Joanna? We are full of happy plans and, yet, you continue to be miserable."

"Oh, I do not know why I find no interest in anything. I am such dull company, I look about me and everyone is amusing himself or herself in the most careless fashion. Perhaps after seeing all the wonders of Europe, it took away my vanity, I feel so insignificant," Joanna answered in a small voice.

Caroline put a finger to her cheek while carefully scrutinizing Joanna. The child did look wan and ragged, her eyes were listless and her complexion sallow. She could not cancel plans to sympathize. Instead, she said, "Your Grandmother can help you overcome your indifference. We will send you for a short visit. She is lonely now that Wilfred and Winifred are gone."

"If you wish." Joanna sighed.

"That's a dear girl, I will talk to Papa immediately."

Within the week, Joanna, her maid and her governess were on their way to Queensgate. Her delightful (gray and lilac) grandmother with calm assurance and kind heart began to soothe the troubled young mind.

One quiet afternoon Joanna reposed in the depths of a great armchair awaiting with delight the sound of rustling silk and sweeping petticoats that announced her Grandmother.

As Kate poured tea for the two of them, Joanna thought of her Grandmother in terms of mellowed roses, soft and velvety. *She wears her age beautifully*, thought Joanna. The past afternoons they had had long discussions and Joanna found Kate's philosophy of life uplifting. Joanna had told Kate of her despair over spending her future in a large home, devoted to wealth, whims and a duty to a snobby society. "Gram, I was not meant for that life, I want to be of some value in this world. I am repulsed at the idea of lounging around in finery being indulged with everything gilded from sauce pans to chamber pots!"

Kate chuckled, "Be patient, dear, life is much like a book, each day a new page. You must not fear for a great Mighty Hand is writing your story. Resigning us to a power greater than ourselves takes strength. There is a controlling force deep within all of us, we want to control our destiny, but it cannot be. This creates great frustration in all of us, so one can either accept the fact or make life a burden. Healthy minds and strong people usually have a calm that comes from knowing a mightier power. Someday you will know, and it will change your outlook."

"I believe in God, Gram, it is just hard for me to think he believes in me," Joanna said soberly.

"Ah, he does, dear," said Kate, peering at her over the rim of the tea cup. "Child, you are about to begin a journey of decisions. Women are doing more and have more independence than I ever had at your age. I wish I could give you the benefit of my experiences, I cannot, so you will have to forge your own future."

"It is all so confusing and frightening. I am, sadly, not a body to settle down yet. I want to see the world, it beckons to me even in my dreams."

Kate leaned over and took Joanna's hands in hers. "Don't despair, you have Holan blood, your ancestors were survivors and they were very strong. You can do anything you wish as long as it does not hurt you or your loved ones. Speaking of survival, I received letters from John and Winnie. The west has softened her a bit. She is very homesick and yearns to return."

"When will that be? How is Willie?"

"She will not return for another year. John has a governess for her. Dear Will is doing remarkably well. John writes the drovers have taken a liking to him. They refer to him as "Wee Will." He has learned to ride and do chores and his speech has improved somewhat. Here, dear, read for yourself," said Kate, handing the John's letter to Joanna.

"Oh, what wonderful news!" exclaimed Joanna after reading the letter. "I hope Winnie is less crotchety to him. It must be terrible to suffer from a disability, but then to have a disagreeable sister add to the discomfort is even worse. Did she ever ask forgiveness, Gram?"

"The little minx did write some weeks ago apologizing for her manner. I don't hold much hope that she will change. It is hard for her to be pleasant; she is so defiant with the world. Anything I did to punish her bad behavior as a child did not have a particle of effect, either."

Joanna crunched on a cookie and let her mind wander. She could imagine Winifred in the big house in Wyoming. It had to be a far cry from this elegant mansion in which she had been raised. She must pine for society as I do for the solitude. As usual, John's letter had been full of colorful descriptions of the wild and scenic country. She sighed, "If only I could change places with her."

Exasperated, Kate said hotly, "Now, Joanna, concentrate on the possibles. You have an obligation to your dear Mama and Papa. Your debut is planned and after that, the door to the world is open. You are a remarkable young lady. You have flowered into a great beauty, but you will not be a woman until a man makes you feel like one. You have this to look forward to…be it Timber, Pierré or someone yet unknown. You must think about returning to New York within a short time. Your mother is planning your debut and Elyce's wedding, both of which involve you. It is imperative you be there to help."

"You are quite right, as always, dear Gram. I will write and make arrangements for my return next week," said Joanna with a small smile, but her eyes were veiled in a mist of tears. "You have been so helpful and understanding, always willing to listen to my concerns. Your kind generosity always recharges me. I am indeed fortunate you are my Grandmother, I love you so."

"I am proud of you, Joanna," sighed Kate, giving her a very tender kiss. "I shall be lonely when you leave, darling. It has been a joy to have you here and I would keep you indefinitely were it not for the family plans."

"I would stay if I could. I am sorry that Daphne is too ill to be of any company."

"Well, be that as it may, we will enjoy the next few days together. Come, let us walk in the garden."

Joanna returned to New York, was attentive to her family's needs and pleasantly went about her duties. She made her fall debut as planned. Her

Worth gown was white damask layered with embroidered lace and tulle and festooned with a garland of pearls and crystal. Her parents gifted her with a double strand of pearls. Her hairdo was designed by Lentheric, worn high on her head in a mass of curls. Throughout her presentation she was relaxed and enjoyed herself. She danced through the gay evening, never lacking for a partner. The society columnists described her as a *stunner* and *an exquisite beauty*…much to her mother's joy.

Following her debut she had a cluster of beaus; was kept so busy socially that the holidays came and went with spring soon to follow. Her dreams of the Golden West and Timber Alexander faded into the long ago.

One of her most persistent callers was Lord William Cowley. He was visiting New York with the Duke and Duchess of Oldcastle. He had been presented to Joanna one evening at the opera and was quite taken with her. He was impressive looking; faultless attire, tall build with wavy blond hair, elegant features and a handsome blond mustache. Joanna thoroughly enjoyed his company. He had traveled extensively throughout the world and his stories captivated her. Lord Cowley was so smitten he proposed before returning to England. Greatly influenced by her mother she informed him she would consider his proposal. Overjoyed, he asked that she and Caroline come to Europe as his guests to meet the family. A favorable sailing date that met with everyone's approval was agreed upon.

Caroline was in a whirl of excitement, Elyce to be married in a posh ceremony in the coming month and then plans to accompany Joanna to meet her future "in-laws" in London. She chattered to friends of Joanna's outstanding catch, of Lord Cowley's attractive fortune and title; Andrew had misgivings about Joanna's feelings; he felt she was more dazed than joyful.

Elyce's wedding was indeed posh and one of the social events of the year. Her gown was a stunning satin creation, the service, performed by the Bishop of the Anglican Cathedral and a huge reception attended by Astors, Livingstons and other notables.

Joanna hugged her starry eyed sister after helping her change into a traveling outfit for her honeymoon. Elyce's comment to Joanna before leaving was, "Dearest Jo, don't cry, I only wish for you the same happiness I feel today. It is a fairytale come true."

Neither girl had any idea that this day would end a fairytale world for both of them.

One morning over breakfast Caroline asked what Joanna was hearing from Lord William. They had postponed the planned crossing, as his mother had become ill with an undisclosed malady.

"Mama, he corresponds on a regular basis and sends considerable poetry. I find it hard to find any fascinating subjects to write about. He moves through such varied levels of society, particularly royalty. I am so young and newly introduced to society, I do not seem to have much in common with him."

"My dear Joanna, to be sure, William loves you and because of your training and beauty, there should be no problems other than some adjusting for you." Joanna had become her newfound treasure following Lord William's proposal and she would see that nothing marred this affair.

Joanna thought, *Too soon I will be married, in a foreign land with a foreign man.* Why was she not pleased with the thought? Over the past few weeks she had been experiencing misgivings over considering William's proposal. There was not another man anywhere in the picture, nonetheless, she wasn't feeling any rapture like he was describing in his love poems! Time would tell.

Caroline was touching her arm to claim her attention. "We should call on Elyce, I believe I will send a note this afternoon to call Wednesday. Don't you find that a splendid idea, we haven't visited since she has been receiving?"

"Oh, yes, I would love to see her now that the house has been redecorated!"

The next Wednesday, Caroline and Joanna were handed into one of the family's custom built carriages. They were to visit Elyce on this particularly beautiful morning. Caroline was smartly dressed in a new Rouff walking costume and Joanna in blue serge calling gown with a fashionable Paris bonnet.

Elyce and Marshall's home was a handsome three story on Charles Avenue. The coachman helped Caroline and Joanna down in the front driveway. Caroline opened her parasol and rustled up the stairs followed by Joanna. A butler led them into the receiving parlor. It was tastefully furnished with delicate pieces of gold and white French and Italian period furniture. Elyce came towards them, arms outstretched. "Oh, darling Mama and dearest Joanna, how happy I am to see you!" Although dressed in a fashionable lavender and white silk gown, she looked drained and very thin. A lovely coffee service graced a serving table and as Elyce poured, Joanna noticed an ugly bruise low on her jaw and throat. It appeared to be layered with powder to no avail.

"Elyce, what happened to you? What a dreadful bruise?" exclaimed Joanna.

Elyce immediately revered the bruise with a hand and her face turned a mottled pink. "Oh, nothing to be alarmed about. I ran into a branch on a ride with Marshall, just my luck."

"Darling, how awful, you must be more careful!" said Caroline. "Open carriages can be dangerous."

Joanna's heart froze and her dislike of Marshall flared anew. He was abusing Elyce! "Where is Marshall?" asked Joanna.

"He is meeting a friend at the Club," said Elyce despairingly. "I told him you were coming and I apologize for his absence."

Caroline was alarmed at how dismal Elyce sounded. It was unpardonable of him not to be host if Elyce had asked him.

Joanna wanted to take her sister in her arms and console her. She knew that Elyce would never admit that Marshall had been cruel, her sense of shame and loyalty would never allow it.

"Don't fret, dear, we came to see you and your home," said Caroline soothingly. "Every man has his little faults, but we must be the first to ask pardon and guard against the little misunderstandings."

"Honestly, Mama, that is ridiculous," snorted Joanna.

"Wives must not use hasty words which pave the way for bitter sorrow and regret, Joanna. Men provide for the household and their masculine ego must be fed at all times, a woman positively cannot survive without a man!"

Joanna laughed, "I will not be a doormat for anyone, be it man or woman!"

Caroline smiled sadly at Joanna, "You are young, my dear. You will learn your place in this world directly. If a woman is lucky she establishes her place in society, with a loving indulgent husband she can become a most sensational hostess. Speaking of this, have you had callers, Elyce?"

"Yes, Mama, we do and I have returned calls and I am exhausted. We go to the Opera and fashionable parties. I work hard to maintain a proper social face." Elyce's face clouded, "Alas, I find marriage not as I envisioned, I am lonely. Marshall spends much of his time at the clubs."

"Come visit us, we can go shopping, calling or just enjoy a luncheon."

"Marshall has a schedule for me to follow and where and whom I call on," sniffed Elyce.

"I am your mother and I would hope he includes me in that schedule," replied Caroline stiffly.

Elyce stood and paced the length of the handsomely decorated room, her hands nervously wringing a handkerchief. "I would never ignore my family, it's just…oh, how can I say it? I miss you so much and I try to be contented, but it is so hard. I don't want to appear ungrateful for my lovely home, but Marshall is so busy and preoccupied."

Joanna face was a mask of fury, "I was afraid of this; oh, leave him and come home!"

This reduced Elyce to a state of despair, which was pathetic to behold. She sat down and buried her face in her hands. Her body shook with sobs. Joanna embraced and rocked her, "Shhh, all is not lost, I will talk to Papa and he can determine what is to be done."

Caroline fell back in her damask chair, her face white with shock.

Elyce composed herself and with a little quiver in her voice said, "I cannot possibly leave. I love Marshall; we will work it out somehow. I do my best, but it seems I irritate my husband more than I please him."

"Elyce, pour me a tea, I am feeling faint," begged Caroline fanning herself furiously.

"Oh, Mama, honestly, Elyce is having the problem and you are making the fuss!" said Joanna crossly.

"Jo, please, it is alright. I should not have lost my calm. I was just being silly and weak. Marshall can be stubborn and I know I try his patience. I have these little touchy days; you know, the female vapors," Elyce said with insistence as she handed her mother a cup of fresh tea.

Joanna hardly heard her. She was convinced that her sister was being mistreated and was filled with anxiety. Elyce was making excuses for Marshall, too many. Joanna would talk to Papa tonight and he would certainly do something! Satisfied with this thinking, she spoke earnestly, "I love you, dear sister, you have more principle and nobleness of character than anyone I know and I hope you are not doing something very unwise. If there is a problem I know it isn't of your making."

"Well, to be sure," said Caroline, "why don't you show us your home, dear."

"Of course, Mama, I hope you find it to your liking, I have enjoyed decorating it." Elyce rose as she spoke and led them through the great house. She had blended antique and neoclassic art and furnishings. Louis XV and XVI pieces vied for attention with warm Audusson carpets and rich fabrics. Fine chandeliers glowed softly. Elyce had embodied the elegance and formality that was required for a wealthy fashionable young couple to entertain.

Caroline was impressed. "Truly, darling. You have remarkable taste." Thinking of more distraction, she continued, "We are going to Saratoga to take the Waters. Would you and Marshall care to come as our guests?"

"What a heavenly idea," cried Elise, then looking a bit doubtful, "Of course, I must ask Marshall so he can check his calendar."

"Do that and I will have Papa speak with him," retorted Caroline.

"Will you stay for a light luncheon?" asked Elise, hopefully.

"Indeed we will if it can be swiftly arranged; I have an afternoon appointment at two." The necessary arrangements were swiftly made with the maid. In short order Joanna followed her mother and sister into the dining room. As she seated herself at the beautifully appointed table, a dreadful chill passed coldly over her. *Elise is in grave danger; I feel it,* she thought to herself. She further studied her sister; the bruise seemed more defined under the light from the overhead chandelier. It had to have come from a blow.

Caroline picked up a piece of sterling flatware. "This is exceptional, Elyce. Mr. Moore's pattern, is it not?"

"Yes. Momma, it is *The Olympian,* produced by Tiffany's."

"Naturally, it is the most expensive," sniffed Joanna.

"Don't be thorny, Joanna," scolded Caroline.

A comely Irish maid who had a despondent air about her served lunch, none ate more than a few morsels. Joanna felt queasy, Elyce seemed to favor her discolored jaw and Caroline was preoccupied. It was a dismal affair.

Following lunch Caroline and Joanna took their departure and as they climbed into their carriage, Elyce stood like a graceful statue before the entrance of her home. The sun rested on her face and head creating a golden halo of her flaxen curls. Joanna's eyes misted as they drove away.

That evening over a dessert of Charlotte Russe and coffee, Joanna expressed her concern to her father about Elyce.

Her mother scowled at her defiantly, "Really, Joanna, this is not the time to bother your father with trifles."

"Trifles, Mother, indeed! Papa, Elyce is being mistreated by Marshall, it is a disgrace!" Andrew lifted his eyebrows and appeared shocked. "What has he done? If he has harmed her, I will thrash him myself!"

"Hold your tongue, Joanna," cautioned Caroline, "you are assuming too much!"

"Caroline, please," Andrew held up a hand, "I will have the truth, if Andrew has done anything amiss, he will answer to me. Now, out with it, Jo."

Joanna told him of the bruised face, of Elyce's apparent unhappiness and also of her denial that Marshall had abused her.

Andrew eyebrows unbent a bit, he toyed with a spoon for a minute, then said in a gruff voice, "If Elyce says it was an accident and does not want interference I cannot, in a practical sense, come between husband and wife. As to his being at the clubs, that is not immoral. A man, if he is to succeed,

.

must belong to several clubs for social and business contacts. I will press Marshall for lunch. As your mother has advised, I will insist that he and Elyce accompany us to Saratoga." He then reached for Joanna's hand and said, "You are excused, Joanna, I wish to speak with your mother."

Caroline's eyes were kindled with anger as she bade Joanna goodnight. Joanna sighed to herself as she slowly climbed the circular staircase to her room. *I wish I had not caused Mama such distress but I fear for Elyce.*

Two weeks later Caroline, Joanna and Andrew arrived at Saratoga, checked into the elaborate hotel and were ushered to their suite. Elyce and Marshall arrived shortly after. The men went to the racetrack to purchase tickets. The three women leisurely strolled about the hotel and gardens admiring the glittering ballroom, the spacious dining room, the luxurious baths and famous fountains. Looking over the posted menus, Joanna remarked, "It is absurdly expensive, Momma!"

"Perhaps, but it is the resort of the wealthy and influential. Those of less means are just not interested," answered Caroline.

"Or wanted nor can they afford it!" retorted Joanna.

"Oh, please, Joanna, you are so contrary at times," Caroline haughtily said. "Let us retire to our suites. The maids should have us unpacked and I, for one, need to rest before dressing for dinner."

The dress for this evening was demi-toilette. Joanna and Caroline entered the main dining room escorted by Andrew. Joanna looked lovely in a gown of rosy lilac taffeta with a necklace of pearls and amethysts; Caroline wore a stunning Worth gown of iridescent turquoise silk accented by a diamonds and aquamarines. Joanna thought her father the handsomest man there. He was attired in a black frock coat, vest and pantaloons. His shoes were enameled and he carried gloves of dove gray. A cane with a gold serpentine head jauntily hung over his arm.

Caroline and Joanna were seated at their table. Joanna was removing her gloves when Marshall and Elyce arrived. Elyce was breathtaking in a sky blue gown with silver trim, her blond hair was ratted softly away from her delicate face with tendrils curling about her ears and neck. The ugly bruises had disappeared and Elyce looked her old self. Joanna relaxed inwardly as everyone chattered happily through the twelve course dinner. Marshall was the perfect gentleman, acting with strict decorum and hung on Elyce's every word. They seemed besotted with each other and asked to be excused early. Andrew kissed Elyce goodnight and winked at Marshall over her shoulder. As they retired from the room, Andrew remarked, "I think you misunderstood the circumstances around Elyce's mishap. I would be very surprised, indeed, to learn otherwise."

Caroline added, "They are just the dearest of love birds, it is wonderful."

"I pray that you are right," said Joanna.

The following day Caroline attended the races with Andrew and Marshall. Joanna and Elyce went to the baths. The girls changed into their bathing attire. Joanna wore a Dickens and Jones ensemble of turquoise. She giggled at herself in the dressing mirror, "Oh, it feels wonderful to have all the canvas and horsehair off. These pantaloons and stockings are so comfortable. I would love to swim naked and feel the water caress me all over."

"Joanna, for shame, what improper thoughts!" blushed Elyce.

"What is improper about that?" asked Joanna, then looking at her sister closely cried, "Heavens, you are so thin after shedding all your petticoats! You have lost so much weight!"

Elyce's navy blue and white bathing dress hung over her pantaloons like a sack. She quickly tied a red sash around her waist making her frail form even more apparent. She pulled on her rubber slippers and turned her back to Joanna. "You might," she said with dignity, "quit trying to find fault with me, Jo. I am perfectly fine."

"I am sorry, I cannot hold my tongue. Forgive me, Elyce, I simply worry about you and miss you dreadfully. We were always so close and shared every little thing. I just haven't gotten used to the fact you are not coming home and that you have another life that I cannot be a part of."

Elyce smiled, with just a faint curve of her lips, but her eyes were serious. "I felt such loneliness after I began my married life. I kept telling myself it would take time to adjust and I am still trying. Not knowing too much about males." she blushed prettily, "in the physical sense, that is, I had no idea what was required of me. Marshall says I lack a passionate side. He was so demanding on our wedding night that having relations was not a bit exciting. I am a dutiful wife, I never turn from him, but I find that part of marriage not as I expected. The rest is nice enough, but I feel like a child playing house."

Joanna let out a big breath to steady her racing heart. Why did she feel such worry over her sister? She must let go for both their sakes. "Come, El, let's enjoy the waters. Here we can do more than just bob up and down like we do while sea bathing."

They spent the afternoon frolicking in the mineral pools like children.

The holiday passed quickly. The days were sunny with cool ocean breezes keeping the temperature comfortable. The family attended the races, bicycled, *took the waters* and, in general, just relaxed.

On their last evening at the luxurious resort, they enjoyed dinner in the ballroom. The conversation was animated with bright snatches of political gossip and social history. Joanna felt about her a warm loving atmosphere. Her mother and father were having a grand time and Elyce and Marshall had eyes only for each other. Joanna waltzed with her father who complemented her on her loveliness and told her how proud he was of her. She and Elyce shared little jokes between themselves like old times. Marshall danced with her and was so proper he was almost rude which suited her fine. It was a happy evening and Joanna was to remember it long into the future.

October was a blaze of color. Joanna always marveled at autumn's palette with its gold, brilliant reds and fiery oranges that dazzled and danced in every direction. Joanna loved to take her maid, Annie, and walk under nature's brilliant canopy when she wasn't attending parties, the ballet and the opera.

Caroline was painstakingly planning an elaborate Thanksgiving Dinner to seat about a hundred guests. She wanted her invitations to be in the post by the first day of November.

It was when the rains of November began and everyone was forced indoors that the dreadful blow fell. Caroline was in her study when her maid entered and informed her two policemen and Reverend Jenkins were in the drawing room. *No, she did not know the nature of their call; the butler had sent the downstairs maid up.*

Caroline rose, brushed down her skirt, patted her chignon and proceeded downstairs. As she entered the room, Father Jenkins came to her his arms outstretched. He took both her hand s and bade her sit.

"Yes, Father, what is the problem?" she asked becoming alarmed.

"Caroline, there has been an accident, it is Andrew," he replied sadly.

"Andrew! What has happened? What kind of accident, is he hurt, where is he?" she cried.

Joanna had been told there was a problem and hurriedly entered the room. She said breathlessly, "Mama, what is it?"

"Pray sit, child. I've just learned your father has been in an accident."

The younger of the two officers began to speak softly, "Mrs. Holan, your husband shot himself. He is dead, ma'am."

"Dear God!" Joanna said, and for a second, realization did not set in. Then a searing pain gripped her body and she felt her head begin to spin. She grabbed the arms of her chair for support. Her mother's scream of anguish followed by racking sobs jolted her back to reality. She rose shakily and went to her mother, sinking to the floor at her feet. Then both women clung to each other weeping in shock and despair.

When the initial shock had passed; the immediate family was notified. Joanna was numb and went about helping her mother in a stupor. Elyce came immediately, John and Kate followed within days. They gathered together in grief and tenderness. Once the inquisition was over, it was determined a bullet from a small revolver entering the right temple had been the cause of death. An attorney brought the suicide note written by Andrew. The farewell note begging forgiveness gave little comfort to the loved ones.

The cause of Andrew's demise was apparent as John began checking the family accounts. Andrew's lavish expenditures and stock speculation had bottomed him out. Metals had dropped to an all time low and railroad stock plummeted for the stock market had been rocky for months. John knew Andrew's loss of status had most likely defeated him. He had borrowed heavily from John and other associates previously. The bank would be calling in Andrew's notes and when John learned of the amounts, he was astounded. He would help Caroline and Joanna relocate, as he was certain the mansion and other valuables would be sold for the debts owing. Waves of shock reverberated around New York. The funeral was a private one because of the scandal.

The family accompanied Andrew's body to Queensgate where it was buried in the family cemetery. Kate and John insisted that Joanna and Caroline make Queensgate their home.

On the return from Rochester, Caroline had little rest. Like locust, bankers and lawyers descended on the threshold daily. The family attorney advised Caroline to sell Holan House and auction the priceless paintings, antiques and jewelry to payoff notes. Caroline then took to her widow's bed. Joanna and Elyce tried to persuade her to eat and dress, but to no avail. When Caroline, pale and sightless from shedding tears, became so weak she could not be roused, Elyce sent for her Grandmother.

"Oh, Jo, I have such misgivings, I know Gram is grieving also, but if Mother cannot be shaken out of this lassitude, she will surely die," Elyce tearfully cried.

"I understand, Elyce, only Gram has the know how to make Mama want to face life again She has lost everything she valued, her husband, her social standing, her home and all her valuables. The fact Papa never discussed any of his financial affairs with her has been devastating. I cannot understand why he never confided in any of us. We loved him, how could he say he loved us and do such a sinful thing?"

"That was Papa, Jo. He never wanted us to worry and he walked the edge for years, so Marshall tells me," shrugged Elyce.

"I will never understand nor will I forgive him!" replied Joanna, her eyes tearing.

The sad weary Grandmother returned to New York and assessed the situation. Once settled in, Kate had cook make broth and tea and took it to Caroline's chamber. Kate spent all afternoon impressing upon Caroline how much her daughters needed her. This was followed by Kate pleading she needed her also, "My dearest Caroline, I am old and tired and Queensgate needs a hostess. Winifred must make her debut and I beg you to assist me in the planning. John places great importance on his only daughter's coming out. I have been quite desperate as I haven't the stamina to carry out all the duties at Queensgate."

Caroline sipped her tea and answered in a trembling voice, "Dear Kate, her debut is two years away. I am forty, I have nothing and I cannot reason anymore."

"Nonsense, you still appear youthful and you are most attractive. Andrew would not want you grieving like this. We are family; we need and care for you. Forget the dreadful deed. Remember Andrew's love for you and the girls. You must carry on, the girls are sick with worry over you. You must be strong as well. Joanna and Elyce have lost their father, and it can't be your wish to have them lose their mother, as well."

Caroline drank and ate and each day found her stronger. As she and Kate shared breakfast trays one morning she said, "I have decided to live. I will help you with anything down to the smallest detail. I must begin by advising the help to ready the house for sale and packing our personal belongings. I will be forever in your debt, Kate. As you well know, I am a vain woman and not the best of mothers, but I will strive to do my duty."

Kate kissed her on the forehead and knew it was time to ready for the return home.

Lord Cowley wrote Joanna of his pain and displeasure over the notoriety and explained how unlikely it was that his parent's would approve of his becoming engaged at this time. He did not offer any condolences and Joanna's only thought was good riddance. She felt a great release after reading his letter and felt no obligation to send a reply. Caroline was crushed and wanted to sail to England as soon as possible to ready the situation. Joanna told her mother she could think of nothing more abhorrent considering the feelings of Lord Cowley's family. "Mother, we have more important things to think about. Please do not pressure me about this."

Holan House was sold within the month; Caroline parted with most of her priceless jewels and furs. The household items, paintings and furniture were sold at auction. Caroline and Joanna's beautiful designer gowns were packed away in trunks and mourning wardrobes of black, gray and lilac were purchased before leaving for Rochester.

When Joanna arrived at Queensgate she had no tears left to shed. Still in a state of shock, she took long walks among the gardens now bare in the crisp winter air. Days turned into weeks and still Joanna was filled with anguish. Her father's untimely death had jolted her senses and torn deeply at her roots of faith. At her father's funeral, the language was rich in continuation. Father Jenkins had intoned that *Love is immortal, life is eternal and death is just a door to a far better world.* Joanna yearned for this to be true for she was filled with bitterness. Her anger at her beloved father tore at her each day. Why, why, why…she asked herself over and over. Before the unthinkable had happened, the family's strong faith had been a protective barrier that kept her safe from uncertainties. The hereafter was a shining promise of heaven and all its rewards for the faithful. Now she realized her father had not been strong, his faith was questionable and her world was shattered. Her father had betrayed them all! Had he truly believed he would still be alive.

The holidays were somber. Queensgate was stark in draped black. The three women attended church services and ate a quiet Christmas dinner. Caroline gave Joanna a mourning pin with a lock of Andrew's hair and Kate gifted her with a braided gold bracelet inscribed with her initials. It was a sad holiday and as dismal as the winter months now were. The New Year came with news from Elyce that she was *in the family way.* Caroline was not delighted, the thought of her being addressed as a Grandmother was not to her liking.

Daphne became very ill and Kate sent word to John. In late spring the frail little woman passed as quietly as she had lived. John and Winifred had returned for the funeral. John mourned for the little sparrow that never learned to fly. On his departure west he said he planned to bring Winifred back in the fall so she could begin to prepare for her debut in the spring. Joanna became melancholy and troubled over this news. For the brief time Winifred had spent at Queensgate after Daphne's funeral, she had treated Joanna abominably. Joanna had endured her scornful remarks in silence, but knew it would become a tempest if Joanna were there when Winifred returned.

After much deliberation, she wrote her uncle:

Dearest Uncle John,

I have given great thought to my present circumstances and I pray that you might consider helping me. Little did any of us realize the grave step Papa was contemplating nor the mortification and grief that followed. Decisions that Papa might have made for me I must now make for myself. I have always longed to go west. Might there be a possibility of my finding a position as a governess or teacher?

Father's estate left me a small allowance that I can use to pay my passage west. I have tried to console myself with the fact I can no longer depend on circumstance only my inner self. I have always endeavored to do my best with schooling and feel quite confident that I have had an excellent education.

Mother is doing well and she and Grandmother are very much into planning Winifred's coming out.

For fear you may think me ungracious, I want to express my gratitude for your kindness to Mother and me in allowing us to live at Queensgate. I do love it here, but desperately need to find my own way. Any consideration you may give to my appeal will be most greatly appreciated.

Ever your loving and dutiful niece,
Joanna Holan

It was a month before Joanna received a reply from her uncle. She opened the letter with trembling fingers:

My dearest Niece,

I know it will please you to learn, after long and deliberate consideration, I have found you a position as a school marm. There are children here and nearby Fort Dix and nearby Snowflake Ranch in desperate need of schooling. The Fort did have an educator, but he moved on.

You must realize you will not enjoy the many comforts of Queensgate. This country is still quite untamed and for that very reason, Winifred is looking forward with great anticipation to returning east. Will, meanwhile, thrives in this atmosphere and is quite content. If you still feel you wish to undertake such a drastic step, I plan to bring Winifred to Queensgate late summer. You will be welcome to accompany me on my return west. I will send you a list of proper attire so you can shop forthwith.

I hope to be further assured by a letter from your mother.

Your devoted Uncle John

Joanna could hardly contain herself she was so exhilarated. She told her grandmother and mother over dinner that evening. Caroline was appalled and began dabbing delicately at her eyes. "Hell's Gates, Joanna, have you lost your senses?" she exclaimed, "I've lost your father and now you wish to go to the ends of the earth?

"Mama, do not feel that way. I am not abandoning you. I want to make my own way and try to make some substance of my life," answered Joanna.

Caroline was trying hard to contain herself as she replied disgustedly, "You have had every advantage, excellent tutors, and are trained to all the social graces. You could be affianced to Lord William yet you wish to throw this all away to go live in the wilds? Whatever is to become of you?"

"Mama, it isn't the wilds, it is the Western United States! It is inhabited, there are numerous towns and cities," Joanna maintained stubbornly, her violet eyes beginning to spark.

"You must have a chaperone, no decent young lady travels alone. We cannot manage that, don't you realize we are practically penniless?" stormed Caroline. "You should be here to receive suitors, you must think of your future!"

"I would not have to look if I wanted a man, I have already been besieged," Joanna exhaled sharply in annoyance. "I will marry when I fall in love or never!"

Kate seeing that the discussion was getting heated intervened, "Don't be so stricken, Caroline. Joanna is a sensible young lady and she would never disgrace you. I will make arrangements for Annie to accompany her when she departs. John will take care of her like his own." Kate reached over and covered Caroline's hand with her own. "It will probably be just an adventure and she will return wiser for the experience."

Caroline heaved an enormous sigh and looked thoughtfully at her daughter. Defiant lavender eyes stared back at her. "I do not want you to go," Caroline said unhappily. "I would never forgive myself should something happen to you. It is so far away and so remote."

"Oh, Mama, I will miss you and Gram, but honestly, what would I do here?"

"Whatever you wished, darling," replied Caroline sadly.

Joanna was not prepared for the emotional stand her mother was taking. She had been so amazed to see her become so involved in helping Kate manage Queensgate including the arrangements and planning of Winifred's debut. She acted as if she had always been here and hardly ever mentioned Papa. Joanna had had mixed emotions about her mother's unsentimental aspects towards her father's death; she felt disappointment and relief that Caroline could recover from such a tremendous blow so soon. Inside Joanna had been sad and resentful, she had held her grief close inside trying to understand her father's desertion. Taking long walks through the grounds of Queensgate in quiet contemplation that had brought some peace. Where she had found indifference in her mother, now she was finding concern and it was a bit disconcerting.

"Mother, if you will give me permission to go with Uncle John for a short period of time, I promise to return and do what is expected of me. I won't disappoint you and I shall be reasonable."

"Oh, my dear girl, you will make an elegant mistress in a splendid home! I will say yes only because I know you will find my thinking correct and thank me for it."

Joanna bounced up off her chair and ran to her mother. "Thank you, Momma," she cried, hugging Caroline. "I will make you proud of me, I think I should have died had you refused me!"

"Joanna, we are too well bred to argue. With an aching heart I give you my leave. Now, until you go, we must be busy about our affairs." Caroline sighed, then added, "So far away!" as an afterthought.

On a warm summer day Joanna returned from a cooling walk in the gardens to find she had a visitor. Pierré de Beaudian sat conversing with Caroline in the drawing room. He rose and came to her with delight on his handsome features. Taking her hands in his, he kissed them and gazed deeply into her eyes. "My sweet Jo, even in your grief you are breathtaking."

"Oh, Pierré, how wonderful to see you!" exclaimed Joanna happily. "Thank you for the condolences, it meant so much to all of us."

"Yes," echoed Caroline, "the flower remembrances and wreaths were so thoughtful."

"Oh, please sit, Pierré. You must meet Grandmother," and she whisked Pierré quickly to a sofa and rang for a maid.

Kate joined them shortly. After introductions her eyes went from Pierré's joyous eyes to Joanna's smiling face and she was overjoyed. She invited Pierré for dinner, which he graciously accepted. Then settling back and smoothing the folds of her black silk dress she enjoyed the obvious delight these two young people found in one another.

That evening they dined modestly on chicken and Beef Wellington. Joanna's animation was heartwarming to Kate and Caroline. She and Pierré happily reminisced about Europe and everyone had a thoroughly delightful evening.

Pierré asked permission to call the next day and Kate was quick to oblige. He became a regular visitor every night for the following week. The atmosphere at Queensgate was now a pleasant one. Joanna smiled and laughed gaily and could be heard humming happily as she went about the mansion. When she greeted him at the door she beamed like a ray of sunlight. On several occasions he took her riding in his buggy and Annie was always the dutiful chaperone. When Pierré learned he must leave within the week to go New York on business he decided to take the situation in hand. He took Joanna for a ride and stopped the carriage beside the river under a canopy of trees. He looked at her, how he enjoyed everything about this exquisite girl. Her complete innocence and honesty was refreshing and her beauty dazzling. Her long lashes threw black crescents against her creamy cheeks and her soft pink mouth curved in a lazy smile. He had observed how the grief had changed her in little ways. It showed in her eyes, a sort of merciful dullness shadowed them and her carriage was now restrained whereas in Europe she had a sort of poetry in her walk. She had seemed like a delicate candle fluttering in the wind. He, oh so wanted to take this lovely lost creature into his arms and kiss the hurt away; to steady her and rekindle the brightness she once had.

She opened one eye quizzically, "Is there a problem?"

"Not really, dearest, I must return to New York, but it will be a short business stay. I would like to return here for a few days before going on to New Orleans." He now had Joanna's full attention and she sat straight up looking at him intently. He continued, "I care deeply for you. I have from the moment I first met you. Do you have any feelings for me?"

"Oh, dear Pierré, I am so tired and confused. My emotions are shredded and I am numb," said Joanna wretchedly. "I am so grateful for your friendship and enjoy your company. I am sorry, but that is all I can give you at present."

An expression of pleasure crossed Pierré's face and his brown eyes were full of love and longing. "Then, my darling, I will give you all the time in the world to find yourself. It has been just a little over a year since you lost your father. I would have called sooner, but when I encountered Elyce at the opera she told me you were betrothed to a Lord someone or other."

"Oh, Pierré, that must have been before Papa's death! Lord Cowley and I had a brief understanding, but following Papa's death, he wrote and said it was an impossibility for us to consider any future plans because of the circumstances surrounding the death. Poor Mama was in a state over that. It was a rather low point, but I cannot despair over someone who would not defend his feelings."

"Damnation, Joanna, he was a fool!" snorted Pierré in exasperation.

"Oh, my dear, I could never marry any man without the cordial consent of his family. I do not have that importance in myself. I most certainly wouldn't want my husband estranged from his family either," answered Joanna fervently.

Pierré leaned over to her and put his hands on either side of her face. He looked into her violet fluttering eyes and then pressed a long lingering kiss on her lips. "I pray when I return you will agree to my proposal. My heart's desire is to make you my wife, to love you as you deserve to be loved. I want to hold you forever."

Joanna shuddered as he kissed her eyelids, her lips, her neck and ears. Exquisite little shocks were running up her spine, through her stomach and up through her breasts. She pushed him gently away. She was amazed at how her quivering body was responding to Pierré's kisses. Turning she saw Annie's eyes as large as saucers staring in shock. Laughing huskily, she said, "It is all right Annie, my virtue is still intact even if my mind is not!"

Pierré snapped the reins and turned the buggy. He said in a low voice, "Joanna, please give serious thought to my proposal."

Her thoughts were in a tumble. *Please heart, stop pounding. I cannot believe I let Pierré take such liberties with me. My body reacted before I could control it and such feelings!* She blushed in spite of herself. She gazed at Pierré in wonderment. They really were good friends and she was so comfortable in his company, was she about to make an amazing discovery? Could this be love? He was so kind, so good, so stable. Horrors, she sounded like her mother!

Pierré asked again, "Will you give my proposal some thought?"

She cast down her eyes demurely, her head awhirl. "Yes, Pierré, I will. I must clear my head to think."

Pierré's warm husky voice answered, "I know, darling, however long it must take you."

Joanna turned and pushed Annie back in her seat. Poor little Annie was still wide eyed. "Don't you breathe one word of this to my mother, hear!" hissed Joanna.

"Yes, ma'am, I mean, no, ma'am," replied the little maid, stuttering.

The week passed quickly. Pierré called every evening bringing flowers and charming gifts. He and Joanna said foolish little things to each other, while his eyes caressed her adoringly. They were never alone as Caroline was always close by.

The evening before Pierré's departure, they had a festive dinner. Pierré placed small velvet boxes next to each place setting. Caroline and Kate were gifted with lovely cameo pins. Joanna's box contained a beautiful pin of amethysts and diamonds. "To match your eyes, my dear," stated Pierré.

"Oh, my, I can't accept this, it is much too valuable!" she said in a shocked voice.

"Nonsense, I had it crafted for you. Accept it with love or friendship, it belongs to you."

Joanna turned the lovely pin over in her fingers deep in thought. She had known Pierré was special from the minute she had met him, but she was also aware she could not have a relationship at this point in her life. In the last two days, she had come to the realization that she loved Pierré as a cherished friend, but she was not in love with him. She dreaded the evening's close, she must tell him and not keep him dangling with hope. She could not say yes out of gratitude for friendship and physical attraction. It would sadden her to make him unhappy and she knew she would. How she wished she could love him as he so desired, but she could not.

Coffee was served in the drawing room. Kate bade farewell to Pierré and retired.

Caroline sat at the far end of the drawing room working on needlepoint.

Pierré reached for Joanna's hand and rambled about many unrelated subjects, then losing his flow of language, he paused. Joanna looked up to find him looking at her questionably. He watched her as he talked. He wanted to touch her, her face, her hair, to hold her in his arms and inhale her beauty.

Her violet eyes began to mist with unshed tears and she said hastily in a resolute tone, "Dearest Pierré, I have struggled with my decision, but I know now that my answer is no."

"Cherié, please, you are breaking my heart!"

"It is no use, Pierré, I wish I loved you as you love me. I've tried, but I cannot change my feelings. Some lovely girl will be so fortunate to have you…" Joanna choked, this was a great deal more difficult than she expected.

Pierré dropped his head and covered his face with his hands. In a muffled voice and in spite of a manful effort to keep it steady, "I have loved you always, I would have told you in Europe, but Elyce became ill, then I planned to visit New York, but learned of your father's death. I waited too long."

"Oh, my dear, I am truly sorry. I hope we can still be friends. You are so very dear to me," pleaded Joanna in an anguished voice.

An ashen Pierré rose. "I must leave, please give my respects to your mother." He walked to the hallway.

"Pierré, wait!" cried Joanna rising.

He stopped short, and Joanna hurried to him holding out the little velvet box, "I cannot accept this, Pierré, truly."

When the last words fell from Joanna's lips, Pierré took her in his arms and held her close "Darling, this pin is yours, a token of my undying love. Wear it in good health, remember always, I love you. If you ever need me, send word. Now dry your lovely eyes and give me my cape and cane." Pierré, regaining his composure and ever the gentleman, kissed her hand in departure.

As he walked into the night, Joanna felt as if she had destroyed part of herself and buried it. She walked slowly back into the drawing room.

Caroline took one look at her stricken face and said quietly, "There is a problem?"

Joanna burst into tears and wailed, "This has been dreadful, the most awful evening! To have to refuse such a wonderful man almost destroyed me."

"Oh, my dear, I cannot bring myself to believe you refused his proposal. I find it difficult to understand you," admonished Caroline raising an eyebrow.

Joanna straightened herself up and dabbing at her eyes said, "Mama, I don't understand, either. I am going to retire." She hastily embraced her mother and fled upstairs.

CHAPTER SEVEN

The spring passed slowly, it was still a difficult adjustment for Joanna. She went to New York with Annie to shop for western wear. Elyce insisted she stay with her. She was beginning to round and on days when she felt well she accompanied Joanna shopping. Joanna shopped as her Uncle John had suggested; daytime skirts of light wool with matching jackets, white blouses, riding skirts, tailored lone wool jackets and a riding habit. She was fitted for leather boots jodhpurs and gloves. Elyce bought her two bonnets, smoked glasses and a parasol. Joanna dashed between fittings for trunks and school supplies, then would rest before dinner with Elyce. It was usually just the two of them. Marshall spent most evenings at the club or elsewhere. Joanna never questioned and Elyce seemed content with the situation.

One particular evening Marshall was in attendance and Joanna sat nervously as his critical gaze swept over her. "God's teeth, Joanna, you look ill." he said. "You should be wearing some color, the mourning period is over. I realize your circumstances are harried, but you must do credit to your remaining family. Notice Elyce, I send her to the finest dressmakers and I expect her to look like a jewel in this splendid setting."

"Oh, Marshall, please don't carry on so," murmured Elyce. "You are embarrassing Jo."

"Look at her in that drab dowdy black—she will never attract a husband wrapped up like a mummy!" Then his eyes glinted, "By Jove, I've got it, I will get tickets for the opera. Elyce, you will buy her a proper ensemble and I will take you both to Delmonico' s after the opera, what say you?"

"Oh, wonderful, darling, it will be just like old times!" exclaimed Elyce clapping her hands together.

A sense of foreboding flickered through Joanna. She had hoped she would not have to socialize with Marshall, then seeing Elyce's happy face she straightened her spine. "It sounds delightful." She lifted her chin and added, "I will purchase my gown."

"Fiddlesticks, it is our treat and we will go shopping tomorrow," retorted Elyce.

The following day Elyce and Joanna shopped. Joanna found a wonderful trailing midnight blue velvet gown with matching opera cape. She was reluctant to quit dark colors altogether. She purchased matching slippers and white opera gloves. "There goes my good intentions," she said as she admired herself in the dressing mirror.

"What good intentions, dear?" chortled Elyce happily.

"I made a promise to myself I would never forget Papa and would dress as such."

"Oh, Jo, he is gone. You are too young to dress so severely and besides, Papa would never have wanted that. He loved life. When he could not enjoy it anymore, he left it!"

Joanna sighed, "It will be wonderful to celebrate a little and this dress is so lovely."

"You look divine, it was made for you. You'll not need, but the tiniest of alterations. I will lend you some diamonds. You will be stunning!"

The evening of the ball was a warm balmy night. Marshall helped Elyce and Joanna into the carriage. He was very impressed by his elegant wife and sister. Elyce's gown was yards and yards of yellow satin trimmed with a deep wine velvet border repeated in her modified sash and neckline trim. It concealed her pregnancy totally with a wine velvet opera cape trimmed in mink edging to the broaddropped collar. Topaz and diamonds glittered around her neck. Joanna shimmered in her velvet and her eyes sparkled with suppressed excitement. Marshall kissed her gloved hand as he helped her into the carriage and she glanced at him startled.

"My dear, you look ravishing," he whispered in her ear.

She froze, her mouth tightened and she glared at him as he settled in his seat opposite her. Marshall smiled at her, running a hand pensively over his jaw as his eyes studied her. He had always had exceptional taste in women and knew where he was heading. Elyce, after becoming pregnant repulsed him, especially as of late. He intended to enjoy what he wanted and he wanted Joanna. Tonight, he vowed, he would have the little sister! His handsome arrogant face gleamed feral in the lamplight and inside he was seething with lust and excitement. His eyes glittered as he thought of his seduction of Joanna. He had waited a long time for this sweet morsel!

"Marshall, I swear, you didn't hear a word I uttered," exclaimed Elyce loudly. "You must be in another world!"

Marshall sighed and pressed himself close to Elyce, "Sorry, sweetie, I was caught up thinking of business. What were you saying?"

"I must shop for more things for the nursery—would you care to accompany me?"

"Elyce, I don't want to be difficult, but I have appointments. Get James to drive you or have the maids do it for you. Perhaps Joanna would stay a bit longer and assist you," he answered, glancing over at Joanna.

Joanna stared at him wide eyed. "I don't know that I can, I will check my calendar," she responded, suddenly afraid.

Marshall gazed hungrily at her. She had been a lovely girl when he first met her, but now she was a beautiful woman. Her chestnut hair curled softly around her face. Tonight her violet eyes were startlingly dark and long lashed and her skin was as smooth as cream. Her body was wonderfully curved and her glorious breasts gleamed ivory above the midnight-blue velvet. She was oblivious to her beauty which made her even more desirable.

The carriage slowly pulled up the driveway leading to the entrance of the opera house. Faint strains of music drifted through the massive portals. A line of carriages and cabs stretched before them waiting to discharge their occupants at the marbled entrance. Beautifully gowned women glittered with jewels and their escorts alighted one after another. Joanna gasped—so many diamond tiaras; so much blinding glitter of jewels. She had forgotten how *best society* primped and preened. Just two years previous, the Holans had been the toast of New York. She thought of Mama and her elegant gowns and jewelry. Ah, yes, but that was the past and with the tragedy they had become declassé. Elyce had *put on a good face*, but her shamed mother and sister left the city. Marshall, (the good catch) and a Davenport made Elyce eligible to still be or the social register.

"Oh, there, Jo, it's Diamond Jim Brady! Who has he on his arm this evening?" squeaked Elyce. A large rotund elegantly dressed gentleman stepped from a carriage with two lovely bejeweled women. "I understand he has made millions from railroads and he is also a gourmet cook! The other evening he gave a splendid dinner. Beside the plates of gold were Turkish cigarettes rolled in *thousand grand bills* for the gentlemen and diamond brooches nestled in gardenias for the ladies!"

"How extravagant, I remember well Papa doing foolish things like that," answered Joanna stiffly.

"Yes, it seems a dream, Joanna," said Elyce quietly. "Come, let us enjoy the opera."

Once Joanna was settled into her plush seat in the Davenport private box, she began to relax and lost herself in the romantic tragedy, *Der Fliegende*

Hollander (The Flying Dutchman) by Wagner. The dark and handsome Dutchman holds her spellbound as he sings his tragic arias across the footlights. *He has been condemned to sail forever on the seas until he has found a woman whose love to him is faithful unto death.*

Joanna is weeping by intermission. The beautiful Norwegian, Senta, has pledged her love knowing she and the Dutchman are doomed.

Joanna and Elyce retire to the dressing room.

"I do so miss the operas and dramas," said Joanna, wistfully. "Of course, I am so fortunate to have been able to see so many of them."

"Well, there is no reason why you cannot again. Return here and we will all go. We saw Puccini's *Madame Butterfly* a few weeks ago and it was marvelous. *Tosca* is coming, you must return for that!" exclaimed Elyce excitedly

"The opera is so touching. Such voices, and Senta, to be able to love like that! Love eternal, shall I ever find it?" Joanna sighed as she plumped her hair and bit her lips.

"You will someday. I would die for Marshall, he is my world!" replied Elyce with great feeling. Meeting Elyce's sad eyes in the mirror, Joanna smiled, "You will have a little stranger to love soon, too."

Elyce's blue eyes brimmed with tears, "Oh, sometimes I wonder if Marshall is happy about the baby. He seems so gloomy at times and he never touches me, now, ever."

"Perish the thought, every man wants an heir. He's probably just being cautious. Good heavens listen to me...I know nothing about babies or birthing or whatever," laughed Joanna, blushing.

Elyce turned to face her, for a second her eyes looked dead and haunted, but then the light returned to her lovely face. It made a chill go through Joanna. So, Marshall had not changed. He was still a brute and in that second she knew her sister was most unhappy!

"Come, let us join Marshall and enjoy the remainder of the opera," said Elyce as she grabbed Joanna's elbow. They made their way through the crowd to Marshall. He was surrounded by acquaintances and as Joanna sipped champagne, she watched him flirt with the women and charm the men. He acknowledged his wife and introduced Joanna to the circle.

There were a few raised eyebrows when the Holan name was mentioned, but Joanna ignored them. The house lights were dimming as they returned to their box. Joanna looked forward to the continuing acts of the opera. Once again she became engrossed with the story and wept as Senta sacrifices herself, breaking the spell cast on the Dutchman. His ghostly ship sinks forever into the ocean. An angel bears the poor wanderer to eternal rest where he is united to the bride who has proved faithful unto death.

As the performers are taking their curtain calls, Joanna is openly weeping. *Enough of this*, she thought to herself and acted half-mechanically…pulling herself out of her seat. She turned to find Marshall holding her cape.

"How wonderful to find a kindred soul who loves the passionate contemplation of beauty; so devoured by the life of soul, the life of mind, and the life of body!" he exclaimed as he put Joanna's cape about her shoulders. "Ah, to see the exquisite tremor awaken your mouth, your abandonment to delight and tears gives me such satisfaction, you are aflame with life, sweet sister."

Elyce looked at him in astonishment, her eyebrows in question.

"Now, little mother, how did the opera affect you?" he asked as he turned and put Elyce's cape about her. He charmed her with, "You look as if you are rising from the sea, all pearly and incandescent, glowing with life."

Elyce beamed, "My, you are in excellent form this evening, yes, indeed."

"Oh, we shall see won't we? Let us risk the crowd, I am famished."

They dined on fresh terrapin, champagne and plover at Delmonico's. The exclusive restaurant was packed with notables. At the very next table sat the jovial Theodore Roosevelt and party. Across from them a group chattered and laughed with a man dressed in white fringe leather. He had long white hair and a goatee to match.

"Who are those people dressed in Western attire, Marshall?" questioned Elyce.

"The man with the goatee is William F. Cody, known by his more popular name, 'Buffalo Bill,' he owns that *Wild West Show*," responded Marshall, sipping his wine. A striking woman with many gentlemen in tow stopped at their table. She was beautifully dressed in crepe and velvet, carrying a long train in one hand and a fan of ostrich feathers in the other. Her dress showed off her ample bosom and hour glass figure to full advantage. Diamonds sparkled in her hair, around her neck, arms and waist. "Hello darling, how good to see you!" she cooed in a silken voice as Marshall jumped to his feet.

"Why, Helen, what a wonderful surprise! You look smashing, as always. Won't you join us?" Marshall asked excitedly.

Helen tossed her beautiful head at her entourage and purred, "Thanks, darling, we have more joining us. The flowers were a delight as always, dear boy…and who are these lovely girls?" she asked pointedly of Joanna and Elyce.

"Oh, may I present my wife, Elyce and her sister, Joanna Holan." He followed with, "Ladies, Miss Lillian Russell!"

Miss Russell's impressive eyebrows shot up, "Are you Andrew Holan's daughter?"

"Yes," replied Joanna, "he was our beloved father."

"Oh, he was a delight…such a dear man and a good friend." She then turned to Elyce, "So this is your sweet wife, Marshall? Charming, charming…well, forgive us our sins, enjoy the evening, darlings."

Marshall bowed respectfully as she swept away with her handsome and arrogant escorts. "What a presence she is!" exclaimed Joanna. "I remember Papa taking us to see her!"

"What flowers was she referring to?" sniffed Elyce.

"I send her flowers for every opening. She is a friend of the family. We know her as Helen Leonard. Quite extraordinary, very beautiful, and sings like an angel," mused Marshall.

The magical evening drew to a close. The women were handed into their carriage and began their return to the mansion. It was a quiet ride home with each lost in their thoughts. Later in her room Joanna sat in front of the dressing table while Annie brushed her hair.

"It is so late. I am sorry you waited up and did not retire to the maid's quarters, Annie."

"Oh, Miss Joanna, I don't mind, it is always a pleasure to take care of you;" protested Annie quickly.

Joanna sighed, "Please stay with me tonight. There is a bed mat in the amoire. I feel very apprehensive about being alone. I can't explain it, just nerves, I guess."

Annie stared at her thoughtfully. Her mistress never expressed concern for herself. "You climb into bed and wrap yourself in dreams. I will be here for you," Annie answered.

Joanna fell into bed exhausted and went to sleep immediately.

She awoke struggling, couldn't breathe…something was over her nose and mouth! "Be quiet!" hissed a male voice. He kept a hand over her mouth, but let her breathe. She could smell stale cigar smoke and strong liquor. "You will be mine tonight, stay still!" The moon slanted through the window illumining Marshall's leering face above hers. Her heart thudded in her chest, this couldn't be happening! Panicked, she lay perfectly still. She could hear his rasping breath…then he ripped her gown down off her shoulders and she began to kick and struggle! He pushed one hand tight against her throat cutting off her oxygen, and his other hand grabbed a breast in a clawlike vise. He fell on her and Joanna felt a knee forcing open her thighs. "No, no, I am dying," she tried to scream, but he covered her mouth with his own and rammed his tongue down her throat. Joanna felt herself losing consciousness as he lifted himself and rammed into her body. Joanna felt her world tear apart.

Suddenly there was a loud thud and Marshall slumped against her in a pile of broken porcelain. Annie lit a lamp. Joanna clawed and pushed to get him out of her and from under his inert body.

"Oh, God, Miss, I hope I didn't kill him!" screeched her distraught maid.

"I hope you did," gasped Joanna, gagging and shaking like a leaf. "We must get him out of here, help me!"

They tugged and pulled Marshall and the satin coverlet off the bed, then rolled and pushed until they got him into the hallway.

Panting, Joanna closed the bedroom door, turned the key and pushed a chair against it. She collapsed on the floor and began to weep hysterically. Annie cleaned up the broken china and stripped off the bedding. She then took Joanna in her arms and crooned to her as she would a child. "Shhh, dear, try to lie down and relax. Oh, gawd, I hope that vase wasn't valuable!" cried Annie.

"Nothing could be as priceless as you are to me tonight, you saved my life, Annie," answered Joanna in a quivering voice and clasped her little maid to her. She finally laid down, but hardly dared to breathe. She lay still as death on the bed, so drained she couldn't even whimper. Then she heard a noise outside the door and a moan and faint rustling. Both women waited with bated breaths, but not another sound was heard. Joanna whispered, "It is nearly dawn. At first light, we will pack and leave."

As the room lightened, the women hurriedly packed the trunks, desperate to escape.

"Hurry, Annie, there is no time to lose!"

Pulling herself together Joanna had Annie pour water into the porcelain basin and she washed as best she could…especially the blood between her legs. She had a deep purple bruise on her throat and her body ached everywhere. She was broken and her mind numb. Annie helped her dress in a high-necked blouse and pulled on a skirt with matching jacket. Joanna dressed her hair with shaking hands. By the time they had everything in order, the house was filled with life. Joanna quietly opened the door with a pounding heart. The hallway was clear. She and Annie crept down the staircase.

"Good morning, dear, did you sleep well?" Elyce was standing in a wrapper at the foot of the stairs. Joanna closed her eyes. She could not look at Elyce. Her hand stole to her throat and she wavered a bit.

"Elyce, I must leave. Where is Marshall?"

"Marshall was gone when I came down. James said he left word he had gone to the Club. Why are you leaving...I thought we were to go shopping for the baby? Have I done something to displease you?" questioned Elyce in a quivering voice.

"Oh, never, Elyce. I forgot I have a most important engagement tomorrow evening. Please don't put any pressure on me, I really must go."

"Oh, tell, tell, you have a secret lover?" laughed Elyce, her eyes sparkling.

"Trust me, someday I will explain everything. Will you have someone fetch my trunks? Elyce, please, please take care of yourself."

Elyce looked at Joanna now with a bit of alarm. "Won't you have breakfast? I don't understand the hurry and you are being terribly unkind not to tell me your secret!"

Joanna hesitated for a brief moment, she would like to tell her sister what happened, but it would be unwise considering Elyce's condition. She could never intentionally harm her.

"I cannot, I love you." She reached out to her sister and with tears in her eyes hugged her tenderly. Elyce hugged her back, her eyes misting.

"Do give my love to Mama and Grandmother. I so enjoyed having you here. Please say you'll return."

"I will try," whispered Joanna. She knew she would never return.

It was two days after the return to Queensgate when Annie quietly opened the chamber door to Kate. Joanna was lying stiffly on the big bed, her eyes puffed and red from weeping. Seeing her Grandmother, she turned her face away and shut her eyes tightly. Kate motioned Annie to bring a chair and she sat beside the bed. She picked up one of Joanna's hands and kissed it. "My dearest Joanna, you must talk to me. Annie told me what happened." Joanna lay silent as Kate continued speaking in a soft persuasive voice, explaining she was safe at Queensgate. "I am here for you. Do you want me to talk to your mother, dear?"

"No, never! Not about this, she would never forgive me!"

"Heavens, child, there is nothing to forgive, you are a victim!" snorted Kate.

There was a long silence. Joanna was thinking of her mother and her indifference. It was hard to remember a gesture of true affection. Joanna squeezed Kate's hand. "Mama would be mortified to know this had happened. It wouldn't matter the circumstances and only add to the shame and dishonor of the family. Mama would feel I behaved improperly and I cannot bear to have her add to the despair and shame I already feel. Why can't she be more caring and understanding like you, Gram?"

"Remember, your mother was born into wealth. I married into it and was raised in a middle class society. Our upbringing was totally different."

"Oh, curses, whatever am I to do? No one is ever going to look at me…WHAT if I get in the family way? Oh, I feel so unclean and soiled!" Joanna began to weep softly.

"That is enough!" said Kate in a stern voice. "At the moment you are going to put some witch hazel on your eyes, then bathe and dress! No granddaughter of mine is going to wallow in self pity because of that devil. We must think this out carefully, Joanna. You should confide in Elyce, the sooner the better."

"Never, I will never tell her! I will never tell anyone. It must be our secret, Gram, promise!"

"I will think on it. By the way, when you are more composed, you will want to read this. It came while you were in the city." Kate pulled a thick envelope from her pocket. It was from Pierré. Joanna opened it slowly with trepidation.

My Dearest Darling,

You were very good, indeed, to write me the particulars of your planned visit to Elyce. Had I stayed three days longer, I would have seen you! I am certain you and your sister had a most enjoyable visit and you are now safely home.

I am off within the month to San Francisco, California, to start a new venture for Papa.

My cherié, how I long that you were going with me. My Mamam feels it is very unwise for me to live so far away, but isn't that just like a mother?

I have been going about with Papa making all the necessary arrangements. I am actually very excited to be able to see more of this great country of ours. Papa wanted me to sail, but I want to go overland to experience it all. I have a fascination with the Red Man and the wild beasts.

I am looking forward, particularly, to visiting this city and it's wonderful bay. I am told it is becoming the metropolis of the west.

You have undoubtedly heard of the Nob Hill where all the nabobs have built their monstrous mansions? Well, if I prosper, I shall build one for you.

I hope and trust you are well. Give my regards to your Mamam and Grandmamam.

I hold you in my heart, lovely Joanna. You know my feelings. I am sick with longing and hope one day you will change your mind. In fact, I pray of nothing else.

Please write before I depart and I will continue to keep you informed of my progress. Hundreds of kisses I send with all my lovesick heart,

    Your devoted and adoring slave,
    Pierré

Joanna's heart turned over with a painful lurch as she handed the letter to Kate. "Oh, Gram, I should never have let him go. If only I had accepted his proposal, I would never have gone to New York!" She sobbed despairingly.

"Joanna, there are always 'ifs' with any tragic circumstances, but it has happened. It is over and you must get on with living. I promise you there will be happier days ahead. Now, if you truly love Pierré, tell him so, if not, begin turning your dreams into reality. Few men are as sinister as Marshall Davenport, but there will be, unfortunately, always one lurking about somewhere. You must never allow yourself to ever be in a vulnerable position again. Now do me a favor, freshen up. I will send tea up and will expect you for dinner."

"I am afraid all the cleansing in the world will never wash away my disgrace," Joanna murmured in a soft voice.

"It is a vile thing that happened to you, but the disgrace is his, not yours!" Kate brushed back the hair from Joanna's wan face, kissed her on the cheek and left the room.

At dinner that evening, Joanna sat frozen and could not eat a morsel. She was certain her mother and all the servants could surmise what had happened. She felt so soiled, she was certain it showed.

"Well, it is good to see you rested so you can rejoin us, Joanna," said Caroline. "I have not had a moment to inquire on Elyce's health. Is she well?

Was Marshall a proper host, did he escort you and Elyce out to any functions?"

The color drained from Joanna's face and with a cry she picked up her skirts and fled the room.

"Well, I never...!" exclaimed Caroline.

"I am certain it is nothing, dear. She must still be exhausted from the trip," retorted Kate, rising and following Joanna. "I will see to her," she called over her shoulder.

Kate found her leaning over the balcony sobbing. "Dear, come with me. This must stop or you will make yourself ill."

"I am ill. I feel evil, dirty, unfit to associate with anyone and branded!"

"Branded, how?"

"Like I have been somehow marked, like I have lost my identity."

Kate led her to the drawing room and pulled the sliding doors closed. She patted a seat beside her on an overstuffed divan in front of a cheerfully burning fire. Joanna sat down dejectedly wringing her hands. "I want you to listen to me carefully, Joanna," Kate said.

Joanna stared into the flames, her voice rang with bitterness, "I wish I were dead."

"Maybe now, but time will heal your sore heart and you will learn to laugh again. I know darling, for something similar happened to me when I was a very young girl. The particulars are not important, but I endured what you are experiencing now. I never spoke of it to anyone but your Grandfather before we were married."

"He didn't mind?"

"He loved me, dear, he wept when I told him and never uttered another word about it all our days together. It made me love him even more, if possible."

Joanna suddenly felt as if a great weight had been lifted from her. If her beloved Grandmother could survive the hurt and the humiliation, then she must. She dried her eyes and blew her nose and replied, "I will be back at the table in a minute, Gram, don't keep Momma waiting. I need to get myself composed, with your help I can make it!"

Joanna walked over to a hallway mirror and looked dispiritedly at her reflection. Her hair was pulled back into a knot and her face was pinched and wan. Her eyes and nose were red from weeping. She walked tiredly back to the dining room and took her seat. Her mother stared at her puzzled. "Joanna, Kate tells me you are not feeling well, should I engage the services of a physician to find the malady?"

Joanna looked over at her Grandmother and felt Kate's strength flowing into her. She turned to Caroline and said quietly, "Mama, I will be better tomorrow, I promise. I am just exhausted and worried about Elyce. Gram gave me a tonic which is beginning to work already." She glanced across the table at Kate with a faint smile and toasted her with her teacup.

Following that evening Joanna was able to put some of the nightmare behind her and began to function. Within two weeks another hurdle was overcome when her body had its monthly depletion; with this behind her she began planning for the trip west.

Winifred and John arrived at Queensgate in late August. Joanna's jaw dropped in astonishment when she saw Winifred. Her cousin was a bit shorter than she was, but she felt as if she were looking at her reflection. Winifred's eyes were different, heavy lidded and cat green. Otherwise, there was a remarkable resemblance.

"My word, you two could pass as twins!" exclaimed Caroline after greeting Winnie. Winifred replied in a cool voice, "Oh, Aunt Caroline, I see little resemblance what so ever," her gaze hardened as she looked at Joanna. There was no doubt about it, Winnie had not changed and her dislike for Joanna was still intense.

Joanna counted the days until her departure. She stood before the cheval mirror in her room examining her reflection. She had dressed in a gown of silk organdy in pale lavender. Bretelles of ruffles began at her shoulders and met in a point at her waist. The skirt was fitted in front and fell into a slight train in the back. Her hair was done in the new Gibson Girl pouffed look with tendrils of curls springing about her ears and nape of her neck. She pinned the diamond star in her hair, used her cologne atomizer, and went downstairs to join her family. Tired of Winifred's constant belittling, she was glad this would be the last social function she would share with her.

Caroline had scheduled this lawn party weeks before. It was to be a combined welcome home for Winifred and a bon voyage for Joanna. Joanna was not in the least enthused. First of all...the young people invited were the cremé dé la cremé of Rochester. Joanna realized that none of her former friends would or could attend. The twilight supper on the lawn was splendidly planned. Caroline was back in form being the extreme hostess. Tables for eight dotted the emerald lawn. Each was draped in exquisite linen edged in lace. Sprays of baby pink roses, baby's breath and white orchids were centered with crystal hurricane lamps. As Joanna stood with Winifred greeting the guests she watched her mother laughing and happy gliding about the tables. Dear Mama, sadly measuring her worth in life by the successes of her balls and parties! Joanna felt nauseated and was glad when her uncle escorted her and Winifred to their table. The crystal stemware and the sterling sparkled in the candlelight as the gloaming darkened. All around were her peers laughing and happy…totally unaware of her. It was all like a dream, no…a nightmare, to be sitting here like a wooden duck trapped in her mother's social web. Her Grandmother smiled at her with understanding, "Darling, your mother just wanted to give you a small send off. Try to pretend you are a bit appreciative."

"Oh, Gram, I will try, but I feel like a fish out of water. I am so looking forward to going on to a new life. I realize I am no longer a rich privileged young lady and I need to come to terms of what I will be doing with my future."

Once the sumptuous gala was over, Joanna prayed she would never put in another such as this one. She missed her father and dearest Elyce and tears sprang to her eyes thinking about them. Oh, life was indeed sad!

John spent three weeks buying supplies and taking care of financial affairs. Most of the remaining time Joanna spent with her Grandmother. Caroline and Winifred were making plans for the debut. The few unavoidable instances when the two cousins came together…such as dinner…was a great effort on Winifred's part to acknowledge Joanna. It made Kate furious and the other guests uncomfortable. The days were drawing closer to departure and Joanna was looking forward to leaving Winifred's company.

The morning arrived…Joanna wept as she left Queensgate. Her Grandmother kissed her farewell with words of encouragement. Her mother hugged her weeping copious tears.

Kate had implored to Annie to accompany Joanna west. Annie had received a very sizeable gratuity for saving Joanna from a fate unknown. Annie, in turn, sent part of the money to her brother, Mickey. She owed him her passage to America. She gladly hoped, as did Joanna, to find a new life in the west.

Having at last turned her heels on the ultra wealthy lifestyle in which she had been raised, Joanna sent prayers to heaven for the safety for herself and family. Elyce, she dearly loved, but could never be close to again because of Marshall. She had to leave her in God's care.

They boarded the vestibule train which was luxurious. George Pullman had founded the Pullman Palace Car Company in 1865 and revolutionized extended railroad travel. Here, indeed, was proof. The parlor car seated ten people. The floor was covered in thick Brussels carpet and the swivel overstuffed chairs were upholstered in plush cut velvet. The woodwork was cherry wood and black walnut. Sparkling crystal chandeliers hung overhead. Linen closets and toilets were at each end of the car. The adjoining sleeping car had compartments with dressers of black walnut and French plate mirrors. Each car had its own conductor and porter. The porter told John the dining car was the Delmonico and served a delectable cuisine. Joanna leaned back in her chair and stared out the window. She was torn with many emotions. She thought of her former home, New York City…America's greatest, and the world's mightiest port. The Northeast was freedom's heritage and her ancestral homeland, but, like many before her, she was going west. Leaving Rochester, then skirting Buffalo, she began to enjoy the beautiful scenery along Lake Erie.

Her thoughts turned to her mother; her earliest memories going back to childhood. She envisioned the beautiful lady she called Mama rustling in to kiss her goodnight. Joanna thought of her as a princess in her lovely gowns and sparkling jewels. As she and Elyce grew older, her mother became the voice of authority. They were taught social graces with great seriousness. Many were the tutors for different subjects. It was her beloved father and adored grandmother who gave her love…who read to her…hugged and embraced her. Her grandmother's gentle ways and teachings had given substance to her life. Kate would always be her stability, her heart the place to come to.

She smiled and thought of Timber Alexander, a little thrill of excitement coursed through her. Over dinner she would quiz Uncle John about him. Dear Pierré also came to mind. She hoped he was established and happy in San Francisco.

The days passed without a moment's weariness or deprivation of any accustomed luxury. John explained the countryside they passed through. She was amazed at the broad plains and the fields of wheat that ran to the horizon. They crossed the Mississippi River (The Father of Waters) where great rafts of logs were floating down to sawmills. This was the region which produced Mark Twain! John explains the continental divide to her; "It is the rooftop of the nation, winding across the crest of the high mountains. It crosses Wyoming and meanders across lofty plateaus cleaving the land. To the east of it streams flow to the rivers, which lead to the Gulf of Mexico. To the west of it, where you will live, streams flow to rivers that end in the Pacific Ocean. So we refer to the *eastern slope* or the *western slope*, depending on which side we have in mind."

Joanna responded, "I recall reading that the Rocky Mountains were first called the Stony Mountains by the pioneers. I cannot imagine rumbling across these plains in a wooden box on wheels...not to mention crossing mountains over ten thousand feet high!"

"Yes, they were brave fools or daring explorers, however one saw them, but the magnificence will leave you awestruck! When I first went west and landed in Colorado I felt so dwarfed by the grandeur of the mountains. It was then I knew I had found the country I would eventually call home."

"I remember reading poet Walter Foss, speaking of the unbroken wilderness that was the primeval West. He said, 'Bring me men to match my mountains!' How true."

"Well, we are almost there, we should pull into Stirrup Crossing tomorrow. Buck, my overseer, will be waiting. We have about thirty miles to travel by wagon, but I know you will enjoy the scenery."

"I am looking forward to seeing the ranch," answered Joanna with feeling. "Locket Springs, I will embrace this land, which I feel akin to already."

The next morning dawned bright and cloudless. Following breakfast Joanna and Annie packed the valises and settled back to await their arrival at Stirrup Crossing. The train puffed into the station early afternoon. The station consisted of two small buildings and a water tank. A town could be seen a short distance away. As John helped Joanna down from the railcar, she noticed a tall rangy man standing to one side with a huge hat in his hand. He came forward with a smile, obviously the overseer. "Howdy, Mr. John, welcome home!"

"Hello, Buck," replied John. "Meet the ladies, my niece, Miss Joanna and her companion, Miss Annie."

"Pleased to make your acquaintance," responded the tall, broad shouldered man. He was dressed in a long sleeved shirt, corded pants and had a kerchief around his neck. He flashed a white smile at Annie, "Welcome to Wyoming." He turned to John and motioned toward town. "Jake and another drover are coming with the buckboard for supplies and the baggage—in fact, here he comes now." The wagon was in sight, approaching fast with a cloud of dust rolling away from it. It rolled to a stop before them.

John handed up Annie and Joanna into a rear seat, then climbed up beside Buck in the buggy. Once seated Joanna opened her parasol as she watched the men load the provisions and trunks. Buck clicked to their team and they passed through the sleepy little town onto a rutted wagon trail. Rolling hills covered in wheat grass, Indian ricegrass and sage rolled by. In the far distance

Joanna began to see jagged lofty mountains. Overall there was an intense silence that almost muffled the crunch of the wheels and drumming of hooves. Joanna dozed and awoke with a start as John admonished, "Hold on, we are crossing a wash out. Flash floods are fairly common in this season and make for rough riding." Joanna held her breath as the buggy tipped and bounced over rocks and brush, then she sighed in relief as the road smoothed. She inhaled deeply the of the tangy sage.

They saw occasional wild turkeys, sagegrouse, and pheasant. John pointed out a herd of pronghorn antelope. Joanna laughed when the beautifully marked animals jumped away startled by the buggy. The wind shifted and the grass became a shimmering sea of gold. The country was everything she had dreamt of.

"We are about an hour away. How are you girls holding up?" questioned John.

"Oh, quite well, thank you," answered Joanna. She noted that the buggy was a fine Heiss. Even so, she would be happy to arrive at their destination. Her buttocks were getting tender from all the bouncing and she was covered with a fine dust.

They began a slow winding climb. Spruce, pine and fir began to appear. A dark evergreen covered with a small bluish berry was interspersed among the larger trees. "What is that strange little tree, Uncle John?" asked Joanna.

"That is a juniper, some people use the berries to make gin," replied John.

"Hmmm," responded Joanna.

The air became cool and fragrant. The sky was blue crystal dotted with a few puffy white clouds. The country was wildly beautiful. The buckboard pulled up short. John put a finger to his nose signaling quiet and pointed ahead to the right. Several wapiti elk began drifting single file to cross in front of them. Joanna's heart pounded and her eyes were wide with surprise. The herd quietly vanished into the trees.

Joanna exclaimed, "Oh, how majestic they were!"

"You will see many herds in this area plus a few grizzlies, wolves and cougars. If you see a grizzly, you make tracks and put a lot of distance between yourself and the bear. They are dangerous and fast."

"Do they come to the ranch?" asked Joanna nervously.

"No, not unless one is sick or hurt, they usually stay above the timberline. They feed on berries, grubs and the like. They enjoy the high meadows."

"Yeah, Boss, but they like horses and good looking girls," laughed Buck.

"Oh, fiddle," said Joanna, her eyes wide, "I don't frighten easily. I am a novice, but I'm willing to learn."

"Joanna, Buck is my foreman and, I promise, if you can overlook his shortcomings, he will be of great assistance."

"You are right, Boss, but these ladies have quality stamped all over them. They will be a handful!" laughed Buck.

"He talks as if I'm a horse!" she said out loud. Mentally she thought, *I'll show him a thing or two!*

They topped a pinion covered ridge and stopped. Joanna and Annie both gave startled gasps. Below them lay a great circular valley partially surrounded by sweeping mountain ranges. In the far distance were scattered buildings and a great house partially obscured by cottonwoods. The meadows of rich green grass were dotted with cattle and horses. The faint smell of wood smoke drifted up from the valley.

"Oh, gracious, Uncle John, is this Locket Springs?" asked Joanna.

"Yes, we are almost home," he answered. They slowly began their decent along a winding canyon road. "If you look over to your right, you will see the springs for which the ranch was named." On the far canyon wall water flowed out of the fractured rock facing. It was covered with a sparkling curtain of water that flowed into a pool some thirty feet below. John continued, "The story goes, the first known white man in these parts found a woman's gold locket shimmering in the pool. No one knows how it came to be here. No wagon trains came this far north at that time. Perhaps it had belonged to a woman held captive by the Indians. Thus it became known as Locket Springs."

"What a mysterious account. Did the locket have any initials on it?" questioned Joanna. "Don't know, Joanna, that is the legend…whether true or not," responded John.

Joanna peered below at the pool. Its far rim was fringed with alders and willows and from the rim ran a ribbon of sheen that wound its way across the valley to the buildings. It was breathtaking; she forgot her discomfort in the beauty of it all.

The sun was sinking as they rolled up the driveway to John Holan's beloved ranch home. The two story house was enormous; massive timbers gave it a rustic appearance and belied its hugeness. As they entered through the large portico a male servant took their valises and a tall striking blonde woman greeted them. She spoke in a German accent to John, "Velcome home, Herr Holan."

John grabbed her hands and beamed, "It is good to be back, Frieda." Turning to Joanna, he said, "This is my niece, Joanna, and her personal maid, Annie. This is my housekeeper, Frieda."

Frieda greeted them with a beautiful smile and said, "You must be tired and famished, I will have a maid direct you to your suite so you can refresh yourselves."

Annie and Joanna followed the maid down a long hallway with walls covered with stuffed game. They entered a huge room, "This is the gathering room," the maid explained. A fire blazed in a cavernous stone fireplace, which stretched to the heavens. Suspended from high ceilings were wagonwheel chandeliers, polished parquet floors were dotted with woven Indian rugs and fur rugs with attached heads. Massive overstuffed divans and chairs were scattered comfortably about the room. Expanses of glass and wood framed breathtaking views of the mountains. A balcony with two staircases circling up to it surrounded three walls of the room. Joanna could see two hallways leading away from the balcony. "Good grief, this is as big as a hotel, I never imagined a ranch like this!" she exclaimed.

A wide eyed Annie responded, "Miss Jo, the Wild West looks awful tamed to me!" The maid giggled and walked them to one of the circular staircases. They climbed to the landing and followed her down a hallway. The maid opened a door leading into a large suite.

"This is the main bedroom," she said, then opening another door she pointed out the dressing room and bath. Walking over to another door she opened it and indicated to Annie it was her quarters. Joanna's room was furnished in Birdseye Maple. Her large canopied bed looked extremely inviting. She wished she could just collapse there and then. Drapes were fluttering at open windows and Joanna went to peer out. "Oh, what a beautiful view, it's heavenly!" she said excitedly as she leaned out a window.

The maid was helping Annie unpack the trunks when a rap sounded at the door. Joanna hastened to open it. Frieda stood holding a tea service. "I thought this would be refreshing, I hope you don't mind."

"Oh, how thoughtful, please come in. I love my tea."

Frieda placed the tea service on a small table and arranged the saucers and cups. "There is enough for your maid, also. I would imagine she is tired, also."

"Oh, good, you must join us, also."

"I will visit for a minute, but I must see to my kitchen," replied Frieda, pouring. "I was taken back when I saw you. The resemblance between you and Miss Winifred is unsettling."

"Yes, I know, but you will find our temperaments are entirely different," sighed Joanna as she sipped her refreshing cup of tea.

"She hated it here. It was good that she returned east," sniffed Frieda sounding relieved.

"Where is Cousin Wilfred?" asked Joanna.

"Oh, that dear, he stays with the hired men. He loves the animals and seems to talk to them. The hands adopted him and he likes being with the men. That sister of his was so vicious to him, I know the hands took pity on him. That girl was hard..." Frieda stopped abruptly, placed a hand over her mouth, then mumbled, "Sorry, ma'am, I shouldn't have said that!"

"Please, Frieda, it is all right, I feel she is a bit of a savage, too," laughed Joanna.

"I will leave you now. We serve dinner at seven."

Following a delicious meal, John took both women into his study. It was all masculine, heavy oak desk, leather chairs and more mounted heads. Motioning the girls to sit, he propped himself on the edge of his desk and lit a pipe. The aroma of rum and tobacco filled the room. "Now, then, my young ladies, a word of caution. The men here outnumber the women about twenty to one. They are hard working drovers, cow men and bronco-busters. I daresay some might not be kind to a female were she to wander into lone territory. You will be shown the riding stock and you are to always ride with a companion. That means, each other, Buck or I, but never alone. Is that understood?"

"Yes, Uncle John," said Joanna, her eyes wide on his face.

He sat down behind his desk and looked at the little Irish maid, "Do you ride, Annie?"

"No, sir, but I can learn," she answered quickly.

"Hmmm, Buck can put you on a good mare. It shouldn't be too difficult."

"Joanna, I also want you to carry a carbine. You will have much to learn in the next week or so."

"What about my teaching and where?"

"That will come later. They have had some trouble up at the Fort, some conflict between a few cattlemen and sheepmen. There are some young lads here you can give schooling to, though."

"No girls, Uncle John?"

"Well, one or two, maybe. There is Frieda's girl, but it's not schooling she needs. Frieda's teaching her cooking and house chores."

"Uncle John! Every child needs to be able to read and write. If she wants to learn, may I teach her?"

John stared at her, then he smiled, "My, dear, you can teach anyone you want as long as they do their chores. Yes, people need to be educated…even the women!"

"Thank you," she sighed.

He nodded and then excused them. "You must be exhausted. I hope you sleep well. I am pleased you are here."

"Oh, I am indeed happy to be here, Uncle John. The ranch is truly splendid. Thank you for bringing me. I will do my best to do a good job." She rose and kissed him on the cheek before leaving the room.

John again sat down and stretched out his legs toward the fireplace. He watched the fire dance and smiled to himself. "Joanna, you will be good for Locket Springs, I feel it in my bones."

This would be a morning never to be forgotten. Joanna stood on the large veranda leading off the kitchen area and inhaled the pure air deep into her lungs. Dawn was stretching its fingers of pink and gold across the eastern sky. Ribbons of orange interwove the gold and pink and little tongues like fire played about the horizon clouds. The silence and the beauty were broken by a prolonged wail of a lone coyote. The answering howl and yips of another coyote shattered the stillness. A rooster crowed to announce daybreak.

Joanna hugged herself wishing she had brought a wrap. Her thin shirtwaist was not enough to stave off the chilly air.

"Here, Miss, you will catch your death," said Frieda as she laid a shawl about Joanna's shoulders.

"Thank you, Frieda, I didn't realize how cool the morning air is here. Isn't it a glorious morning?" asked Joanna, watching the dawn clouds turn to a fiery palette.

"That it is."

Joanna leaned against a support pillar still marveling at the fading brilliance of the sky. "You speak with an accent, Frieda, did you recently come to America?"

"I have been here seventeen years, originally from Deutchland, Berlin," answered Frieda with a far away look. "My father was Herr Doctor Professor at the University. We were a happy family until Chancellor Bismarck formed the First Reich. My mother's parents, the Baron and Baroness Von Hildebrand, lost everything to the new regime and then came to live with us. That very summer I met my Albert. He was in the army; I never forget my first look at him. He was in gray trousers, a blue tunic, spit-polished boots and wore the Pickelhaube…the spiked helmet. His eyes were gray and his smile was as broad as his face," Frieda sighed sadly and continued, "He was trim and erect and I fell in love with him there and then. I was but sixteen and Father forbade me to see him. I was so in love as was Albert and we arranged secret meetings. My beautiful Albert with his gold hair and gray eyes…ach, such a man!" Frieda fell silent and said no more.

"Oh, pray, go on, Frieda," coaxed Joanna turning from the faded sky, "Then what happened?"

"We decided to run away, I told my mother and she cried and cried. Things were getting worse in Prussia, nationalism was the start of a major depression. With me gone there would be one less mouth to feed. Mama gave me her ruby ring and some gold she had saved. We were married at the Rathaus (town hall) and left for America. Albert first worked in the coalmines in Pennsylvania and then we came west. He worked the mines in Virginia City, Nevada. I cooked. I cleaned and did whatever I could to help. The years were hard; we never could get ahead. Albert was proud, sometimes I think too proud. He never let anyone help him, even a fellow German! One day when he was in the mine, a fire started in the shaft and by the time they got the fire out he was dead with a group of other men. I just learned I was pregnant after hoping for three long years! I wanted to die, too. I went to San Francisco and got work in a mansion on Nob Hill. They were good to me and kept me on after Ella was born. When your Uncle John hired Molly, the cook from the mansion…he hired me, too. A good man, your Uncle."

"Yes, yes, he is…"

Abruptly Frieda turned away saying, "I have to see to my bread."

Joanna walked the length of the veranda and then walked into the huge kitchen. Molly, the Cook was a rotund woman with a booming laugh. She was Celtic and had already taken Annie under her wing. The two of them were seated at a large oval table sipping tea.

"Morning, Miss, breakfast sideboard is in the dining room and I will check the water for tea. The coffee is still hot," said Molly, rising and taking her cup to a soapstone sink.

"When does Uncle John eat breakfast?" asked Joanna.

"Lordy, he has been up and gone quite a spell ago. He and some of the hands are riding to a homestead in Snail Valley. Mr. John was told they are stringing Devil's Rope."

"I am hopelessly at a loss for words. What is Devil's Rope? Why does everyone get up in the middle of the night?" asked Joanna with a bewildered expression.

"Well, deary, it's like this. As long as the weather holds, everyone prepares for the long winter. We can, we store and stock the cellars. Wood is hauled in and cut, cow chips are stored, and hay is stacked. There is always something to be done while the weather holds. The boys ride for late calves and when fall comes, they bring the cattle down from the range. Now, Devil's Rope is barbed wire. The ranchers hate it! Animals get tangled in it and die. The fencing cuts off trails to water, too. The homesteaders use it because the cattle destroy their crops. It is cheaper than wood so more and more is being used. Mr. John vows it will never be strung here at the Springs."

Trying to absorb all of this, Joanna excused herself to go the dining room. Lifting lids off chafing dishes she selected a small portion of breakfast and sat down in the huge room. Here, again, another room of masculine dominance. More stag's heads look sadly down from the walls. The large mantel over the fireplace sports stuffed pheasants and other fowl. The massive dining table, chairs, the sideboard and wainscoting surrounding the walls are all dark walnut. It has a warm and inviting feel, and large potted plants add to the ambiance.

After finishing her lonely meal, she wandered through the first story of the big rambling house. Some of the floors were parquet while others were planed and polished oak. Off the gathering hall was a music room with an organ, pianoforte and harp. Continuing down the hallway she entered the library and found, to her delight, beautiful bound literary works with titles and author's names stamped in gold. After leafing through a few editions, she continued on her inspection of the downstairs. She peered into a game room with card tables and billiards table and then opened the huge doors leading to the veranda. Stepping outside, she marveled at the foot thick logs that were hewn and counter hewn to make the front portico. Pillars of polished walnut that support the veranda extend the full length of the building. Remembering John's words of caution, she turned back into the house to find Annie. Annie was tidying up the sleeping quarters. "Annie, please come, I want to explore the grounds. It is all so exciting and large. Goodness, it is not at all what I expected!" exclaimed Joanna.

Putting on bonnets and gloves, the two women left by the great doors and descend the steps. There is an incredible canopy of green formed by tree branches over the driveway. Dogs yapped and jumped about them as they walk toward the corrals and barns. A pretty blond girl came out of one of the buildings. She stops short when she sees Joanna and opens her mouth in astonishment. "Hello," said Joanna, "you must be Ella. My name is Joanna."

"You are Mr. John's niece?" the girl asked, her eyes wide.

"Indeed I am, I am here to begin a school and I do hope you will attend."

Ella's pretty eyes narrow with suspicion, "What do I have to do there? What kind of work?"

"Oh, my, you will learn to read and write, that is all. Wouldn't you like that?" smiled Joanna.

"Well, I can write my name. Mama taught me that and I can spell some words. I guess so, but I have chores and I help Mama in the kitchen," answered the young girl, chewing nervously on her lower lip.

"It will be possible, even so. Uncle John will let you attend and we will make time for the chores," said Joanna, placing her hand on Ella's shoulder.

Ella gazed up at her in a bewildered way. "You look just like Miss Winifred, some higher. She didn't like me. She called me a little beast. Mama told me to keep away and never bother her."

"Blessed heaven! Dear child, I am not Winifred and I will never call you anything but Ella," smiled Joanna. "Now, what have you in your basket?"

"Onions and carrots for Molly."

"Ella, would you like to show Annie and me about this big old place? I'll bet you know every nook and cranny around here. We would certainly appreciate it."

The girl cocked her head to one side and smiled, "I'll hurry up to the house and be right back. Are you sure you want me around?"

"Yes, absolutely certain. Now, be off and we will wait for you."

Joanna and Annie leaned against the split rail fence and watched a small herd of horses in knee high grass. "Oh, look, there are other animals!" said Annie, pointing.

Joanna was astonished to see elk grazing among the horses. What a beautiful sight, she could understand why her uncle loved it here.

Ella skipped down the driveway, and then what a tour she gave them! First, the spring house and pantry behind the house. Standing next to them was a mountain of corded wood. Judging from its size, Joanna concluded the winters must be extremely harsh. Ella led them to the chicken houses, stables, barns, gardens, cellars, bunkhouses, stone house, blacksmith shop and corrals. Joanna was quite exhausted on her return to the main house. All this to run a ranch, my, oh, my. She hummed a tune because she had made a wonderful discovery. An old freestanding shed was located halfway to the orchards. At one time it had most likely been used for storage. It was open on one side and had no flooring, but Joanna could visualize her schoolhouse. A small brook lined with willows ran behind it and a large cottonwood provided shade.

That evening at dinner Joanna inquired if the little run down building was being used for anything in particular. John said it had never been used while he owned Locket Springs.

Joanna excitedly explained, "With a floor and an enclosure, it could be ideal for a school house. It will need benches, a stove and a small window on the east to provide sufficient light. I can purchase black paint for a blackboard. I purchased small slates, chalk and primers in New York. I must also have a recitation bench and, of course, a desk and…"

"Whoa, young lady, take it a bit slower for this old man," said John with a smile. "I readily agree to your having the shed and I will have a hand or two help refurbish it. The stove will have to be ordered."

"Oh, Uncle John, you are a darling! I promise to you repay every expense. I ordered pen and inkwells, but they will not do at first. I have nine lesson plans and a terrestrial globe. These supplies should be arriving in a couple of weeks."

"What will you teach, Joanna?"

"After the pupils learn to read and print, I will follow with sums, grammar and geography. Hopefully, I would like to teach at least five hours a day. Meanwhile, I will write for the information I need for becoming certified."

"Splendid, I am proud of you, I will assist in every way possible. A school for Locket Springs, now that is admirable!" said John, smiling and twisting his mustache with satisfaction.

Joanna had Annie accompany her every day to the shed. Tony DeBernardi, the blacksmith, worked on the little building when he had spare time. He was a powerfully built Italian with muscles of iron. He had replaced the roof with tin and was planking the floor. On a particular day when Tony could not work on the shed, out of curiosity, the two women went to the blacksmith shop. Joanna was amazed when she saw the forge bellows and anvil. They found Tony busy shoeing a horse, and indeed it was an art.

"Do you mind if we observe, Tony?" asked Joanna.

At first he glowered at her, but thinking better of it, replied, "Naw, if you really have an interest."

"Doesn't it hurt?"

He rolled his eyes, "Miss, if it hurt, this mare would be outta here and long gone. Their hoof is like a fingernail to us. The nailing don't hurt as long as it isn't driven into the sole…that is sensitive. I have to be careful when I pare the hoof, especially here at the coffin bone and I can't drive a nail too deep, we call that quicked. You have to pull the nail immediately so the hoof won't abscess."

"Why do you shoe a horse?" asked Annie, stooping closer to watch as he filed and cleaned the hoof.

"Well, Miss, there are several reasons. The main one is traction. A shoe has a crease in it and protects the foot from contacting the ground. When the crease fills up with dirt, that provides traction, especially here when they take the horses into the mountains."

"Gracious, I would have thought it would do just the opposite," said Joanna thoughtfully.

"Generally, it makes the animal feel good. A good horseman can tell if his horse is sore-footed. I pretty much can tell within a day if the sole pressure is wrong. I don't mean to brag, but I do a good job. If a blacksmith knows his business a horse should never be hurting."

They continued to watch as he heated each shoe until it glowed orange, used tongs to remove it from the forge and worked the heated metal on the anvil. Satisfied with the fit he plunged the shoe into water and let it cool. He continued to work and held the horse's hoof between his front legs and hammered the shoe onto the hoof. He showed the girls the different types of shoes, very distinctive groves and thickness for working teams, thinner for the saddle horses, filed for mountain terrain and light and smooth for the valley.

"Startin' to feel like fall," said Tony when he had finished with the horse. He wiped his hands on his apron and squatted down to pick up a sickle. "Got to get these sharpened and the shovels, everyone works to get the vegetables in before the first frost."

"We will help, I'll tell Frieda to tell us when we are needed," responded Joanna.

Tony grunted at that and stood up. He looked at her, "It is a backbreaking job, you pull potatoes, carrots, beets and turnips. Gather pumpkins and squash…big jobs for city women."

"Fiddle, we can do it. I want to do something besides wander like a lost sheep around here. My school supplies haven't arrived nor the stove. I can't do a thing at the shed until then. When the floor is finished, I'll use sand and brushes to get it smooth."

Annie stood with her hands on her hips defiantly and said, "Sir, I'll have you know in my native land of Erin, I worked in gardens, I cut peat, I hauled wood…I am a good worker!"

Tony shook his head, "Ah, ladies, you are taking on a big project. You are plucky, I give you that!"

"Against all odds, Mr. DeBernardi, I will have my school!" exclaimed Joanna, her violet eyes flashing.

"It gets freezing cold here in the winter and that shed is old and was never well made. The roof will likely leak and the walls need chinking, even with a roarin' fire, you'll be freezing."

"I must make an attempt, these children need schooling."

"Yes'm I agree," Tony turned on his heel and strode away, whistling.

"Well! I feel like a failure before I've even begun," said Joanna quietly.

It was obvious that Winifred had demanded she be regarded as royalty and now Joanna was being treated in a like manner. Everyone, that is, but her beloved cousin, Willy. He had shocked her very soul. The pasty pink headed lad of the past was gone and replaced with a young man tanned like shoe leather and hair the color of a rusty nail. He still had a stammer, but sat a horse like a pro and had been adopted by everyone on the ranch. Locket Springs had done wonders for him. He came often to see Joanna, happy as a puppy.

Joanna found, she also, had fallen in love with the large ranch. Soon she would learn the harsher side of ranching, but for now she was enjoying the pleasure of new found freedom. Hers was primarily the out door life. Time was spent exploring. The three enormous barns were fashioned around a square enclosure. They were the finest of barns and her uncle had spared no expense and was enormously proud of them. The main barn was on the west side of the square. Great doors opened into it from the meadows where loaded hay wagons were emptied into a huge hay bay and then stacked to the roof far overhead. There were stalls for the milk cows and at the lower end, a machine and tool shop. Around a corner was the South Barn where a feed room and a calf pen were located. Inside a sheepfold and hog pens lined the outside wall. The East Barn housed the horses. Rows of box stalls lined the east wall. Attached at the far end was the Buggy House where two sleighs, two carriages and a wagon were housed. The animals could be unhitched and go from the Buggy House to their stalls…a blessing in winter months. There was as adjoining tack room with polished saddles; bridles and harnesses all kept in excellent condition by a young black boy named Lionel. Lionel's father, Madison, was Tony's helper and becoming a blacksmith. He often helped at the school building and Joanna found him to be a quiet gentleman for his immense size. Maddy (as he was called) was a burnished black man, over six feet tall and had forearms as thick as a ham. He had expressed a desire for his son to learn to read and write. Joanna assured him Lionel would attend school.

Joanna and Annie explored the root cellars, chicken and turkey enclosures and the springhouse, which intrigued Joanna. It was dug deep into a side of a hill where a stream gurgled through making it very cool. Two small lanterns gave light. Joanna ran her hands over the gleaming red and silver milk separator and the large wooden butter churns sitting along side of it. Shelves on one side of the room held cheesecloth covered pans of milk with rising cream. Lower shelves held rounds of salted butter the color of buttercups. On the opposite wall round yellow cheeses covered in paraffin sat on shelves. Cottage cheese tied in cheesecloth sacks dripped whey into collecting pans. Crocks of milk sat to the back, immersed in the stream. Joanna lightly put her hand on one and found it cold to the touch. A curtain of wet burlap covered the entrance.

Each day was a new learning experience for Joanna. At first she had viewed this lush land with the romantic eyes of a woman of privilege. She now realized one had to work with others for survival.

She and Buck began teaching Annie to ride horseback. Joanna became acquainted with a western saddle. She laughed! How appalled her mother would be if she saw her straddling a horse in her bloomers!

Riding became a passion for both girls and an outlet for their energy. Buck kept a watchful eye on them, demanding to know when they were leaving and where they would ride. On some days Joanna would wear a riding habit with a black silk hat and be properly mounted on a velvet sidesaddle. Her delight in her surroundings made her radiate and she felt really free for the first time in her life.

By the middle of September, Tony and Madison were almost finished with the shed. The days were turning golden, as were the aspen in the mountains. Shrub oak began to glow red in the canyons and the nights were turning cold. Joanna and Annie joined the others in pulling vegetables. The first day went well, but by evening the muscles in Joanna's back and upper arms began protesting. She refused to quit and joined the group again next morning now wearing a tattered big brim straw hat from Frieda to cover her sunburned face. She ignored the sympathetic looks Frieda and Ella gave her and found squatting like the other women relieved her back. The following day she wore her cycle bloomers for comfort. At noon she ate a sandwich, stretched out under a cottonwood tree to rest her aching muscles and fell fast asleep. She awakened to deep masculine laughter. Opening an eye, she peered up to see the source of the laughter. Stars! It was Timber Alexander! She sat up abruptly...horrors, she must be a fright...sunburned nose, hat askew, bloomers how perfectly ghastly!

"Well, well, if it isn't Joanna! John told me you were out here. The same fascinating rebel I found in New York! Pulling turnips and potatoes, I declare!" He stared at her, smiled and then laughed uproariously…that wonderful laugh! "You look like hell, what are you doing in the fields?"

Mortified, she answered in a muffled voice, "Doing my share of chores."

"Sleeping in the dirt?" He held out his hand and pulled her up, then stood back scrutinizing her. "So this is the new school marm?" Shaking his head and grinning he said, "Come along Joanna, I want to converse with you over a cup of tea."

Back in her room, Joanna had Annie pour a bath and washed body and head. Donning a shirtwaist and a gored skirt with a small train, she viewed her reflection in the mirror. Sakes Alive! I look a sight! A suntanned face with wet curls of hair striated with sun bleach looked back at her. *Well, at least I look healthy!* She tied back her hair at the nape of her neck and proceeded downstairs.

She and Timber discussed the school until dinner was served. Joanna found she could hardly touch her food. She was so delighted to see Timber and her eyes devoured him.

John and Timber discussed land, railroads, cattle, and stock and finally Timber turned to her, "How is Elyce, Joanna? I have thought of her often. I was quite taken with her, you know."

"Oh, doing well. She is happily expecting her first child. I miss her dreadfully. She has become a most capable wife, an outstanding hostess and charmed the aristocracy."

"Certainly she would. A lovely lady, indeed," answered Timber a bit sadly.

Joanna suffered a tiny pang of jealously. Elyce, her beautiful, fascinating sister had made a very long lasting impression on Timber!

"My dear Joanna," John began, "I received word the school superintendent will be here within the month to test you for your teaching credentials. This must be pleasing news."

Joanna became as rigid as a board. "Oh my, oh goodness, I must study to pass the tests."

John reached over and placed his big hand over her small one. "You will do just fine. With your extensive schooling I find it highly unlikely you will not do well."

Joanna moaned, "Oh, I do hope so. Thank heavens my books and supplies arrived, I shall need them."

Timber studied her thoughtfully; "You do amaze me, Joanna. With your privileged background, it is difficult to imagine your wanting to be a spinster and teach. Not only that, pulling weeds in the fields, very unladylike!"

She blurted out, "Curses, I was just helping with the vegetables! Must a woman just sit to be a lady? Is it wrong to teach and make my way? My uncle and grandmother should not be responsible for my livelihood!"

Timber laughed, "You certainly are a survivor! I suggest you take pity on the superintendent. He will be bowled over with your attitude and intelligence."

Joanna brightened, "Oh, Timber, you are generous with your compliments, especially when I feel so inadequate and incomplete. I have had such a hard time adjusting to Papa's death and Elyce's marriage. The move to Rochester left me so drained and lonely. Thanks to my beloved Uncle John, I feel reborn here. I have come to believe that there is a purpose for everything. One cannot help but feel the presence of our Maker. I so want to be a part of it all."

Timber chuckled, "You have just begun. I hope you still will be as impressed with the west come spring; Our winters are long and hard. Of course, during the white months you can put your intellectual qualities to the test…teaching. Where are you planning to hold classes?"

"Oh, you must see my gala little school house! Tony and Melchoir have done a remarkable job. Uncle John, will you accompany us in the morning? It has been some time since you have seen it."

"You are a perfect nuisance, my darling. Nothing would please me more," answered her uncle with a twinkle in his eye.

After breakfast the next morning they rode to the transformed shed. Timber was amazed at what had been accomplished. The board walls had been battened. A large pot bellied stove sat on one side of the room. Joanna's desk was on a raised platform at the front with five benches facing it. Tony had framed boards for a fair sized blackboard. Joanna had painted it thickly with gummy blackboard paint. *Good Morning* was written in white chalk across its face. To one side of her desk was a small bench for recitation. An east window had been installed for light. Primers were stacked on Joanna's desk. A plank floor had been laid, smoothed with sand and soap. Coat pegs were in evidence by the front door. Tony and Melchoir were adding more tin on the roof.

"Won't that be noisy when it rains?" asked Timber.

"Very likely, but better than drowning," laughed Joanna.

108

Joanna continued the tour pointing out the recess area and the new privy that had been dug; Melchoir had limed it yesterday.

John was beaming and proudly said, "Locket Springs School, I must admit it looks very impressive. I will add a little more to it for you, Joanna. I will order a bell and a flag. Tony can build a small steeple for the bell."

"Oh, thank you, Uncle John. You have been so kind to me, whatever would I have done without you?" said, Joanna, her eyes misting.

"Hush child, I am happy to be able to do it," he answered, "Your father would have done as much for me."

She turned to Timber, who had his chin in hand, deep in thought.

"Well, kind sir, what say you?" she asked.

"Serviceable, for a start. I was just thinking, I will purchase a ton of coal from the railroad and have it delivered. It will give you a good warm fire with your wood."

"Good thought, Timber. I will order some extra myself," agreed John.

"It is a start, isn't it? I will endeavor to do my best to establish a good school," stated Joanna.

"Best we take our leave, I have some business I want to discuss with you, Timber," said John and they returned to the big house.

Timber stayed a few days more. Joanna looked forward to the few times she was able to visit with him. He loved teasing her and then looking at her with a saucy grin awaiting a response. Joanna would not disappoint him, she enjoyed banter and their friendship grew.

The day Timber was to depart the mail arrived. Joanna was conversing with Timber when John handed her a large envelope.

"Please excuse me, it is a letter from Mama," she said, opening it. She cried out in anguish as she read it. John and Timber abruptly stopped a conversation.

John rushed to her, "Whatever is the matter, child?"

"Oh, that beastly man, that vile, dreadful cur!" sobbed Joanna into a hankie handing the letter to her uncle.

John read it aloud to an alarmed Timber.

My dear Joanna,

I am sorry to relate very distressing news. Our dearest Elyce has lost the expected child. I have been with her since the sad happening and just now returned to Queensgate. This has been a most trying and depressing time for all.

Elyce somehow fell the entire length of the staircase and was in a critical state for days. Your grandmother came and we sat with her day to day with great anxiety.

Marshall did not attend her and I confess I was much disturbed by his behavior.

I eventually confronted him, asking why he was avoiding our dear Elyce. Vehemently, he assured me that wasn't the case; he was over burdened by business! "Indeed," said I. "Hard to imagine." Furthermore, his family never called on her once! I feel this entire behavior most unnatural and unkind. I know your father's death was scandalous, but to make Elyce suffer because of it is infuriating.

Elyce has been deeply hurt and her heart is hardened against Marshall since the accident. It is a house of great sorrows, seemingly, the death of a marriage as well as that of a child.

Your Grandmother had implored Elyce to leave Marshall, but to no avail. Perchance harmony may again be restored, my earnest prayer, although I gravely doubt Marshall has her welfare uppermost in his mind.

Please keep her in your prayers and send condolences.

Give my regards to John and relay to him that Winifred is content with her social life. Although she has a vexation of spirit, it attracts men to her like moths. I have been a busy chaperone on her many outings.

We miss you dreadfully, darling, God be with you.

Your devoted mother.

"The unspeakable cad, I could kill him!" roared Timber, his fists clenched.

John went to a side bar and poured cognac for the three of them.

Joanna was consumed by fury. "He is a distorted, twisted man! He didn't want the baby! He hated Elyce's condition! He made nasty, vile comments about her appearance when I was visiting her. Oh, I begged her not to marry him! My poor sister."

Timber reached out to her and took her in his arms. "Shhh, we will help her, Joanna." He rocked her gently and sat her down. She shook herself, a strange smile crossed her face and she said in a guttural tone, "I will kill him one day!"

John handed her a crystal globe partially filled with cognac. "Drink it, you need it," he insisted.

Joanna lifted it to her lips with trembling hands and sipped it. She finally composed herself. John had rung for Annie and she took Joanna upstairs to her room.

At dinner that evening she found a folded letter lying next to her place setting. She read it with a sinking heart.

> *My Dear Joanna,*
>
> *As you know, it is imperative I leave. I hope to return before the snow flies as John and I have business dealings.*
> *I was very saddened to learn of Elyce 's great misfortune. Convey to her my heartfelt sympathy. If she should ever need assistance, I will go to her immediately regardless of the circumstances.*
> *I, of course, would do the same should you need me. I congratulate you most heartily on your school. I know you will be a dedicated teacher.*
>
> *Sincerely,*
> *Your friend Timber*

Hell's bells, he's besotted with Elyce. I truly wish he had found her first. Ah, well, if he's to be only a friend, I must accept it. I am numb to heartbreak. Godspeed, Timber, she thought as she folded his note.

The sun had not yet risen next morning when Annie brought a tray with coffee. "Miss Joanna, the school gentleman arrived late last evening and wants to see you. He is having breakfast."

Joanna dressed quickly, her heart in her throat. She nervously entered the dining room. John introduced her to Mr. Dexter Winters, a short stocky bespectacled man with a generous smile. Mr. Winters informed her he could only stay the day to give her the necessary tests for her certificate. After finishing breakfast they went into John's study. Joanna sat very straight with her hands folded in her lap.

"Miss Holan, shall we begin with the written this morning and do the oral after lunch?"

"Whatever you wish, sir," replied Joanna, biting her lip nervously.

So began history reviews, geography outlines, diagramed sentences followed by grammar with long complex compound sentences full of adverbial phrases. Then came the arithmetic. Joanna disliked mathematics and her upper lip began to bead with perspiration as she worked through long division, multiplication and Algebra. Her face was strained and pale when Mr. Winters said, "Time is up."

After the lunch hour the oral exam began. There were questions asked about the Congress of the Confederated Colonies, Spanish and French explorers, Raleigh's lost colony, English settlers in Virginia and Massachusetts, the War of Independence, The Constitution, George Washington and on and on it went; laws passed by the First and Second Congress, the Declaration of Independence, War of 1812, historic sea battles, the Spanish American War and the push to open the West. Joanna began to tire, her voice shaking a bit. Mr. Winters gave her a short rest and then launched into Latin and French. Joanna translated carefully and finally through a blur heard his voice say, "Enough, Miss Holan, you may sit."

She weakly sat down relieved the ordeal was over. Mr. Winters spread a blank certificate on Uncle John's desk and picked up one of his pens. The only sound was the ticking of the mantle clock and scratch of the pen on the parchment. Mr. Winters blotted the paper, corked the ink bottle and stood up. Joanna rose as well.

"May I present you with your with your elementary certificate, Miss Holan. Congratulations, you did very well," he said cordially, extending the rolled parchment to her.

"Oh, thank you, sir," Joanna said gratefully, tears shining in her eyes.

He began to walk from the study then turned, "I wish you well in this harsh country. One more thing, be certain you form a School Board when you start your school. We will keep in touch."

Joanna sat down again and unrolled her certificate. Tears of relief poured down her cheeks. At last, she would be able to do something worthwhile! She smiled, *Oh, to help a young mind to read and write, how fulfilling!* She also felt a flicker of independence and it was exhilarating.

Days were growing shorter, the leaves were floating down from the big trees along the drive and nights were chilly. The fields became diamond grain and rime lined the wagon ruts. The encircling mountains tops wore a splattering of white, winter was fast approaching.

The Locket Springs Outfit came in from the range. The ranch seemed over run with bowlegged, bronzed men. Most of them were long limbed, small hipped with broad shoulders. They wore crumpled ten gallon hats and colorful kerchiefs around their necks. The slap of leather chaps and ring of spurs became a familiar sound. Joanna was amazed at the high heeled boots they wore. Buck explained that the boot heels kept the foot from slipping out of the stirrups. The chaps protected the legs from insects and brush and the kerchiefs were used to cover mouth and nose from dust. The cowboys appreciated the comely young women and raised their hats at every opportunity. Joanna and Annie smiled in return secretly pleased at the attention.

There were so many hands she asked her uncle why he needed them. He told her of his lucrative contracts with the railroad and government to supply beef. Between two outposts, the town of Stirrup Cup plus the railroad, he did not have to worry about a market. He also supplied saddle horses to the outposts. They had to be broken and be good quarter horses. Some of the officers wanted finer stock such as Morgans, especially if they lost their personal steeds to death or theft.

The remaining cattle would be kept at the ranch through the winter. The mares, fillies and stallions were also wintered. Thus the hands were kept busy feeding, watering and breaking horses plus tending and feeding the cattle. Repairs needed to be done such as riding the fences and barn upkeep, etc. Many jobs for many men.

Joanna took Annie with her and readied the schoolhouse for the three months of winter schooling. Buck would stay close and walked them to and from the school. It amused Joanna to see how protective he was of Annie. Joanna commented to Annie, "I think Buck is sweet on you."

"Do you really think so?" Annie asked, blushing.

"Do trees have leaves, of course he is! Do you care for him, also?"

"Sort of," answered Annie.

Joanna snorted and hugged her, "You could do worse."

Joanna learned children from a neighboring ranch would attend as well as Ella, Lionel, Willy and Annie. She sent a letter to the Snowflake Ranch informing them of the date of registration.

Meanwhile Joanna was very concerned about Elyce. She had written a letter of condolence and her sister had written in return. The news had been discouraging. Elyce wrote of Marshall's displeasure with everything she attempted. He expressed constantly, his disgust over her father's suicide, and insisted the scandal had stained his family's social standing.

Her mother wrote that Elyce's delicate appearance was upsetting. She had visited Queensgate and Kate and Caroline had pleaded with her to stay, but to no avail. Elyce returned to New York City as she felt her place was with her husband.

Joanna was heartsick over her sister and tried to keep busy until school started. She begged Frieda to let her help take inventory of winter supplies. Frieda, at first, was horrified, but relented and welcomed her help. She gave Joanna a clipboard and Joanna followed her and Molly into the vast storeroom adjoining the kitchen. Walls were lined with shelves full of glass jars, sparkling like multicolored gems. They were filled with jellies, jams and fruits all precisely labeled. Under the shelves were barrels of fat white pork covered in brine. There were wooden boxes of soda crackers, salted fish, dried apples, pearl barley and tapioca. Piled against the opposite wall were sacks of flour, beans and dried peas. Five gallon tins of coffee, sugar and tea were stacked in rows. Large stone crocks were marked as lard.

Joanna considered all the work this represented particularly when Frieda showed Joanna crocks of mincemeat. Weeks before, Joanna had watched her and Molly chop cooked beef and mix it with suet, raisins, spices, sugar and vinegar. They then added chopped apples and brandy to the mixture. Frieda referred to the mincemeat as "holidaymeat" and it smelled heavenly.

Beneath this room was the *potato cellar* with two entrances. Inside a trap door lifted to reveal stairs disappearing into a dark hole. Outside a door opened to stairs for the men to carry down large sacks. Frieda lit two lanterns, handed one to Molly and they carefully descended the wooden stairs. Now Joanna could see the results of her backbreaking work in the garden.

Burlap sacks of potatoes, carrots, turnips and beets were double stacked against one wall. Pumpkins and squash were piled in high green and gold heaps. Braided ropes of onions and garlic were hung under the stairs. Waxed paper wrapped smoked hams and venison jerky hung from the cellar rafters. Great bunches of dried herbs tied in cheesecloth gave the cellar a musty spice odor.

"Goodness, will all of this be eaten?" asked Joanna marveling at the store of provisions. She would never eat another meal without respect for its origin.

"Oh, my yes, most all of it by spring. We lay in heavy for winter. One never knows," replied Frieda, brushing away a cobweb from a rafter. After the count of the cellar, they walked down a short path to a building made of stone and cold as the cellar. Blocks of ice covered in straw were stacked against one wall of the narrow long building; it was used for storage of meat. Sausage balls and slabs of bacon were wrapped in cloths and neatly stored and sacks of cloth covered quarters of beef and venison haunches were hanging from huge hooks.

Frieda said, "As soon as we get a hard freeze, the meat will be frozen solid."

"Really, it gets that cold?" asked an astonished Joanna.

"Mien Gott, child, you have yet to experience such a winter! We had snow in Germany, but nothing like here. The blizzards can be frightening. Come, on to the spring house."

Butter tubs were now covered with white cloths. Frieda stated there was at least two hundred pounds of golden sweet butter! They made a count of the round yellow and orange waxed cheeses, then of waxed blocks of Jack and Swiss cheese. A pleased Frieda and she herded them back to the kitchen where they refreshed themselves with cookies and tea.

"Now we go down the hill to the bunkhouse storeroom," said Frieda.

It was a dry one stocked much the same as the main house, the only difference being more flours and beans.

Joanna was introduced to Dusty Whitcomb, the cook for the outfit. A big man with protruding eyes and a handlebar moustache, he prided himself on his sourdough bread and pies. He drove the chuck wagon during the spring and summer months. He had two young Mexican boys for helpers, one called Tomas and the other, Jose.

Jose followed them around as they took inventory and then quietly spoke to Joanna, "Senorita, you are the teacher, si?"

"Yes," answered Joanna, "Is there something I can help you with?"

The young lad looked at her with soulful brown eyes and wistfully said, "I wish to write my name."

"Can you not write in Spanish or English?"

"No, Senorita, but I wish to learn."

"Hmmm, let me talk to my uncle and maybe we can arrange some time for you at my school."

"I do not think Senor Dusty would like that," he said in a quavering voice.

"We will not tell him until I talk to Senor Holan, I am certain something can be done," answered Joanna firmly. "Now, go about your chores and I will get back to you."

"Gracious, thank you, Senorita," the young man bowed and turned away.

Dusty and Frieda were discussing recipes when Joanna joined them. "Mr. Whitcomb, how old are Jose and Tomas?"

Dusty scratched his head and replied, "Gosh, Miss, I don't rightly know. They have been with me for two years, Mr. John brought them to me to help."

"I see, well now, they need to be educated."

"Hell, ma'am," Dusty rolled his eyes and put his hand over his mouth, "Excuse my language, but these lads are Mexicans!"

"They are human beings and if they are going to reside in this country, they should have an education," retorted Joanna.

"Wal, I don't see as how I can spare them for any learnin', this be different country than the East, if you will excuse me for saying so, ma'am."

"Yes," snorted Joanna, "It certainly is, a bunch of uneducated galoots if you will pardon the expression, Mr. Whitcomb!"

Frieda quickly interceded, "I will order the supplies you requested, Dusty. We best be on our way."

As they walked back to the big house Frieda said, "He is a good cook, Joanna, and the men like him. Mr. John would not be happy if we displeased him. Mr. John runs an orderly ranch, he believes in stocking well for winter and feeding the hands well so there are no disgruntled men. The blizzards and drifts can be deadly. Sometimes the supply trains are weeks getting through."

"I can understand that, but with all the hands, certainly one or two could relieve those boys for a couple of hours to come to school. I will talk to Uncle John," answered a determined Joanna.

Frieda smiled to herself, this girl was as fiery as Winifred, but with great compassion. She would be a teacher to reckon with.

When they reached the big house Joanna asked about her uncle's whereabouts. She was told he had gone to the upper meadow.

After a quick lunch Joanna had Annie ride with her to find John. Haystacks high as a house dotted the upper meadow; even the high grass in the slough by the springs had been cut and stacked! The smell of alfalfa and timothy greeted the women as they rode down the hay town. The area between the stacks was wide enough for hay racks or sleds to pass. With this and the hayloft full, John hoped it would get them through another long winter.

Joanna found her uncle with some hands tying down the last of the lofty stacks. John was surprised to see the women.

"What brings you ladies here? Searching for a fox to chase?" he asked with a laugh.

"Oh, Uncle John, be serious, we were looking for you," answered Joanna with a twinkle.

"I may look like a fox, but I'm not one," he chuckled. "Get off old Dobbin and come over to the wagon, we can talk there."

Joanna seated herself on the buckboard and began to ask her uncle about the two Mexican boys.

"Where did they come from, Uncle John? Do they have family?"

"The owner of the Snowflake Ranch brought the family up from New Mexico. The mother died three years ago with consumption and the father drank himself to death. The boys were a handful. Phillip, the owner, drives cattle and horses for his father in New Mexico and the overseer at Snowflake didn't want the responsibility while he was gone. Phillip ask me if I had work for them and I gave them to Dusty. He had to raise leather to them a few times, but they work well now. Why do you ask?"

"I want them to attend school," answered Joanna.

"What!" John turned to her and his eyes were intense. "Joanna, we don't educate Mexican workers. I pay them their room and board, do not interfere with me on this issue!"

"Uncle John, the one boy wants to learn to write. What harm is there in that for goodness sake?"

"Joanna, I am not paying to educate an Indian and that is my final word on it!"

"Why, are the white men afraid of educating others of color…any color, because they might be as intelligent as they?"

"Joanna, I have never prided myself on prejudice and I am not about to sit here and discuss this with you," replied John, climbing down off the buckboard. He looked up at her and said, "You have yet to begin, girl, do not put more on your shoulders than you can handle. You have Lionel, see how the others handle that. If it works maybe we'll talk again someday."

Okay, for now Uncle, but I will find a way to help that child. He asked and that is enough for me! she said to herself defiantly.

The bell arrived for the schoolhouse and Tony hung it from the small steeple he had built. Joanna noted he had also built a small lean to at the back of the school. Kindling and chopped wood were stacked next to the coal. She and Annie uncrated slates and chalk for the students and polished the building until it sparkled.

It was a crisp morning when Buck strode up the path to the schoolhouse. Joanna and Annie were hanging curtains when he came in the door. He pushed his hat to the back of his head and leaned against the wall.

"Good morning, Buck, and what do we owe the pleasure of your company?" chirped Joanna mischievously for she suspected Buck was smitten with Annie.

"Well," he answered as he twirled his hat by the brim, "it's a fair morning and I have to ride the ridge to look for a filly. I thought you two might enjoy a canter before the snow flies." Buck had never had anyone affect him like this little Irish lass. He was gone on her.

Annie felt much the same and it showed when their eyes met. She turned her face quickly, her cheeks flushing.

Joanna chuckled, "Give us a few minutes and we will meet you at the barn."

The girls hurried to the house and changed into split skirts and boots. Grabbing jackets and hats they pulled on their gloves as they entered the barn. The horses were saddled and waiting. Once mounted, Buck led the way at a fast trot. The path they took was a game trail that led up the mountain through aspen groves and into pines. Buck would pull up now and again to listen. "If the cats or wolves didn't get her, she will likely be in one of these canyons. Keep an eye peeled. She is a sorrel with a white blaze."

They saw nothing. They entered a wild and broken canyon, and walked the horses up a dry streambed. Great boulders were scattered amid cedar and pine and eventually Buck had them remount. The warm sun and creak of the saddles became hypnotic; Joanna fought to stay awake. Suddenly Buck pulled up short. High above, on a cliff about thirty yards away sat a rider on his horse. A long and melodious *Hallo* bounced off the canyon walls. Buck swung an arm in a wide circle.

"It is okay, it's Phillip," he exclaimed, urging his horse on. The horses picked their way to the top of the canyon and cantered over to the rider.

Joanna stared at the man. She was instantly aware of two things…he was handsome and he was arrogantly staring at her! A quick stirring deep within her left her breathless.

"By all that's holy, what are you doing this far north this time of year, Phillip?" asked Buck, leaning over to shake hands with the rider.

"I came to Snowflake to check on the building and see if the haying had been finished. Got a late start, we drove a big herd to Cheyenne. Lost quite a few to the drought," stated the stranger.

"You gotta' run more shorthorns up here, Phillip. Those long drives are too much and the price is way down for those rangy longhorns. No meat, no way," Buck said as he turned in his saddle to the women.

"Ladies, this is Phillip de Leon…Miss Holan and Miss Kelley."

"Pleasure, Miss Kelley." Looking at Joanna, he lifted a match to a thin cigarillo and looked through the flame into her eyes. He leaned forward in a lazy insolent manner, the cigarillo between his lips, and his narrowed blue eyes bored into hers. "So, Senorita, we meet again!" he sneered.

Joanna averted her face, her cheeks hot. *How dare he, I do not know this rude person!* Phillip turned back to Buck who was describing the missing filly. Joanna's eyes wavered back to Phillip. He looked to be very tall. He wore a black flat-crowned hat, buckskin shirt, tight fitting black pants with boots and huge roweled spurs. His saddle was tooled black leather richly adorned with silver. An ivory handled revolver was at his waist and a carbine was jammed in a scabbard. His horse looked to be a magnificent Arabian. Yes, indeed, he was a dashing figure! There was something that went beyond the handsome darkness of his face; it was the obvious strength of his body and the hard strong maleness of pride. Joanna was speechless and also angry.

"I haven't seen her, Buck, but I did hear a horse neighing earlier. Diablo was answering and blowing so it most likely was a mare. I'll ride with you a short distance and maybe we can spot her."

The two men rode a distance ahead. Annie observed, "Blessed Mary, he is a most handsome man, Miss Joanna. Did you see those cheek bones?"

"Yes," answered Joanna, "he is quite remarkable."

"Beautiful, you mean! Where did you meet him?"

"I have never laid eyes on the man before. He has either mistaken me for someone or just dreadfully rude," sniffed Joanna.

"There she is, Phillip!" yelled Buck pointing below the rim. "You girls stay here!" he called over his shoulder as they hurriedly rode down the canyon.

For an instant Joanna hesitated then started her horse down the cut the men had taken. Annie soon followed. When they reached the bottom of the draw Buck had the filly roped to his pommel. The little sorrel stood with bowed head.

"She is tuckered out, something has been running her, she's mighty pleased to see us," said a relieved Buck.

Phillip's horse came broadside Joanna's and he said in a husky low voice, "Don't start anything out here or I'll make it very embarrassing for you." He looked into her face and his eyes were glinting with a cold blue green light.

Joanna stopped her horse and slid to the ground. "Sir, I think you are rude and impertinent. What ever is your problem? I have never laid eyes on you before in my life! How dare you speak to me in such a manner!"

Phillip wheeled the Arabian and jumped down. He grabbed her by her arms and held them at her side. "Winnie, I've warned you before, I've had enough!"

"Oh, my God! You have mistaken me for my cousin!" gasped Joanna.

Phillip momentarily stepped back, confused, he swore softly staring at her. The eyes were different, she was taller and her face soft and lovely. Her shapely rounded body made him very aware this was not Winifred Holan! This woman had a proud lift to her chin, a beautiful mouth and hair shimmering with glints of red and gold. Her lavender eyes were sparking fire and ice.

"Who are you ?" he whispered leaning into her.

"I am Joanna Holan, John Holan's niece," she spewed.

He smiled showing perfect white teeth. "You are the most beautiful thing I have ever seen, I deeply apologize for the mistake...there is a resemblance...." His voice trailed off and the two of them seemed to blend together. His heart pounded, her ears roared...body folded into body caught in an on-sweeping tide of passion. Closer, he pulled her closer...their lips clung together, he felt her full breasts heaving against his chest, she felt his thrusting manhood...she tore herself free, staring at him.

"I am truly sorry," he said. He started toward her.

"No, please!" She brushed a strand of hair from her eyes and turned away.

A wide eyed Annie and a chuckling Buck still sat their horses.

"Some chaperone you are!" hissed Joanna at Buck as she mounted her horse.

At this he guffawed and said, "We had better head home. Thanks for the help, Phillip, appreciate it."

"Glad I was in the area," answered Phillip as he mounted his stallion. He then took off his hat, sweeping it in a half circle bowing his head, "Ladies..." he said as he turned his magnificent horse and galloped away.

Buck led them down the long canyon back toward Locket Springs. Joanna finally was able to rein in beside him. "Buck, tell me about Phillip, who is he, what does he do?" she asked breathlessly.

"Now you ask?" grinned Buck. "Well, he comes from Spanish aristocracy, his great grandfather was a count or something of Argon. He was given a Spanish Grant located in the Southwest Territory. Don Luis, Ramon's father, lives on the Ramada. Phillip and his brother, Antonio, manage the large spread. Don Luis sent both sons to Europe for schooling and Phillip brought back a French bride, just like his Mama she's French. His wife was a pretty little thing, her name was Leonora, and Phillip adored her. He bought the old Redland's homestead up here and called it Snowflake. The original house burned so he was having it rebuilt. He and Leonora were going to live up here."

"You keep referring to her in the past tense," questioned Joanna. "Why is that?"

"She died in childbirth over a year ago. Ramon floats between here and the Ramada since then. A kind of lost soul, so to speak."

"How tragic!" exclaimed Joanna. "What about the baby?"

"It died with the Momma."

"I am very sorry about his loss. Tell me about Winifred, what is the connection?"

"Hmmm, well, Phillip and Mr. John are good neighbors. Phillip would come often to visit with the boss and danged if that Winifred wouldn't follow or ride out after Phillip. It made him very uncomfortable, I can tell you. He stopped coming to Locket Springs. Your cousin is brazen and shameless, if you pardon my saying so," retorted Buck hotly.

"She can be appalling by turns. I cannot defend her behavior, she is like a fire out of control at times."

Joanna then blushed recalling her behavior with Phillip earlier that very day. She said no more on the return to the ranch.

As she dressed for dinner, Joanna sat contemplating her image in her dressing table mirror. She traced the outline of her face with a finger. *Whatever is to become of you? You disgraced yourself today, well, at least it was in the presence of help!* Her image reflected shock. *Dear God, I sound like my mother! Annie and Buck are dear friends and what about the sensual Phillip? What thoughts does he have of me?* Her face flushed red and tingled. He was certainly the handsomest of men, a spectacular horseman and a son of a family of distinguished Spanish aristocrats! She touched her lips in memory of that kiss and a smile played around her mouth.

She finished her toilette and went down to dinner. The upstairs was chilly and she welcomed the warmth of the downstairs area. It would seem winter was on its way.

She told her Uncle John of meeting Phillip. "Fine young man, I wish he would come around more often. That vixen of a daughter of mine ran him off. She was so young and uncontrollable. I failed her miserably," sighed John taking a deep drink from his wine goblet.

"Oh, she will find her way, Gram and mother will see to that," answered Joanna, smiling.

"I pray to God that she will turn out to be a lady. She seems happy in her letters so she may be growing up, after all," John cynically replied.

The next morning when Joanna pulled back her drapes, the world was white with frost. She ate a quick breakfast and hustled out to the little schoolhouse. Buck had the road dragged so the walk now was an easy one. The sun was a bit higher and melting the light frost. She passed Ella and Lionel pulling up blackened tomato vines in the garden. "Good morning," she called.

"Morning, Miss Joanna, when does school begin?" called Ella.

"Next Monday," she answered over her shoulder.

The little schoolhouse was frigid. Joanna kindled a fire. Her nose was cold and her hands felt frozen. She hadn't worn her knitted mittens, which were much warmer than the white cloth gloves she had worn. Shortly a fire was roaring in the new pot bellied stove. She filled a teakettle from a water pail and set it on top of the stove. When the water was hot, she made a cup of tea and sipped it as she arranged books. She loved the smell of the new print, the lovely illustrations of the First and Second Readers; marveled at the Ideals of History of America, the Civics Books, and Natural History. She unpacked books of poetry, geography and arithmetic that had been used by her and Elyce. She studied the lessons.

She had a dread of Monday. What if the children would not mind her? She really had no idea of discipline, as she had never attended a public school. She and Elyce had nurses and governesses since birth. Her grandmother's voice echoed in her mind, *Have confidence in yourself, Joanna, and you can overcome anything. If you appear confident, others will have faith in you. When things seem impossible, pray. The answers will come.* Joanna laughed out loud in the stillness and immediately felt better.

She finished her tea, closed down the stove damper and put on her wraps. The schoolhouse looked tidy and neat waiting for the children.

Rain began falling as she walked back to the house. It fell steadily all night and the next day. John complained of feeling winter in his bones and sat close to the fireplace in the big room. He didn't come to dinner that Friday evening and Frieda took a tray up to his room.

When Joanna looked in on him the following morning he was burning with fever. Alarmed she and Frieda sent Buck for the doctor. Dr. Tuttle arrived mid-afternoon. He was a jovial, rotund man and medicated John for the grippe. He took Joanna into the kitchen and instructed her and Frieda in the making of mustard plasters. Joanna watched carefully as he put ground mustard and water in a bowl and made a smooth paste. He spread it on butcher paper between two pieces of cloth and cautioned them about getting any of the mixture on the skin. Frieda was instructed to made a beef tea custard. The doctor then made a salve out of camphorated and eucalyptus oil adding turpentine and Vaseline. He heated the oils together and had Frieda grind onions and place them in flannel sacks. The three of them climbed the stairs to John's chamber. The doctor carefully applied a mustard plaster and left it on for an hour. When the plaster was removed he dipped the onion sacks in the oil solution to be left on the chest overnight. He gave John pine tar syrup and horehound candy for his cough.

Eyes weeping and nose highly irritated, Joanna mused, *Perish the thought of getting ill in this country, the stench of the medications alone would kill one!*

By midnight John's fever had broken and the congestion began to break up. Joanna was overcome with relief. She couldn't abide the thought of losing her beloved uncle.

The good doctor left Sunday morning after instructing Frieda and Joanna on using the powders and salves. Frieda stayed by John's side leaving only to make tea and broth.

Monday morning was coldly blue and white. Everything glittered with a heavy frost. Joanna looked in on her uncle and was happy to see him propped up in bed eating gruel. She blew kisses to him and trotted downstairs to eat and prepare for school. The air scorched Joanna's cheeks with cold and her breath blew out in frosty puffs. The bitter thick frost had left every green living thing dead except the trees. The mile walk seemed much longer in the cold.

The frost had crept up the walls of the school and to Joanna's astonishment, blacks smoke rose from the stovepipe and she could hear voices. She gathered her courage and opened the door. The big stove was cherry red and standing around it was her scholars. There were nine in all, four boys, four girls and dear Willie!

"Good morning," her voice squeaked.

Everyone answered, "Good morning, Miss Holan!"

She took off her wraps and went to her desk. Her small clock chimed eight thirty am. "Glory be, you are all early and what a wonderful fire! I hope you will soon be warm in your seats."

They shuffled away from the stove and sat down. Ella and Willie sat in the front bench or the right side, on the left sat a tall girl and a little boy. Directly behind Ella and Willie were two boys, obviously brothers. A pretty dark haired girl sat with Lionel and another boy and girl sat together across the aisle from them. Joanna asked for names and ages.

The tall girl was Sarah Smith; she was twelve years old. She was blond with sparkling blue eyes. The little boy beside her was her brother, Howard.

He had bright brown eyes, round rosy cheeks and thick and unruly hair. He was seven and quick in movement and speech. The two brothers were Jacob and Randall Clarke and were eleven and ten...both chunky husky boys with copper red hair. Their speech was saucy and Joanna knew they would require watching. The older boy, Jacob, informed her his father was the overseer of Snowflake ranch. The pretty dark haired girl sitting with Lionel was Mary Angela DeBernardi. She was nine with black ringlets and soft brown eyes.

"Are you Tony's daughter?" asked Joanna in amazement.

"Yes'm," answered the child, "I am not called Maria, but Angela because my mother's name is Maria and Poppa says it's too confusing."

"That is perfectly fine, Angela is a beautiful name," answered Joanna, smiling at the adorable girl. She hadn't even inquired of Tony if he were married, how thoughtless of her!

The other boy and girl were brother and sister, Bonnie and Bobby Nelson. They were fraternal twins with silvery blond hair and gray eyes. They were obviously Scandinavian, ten years old and their father was the caretaker at Snowflake.

Dearest Willie looked at her with great anticipation, his blue eyes bright and lively. Joanna knew she must give him extra attention for his speech was slow, it would take great concentration for him to learn to write and read.

After sorting out how much education each student had and what lesson to start them on, Joanna passed out the books. None had studied grammar, geography or history. Three had never learned to spell or write.

"Very well," Joanna said, "School will come to order. It is now nine o'clock. Randall will ring the bell and Sarah will lead us in the Pledge of Allegiance, after which, I will lead us in prayer."

By the time Joanna assigned lessons and drew up a chart board, it was time for recess. They all put on wraps and went outside to play. After fifteen minutes she rang the bell. Until noon she listened to the readers, then rang the bell for lunch. The students ate from their lunch pails and the boys went outside. Joanna shared a sandwich with Willie and had tea. When the lunch hour was over the boys came in glowing from cold and exercise. The afternoon followed with recitation. The three beginners began the ABCs. Four o'clock chimed and she sighed with relief.

"Put away your books neatly, school is dismissed."

Joanna stood by the door watching them go. A wagon was waiting for the children from Snowflake. Lionel, Ella, Angela and Willie left on foot wrapped well against the cold. She erased the blackboard and swept the floor.

After shutting the drafts in the stove she put on her hood and coat, closed the door carefully behind her and hurried down the path. Her first day of teaching was completed! She felt a deep joy.

John recovered slowly under the competent care of Frieda.

Returning from school Thursday afternoon, Frieda told her Timber was visiting with her uncle. Joanna rushed up to her room, patted her hair, changed her shirtwaist and bustled down the great hall to her uncle's room. She knocked gently on the open door and entered. Timber was sitting in a chair by John's bed and both men were speaking in hushed voices. Timber stood as Joanna approached. Her uncle was still wan, but much improved.

"Joanna, it is nice to see you. May I congratulate you on receiving your certificate, John tells me you are now teaching."

"Thank you, Timber, it is wonderful to see you again," answered Joanna, her face radiant. She seated herself on the edge of the bed and turned to her uncle who soberly began to talk.

"Timber is leaving for New York, Joanna. I sent for him. Elyce has had an unfortunate accident. She is in an infirmary, now apparently out of danger. Mother cabled, Elyce needs financial help and legal counseling. Timber is going in my stead."

Stunned, Joanna exclaimed, "I must go, also. She will need me!"

"Nay, child, you've signed a contract and must continue your teaching. Your mother is with her as well as your grandmother. Timber will handle this," answered John in a stern voice.

Timber leaned over and grasped Joanna's hands, "Joanna, I promise you, Elyce will get the best of care and I will bring her back with me. I give you my solemn word if she has need of you, I will cable you. I can understand how you feel, but this must be handled legally and you would only add to the problem at present."

Joanna looked up at him with hurt in her eyes, "But she is my sister, Timber, I would comfort her, we have always been close."

"No," Timber replied, "not now, perhaps later, but not now."

"What happened to her, Uncle John?" she queried.

The two men exchanged glances and John hesitated before answering, "Mother stated she had been burned, but is doing well."

Joanna's face became stiff and white. She shakily stood up and reached out to Timber, took his hand and squeezed it lightly. "Thank you for going, whatever has happened, indirectly or directly, her husband must have been the cause. Please get her away from him, he is a brute!"

Timber looked down at her and gave her a smile, "Dear girl, you can count on it. Now, take care of your uncle and your pupils, I'll see you upon my return."

Joanna turned and fled to her room, tears streaking down her cheeks. She flung herself across her bed. *Why, God, why? Papa, now Elyce, I cannot understand this! My dear sweet sister who loved life and everyone. How did she become burned and where? Something very grave has happened for Uncle John to have Timber go to New York. Did she hurt Marshall...maybe she killed him!*

"Miss Joanna, it's Annie, can I get you a cup of tea?"

Joanna rolled over and sat up. She had cried herself to sleep. Annie was bending over lighting a fire; a lamp was burning above the mantel. She looked at her lapel watch, almost eight thirty! Her head was splitting and her eyes were swollen.

"I will bring up a tray for you. You should prepare for bed."

"Has Timber left?"

"Yes, quite a while ago."

Joanna paced the room, looked out a window and saw whirling snow. She undressed, washed her face and donned a flannel dressing gown.

Annie returned with a tray.

"When did it begin to snow, Annie?" she asked, pouring a cup of tea.

"Just a short while ago, at the most a half hour," answered Annie as she uncovered a bowl of soup and toast.

"I hope Timber made it to Stirrup Crossing."

"Now, don't worry your pretty head. Tony and one of the hands drove him back in a carriage. They will be fine...just rest awhile."

"Annie, Elyce was burned. I just know Marshall has done something to her."

"I know, Frieda told me. She was worried about Mr. John, he was so upset. Mr. Timber's arrival helped soothe him. Mr. John sent for him yesterday."

"Yesterday and he told me nothing! Why did he do that?"

"Frieda said Mr. John didn't want to alarm you. He was concerned that he might not contact Mr. Timber."

"Oh, it is all so confusing! I wish I could get my hands on that Marshall, that fiend!"

"Shhh, we don't know all the particulars so you must wait until your uncle has more word. Now, eat your soup."

Next morning the sky was a brilliant blue and the ground was blowing white. Joanna put on her hood, coat and mittens. She pulled galoshes on her feet and covered her head with a large shawl that she secured with a shawl pin under her chin.

Annie was dressed similarly and stated, "I am going with you, you promised to teach me to read and write, no time like the present."

Joanna hugged her and huskily said, "You are my dearest friend, thank you."

Outdoors the sun glitter was blinding. Joanna had to squint to see around her. There were footprints leading to the schoolhouse from the lane. They were spaced too far apart for Joanna and Annie to walk in so they floundered through a foot of snow. The footprints were all around the school. Joanna opened the door and peeked in. The pot bellied stove was red and sitting expectantly were Sarah, Howard, Jacob, Bonnie and Bobby.

"Oh, my dears, you must have frozen coming this morning!" exclaimed Joanna as she and Annie walked into the room.

"It wasn't too awful bad, Miss Holan," said Sarah, smiling. "Mama heated us bricks for our feet, gave us hot baked potatoes for our hands. Papa said if it snows more he will come early for us."

"Potatoes, how interesting, and they really kept your hands warm?"

"Gosh, yes, and we put them close to the fire so's we could eat them for lunch!" giggled Howard.

"I must say, you have a smart mama, I think it is a brilliant idea," laughed Joanna, taking off her wraps.

A blast of cold air rushed in as the door opened and Willie, Lionel, Ella and Angela entered the room. Joanna now knew her Uncle John had made the right decision in having her stay to teach the children.

The day went smoothly and by that evening Tony had returned and reported to John that Timber had left for the East by rail.

There were two more storms within the next few days. Joanna and Annie had to break a path to the schoolhouse again. Tomas and Jose came to school...Joanna could have wept.

That Friday afternoon Joanna was helping Willie with his phonics when she heard a tinkling silvery sound. Everyone listened as the sound grew nearer and the air became filled with chiming of tiny bells. Joanna walked quickly to the door and found Buck sitting in a sled with a pile of furs behind him. He was in a buffalo coat and a fur cap. The horses were stamping and a few bells would shake small tinkles as the horses turned their heads.

"It will be a few minutes," called Joanna. Buck waved an arm in response.

Now came another sound, clop, clop, clop of hooves and the squeak of sledrunners on the hard packed snow. It was a big sled from Snowflake.

127

Jonathon Clarke, Randall and Jacob's father, was driving the sled. All the children quickly put on their wraps. The children from Snowflake climbed under robes in the big sled and were off.

Buck lifted Angela, Lionel, Tomas into the sleigh then motioned for Jose to come.

"I'll be back in a flash for you, Willie and Annie," and the bells tinkled merrily as the cutter flew away. Joanna and Annie shut the drafts, picked up the schoolhouse, arranged slates, and then dressed bundled warmly. Joanna picked up her lunch pail and books. She turned to Annie whose eyes were sparkling with excitement.

Joanna remarked, "I am afraid, my dear Annie, one of these days, I am going to lose you to that good looking cow poke!"

Annie suddenly looked very dreamy. "We have only made polite conversation, but he did ask me to the Harvest Dance."

"Oh, and when is that?"

"In a couple of weeks at Stirrup Crossing. He says most everyone goes from Locket Springs. He says your uncle goes and stays in his house there. Buck says they have a midnight supper and everyone from miles around comes. He says they dance 'til dawn."

"Hmmm, well, it does sound like fun. Uncle John is so much improved I would wager he will go."

The sound of bells announced the sleigh's return and they were soon gliding toward the big house.

The next morning John asked Joanna to come with him as he had something he wanted to show her. They went up to the attic where John opened a large trunk and pulled out a silver blue fox coat. "Here, child, try this on. It is warm and only worn once," he said, holding up the beautiful wrap. "I had it made for Winifred and she turned up her nose."

Joanna slipped into the fur and turned slowly for her uncle to pass judgement.

"It fits perfectly and it will keep you warm. You have made me very proud, Joanna. It is a fine thing you are doing here."

"Oh, Uncle John, I love teaching and the children. It is so rewarding to see a child learn to read, the look of wonder in their eyes is so inspiring!" Then she hugged him, "Are you certain you wish me to wear this? I wouldn't want to have Winifred upset."

"Joanna," he answered, closing the trunk, "she did not like it, would not wear it and all but threw it in my face. It is yours, wear it and enjoy it."

"Thank you, it is beautiful and very thoughtful of you to want me to have it," she retorted, "we best get back downstairs, it is chilly up here and it would never do should you get a chill."

Joanna hurried to her room and twirled in her coat for Annie. It had a hood, which made a silver blue halo about her face, it was most becoming.

Annie patted and stroked the wondrous fur. "My, gosh, it is so soft and warm. You look most elegant and royal."

"I feel badly for Uncle John. He had this made for Winnie and she refused it. Can you imagine?" said Joanna. She then went to her armoire and took out her horsehide coat. It was practically new and still very fashionable. "One good turn deserves another; you shall be warm also, Annie!"

"Blessed be, this is the nicest thing I have ever owned," the astonished Annie replied.

Both women were pleased with their new acquisitions and used them to good advantage as the winter turned colder.

Joanna had her first meeting with her school board. It consisted of Jonathon Clarke, Martha Smith and Tony DeBernardi. Martha was the cook for the Snowflake Ranch and her husband was the blacksmith. She was a tall rawboned woman, old for her years; Joanna was shocked to learn she was only twenty-eight. At one time she had no doubt been pretty like her Sarah. Martha was happy that Howard and Sarah could attend a school. It had been three years since they had a teacher close enough to help.

Jonathon Clarke, a rangy, leather-skinned man, had a twinkle in his eye and a smile as wide as his face. He informed Joanna his wife had insisted that his two younger boys attend. His two older boys were working at the ranch.

"Mr. Clarke, can they read and write?" asked Joanna.

"Well, they can write their names," he answered. "They can't read; I can't spare them, either."

"Is your employer that difficult?" inquired Joanna, thinking of the handsome Spaniard who was haunting her dreams since their encounter.

"No, ma'am. He is a good man. We are finishing the roof on his house before another storm."

"When the roof is done, can you spare them?"

Mr. Clarke looked very solemn, scratched a bushy eyebrow and replied, "Maybe Johnny, but Jedediah must work with me."

"I must abide with your decision, but learning to read and write should be a choice every child should have."

"Well, ma'am, you can't do neither if you have no food or work!"

"Do what you must, I'll work with either boy when you can spare them. I will speak with your employer. Maybe he will assist so the boys can still earn and learn."

Mr. Clarke laughed a mocking laugh, "Why, you are a poet, too!" Then, "I wouldn't count on too much help from the patron, he isn't around much."

School progressed, but not without headaches. At times Joanna was in despair. There were days when the children were not able to study their lessons because of chores. Many days she had to reassign the lessons. Only three pupils were at the same grade level. She never had the time to give her full attention to a student. She made Annie a monitor and wished with all her heart that Annie were better educated. On weekends she spent time with both Annie and Willie. Annie was a fast learner while dear Willie struggled to even write his name. She had none to turn to for advice so she did the best she could. She wrote the school superintendent for literature and he mailed primary plans and instructions for a Normal Teacher. They were of little use for a rural teacher. One blessing was the fact that her pupils were well behaved and never took advantage of her. They soaked up learning as they could. It heartened her a bit when they could finally give recitations.

There were two weeks were bitter cold. Bands of gray clouds lay low along the mountains and their tops concealed by blowing snow. The wind blew monotonously. Fortunately the trains got through which meant mail and provisions. Mail always made for excitement as newspapers and letters from loved ones brought the outside world in.

A huge crate of machinery was sitting on a freight wagon as Joanna came from school. Buck and Tony were cutting straps from the crate.

"What in the world is that, Buck?" asked Joanna, looking at it in amazement.

"It is a gee-haw engine of sorts to make electricity that you uncle ordered."

"I declare, isn't that something!" answered an astonished Joanna.

Later she joined her uncle in the big room. He was busily going through the mail, sorting letters into one pile and papers into another.

He greeted Joanna. "I should be in the study, but it feels much warmer in here."

The big ornate stove had flames blazing through its isinglass window and the stone fireplace had a roaring fire. The room was toasty and cheery.

"Here is a letter for you, Joanna. Timber wrote me of Elyce's welfare, I am certain you will want to read it." One of the servants brought John a brandy, lifting the snifter, he asked, "Would you like tea or a drink?"

"Tea would be lovely," she answered and settled comfortably in a chair with the two letters. Her letter from Pierré had a San Francisco postmark. She would read it later. She took Timber's letter from the large envelope.

My Dear John,

I am happy to report that Elyce is in a much improved condition. She is resting comfortably here in Boston with mother and me. Caroline was here for a week and your mother is to arrive shortly for an extended stay.

Elyce is under the care of Dr. Max Frieberg. He works with burn victims using a plant from South America called the "Aloe Vera." He pointed out it has been used for its curative powers for more than three thousand years. He even quoted the Bible, John: 19:39

"Nicodemus, also who had at first come to him at night, came bringing a mixture of myrrh and aloes." He claims it is a pain inhibitor and promotes the healing of injured surfaces. He has made progress with Elyce's healing.

I am so thankful to God for his goodness in preserving our dear Elyce. The burns on her face and neck are now healing. The shoulder and upper arm, having been more protected, were not as deeply burned. Mother changes the bandages as Dr. Freiberg wishes and sadly, there will be scarring and most likely, troublesome after effects such as some pulling and puckering. Luckily, the scalding water missed her "My Beautiful Face."

She was extremely depressed and sat silent for hours. How dark were those days! Her reaction to her face was one of horrified shock. Dr. Freiberg was very angry when he learned a nurse had let her view her face when bandages were changed. It has been ghastly for her, poor darling.

I have decided to stay on in Boston indefinitely. Mother is delighted to have me here and I want to be near Elyce and reassure her. I have made a dramatic decision. I would like to marry Elyce as soon as she is well...if she will have me. I have loved her since the first time I laid eyes on her.

Marshall Davenport has engaged the services of Downey, Lake and James; Esq. The marriage is to be annulled on grounds of financial misrepresentation citing the pre-marital contract concerning Elyce's dowry. They claim the contract was not fulfilled because of her father's death and bankruptcy. The annulment will not give her any rights to her husband's estate or any share of his property. The scoundrel has only agreed to pay her medical bills!

She will never need anything as long as she is in my care.

By the way, the young woman, involved, had no charges filed against her. She told the court she threw the water, but I have my doubts. The Davenports have gone to great lengths to have the whole affair quietly settled. We are still in a state of continual apprehension never knowing what to expect from one moment to the other.

I pray you are much improved, John. I know Joanna must be a great comfort and joy to you.

I have written of my fondest hopes and wishes concerning Elyce. I hope I can bring it about. I know you will be very surprised and possibly find it hard to understand how an attachment so deep could have arisen in so short a time. I feel she is the one I have been waiting for all my life and I love her with my very soul.

When her health has improved enough for her to consider my proposal, I should like your blessing and approval.

Mother is most insistent that I become more involved with her estate. As you know, I am the only heir, so I feel inclined to abide with her wishes.

I have every confidence in this kind doctor and entrust Elyce's care to him. I hope you will also.

Bearing in mind the west is my true home, I hope to return in the future if only to visit.

Your devoted friend and servant,
Timber Alexander

Joanna had very mixed emotions after reading Timber's letter. She felt a tear rolling down her cheek and quickly wiped it away with a finger. A sense of great loss compounded with thankfulness that Elyce had Timber washed over her.

Sipping her cup of tea, she opened Pietré's letter. He was doing well and liked San Francisco. *What a gay city,* he wrote, *a city of grandeur, extravagant in every sense. The fetes are brilliant and the homes of the "Nobs" on the hill are castles in every respect, demanding great social prestige. I am having a home built with gardens facing the ocean. It is in an area called the Palisades.*

Sweet dear, it has been weeks since I have had a note from you. Please write me particulars of all that is happening. How is your school progressing? He pledged his love and closed, once again imploring her to write.

She fixed a smile on her face so her Uncle John would not see how upset she was. She had control over her outward signs of agitation, but she could not stop the images running through her mind. She envisioned Elyce's horrible burns and how terrified she must be. How fortunate Elyce had Timber and that he was devoting himself to her healing and well being.

Joanna felt a great sense of loss. She asked to be excused and fled to her room. There she paced restlessly from corner to fireplace to chaise lounge. *I feel like I am walking out of step in time*, she thought. *Where do I belong? Who am I? My beautiful blonde and dreamy sister...what will life hold now for her?*

Elyce had been openly admired for her beauty. This latest disaster obviously had changed her appearance. Could Elyce cope with this?

A knock came at the door, it was Annie. "Can I do anything, Miss Joanna? Aren't you going to dinner?"

"As a matter of fact, I'm not. Would you tell Uncle John I have a splitting headache and tell him I ask to be excused."

Noting Joanna's look of utter despair, Annie said quietly, "I will bring up a tray."

"Make it light and a glass of warm milk. Thanks, Annie."

Joanna undressed, washed her face and prepared for bed. Annie brought a tray, then turned down the bed. Joanna climbed under the feather comforter and nibbled at the food on her tray.

"I am putting a hot water bottle under for your feet. You are shivering, drink your milk and I will build up the fire," stated Annie.

Joanna slowly warmed and fell into a fitful sleep. She awoke with tears streaming down her face. She pulled on her wrapper and added more wood to the embers. Pulling up a rocker she watched the flames lick the logs in small orange ribbons then curl and wrap around the logs in tongues of yellow and red. She shook more from emotion than cold. Weary and weepy she twisted her hands in her lap. There were so many things running through her mind; she had never been able to break from the grief of her father's death. He had been such an influence in her life, indulging her and Elyce with gifts and love. She smiled as the memories tumbled and played in her head. She recalled the beautiful Christmas when she had been thirteen. Papa had insisted she and Elyce go for a ride with him. He hustled them into their wraps and they hurried down the marble front stairs to the surprise that awaited them. A groom was standing by a beautiful red and gold sleigh. The cutter was small, about six feet long and thirty inches wide at the bottom.

"Oh, Papa, it is beautiful!" Joanna and Elyce snuggled under a fur robe. The groom gave Elyce the reins and the two girls skimmed over the snow. It had been so exciting, the matched blacks named Midnight and Starlight had settled into a brisk trot with music streaming from their collars and bells. The girls took turns driving while laughing and waving as they flashed along streets of store windows and large houses. The little sleigh had been enjoyed all winter much to Mama's chagrin. She reminisced fondly about the Christmas of her sixteenth year. It had been a blustery cold winter with deep snowfalls. After Christmas Eve dinner, it had been traditional to attend midnight services and then open gifts on Christmas morning This particular year Papa wanted the three of them to open three large elegantly wrapped boxes on Christmas Eve. Mama had protested saying, "But Andrew, it isn't Christmas yet!"

He had answered, "Caroline, every day is Christmas if I can afford it. Now, open your gifts!"

Joanna had removed the red velvet ribbon off the gold box, lifted its lid and pulled out a mink coat with matching muff. Elyce' s was identical. They had stood quietly in their coats watching their father help Mama slip into a magnificent Russian sable with a matching pillbox hat. Oh, they had felt like royalty attending mass that magical evening! The most memorable part was that Papa had been so happy with giving, he spent the whole Christmas holiday at home!

Immense sorrow overcame her, remembering was so bittersweet. She had felt so secure then, now she felt like an intruder…an imposing guest. She snorted to herself, *A teacher, my pay a month, twelve dollars after giving Uncle John three dollars for board! I will never be self supporting. Now if I were a male teacher my salary would be double. Why are we women treated so inferior?* The fear dug into her with clammy claws and she could hardly breathe. The tears began to flow again.

"Miss Joanna, I had a feeling you were too upset to sleep. I, too, am restless," came a whisper.

Joanna shifted her gaze from the flames to the door. Annie stood wide eyed in her wrapper at the open doorway.

"Oh, Annie, I am so dreadfully depressed, I cannot sleep. I feel so alone and lost!"

Annie crossed the room and pulled up a chair beside her.

"I am so afraid of life," Joanna said quietly. This caused Annie to take Joanna's hand in hers. "Annie, how did you ever come to America? You left your family, weren't you frightened?"

Annie felt the prickle of tears at the back of her throat, but her eyes remained dry. "I have never stopped being frightened. I have lived with fear nipping at me heels since I was old enough to remember. We lived in desperate poverty. Poor Ma and Da had both been raised during the Potato Blight. You probably know about that."

"I have read about it, not to a great extent."

"Over a million died in Ireland from starvation and disease. The land ownership was terrible...it still is. Tenants are treated like slaves; most owners are Irish or English Lords. The landowner takes all, but just enough to keep a stew pot bubbling. Da worked extra in the peat fields to send my oldest brother, Jack, to America. Within a year Jack sent passage to my brother, Mickey. I was the oldest girl so it was decided I would go the next year with brother Patrick, a year younger. Donovan, my youngest brother, and my baby sister, Mary Kathleen, stayed at home. Donovan is now a priest and Kathleen got married at fifteen." Annie leaned into the fire staring hard at the flames, her pretty face a mask of sorrow. "I was so filled with terror when Pat and I got on that rotting old ship I felt like I had a stone on my chest. I cried myself to sleep at night when I wasn't retching from the ship's pitching. I missed my country, my home and my family. I had such panic I would wet myself adding humiliation to terror. Pat would hold me and then we would say our rosaries together, that helped." The shadows from the fire danced across her features. She pressed her lips together to keep them from trembling.

"Mickey met us, took us to his flat in shanty town....we became 'shanty Irish' then. I was called that wherever I went. The flat was tiny and grubby.

I slept in Mickey's bed and he and Pat slept on the floor. My first job was in a boarding house where I cleaned, made beds and emptied slop jars. The owner was a lady by the name of Mrs. Megan O'Hara. She took a liking to me and took me to her sister, Peggy, to train me to be a lady's maid. The lady of the house was very demanding and her husband was very demanding in a different way. He chased Peggy from room to room. Peggy encouraged his advances and I found them in various states of disarray more than once. Peggy said granting her favors to the man of the house helped her get by. He tipped her very generously. One day he tried to force me into a compromising situation and I vowed he would never have his way with me and I quit. God was very good to me when your parents hired this 'Shanty Irish' girl."

"Oh my dear, how selfish! I have been thinking only of myself!" Joanna drew in a long quiet breath.

"I know lots of bad things have happened, Miss Joanna, but it could be worse. Your Uncle John loves you like his own and this country is good, you must know that. We have shelter and food and we are surrounded here with caring people."

Joanna's heart ached for the winsome Irish girl whom she loved dearly. Annie had given up her family and in all probability, would never see her mother or father again or her homeland.

"Let's go downstairs and see what we can find to eat. We will heat some more warm milk and you sleep with me tonight, we will chase each other's nightmares away," said Joanna, rising from the rocker.

Annie rose with a smile and they tiptoed downstairs to raid the kitchen.

Next morning John told his sleep deprived niece that the Harvest Ball was being held that weekend. "I want you, Annie, Frieda and Ella to go with me. We will stay in my house in Stirrup Crossing so bring a valise."

Joanna packed a black cashmere gown, well made and plain. She put a strand of pearls with it, not feeling festive in the least. School had been tedious this week so she would be happy to forget lessons for the weekend. She might be able to put Elyce out of her mind for a few hours.

It had snowed again so the snow pack was considerable and they would go by sleigh followed by Buck, Willie and a few hands in a hay sled.

Saturday morning the whole outdoors was sparkling brightly in the cold sunshine. The women were helped into the sleigh. Flatirons and hot bricks wrapped in flannel were placed at their feet. John and Buck tucked them in lightly with buffalo robes then the two men climbed in. They were on their way to the dance! The morning passed swiftly with everyone was in a cheerful mood. They shared hot chocolate, coffee and sang songs. It was mid-afternoon when they arrived at John's modest house in Stirrup Crossing. It had been built before the Locket Springs ranch house went under construction. It stood by itself on the west side of Main Street, a two storied house with lots of gingerbread.

"Here we are," said John, handing them out of the sleigh. "I'm certain dinner will be prepared. Mrs. Mead became my caretaker after husband was killed by a run away team."

Julia Mead met them at the front door, a pleasant woman with a hearty laugh. "I'll bet you are plumb frozen!"

John made the introductions as everyone removed their wraps.

"Come, Lambs, I will show you to the guest rooms. You will have to share as there are only the two," the caretaker said as she led them upstairs.

"That will be fine, Frieda and Ella can share one and Annie and I the other," replied Joanna.

After refreshing herself Joanna went downstairs. The house smelled of good things, she peeked into the kitchen through the dining room door. Frieda and Annie were busily helping Mrs. Mead. A cupboard held large golden crusted loaves of bread, a sugar frosted cake, two crusted pies and a large platter of cookies.

"Oh, yum," said Joanna, wrinkling her nose to sniff the goodies.

Willie and Buck came to join them for dinner. They sat at a large oval table. Mrs. Mead placed roast chicken, bowls of fluffy white potatoes, gravy, stuffing and applesauce on the table. John said a blessing and began heaping plates. Following dinner, Frieda helped with the dessert and Annie refilled cups. They sat for a short time talking of the winter and of the spring to come.

Joanna could not take her eyes off Frieda who had wrapped her blonde hair into a coil on top of her head. She had also curled bangs over her forehead which was most becoming. There was a definite glow about her.

Everyone retired until early evening and then left for the dance about nine o'clock. The dance was held in a large wooden building with a painted sign that read Opera House. Upon entering the hall, fiddles were heard being tuned and a trumpet being fingered for clarity.

Long tables lined the back wall while chairs lined the two sidewalls. Gas jets sputtered here and there along the walls and a brass chandelier glowed from above.

There were all shapes and sizes of people, they were laughing, talking, gossiping and in general, enjoying each other's company. Some of the men were in suits, some in army uniform, and many in shirts and corduroy pants. The women were a mixed group, some in satin adorned with jewels, others in non descript gingham and calico dresses.

Joanna and the women from Locket Springs found empty chairs. Annie looked especially pretty and her eyes were sparkling, Joanna had dressed her in blue cambric and curled her hair.

The dancing began, Annie was tapping her foot to the music when Buck touched her arm and swept her away to waltz.

Frieda sat to Joanna's left. She was dressed in dark navy faille that set off her pale hair and blue eyes. She smiled at Joanna as she swayed to the music, "I particularly like waltzes, don't you, Joanna?"

"Oh, I love to dance, Frieda," she answered. "It has been ever so long."

The next dance was a Waltz Quadrille and John led Joanna out on the floor. They changed partners to waltz to places. "Right hand your partner and Grand right and left," sang out the caller. "Meet partner, waltz to place, change partners."

Joanna looked up as her uncle handed her off and found herself staring into impossibly blue eyes, Phillip! That compelling face with skin gold from the sun and that wonderful mouth with the quirk of a lop sided grin!

"You!" she hissed.

"In person," he nodded which made his mane of ebony wave about this face accenting his long bones. "Miss Holan, how good to see you again."

He continued to smile down at her while he waltzed her back to place and handed her to her uncle.

When the quadrille ended and she was once again seated, she whispered to Annie, "That Phillip de Leon is here!"

"Oh, I spied him as did about every woman here. Look at those women flirting with him, but then who can blame them, he has incredible eyes and lashes!" said Annie.

"Oh, do stop, be serious." Then, "Why, my goodness! That's Frieda and Uncle John!" exclaimed Joanna, her eyes wide with surprise at seeing the couple dancing. John was smiling at Frieda and she looked positively radiant. "Hmm," Joanna lifted a brow, "do you suppose?"

Annie smiled an impish grin, "Does this trouble you?"

"Oh, heavens, I should hope not! I love them both, I am happy they are enjoying themselves."

In the meantime three young women had surrounded Phillip and were vying for his attention. He hardly heard their chattering as he studied Joanna across the room. She was so unconscious of her beauty, such an elegant cameo face surrounded by a halo of autumn hair. The severe black she wore emphasized her lovely figure and her amethyst eyes flashed like jewels. He excused himself to the ladies and swore viciously under his breath as they clung to him. He pushed them away politely and crossed to Joanna.

She sensed he was there before she turned from Annie. His scent hit her first, the elegant sting of rich tobacco, exotic, imported. His physical aura shimmered about him. Here was a man a woman shuddered over, yearned for.....

Her heart did a jig when he asked, "Miss Holan, may I have the pleasure of this dance?" His sensuous voice sent tiny shocks down her spine. She said nothing at all, just rose into his arms. He was a marvelous dancer, smooth and graceful. He dipped and whirled her about in large circles.

He whispered in her ear, "You are beautiful. It is so strange that I mistook you for Winifred. She is like glass, cold and transparent," he held her closer. "You, however, are like a lovely flame, luminous and glowing with life."

Joanna flushed and felt her heartbeat quicken. *Oh, he was smooth and doing such delicious things to her!* She pushed herself back against his arms. "Sir, you have a glib tongue!"

"And, you have a luscious mouth."

"No, please." She again eased back and raised her violet eyes, imploring him to stop. "I must return to my seat."

"I apologize for falling under your spell, I shall keep my distance in the future." He smiled, whirling her back to Annie and Buck.

Before Joanna could catch her breath she was caught up in another dance. There were more men than women in attendance and she was not allowed to sit out a dance. She just knew she was wearing holes in her slippers from dancing so exuberantly!

The music stopped at midnight and long tables began filling with platters of food. Such a plethora of edibles! Salads, meats, fish, casseroles, soufflés and dishes new to Joanna called head cheese, garnished tongue and game pies...ugh! There were breads and rolls of every description, pies, cakes, Nesselrode puddings, ices, and even ice cream. People began filling plates, chattering gaily and wandering about finding places to sit.

Annie and Buck were obviously fascinated with each other. Their food was ignored as their heads touched and they whispered and giggled. Joanna sat beside them drinking a glass of punch. Annie eventually turned and smiled at her. Joanna said, "Truth be told, dear, you must be in love...you radiate."

Annie laughed as Buck pulled her up, "I do like the big rascal!" They disappeared into the crowd.

Phillip sat down beside Joanna. "Miss Holan, we got off to a bad beginning, perhaps we can overlook our first encounter and begin a new relationship?"

Joanna shrugged her shoulders in a careless shrug. "Of course, Mr. De Leon."

"Please, the name is Phillip."

"And I, Joanna," she replied with a wicked grin. *Oh, Lord, he was so handsome, almost too much to bear.*

"I know you are the school marm at Locket Springs and John Holan's niece. Tell me more about yourself. Why did you decide to come west?"

"Well, you have done your homework!" she laughed and then soberly, "Truthfully, I am here to get away from many dreadful sad memories. My father took his life after losing his fortune. It broke my heart. To add to it, my sister married a rogue and I had to seek new surroundings. I do love the west, though, its vastness and wild beauty."

Phillip swirled his drink, then replied quietly, "I am sorry about the loss of your father. In a way, I understand your feelings. I lost my wife a year ago. She died in childbirth and my world was buried with her," he drew in a long breath, "I can never bring her back so I must find some purpose in living."

Joanna closed her eyes. "Grief is such a terrible emotion. I can not think of any pain worse than having someone you love torn away suddenly. Knowing that our love was not enough to keep Father alive has been devastating. We all have such guilt and misgivings."

Phillip nodded, "Regardless of the circumstances, everyone has guilt imagining how one might have done things differently. I have cursed the day I brought my wife to this desolate country. The baby came early and I could do nothing for either of them. She died in my arms calling for her mother. The doctor arrived too late to help and told me he could have done nothing, she bled to death. I have purposely kissed death over and over again, but fate has not been kind and taken me."

"Oh, Phillip, you are young, your wife would not have wanted you to follow her into heaven so soon!" exclaimed Joanna.

"I must tell you, there have been many women, nameless and forgotten since she died, but you have awakened something deep within me. I haven't felt the will to live for months, but I feel you gave me the kiss of life."

Joanna blushed furiously and lifted a hand to her face.

Phillip grasped it and held it tightly, "Please, Joanna, believe what I tell you." He searched her face fighting against emotions to kiss her brow, her eyes, and her lovely trembling mouth at that very moment. She was so unbelievably lovely.

"This is very unsettling, everything is happening so quickly. I know I acted shamelessly allowing you to kiss me. I have no explanation for my behavior other than it happened."

"Are you sorry?" Phillip asked carefully.

"What about you?"

When he spoke again, his voice was husky and low, "I told you, it was the kiss of life, your very touch inflames me, I want you."

"Stop!" Her eyes frosted over and she pulled her hand free. "No more, do not play with me, sir. I know I acted improperly, but I am not a loose woman!"

"My God, Joanna, I never for a moment thought that....."

"Yes, you did!" she interrupted vehemently jerking away. Fury flamed in her, "You mistook me for Winifred who has very impulsive, naughty ways! I will have you know my mother reared me to be a lady!"

Her eyes sparked with tears of fury. Phillip removed a linen handkerchief from his coat pocket and handed it to her. "My dearest girl, I am sorry I have made you cry. It was not my intention."

Rebelliously she refused his handkerchief and pulled one from her purse and dabbed at her eyes. *'Oh, what a mess! How dare he assume she was fast!* She looked at him with a sense of shame in her eyes. *That horrid kiss!* She was shocked to see nothing, but love and concern in his eyes. He waited on her words, but none came.

"On the occasion of our first meeting, I thought to myself I had met not only the most beautiful girl in the world, but also one who had the courage to show her emotions. You were not like some silly pretty little fool who concealed all her thoughts and desires. You felt as I did…that doesn't make you or I ill bred. I am sorry if I have insulted you."

She looked again at Phillip and he had a small grin on his face. One eyebrow was raised quizzically and he whispered, "Forgive me?"

He took her hand; she began to tremble, her knees felt weak. He lifted her hand to his lips and kissed it. His expression was so woe be gone she suddenly found herself smiling, a sweet and charming smile, "I cannot stay angry at you, you are quite beyond all comprehension."

He drew a finger along her brow and down her face, she held her breath.

"Well, you two, what's happening?" Buck and Annie were standing looking at them and both were grinning like fools.

Joanna turned from Phillip dropping her eyes. Phillip stood and offered his seat to Annie. He leaned over and whispered into Joanna's ear, "My dear girlie, I will be back to claim my dance!"

She met his eyes unwillingly and saw they were twinkling with merriment. She finally laughed at the absurdity of it all and he laughed too. "You are a rascal," she said.

"Whatever were you two whispering about?" asked Annie as she seated herself. "All the young ladies had their eyes on the two of you and were probably cursing you for keeping Mr. Phillip's attention so long."

When Joanna answered, she quietly said, "I am most likely headed for another heartbreak, Annie. That man makes me feel positively wicked!"

Annie laughed, "Perhaps the school marm is just falling in love!"

Joanna said, "Oh," in a stunned voice and then agreed meekly, "It might be, I am so confused. I want to believe he is sincere, but I don't know him. Thunderation, Annie, he has never even called on me! My mother would be mortified."

"Well, I know this isn't the East and manners and habits do fall by the wayside out here, but you can fall in love at first glance, though. It happened to my Ma and Da. They swore the first time they laid eyes on each other the world stopped turning."

"Well, I just don't know about that, Annie." Then to change the subject, "It is hard for a lady to remember all the social graces when not exposed to everyday society. I miss that, Annie, I do indeed. I feel both man and woman should treat each other with all respect. I also miss being fashionable. The women out here all wear out of date dresses, just look around! I realize true finery is saved for special occasions and I suppose fashion is impractical, but they could wear their best even if it is years old!"

"Miss Joanna, you sound just like a snob! These women have worked themselves to death trying to raise a family and take care of their men folk. A fine dress is probably the last thing on their minds."

"True, some of them may be poor, but they can order Godey's Ladies Journal and seek to copy the newest styles. I have every intention of doing just that as I received my first copy last week!"

"I don't mean to be rude, but it is hard for many of these poor souls, Miss. They probably can't afford the book, even."

"And just look at that, Annie!" Joanna snorted as the dancing began again. Due to the shortage of women some of the men had tied handkerchiefs around their arms and assumed the role of a *dancing belle* for the evening. "I find two gentlemen dancing together abhorrent!"

Annie smiled, "You would be shocked to be in good old Ireland! The women dance together and so do the men. Everyone loves music and no one thinks a thing about it. It was great fun; I danced with my sister and my Ma many a time and my brothers danced together too. It may be unsettling, but if they enjoy dancing what harm is it doing?"

Joanna pursed her lips and did not answer. Evidently she had much to learn! Annie possessed all the vivacity and energy inherent to her race and she was soon whirled away by a happy male.

Joanna pleaded exhaustion to offers and had actually worn a hole in her leather slippers. Then that irresistible voice set her heart to fluttering again. "Joanna, I have come to claim my dance."

Joanna looked up and smiled into Phillip's blue eyes. "I am honored, but I must decline. I have worn a hole in my sole."

Phillip chuckled, "I am not surprised, you've been much sought after. I will buy you the most elegant dancing slippers I can find. Can we try for a slow waltz...just a few turns?" he pleaded.

"Perhaps," Joanna answered as they sat watching dancers enjoy a Virginia Reel. "This must be quite an adjustment for you, no orchestra or flowers, no crystal chandeliers, dance cards and no chaperones. It must have been hard to leave the conventional role of eastern society."

"Let me put it this way, I resent living in a male dominated society whether it be east or west. One thing I can do in Wyoming is vote. It would be nice to be accepted as an equal. I doubt it will ever happen on the east coast, but maybe it can happen in the untamed west," reflected Joanna.

Phillip eyed her warily; "Women have always been placed beneath men, socially, politically and...in bed. I believe women should be allowed to express their desires and political viewpoints, but I want my woman in the home."

"There you have it," stated Joanna, her eyes flashing. "If I had not been fortunate to have become a teacher, society would demand that I marry or become a 'soiled dove.'"

"Do you realize what you are saying? You would even consider such a thing over marriage?" Phillip murdered her with a dark stare.

"I dare say, sir, I was only making a comparative statement! I shouldn't worry about it if I were you; it will never take place. I may act recklessly at times, but I would never disgrace my family or myself even by discussing it again."

"You are a bewildering women, your brilliance is amazing. You spellbind me with your beauty and scandalize me with your tongue!"

"I have always made my opinions known. My Grandmother taught me that," replied Joanna defensively.

Phillip sat quietly enjoying her classic profile as she sat staring straight ahead. Finally, she turned to face him, an eyebrow raised questionably.

"I was studying your profile, my dear. How alluring you are and yet you seem totally unaware of it. It amazes me," he commented.

At that moment a smiling John and a flustered Frieda appeared. Joanna realized she hadn't seen them for hours. "You both look as if you have the spirit of intrigue about you. Are we missing something?" asked Joanna with a smile.

"Oh, it is a surprise, we will tell you later," answered her uncle. Frieda was blushing radiantly. She sat down and began fanning herself. John stood behind her, his hands placed possessively on her shoulders. Joanna was a bit shocked at her uncle's behavior. She was very fond of Frieda and hoped he had not put her in a compromising position.

Phillip gently reminded her of their dance. It was indeed a slow waltz and she rose into his arms. He was silent as they began circling. Looking over her head, he said, "I would love to see you beautifully gowned with jewels at your throat, standing at my side and welcoming guests to Snowflake."

"Please," she said, "please don't tease."

"You wish me to speak more bluntly, surely you know by now I am enamored with you. Have you ever considered being married?"

Joanna stared up at him in astonishment. "Perhaps, Phillip, it would be wise to become more acquainted before we speak on these terms. I am trying to be a responsible woman. I now have to make my own decisions and consider the occupation I have begun."

"Indeed," he appeared to be genuinely amused. "Do you not think we have gotten to know each other quite well this evening? You have said more to me in a few hours than most women do in a year of courting. They sit simpering like silly little fools with their hands folded in their laps making goo goo eyes. Then Daddy says, 'Dear, play some music,' and they tinkle the ivories and still say nothing. I enjoy knowing the lady I am going to marry."

Joanna regarded him helplessly.

He twirled her slowly toward the open door leading to an outside portico. He led her to a dark corner, cupped her chin in his hand and raised her face to him. "You are my heart," he said softly. His voice was a caress. She felt his fingers on her throat then he dropped his hands to enclose her in his arms. Joanna drew a shuddering breath and reached up to meet his mouth. "You were born to be mine," he said huskily.

She was lost in that sweet kiss, she pulled away for an instant and he pulled her back and kissed her so deeply her legs gave way.

"We will go in, my querida. You are shaking, perhaps from the cold?" Philip whispered against her mouth and he took her hand and led a dazed Joanna back into the light and music.

This time he whirled her around the room and she laughed aloud as he dipped and pivoted gracefully asking, "Are you warming up, my swan?"

The dance ended and he returned her to her seat.

"My sole is truly gone," said Joanna as she smoothed her skirt, looking at her slipper.

"The soul you are giving me or the sole of your shoe?" queried Philip, smiling down at her.

"Both, sir, I'm afraid," she answered, her lovely face flushing.

The last dance was announced and following it, John and Buck led the women to collect their wraps. At the door, Philip asked John permission to call on Joanna.

"Son, you are always welcome at Locket Springs...anytime!" beamed John.

As Joanna entered the sleigh, Phillip grabbed her gloved hands; "I will see you presently. I must look to replacing your slippers. Until then, Joanna," and he raised her both hands to his lips.

Annie wakened Joanna after about an hour's rest. "Mr. John wants to leave as soon as you can make ready. He is fearful that a blizzard is on its way as the station agent sent word a wire says a large storm is headed this way."

They left after a quick breakfast. Joanna tried to force her eyes to remain open, but to no avail. She was exhausted from the dance. She snuggled down into the furs and slept.

"Joanna! Wake up, we are almost home...Joanna!" Frieda was nudging her. She was numb with cold. "Come, move your arms, stretch your body!"

Joanna tried to do as she was told seeing nothing but swirling snow. Squirming deeper into the fur lap robe, she flexed her legs and feet. *Dear God*, she prayed silently, *Help us find our way and let us not freeze to death.*

The snow was coating the robes and when Buck turned his hat was covered with ice and snow. Both he and John's lashes were coated with white and they had bandanas tied around their noses. She could hear them both yelling encouragement to the team. She felt the first stirs of panic. How glibly she had assured herself she would be fine in this vast country, oh, how confident she had been! She knew the animals' blind instinct should get them through the pass if the snow did not become too deep. The horses strained to pull through the drifts, and then above the loud winds she heard a bell. John yelled, "It is the school bell, we are going to make it."

Joanna said a prayer of thanks and wiped a tear from her reddened cheeks. She looked at Annie who was praying over her rosary. Joanna thought of Phillip, his endearing blue eyes and beautiful mouth and felt great joy in knowing she would see him again.

The sleigh lurched, then slid and righted itself. The bell was more distinct, clearer now. The storm seemed to be abating; she could see the horses' broad backs in the flurry whiteness.

The sled slowed and Joanna sat up in the gray dimness. The bell was very loud now, they must be home! Heavy barn doors swung open and the sleds entered the dim cold expanse of the big barn. Buck and John helped them out of the sleigh. Joanna had no feeling in her feet.

Madison and another hand were unhitching the teams. "How did you know to ring the bell, Maddy, you saved our lives!" John asked.

"We had a feeling you would try to beat the storm so we started at noon ringing the bell," answered Maddy with a huge smile on his black face.

"Bless you all, you are good men!"

"Yessuh, so are you!"

"Frieda, get yourselves to the house, Joanna, you grasp the rope and do not let go until you are at the door!" roared John.

The women left the barn into the swirling white. Cold crystal flakes pelted Joanna's face as she clung to the rope strung from the barn to the house. Small bells were hung at intervals. They found the back door and entered blessed warmth. Molly was there to greet them. "Get those wet clothes off and I have coffee, hot tea or chocolate for you. My goodness, little Ella, you look like a snow princess with your frosted bangs and lashes."

Frieda had Molly put Joanna's feet in a bucket of water until they began to tingle, then she rubbed them briskly with snow. Joanna dried her feet and hobbled to her room. She changed into fresh clothes and stockings and then went down to the big room to sit in front of the massive fireplace. Molly brought her hot tea, oh, how wonderful to be in out of the smothering whiteness. Winter had come with all its intensity to the ranch.

The harsh ferocious wind was lashing the big house when Joanna crawled under her goose down quilt. The storm was rising again and the wind's mighty breath seemed to shake the house. Branches scraped the windows filling the upstairs with eerie sounds.

146

Joanna slid deep onto the warmth of her bed and fell into an exhausted sleep.

For two days the sky was filled with dizzy whirling whiteness and searing cold wind. It moaned in the chimneys and stove pipes. The windowpanes became a crystallized whitish gray.

On the morning of the third day, Joanna heard the clatter of stove lids as she walked through the dining room towards the kitchen. As she opened the swinging door the chatter of happy voices greeted her. The wind had lessened, but it was still snowing.

The fire was burning brightly in the big iron Aga stove. Frieda, Molly and Willie were sitting at the big round table.

"Willie, how happy I am to see you here! I hope you will stay and we can go over some writing and spelling!" Joanna exclaimed happily.

"Yeah, h-h-here I am, Poppa sent for me, h-h-he w-w-was afraid I w-w-would h-h-have trouble in the storm. Gosh, I was fine, the boys w-w-watch out for me!" he flushed.

"That is good, but your father has a right to be concerned, it has been a terrible blizzard and he certainly would not want anything to happen to you! If you are here in the house, he won't worry so," answered Joanna, smiling.

"Shucks, n-n-nothing is going to h-h-happen to me!" Then he eyes got big; "Will you really h-h-help me study?"

"Nothing would please me more, but first, I need some breakfast. Has everyone eaten?"

"Most everyone. Why don't you go into the dining room and I will fix you something?" Frieda beamed.

"Aren't you the chipper one?" Joanna said. The lovely German blushed.

Frieda ignored her remark. "What do you want for frustuck (breakfast)?"

"I will have a boiled egg and some of the oatmeal that is left. I am not eating in the dining room, I am staying right here."

Household members came and went as Joanna ate and Willie finished his coffee. The wind howled suddenly into the kitchen as the back door slammed hard. John came in, snowy but smiling.

"I think it is beginning to lessen, the wind is dropping," he said, relieved.

Frieda took his mackinaw and carried it out to the porch. "Just as long as you are alright, John, that is all that matters," she murmured.

Joanna noticed immediately Frieda's elimination of addressing her uncle with the more common *Mr. John*. Something was definitely happening between the two of them!

By mid-afternoon a cold sun shone with a feeble light. The world looked like marshmallow frosting; swirls and drifts of dazzling white covered everything.

"We will be using nothing but sleds now as this will freeze solid. Buck and the boys are dragging to clear some of the roads. Maybe you can open school tomorrow, Joanna," said John.

Joanna bent over Willie instructing him in the alphabet answered, "Oh, I do hope so, Uncle John."

It was not to be, another icy blizzard shrieked in the next morning. The outdoors became a formidable place where only the bravest dared venture. Buck came in midmorning and dropped into a kitchen chair to regain control of his breathing. Frieda poured him a cup of coffee and he sipped it gratefully.

"It's a humdinger, really bad because of the sleet," he commented.

Joanna mused, "No school again…"

"Hardly, ma'am. It is a no man's land out there. John should be along shortly; he was in the big barn checking on the stock. The men have everything pretty much under control."

Shortly thereafter John came in with ice crystals in his beard and eyebrows. A concerned Frieda helped him out of his heavy wraps and placed a steaming cup of coffee on the table for him. He sat down and rubbed his beard, "I quite forgot how suddenly blizzards can arrive out of nowhere here."

The search for conversation ended in silence as this latest storm inspired a feeling of deep melancholy. Joanna got up and walked from room to room listening to the wind howl down the chimneys. She finally decided to do some needlework as Willie had tired of his ABCs.

This blizzard raged for two days burying everything in a hard frozen white;. Familiar landmarks were now unrecognizable. This was followed by a cold, monotonous silence. Finally Joanna and Annie could be driven to the school. The students from the ranch huddled around the big stove and studied. The pupils from Snowflake were not able to come for a week. Joanna was amazed they arrived despite the dreadful cold. She made hot chocolate every morning and dried their mittens and wet wraps by the big stove. She was so grateful to Timber for his coal as it lasted and gave off radiant heat.

Thanksgiving came and was celebrated with the traditional turkeys and all the trimmings. The snow laden trains were arriving on schedule at Stirrup Crossing. It was wonderful to get family mail and made for a festive day. Joanna's mother wrote that Elyce was improving mentally and physically.

Caroline was excited about accompanying Winifred to Paris in the coming spring. Joanna smiled to herself; she could picture her mother's excitement at shopping aboard again.

Then Joanna received a letter from Elyce, herself. She wrote she had received a friendship ring from Timber. Her letter had terms of endearment for Timber and his mother, Lady Adelaide.

John received a rather unhappy letter from Winifred.

> *Dearest Poppa,*
>
> *I feel very dull and school is boring.*
> *I do so long to see you, dear Poppa. Grandmother and Aunt Caroline now discourage my going out. They feel I do too much and object to late evenings. I have quite worn out Aunt Caroline so I am now spending much time at home. I have not done anything seriously naughty; I just have lots of energy... "*

Kate wrote:

> *"Do not mind if you hear I am strict and discourage Winifred's venturing out. We keep her in order.*
> *She is a dear child, but needs a firm hand. She can be a handful, John. Her motives, at times, are willful and a bit underhanded. My dear grandchild can also be very hostile when not getting her desires!*
> *The goods news is that she is doing well with her lessons and we do make allowances for her. We let her socialize in ways which we consider respectable.*

John chuckled heartily. He could picture his pretty daughter in defiance of her restrictions, tossing her head and stamping her feet with her green eyes flashing. Encountering the will of her silver haired grandmother would be overwhelming. Winifred had deeply wounded Kate previously and Kate would never allow her to do it again. *How did I bring two such opposites into the world?* He mused, *Winifred has a lot of the devil in her and Willie has the innocence of an angel.*

Although everyone went out of their way to make Joanna comfortable and feel welcome, the winter began to take its toll of her patience. The children were becoming high strung and excited about Christmas.

Joanna wrote her mother requesting that she shop for her students. She suggested warm gloves and scarves for the students and assorted gifts for Uncle John, Annie and Willie. She also sent a list of the household help and wanted something nice for Buck, Madison and Tony in appreciation for the work done on the schoolhouse. She sent most of her paycheck and hoped her mother could stretch it for Christmas.

She wanted a small tree for the school. Buck and three of the boys cut a small spruce and made a stand for it. She and Annie bur roughed through the attic of the big house for ornaments. The pupils strung popcorn and glued paper into links for the tree. Her requested gifts arrived along with many other packages for the holiday. John had ordered a crate of oranges, candy canes and taffy for the school.

Two weeks before Christmas she gave each of the children their gifts with an orange and a candy cane. Oranges were such a wondrous gift in winter that the pupils squealed with delight. Joanna, in turn, received a box of cookies, a fruitcake and a knit muffler from the pupils from Snowflake. Angela's mother had crocheted an exquisite lacy collar for her and Maddy had tooled a belt with her name on it. She was overcome with emotion and felt a fleeting wistful longing for home, then thought, *I have no home, my home is in my heart and today it is with my new family!*

That evening John asked Joanna to come into his study following dinner. She knocked softly and entered. Frieda was standing quietly before the fireplace, her hands clasped, staring intently into the flames.

"Come in, come in!" beamed her uncle. He went to Frieda, she turned and he put his hand in hers. They faced Joanna and he stated, "I have asked Frieda to be my wife. We are to be married a week from tomorrow, the Saturday before Christmas."

Joanna eyes glistened with tears, "Oh, I am so happy for the both of you! What a wonderful turn of events!" She hugged each of them in turn and said, "Oh, we must begin preparations at once…it is only a week away!"

"This will be a quiet ceremony. In the spring I would like you to travel with Frieda to Denver and San Francisco to help her purchase a new wardrobe befitting her title. When we go east for Winifred's debut, I want Frieda dressed in the latest!"

"Oh, it will be a pleasure, how perfectly exciting, Frieda!" Joanna exclaimed.

Frieda leaned into John and wept tears of joy, then wiping her eyes she said, "I never dreamed I would ever love again. God has blessed me."

John kissed her nose and then her mouth and Joanna quietly left the room. She began climbing the stairs when Annie came up behind her. "Miss, Joanna, may I speak with you?" she whispered.

"Of course, anytime," answered Joanna as they entered her bedroom. Annie lay wood on the coals and Joanna motioned her to sit. Annie twisted a handkerchief in her lap keeping her head down.

"Lord, Annie, what is it?" asked Joanna, alarmed.

Annie raised her eyes and looked at Joanna piteously. "Buck has asked me to marry him and I have accepted."

"What? First Frieda and now you!" Joanna cried in a stunned voice.

"Oh, Miss, we won't be marrying 'til summer. Buck wants to build a house on a parcel of land Mr. John gave him," answered Annie in a small voice.

"Oh, Annie, I am sorry! How stupid of me not to think of your welfare. My dear, I am happy for you, really I am! You love him, don't you?"

"Oh, yes, with all my being. He's a g-r-a-a-n-d man and he be a fine catch!" replied Annie, lapsing into a brogue. "Here be my betrothal ring," she said, holding up her left hand upon which sat a large gold band with a small ruby atop it. "You aren't angry with me, are you?"

"Lord, no, a bit envious, maybe, but never angry. You are so deserving of a good man and Buck is that."

They hugged each other and talked late into the night.

After Annie retired, Joanna lay in the big bed watching the shadows from the flames dance along the ceiling. Tears began to roll down her cheeks, she felt so dreadfully alone. She thought of her father and the anger returned. He had been so young, he should have lived to enjoy his grandchildren and loved her enough to want to. Damn him!

The loneliness for family assailed her as she wept quietly. She missed her sister, her grandmother and even her mother! *Stop*, she said to herself, *I am not weak like Poppa, but strong like my grandmother and this will pass!*

And indeed it did. It was Thursday; the wedding was two days away. Everyone had worked like demons to clean and bake for the affair. As Christmas would fall three days after the wedding, the house was alive with the splendor of the holiday. A huge evergreen shimmered and sparkled before the large windows in the big room. Garlands of holly and evergreen graced the mantel and the balustrades of the grand staircase. Wreaths adorned the windows.

On Thursday Molly and the kitchen help were decorating a huge fruitcake for the wedding. Joanna and Annie were upstairs finishing alterations on a watered taffeta gown of sapphire blue that Frieda was wearing. It was to be her wedding gown and was one of the few Worths that Joanna had brought with her. It was beautifully made and did justice to Frieda's striking figure.

"Time is getting short, are you nervous, Frieda?" asked Joanna through a mouthful of pins.

"Ach, that I am, but I am so happy," she replied, her blue eyes sparkling.

"You are going to be a stunning bride and you will make Uncle John a good wife."

"He is a good man. I respect and admire him."

"Do you love him?" asked Joanna, smoothing the flounce in back of the gown.

Frieda laughed, "But of course, I would think everyone could see it written all over me," she sighed. "How much longer, dear? I have to make a Stolen for Ella, it is traditional with us."

"I am finished, you can take it off and Annie and I will sew the necessaries. By the way, do you have a dress for Ella? If not, I have one that we could pare down."

"I do have one for her; I kept it for her to wear someday. It was only worn once on my sixteenth birthday. Mama bought it for me. I will feel her with me when Ella wears it," answered Frieda as she handed the gown to Joanna.

Joanna and Annie put the finishing touches on the dress before dinner.

"I am so relieved that this is finished," Joanna said, sewing was not something she enjoyed. "Tomorrow you can iron the dresses, it is too late now, Annie."

The Lutheran minister and his wife arrived the next morning driven by Buck in a Springs' carriage. Joanna laughed to herself; her uncle was taking no chances on inclement weather!

Joanna, Buck and Willie fashioned an arch in the big room and covered it with fresh evergreens. Joanna placed candles in wrought iron candle stands and tied bows of white satin here and there. Baskets of flowers will be placed below the candle stands tomorrow. John had ordered flowers expressed from Denver for the occasion.

Lord Peterman and his wife arrived late afternoon. The Powder Valley Ranch was owned by the lord and he was a good friend of John's.

All seemed in readiness for the evening wedding as Joanna retired for the night.

The ceremony went without incident. A beautiful full moon caused the crusted snow to glitter in reflection through the large windows. The minister, John and Frieda stood beneath the arch of evergreens while tiers of candles glowed on both sides and the fragrance of flowers added to the ambience.

Frieda looked resplendent in the sapphire blue. A veil of aileron lace was tucked under her coronet of braids. John had gifted her with the pearl necklace encircling her throat and she carried a nosegay of roses.

John was dapper in short tails and a corsage of roses.

Ella looked dear in her mother's pink satin dress. The overskirt was gathered in drapes with rosebuds at each side.

Joanna and Lady Peterman were in velvet. Joanna in deep emerald and Lady Peterman in crimson.

Following the wedding vows everyone sat down to a full course dinner. The newly weds were lauded with many champagne toasts. Buck and Annie had been invited and looked radiant. Obviously, Buck had asked John's consent.

Willie sat next to Joanna and beamed with happiness. "I am so h-h-happy for Papa; F-F-Frieda is so good. Now I h-h-have a Momma!"

"Yes, dear, you have. She is a wonderful lady and will be very good to you."

"Like you and G-G-Grandma Kate, not m-mean like Winnie."

"Not mean like Winnie. Now eat your dinner, Willie."

Later they gathered around the piano and sang while Joanna played.

The newly weds retired and shortly thereafter Joanna excused herself and went to her room.

Christmas morning dawned cold and crisp, but the big house was warm and full of cheer. Gifts were exchanged followed by breakfast.

Joanna asked Annie if she would take a walk. The women donned warm wraps and laughed and talked as they walked down the lane. The snow had drifted like sculptured frosting over the landscape.

"How beautiful and deadly the winter is. This is such a fantastic scene!" exclaimed Joanna breathing deeply.

"Do you hear drumming?" asked Annie, cocking her head to hear better.

"Must be Buck returning from Stirrup Cup," answered Joanna.

Then they could see in the distance a cutter and a team of horses gliding over the snow. "Hmmm, that is not Buck, really don't know who that is," observed Annie. Joanna said nothing. *Could it be Phillip? Please, God, let it be him.*

Annie turned to her with a big grin. "I think it is Phillip de La Cruz."

The girls stopped as the sleek cutter sped towards them. As it came abreast the team was halted and pushing out from buffalo robes was the handsome Spaniard, his blue eyes dancing in recognition.

"Well, glory be, I know it's Christmas, but I didn't expect to find two such lovely angels on the way side." he laughed.

"Senor Phillip, you are as full of blarney as any good Mick, I swear you have a touch of the green in you!" giggled Annie.

"Ah, to tell the truth, I am half-French and half-Spanish, but who knows? After all, the conquering forces of Europe mixed their seeds in every country...I could be anything." He laughed.

"Joanna, 'tis I, you haven't even looked at me," said Phillip, pulling off his fur cap. "See, it is your true love!"

"Silly, how could I not know you? You stole my dignity with your impudence. And never a word after...not a word!" Joanna did not mean to be short tempered, but it had been weeks since the ball and he had infuriated her with his silence.

"Dearest Jo, I have been busy. I was away on a business trip and just recently returned. Please don't be difficult."

"Difficult? Really, sir!" She stared at him with defiance perturbation.

Phillip's black brows shot up and his blue eyes looked troubled. "I will see to my team and meet you at the house," he replied as he turned the cutter to the barn.

"I cannot believe how he brings out the worst in me." Joanna suddenly laughed. "Mon Dieu, I must be a fright! Let us hurry, Annie, I must make myself presentable."

The two women dashed to the house...Joanna hurried to her room. She put on an elaborate mousse line de soie gown in the latest tint of jade. The dress was a gift from her Grandmother Kate. She turned this way and that before her mirror. The skirt gathered around her hips and terminated in flounces ending at the hemline. The bodice was encrusted with jade beads. She brushed her hair into a Gibson girl roll over a mouse.

"You look like a queen, Miss Joanna. Go knock his highness off his pins," giggled Annie.

Joanna's violet eyes danced, but then a slight chill entered her heart. Suppose Phillip was just toying with her. She caught her breath and then became annoyed with herself. "He is here, it's Christmas and I will treat him as a guest. I will be a lady and conduct myself properly," she said out loud before she swept down the stairs.

John and Frieda had received Phillip in the big room. Phillip was leaning against the fireplace, his powerfully built body relaxed. He was listening intently to John. When he saw Joanna he instantly came toward her, a smile on his handsome face. His bold, blue eyes appraised her admiringly.

"My dear, you take my breathe away," he said as he bowed and lifted her hand to his mouth.

She tried to think of something to say and could not. She began to tremble. For an instant there was a silence so profound that neither of them took a breath. She felt her knees buckle, but Phillip grabbed her and walked her over to Frieda and John. Frieda had a box on her lap and from the tissue she was lifting an ornate sterling coffee and tea service, a wedding gift from Phillip.

Joanna quickly sat down on an adjoining velvet divan. Phillip sat beside her and asked, "Are you all right?"

"I walked a bit too fast and far and perhaps I got a chill," she lied.

Phillip presented her with an elegantly wrapped box. Upon opening it she found an exquisite pair of champagne satin slippers. The craftsmanship was extra ordinary with sunbursts of seed pearls over the instep and also at the back of the slipper above the French heel.

"You remembered that I danced through my sole!" she exclaimed as she tried on one slipper that fit beautifully.

"Yes, Cinderella, your prince remembered," laughed Phillip, his blue eyes twinkling. "You didn't read the message, Joanna!"

She lifted the folded paper and read the words written in a flourishing hand: *Dearest, these are to be worn on our wedding day. Phillip.*

The blue eyes flickered over her, waiting for her reaction.

She stammered, "How did you know my size, how...?

"Annie spirited away a pair of your slippers and I had these made. Joanna darling, I have been negotiating with your uncle for your hand in marriage. Will you listen to the terms ?"

Joanna's eyes sparked with indignation. She snorted, "You are marketing me in terms, sir? What say I in all of this? Pray tell me when I consented to be your wife?"

Phillip's face went white. He sprang to his feet towering over her, his hands clenched. "I see I have made a terrible mistake in coming here. I believed you cared for me as I do you."

Phillip turned to a stunned John and Frieda, "Forgive me, I will see myself out." He was gone before Joanna before she could speak again. She heard the large door in the entrance hall close loudly after him.

Frieda exclaimed, "Oh, my dear girl, how could you be so insensitive? He traveled all the way to Denver to have those shoes made. It took some doing with this terrible winter. He adores you so!"

John stated with a frown, "He will not forget you shamed him, Phillip is a very proud man. I will try to speak with him and apologize for your lack of manners."

Joanna's rage was gone and there was desolation in her heart. Phillip's stricken face would haunt her evermore.

"What have I done? I do truly care for him?" moaned Joanna as she ran from the room.

She went up the stairs so swiftly she felt faint. Her heart hammered so hard she felt certain it would leap through her chest. Once in her room she ran to the window and she could see Phillip's cutter flying over the snow. She sat down on the edge of her bed until the sickening feeling began to depart and then collapsed to the floor tears streaming down her face.

Annie found her later still in the same position, her face paper white and her eyes a dull glow.

"Come, Miss, get up. You'll catch your death on the floor, it's freezing in here. I will lay a fire."

"Oh, Annie, did you hear what I did? My foolish mouth turned my love away!"

"Umm, come, we will talk more once I get you warmed up," answered Annie as she helped Joanna to a chair. Joanna looked at Annie oddly, her hands shook violently and her teeth chattered. Her thick sooty lashes sparkled with tears.

Annie soon had a fire crackling in the fireplace and she covered Joanna in a shawl saying, "This will help the shivers."

·Joanna grabbed Annie by her arm, "Do you suppose he will forgive me? I disgraced him in front of Uncle John, I had no idea he was so serious. He mentioned marriage, but I am accustomed to men with clever tongues with no meaning. Oh, I am so bewildered!" She looked up at Annie in sudden anguished apprehension. "You don't suppose Uncle John will send me East?"

Annie looked mournfully at her beloved mistress. "I can't say, Miss."

Joanna struggled out of her dress and donned a wrapper. She remained gloomily in her room for the rest of the afternoon. Life certainly was not worth living!

As dusk began to fall a knock sounded at the door and Annie opened it.

"Permit me," said Frieda, carrying a large tray covered in a snow white cloth.

"Annie go down and spend some time with Buck, I will see to Joanna." She put the tray on a table by the fire and poured tea.

"Come liebchen, join me."

"Oh, Frieda, I have ruined Christmas and made such a mess of everything. It all happened so quickly. I have only seen Phillip on occasion; he has never called on me. I am most attracted to him and I believe I love him, but..." Joanna raised bleak eyes to Frieda and pleaded for understanding. "He could have told me, he could have!"

"Yes, dear, he could have, but this is the West where things are done hurriedly. Life here is uncertain and harsh; therefore, no one stands totally on propriety. He and John had agreed to a long engagement, Phillip wanted to finish the house at Snowflake and he had a ring for you."

"I will never understand men, I have already lost one and now I am losing another. It never occurred to me that any of this would happen. A woman has no voice in anything. Oh, how I wish Phillip would have said or done something so I would have been somewhat prepared."

"You must remember you are your uncle's ward. You must speak with him tomorrow. "

"He must be furious with me!"

"Nein, he was surprised by your reaction. John is a compassionate good man. I believe he feels Phillip would be a good husband for you."

The morning sun burnished the snow with coppery glints and the sky was opalescent. Joanna stood watching high wispy clouds speed eastward through the large windows in the big room. She has been summoned to her uncle's study and she dreaded the encounter. Inhaling deeply she turned and made her way to the study, then rapped on the door and entered. John motioned her to sit and leaned back in his leather chair. He was astonished at her appearance. She had the look of a stricken animal, her head hung down and her hair undone. She twisted her hands nervously in her lap.

"Joanna, please look at me. My dear, I can see your anguish. Now what can we do to remedy this situation?"

"Oh, Uncle John, I never intended to hurt or disgrace anyone. I was breathless with surprise at his gift and words. I felt he had been very presumptuous talking to you and nary a word to me."

"Good Lord, Joanna, he told me he talked to you of marriage at the dance!"

"He did, but I did not take him seriously, he seemed to be jesting with me."

"You kissed him!"

"Yes, I did, indeed," cried Joanna stricken with guilt. "I didn't understand, I-I do care for him, it all happened so fast." Indignation at not being understood flashed through her. Her forlorn feeling of being the only one to feel her pride had been injured was overwhelming. She had mixed emotions. She would never intentionally do something hurtful, not to Phillip not to herself….but it had happened. She blinked back tears.

"Interesting," said John, fastening a sharp eye on her, his moustache twitching. "Times may be changing, but a proper woman of culture does not go about compromising herself unless she intends to marry the gentleman. I hope this was your intention, obviously Phillip considered it to be. He left within the week following the dance to go to Denver. He purchased a ring for you and had your shoes made. When one is given the stimulus or the motive to impel one in a direction such as Phillip took, he must have had reason to believe he could honor you with marriage. You certainly know it is considered an irrevocable law of etiquette that a young man obtains the formal consent of a young lady's guardian or her parents before asking for her hand in marriage! Phillip did just that very thing, not only to me, but writing to your mother a week ago. She must be delighted of course. Phillip comes from a titled family; both the French mother and Spanish father are nobility."

"That doesn't matter to me; I care for him only as a person. However, Elyce was proposed to before Mother and Father gave their consent!"

"Let me continue. Love is sacred, any public display of affection anywhere, at any time is grossly unrefined. It should not be thrown open to the rude comments of strangers. You must conduct yourself with quiet dignity and reserve, Joanna. You cannot indulge in caresses if you wish to continue teaching. Obviously you are not considering marriage so you had best conform to social etiquette standards befitting a school marm."

Then as an afterthought, "By the way, Phillip left this behind, you may wish to return it with some explanation." He pushed a gray velvet jeweler's box towards her.

Joanna picked up the box and pushed a spring. The lid snapped open to reveal a sparkling diamond ring; she began weeping, "Oh, what have I done?"

"I have made you think, have I not?" questioned her Uncle. "I aimed to do just that."

Joanna sank back in her chair weeping quietly, "It is too late."

John rose and walked over to Joanna. He took one of her hands in his. "Honey, if I were you I would ask Buck to take you to Snowflake. Get this misunderstanding resolved. As I mentioned before, Phillip is a very proud man. If you wait too long you will never see him again."

At that Joanna smiled a little and her heart quickened a bit. She stood and hugged John. "I will do just that tomorrow with your permission. I will go find Buck and I will take Annie with me. I am sorry Uncle John, I have acted a fool."

"Nay, girl, we all find growth in different ways. You aren't the person today you were yesterday…be gone with you and don't lose that young man. I have a great fondness for him."

Unfortunately more snow fell and it was three weeks before Buck could take Joanna and Annie to Snowflake. Drifts had closed the pass to the other ranch and a wagon plow had to be used to clear the roads.

The day was bright, the blue sky a cobalt blue with mottled puffs of white floating gently high above. Joanna and Annie were nestled in buffalo robes and Joanna clutched the velvet box with the sparkling ring close to her heart. The cutter sped like a feather over the snow. Joanna was looking forward to seeing Phillip and explaining away her thoughtlessness.

As they neared Snowflake her heart was leaping with anticipation. Buck pointed out the house still under construction. It stood on a small knoll. Its high mansard roof had a wrought iron fence on top and a tower at each end with leaded glass windows. Fancy wooden scroll work hung from the roof of the large porch and framed the porch banisters. Snowdrifts not touched by a shovel indicated it was not being lived in.

Smoke drifted from a two story log house located down a slope away from the big house. As the sleigh neared the log house, dogs ran out to greet them barking and frolicking in the snow. Mr. Smith came out the front door and helloed at them, "Well, I'll be durned if it isn't Buck and Miss Holan! Come on in." Then he yelled to the inside, "Martha, put the kettle on!"

Annie and Joanna stamped their feet and removed their galoshes. On entering Joanna observed how clean and spotless the interior was. It was cherry and warm with oval hooked rugs scattered about planed wood floors and colorful chintz curtains hung from the windows. A large pot bellied stove gave off waves of heat.

"Come in, come in," called Martha Smith from the kitchen. She was putting an agate tea kettle on a large range. "We will have hot coffee in no time."

Martha indicated they sit a long table that could easily seat twenty. "I cook for the hands; they live in the bunk house behind the hill. Mr. Smith and I and our kids live here. When the boss is here he stays in the main bedroom upstairs."

"Where is Phillip? We have come to see him on business," queried Buck.

"Oh, he's gone til spring. He high tailed it outta here a few days after Christmas. Never saw anyone so het up. He went to the big ranchero in New Mexico."

John and Frieda were kind and solicitous. In private they discussed plans to include Joanna on a trip to San Francisco. John then decided he could not go as government contracts were to be renewed and he needed to get all his legal affairs in order before he and Frieda went east for Winifred's coming out. He made travel plans for Frieda, Joanna and Annie. It was high time for Frieda to purchase her long overdue trousseau.

Toward the end of May the women boarded the train. They were soon speeding over the rails of the Central Pacific Railroad built by Leland Stanford, Charles Crocker, Mark Hopkins and Collis Huntington. Their accommodations were the very best and they enjoyed the vistas of the beautiful Rocky and Sierra mountains.

Joanna had written Pierré of her arrival. He had wired her uncle opening his home for their visit. John had wired in return his deepest thanks, but informed him suites were already reserved for the ladies at the Palace Hotel. He would appreciate Pierré meeting them at the ferry.

As they stepped off the ferry Pierré was there to greet them. He had roses for Joanna and Frieda. He handed them into his carriage and they headed toward Market Street and their hotel. On the drive he described the Pacific Coast Metropolis. "I have fallen in love with this lovely city. It is one of the most beautiful and picturesque cities in America. Her location is particularly attractive, inasmuch as the peninsula it occupies is swept by the Pacific on the west and the beautiful bay on the north and east. They call it the 'City of the Golden Gate,' which is richly deserved for the bay is tinged with gold not only from the sun, but the great washings of the mountains."

"Real gold?" asked an astonished Annie.

"No, but the soil and clay give an appearance of gold especially at sunrise and sunset," laughed Pierré.

Arriving at the Palace Hotel Joanna gasped as they entered. She had forgotten the teeming commotion of people and how the aristocracy paraded their finery.

She was tired from the trip and once in her room had the maid draw a warm bath to luxuriate in. Her thoughts drifted to Pierré. Tomorrow evening they were dining with him and she was looking forward to it. It had been a long while since she had been in male company in a nice atmosphere.

The three women ate dinner together in the suite and retired at an early hour.

They shopped at the most fashionable boutiques in the city. Frieda was fitted for tea gowns, afternoon gowns, opera costumes and walking dresses. The elaborately designed wardrobe featured the now fashionable puffed sleeves, slim waists, high molded bodices and long graceful skirts. By mid-afternoon they returned to the hotel to rest before dinner.

"We have ever so much to shop for, accessories, hats, lingerie, ball gowns and shoes! It will take days and then the fittings!" sighed Frieda unbuttoning her shoes.

"You deserve every bit of it and more. Enjoy it all and be beautiful for Uncle John," laughed Joanna as she watched Frieda rub an aching foot.

That evening Pierré escorted them down to the Palm Court. Joanna glided on Pierré's arm across the creamy carara and serpentine marble floor. Tables were conveniently placed amidst the potted palms. The roof was a vast expanse of domed glass. Cut crystal chandeliers cast hundreds of reflections that sparkled off the roof. A Sevres vase overflowing with iris and orchids centered their table. Irish damask napkins, handsomely wrought Tiffany silver, Baccarat crystal goblets of various shapes were at each setting. Flickering tall tapers added to the intimacy. Pierré was ever the charming host and the women basked in the atmosphere. The menu lived up to its reputation as they ate and drank slowly savoring each entreé. An orchestra played softly in the background.

Joanna felt almost her old self. She had forgotten the feel of silk caressing her skin, the forgotten glamour of seeing admiration in men's eyes.

Tonight was a lovely dream and she would long remember it. Dessert came in a masterpiece of strawberries in crust with cremé de cocoa poured over Chantilly cream. Champagne was poured and Joanna felt relaxed and content. Pierré and Frieda were conversing in French and Joanna listened quietly. Frieda looked every inch a countess, her blue eyes sparkled and the silver blond hair added an aura to her heart shaped face. She was explaining to Pierré where her previous employment had been in San Francisco. He answered he would do everything in his power to show Joanna all the city and he wanted them to see his home.

Suddenly the goblets began to shiver and Joanna felt her seat sway. "Whatever is happening?" she asked in a startled voice.

Frieda and Pierré laughed. "That was only a little shake, the city has them fairly often, but nothing to worry about, Cherié," answered Pierré.

"When you live here, you become accustomed to them. They used to frighten me at first, but I hardly noticed them eventually," added Frieda.

"I must say, it is a bit unsettling!" exclaimed Joanna.

"Oh, to say the least!" laughed Pierré. "By the way, Joanna, do you now have a gentleman friend?"

For a long moment there was silence between them. Joanna did not know how to answer. Finally she said, "There was someone, but I foolishly did something to turn him away."

"Was it Timber?"

"Oh, no, Pierré! Timber married Elyce in February!"

Seeing his surprised and perplexed look, she added, "It is a sad story, but with a happy ending," and proceeded to fill in the details.

"Did you ever hear from Lord Woo Who?"

"Heavens, Pierré, when Father lost his fortune that was the last of those royals!"

"So-o-o you are still truly a princess waiting to be carried off and made a queen?"

"Oh, dear friend of my heart, how I have missed your golden tongue. I am so blessed to have you in my life," giggled Joanna.

"Am I not handsome, dashing—a rising star in this new west?" replied Pierré wickedly. "Dear lady, I still love your beauty and brilliance and have always been fascinated with your independence. I say again, sweet princess, will you be my queen?"

Joanna was at a loss for words. Her violet eyes sparkled with tears and she chose her words carefully. "At one time, Pierré, we would have been a splendid match, but I have changed. We all have our complexities and problems. I am still searching…for me. What I really want and who I am. I realize women in this age are not to be complicated. We are taught to be good wives, good hostesses and bear children. I want to be independent and do something with my life other than pour tea. Can you understand a little of what I am saying?"

Pierré stared hard at her, his expression sober and concerned. He sighed as if he had made a great decision. "It is settled then; I shall put this behind me and carry on with my future. I wanted to make certain that you had no illusions about being my wife."

"Pierré, I want always to be your friend. I am just not ready to accept the responsibilities of marriage, perhaps I shall never be."

"Someday, Cherié, someone will change your thinking." He twirled the golden liquid in his goblet thoughtfully. "Then it is settled, I want you and Frieda to meet a very dear friend of mine. I believe I will make her my wife. Will you have dinner tomorrow evening at my home?"

Frieda answered, "Sounds delightful, Pierré."

"I will send my carriage for you around seven."

Joanna sighed with a sense of relief. The evening concluded with a sense of harmony restored.

A cool breeze wafted in off the bay and the roll of waves pounding on the beach could be heard from the cliff as they drove to Pierré's home. When they arrived Joanna was stunned in spite of herself. The villa clung and flowed along the cliff as though it had been there forever. The huge French house was framed by partérre gardens and had a stunning view of the Bay.

A servant bowed them in and took their wraps. The soaring foyer was flooded with brilliant hues of the setting sun spilling through the stained glass skylight. Persian rugs lay over marble floors with peach colored silk walls hung with ornate paintings.

"Please follow me to the lift," said a maid, taking them to a wrought iron cage encased in lovely etched glass. The grille moved into place and the elevator groaned up three floors.

Stepping out of the cage, Joanna caught glimpses of the bay through huge broad windows. They followed the maid down the hall into a magnificent dining room. One entire wall was glass doors opening onto a terrace. Palms and sprays of flowers were carefully displayed around the room and a cheerful fire blazed in a beautiful Louis XV marble fireplace.

"My, how lovely," remarked Frieda as she beheld the mahogany table set with tapers, Baccarat crystal and silver. A large silver epergné brimmed with exotic orchids.

The women were handed flutes of champagne just as Pierré appeared with a doll like woman on his arm. She had the face of a dimpled child and was almost swallowed in an elegant ball gown of blue damask with layers of embroidered lace and tulle. Her ample bosom sported a huge diamond pin and a diamond coronet encircled her head of dark ringlets. As if that was not enough finery, she carried a fan of ostrich plumes. Following her was an older rotund lady dressed in pink satin and sparkling with jewels.

"Dearest friends, may I present Mademoiselle Giselle Gezlin and her mother, Madame Gezlin," said Pierré, "Mademoiselle Joanna Holan and her aunt, Madame Frieda Holan."

Giselle extended a small dimpled hand in welcome and smiled prettily.

The dinner cuisine was excellent and served with pomp. Following this Pierré gave them a tour of the magnificent house. It was impressive with imposing French furniture and statuary.

"You have built quite a monument, Pierré. It is indeed lovely," commented Joanna as she looked at the panorama of the bay glittering with night reflections of the city.

"Come, let me show you the veranda, it is quite breathtaking," said Pierré, grabbing Joanna's hand. Frieda followed closely.

They wound around plants and wicker furniture and then Pierré stopped and faced Joanna. "Do you like Marie?"

"She is very sweet, Pierré."

Looking out to the water Pierré said, "I must have someone to care for....and I cannot have you."

"You will always be my dearest friend, Pierré. Be happy, you deserve that."

"She is dear, but I will never love anyone as I have loved you." His voice trembled and he was a bit overcome with sadness.

"Please, Pierré, we have been all through this, don't spoil a lovely evening." Tears flooded Joanna's eyes and she blinked them away.

Pierré held her close then turned to re-enter the villa. Joanna and Frieda followed him in. Pierré poured a goblet of brandy and almost shouted, "This is nothing, wait 'til Pierré shows you Nob Hill! The Railroad Baron's and the Bonanza King's palaces are unimaginable! Eh, Frieda, have you told her?"

Frieda smiled and nodded, "Oh, Joanna, these palatial residences are most imposing. These nouve rich vie with each other for the most luxurious grandiose homes. Some without any regard for taste, whatsoever. Never have you seen so many great homes crowded on such a small hill!"

At the end of the evening they agreed Pierré could take them sightseeing when the fittings and shopping was done. They visited over cups of café laced with liqueurs.

"We will dine at the Cliff House and tour Nob Hill."

"Please tell me about the Barbary Coast, I have heard so much about it. Will we see it?" Joanna inquired.

"Hmmm," Pierré rubbed his small moustache and sighed, "The waterfront is a melting pot of races. A colorful sight are all the fishing fleets. Sailing in under lateen sails are the Neapolitans who have brought their customs with them. Their lateen rigs are shaped like the ear of a horse and stained an orange brown. There, also, are Kanakas from the Sandwich Islands; Lascars in turbans, Alaskan Indians, Gilbert Islanders, Spanish Americans and all the European races. They come in and out in queer craft and lose themselves in the disreputable tumbledown, but always mysterious, shanties and small saloons. In the backrooms South Sea Island traders, captains, whaling masters meet to begin expeditions and trade adventures.

"Portsmouth Square is an old plaza. It has Chinatown on one side and the Latin Quarter and the Barbary Coast on the other. Here men prevaricate and tell strange tales of the sea. Stevenson lay with them for a time and learned many of the things he put in *The Wrecker* and other stories he wrote. The Barbary Coast is a loud bit of hell on earth, Joanna. No one knows who coined the name. It is simply three blocks of solid dance halls with girls of every persuasion for the delight of the sailors. Dance music blares from orchestras, steam pianos and gramophones.

"The din on the street is unbelievable. Behind the swinging doors anything happens. Innocent young men and women are shanghaied never to be seen again. A white woman in China is worth her weight in gold."

"How awful," uttered Frieda. "Do continue."

"The dance halls have rather odd names...The Eye Wink, Little Silver Dollar, Gold Dust, South Seas Trader, Mary's Tooth, etc. The saloons that hang out over the water give strangers a drink called a *Mickey Finn*, which knocks them out. Then they are lowered through the floor into a boat and usually end up on a whaler bound for the Arctic."

"How dreadful, what about the women? Do any of them ever get out of this wild place?" asked Joanna miserably.

"Some in time.....alive or dead. These poor souls have had to compromise themselves. Some came with husbands to seek a fortune in gold, then the man died or disappeared and the poor wife ends up in San Francisco. Could be a woman came around the Horn on a Windjammer with family; then perhaps disaster or sickness overtook the companion or family member. She then is enticed into a job on the coast. This hardly an exaggeration...all races, all languages and some of these women are unbelievably beautiful. The lucky ones find someone to care enough to help or take them out of the filth. Most end up in the opium dens of the Chinese passed from one man to another."

"Where are the authorities?" asked Joanna indignantly.

Pierré shook his head. "It's a futile thing, until something is done to close the area it will continue. Don't ever go near the area, ever!" he admonished.

Giselle daintily yawned and batted her eyes at her host. "Mon Cher, it is getting late. Mama and I wish to retire. May we be excused?"

"Of course, my dear," Pierré immediately rose and bowed to Giselle and her mother.

"Delighted to have made your acquaintance," dimpled the doll faced young French woman.

"My pleasure, also," heaved the rotund Madame Gezlin.

"Oh, indeed ours also," acknowledged Joanna smiling.

"We must take our leave, there is much yet to be accomplished. Pierré, your hospitality has been overwhelming. I cannot thank you enough for such a lovely evening," acquiesced Frieda.

"My dear lady, it has been a great pleasure to have had you in my home. Shall we plan on Friday to tour the mansions?"

"We will look forward to it."

Pierré escorted them to the elevator and down to the foyer. He helped Joanna with her cloak and she turned to face him. He placed a kiss on each cheek and then looked deep into her eyes which conveyed to her all the hopes and dreams he now renounced. He whispered, "Adieu, my love."

The week was foggy and overcast with intermittent rain. They were so busy shopping the women hardly noticed the weather. Frieda found an elaborate custom designed ball gown suitable for being introduced into society as John's wife. It was made of sky blue silk with layers of pearl and crystal embroidered lace and draped beautifully over her shoulders and across the bosom.

"Frieda, Uncle John must buy you a collar of diamonds or pearls to set this off. You will look divine," said Joanna as she cocked her head in admiration.

"Now dears, I want both of you to pick out a gown. John gave his consent before we left. Make a selection while I am being darted and pinned."

Joanna helped Annie select a pale lilac taffeta enhanced by a cream colored chiffon and lace overskirt. It highlighted Annie's eyes and coloring.

"Annie, it will make a lovely wedding dress, do you like it?" asked Joanna admiringly.

"Oh, Miss, I have never had something so lovely. It has always been hand me downs and off cast clothing. I feel like crying," Annie answered, her eyes sparkling with joy.

"Don't you dare, it would spot the gown!" laughed Joanna hugging her.

Joanna fell in love with an off white layered chiffon trimmed in black and lavender beading. It had a decided train. She looked elegant.

After handing the gowns to the Frieda, Joanna walked Annie to the shoe department.

"You must have gloves, slippers and a mantel. It isn't every day one gets married!" Joanna smiled fondly. "These will be my gifts to you for I owe you so much, more than I can ever repay."

"Lah, Miss, don't talk that way. You and your kin have given me a life and aren't I the lucky one? I could be down on my luck like those girleens you talked of down at the Barbary Coast!"

"Thank God, you came to us, love. It was a lucky day all around."

Late afternoon the happy trio returned to the hotel unmindful of the rain. Pierré had left a message he would call for them at ten the next morning.

Frieda excused herself from the next day's tour. She had seen the Nob Hill splendor while working at the Gould Mansion and had no desire to return.

The rain had stopped and the sun was beginning to glisten through the mist when Pierré came for them the following morning. He enjoyed explaining the history of his adopted city to Joanna and Annie. He gave them the story of how Nob Hill got its start.

Years ago the elite of Rincon Hill were astounded to see one Arthur Hayne building a house on what they referred to as "the big hill." This hill was the steepest in the city and horse drawn vehicles struggled and slipped trying to make it to the top. Most often the wagons would slide down the sandy knob with the poor horses trembling in harness. Hayne's bride was a former actress, Julia Dean, and when they married he had promised her a house on the highest hill of the city, supposedly to overlook some who had looked down their nose at the actress. His good friend, mining car designer, Andrew Hallidie, responded with a great feat of engineering, the California Street Cable Railroad. Thus the house could be erected!

Nob Hill had a greater impact on the nation than that of the trans continental railroad. Following this feat, four Sacramento merchants, Charles Crocker, Mark Hopkins, Collis P. Huntington and Leland Stanford combined their resources to create the Central Pacific Railroad which *annexed* the United States to California. Their wealth was staggering. For removal from the din and noise of the city, of the four, Charles Crocker was the first to build. Directly across the street on California Avenue Stanford then built a veritable palace. Mark Hopkins built his castle on the hill itself and Huntington built on the crest of Nob Hill.

Following this, other Bonanza Kings who made millions on the discoveries of the Comstock, began to erect massive estates on the prestigious Hill.

On arriving at the top of Nob Hill, Pierré handed down Joanna and Annie from the carriage. "The only way to see these impressive castles is to stroll at leisure," he recommended.

The two women opened parasols and began to accompany Pierré. Nannies and their charges were strolling through formal gardens on the estates. Marble sculptures and fountains graced the grounds.

Most of the homes were characteristic *Carpenter Gothic* noted for the steep gables and elongated pointed windows. The huge mansions were astounding. Each owner had had his carpenter/architect create his fanciful design. The ornate wooden details were works of art in themselves. Collectively called Victorian the mansions were combinations of Italianate, Second Empire, Queen Anne and Gothic. Square bays, flat roof lines, corniced eaves, angled bays, towers, gabled roofs, and turrets were all mingled in some mansions, each seemingly more elaborate and flamboyant than the last.

As the three paused before a monumental edifice of granite and marble, Annie exclaimed, "This is a home?"

"Ah, this is the Huntington Estate, incredible is it not? I understand even the horse stables up here have marble mosaic floors and crystal chandeliers!" Pierré laughed.

"How quaint!" sniffed Joanna.

Continuing on their way they passed the Flood mansion and others too numerous to remember. Joanna began to weary and her shoes were pinching her feet. They once again stopped at a huge foundation, surpassing in size anything they had seen previously. This was to be the James Fair Palace, but rumors had it domestic troubles had put a halt to the building. Mrs. Aelrichs, daughter of the late owner was going to erect a hotel in its stead to be called *The Fairmont*.

"I must find a place to rest my feet, Pierré," said Joanna, grimacing.

"The carriage is around the corner and there are also benches in the next block. We can continue or I will go for the carriage," answered Pierré with a look of concern.

"Oh, let us find the benches, it is such a lovely day and I am enjoying all this magnificence. I must walk slowly. Sorry, but these new shoes are not comfortable."

They sat across from the Hopkins Palace on a wrought iron bench. As Joanna eased a foot from a slipper, she asked, "How many rooms would you say that mansion has!"

"Hmm, hard to say, but I imagine with the servant quarters and all, possibly three hundred or more. It has a ball room, I'm sure it is truly enormous."

"My heavens and I thought our New York residence was large! Must be hard to find one another at times!" laughed Joanna who then crossed her legs and leaned forward holding her chin in her hand. "I must say, San Francisco is like a frivolous woman in many ways. She is like New York City's western counterpart, but still different in so many ways. What a time to be alive and to live in all this magnificence!"

Pierré answered with a bit of a frown, "To be sure, but behind some of the facades there are many sad stories of ill conceived fortunes with much future agony to come."

"It is distressing to be one of those less fortunate and especially, a woman in this time and age!"

Pierré was shocked at the note of bitterness in her tone. He began to speak, but thought better of it and watched a fashionable couple walk two Russian wolf hounds. Large glittering collars encircled each animal's throat.

"Do you suppose.....?" Joanna began.

"Yes, they are diamonds," stated Pierré.

Annie blurted, "Lah, I could live in comfort for the rest of me life if I had one dog collar, imagine, the shame of it all! I should have been born a hound instead of a poor Irish lass!"

Whereupon Pierré and Joanna laughed heartily.

On their return to the hotel Pierré insisted they eat an early supper at Tate's Palace Grill. They laughed and reminisced over their cruise and tour of Europe.

Nearby at a table partially hidden by potted palms, two very distinguished gentlemen were observing them. The younger of the two stared at Joanna with shocked recognition. His gaze rested on that flawless face with its violet eyes framed in sooty lashes and the soft lips that had once reached for his own. Phillip's heart turned over in his chest and he had trouble breathing.

Damn her, he thought, *she is obviously enjoying her male companion's presence. She is laughing gaily and seems to be thoroughly enjoying herself.*

"What madness has seized you, Phillip?" inquired the elder gentleman. "You look as if you have seen a ghost!"

"I have, Father, a copper headed vixen I met in Wyoming. She is John Holan's niece."

"You must reacquaint yourself and introduce your father," said Don Luis with quiet dignity.

"I think not, Father. She made quite a fool of me and I care not to repeat it."

"Aha, so she is the reason you left Snowflake in the dead of winter to come to the ranchero! You have been so reticent to speak of Wyoming." Phillip toyed with his wine glass deep in thought.

Don Luis studied his beloved son. Relations between them had been painfully strained since the death of Phillip's wife. Phillip had been like a bird lost in flight, alighting thither and yon. Such a handsome lad he was with skin tanned deep copper and his eyes so like his mother's…cobalt blue, a startling contrast to his ebony hair. Yes, indeed, he resembled his beautiful mother, Mercedes Maria Eugenia, a descendant of strong Bourbon blood.

Don Carlos chuckled to himself as he recalled asking his father, Duke Carlos Luis Del La Cruz de Castillo for his blessing on the union to Mercedes. His father had answered, "Well, why not, the House of Bourbon has ruled Spain since the 1600s. If French blood is good enough for the throne, then it should be good enough to enrich our family." His beautiful Mercedes had added great charm and luster to the De La Cruz name. She was still the loveliest thing in his life. Antonio and Phillip were extensions of his and Mercedes love and he still marveled at what they had created. It had broken Don Carlos's heart when Phillip's Leonora had died. Phillip had then turned into a brooding, quiet ghost of himself drawing away from his family.

Don Luis inhaled deeply of the odor of the tantalizing food set before him. Before beginning his meal he again looked at the lady in question. She had an exquisite face with delicately tinted skin stretched over fine bones. Her eyes sparkled with vivacity and she was demurely clad in the latest mode.

"She is quite striking, Phillip, surely you can rectify the misunderstanding?"

"Father, she refused my hand! I went to her uncle for permission to marry and when I approached her, she was furious." Phillip looked aside, pain written over his face.

"Why was she furious?"

"I had not formally proposed. I had not contacted her for over two months. I know I should have called on her. We had been to a dance; we kissed, and confessed our love! Surely, that should have been sufficient."

"Women, my son, are the most confusing of creatures. If you dote on them, they become indifferent; show indifference…..they become angry, you cannot win."

"Was Mother like that?"

"Ah, your mother, there is no creation on earth like her! Perfection, I wish only for you someone half as perfect. It will happen, Phillip."

Phillip gazed at his father in silence for a minute then said, "It has already happened…too late."

The two men turned their attention to the delectable food and seemingly forgot the topic of their discussion.

The evening came to a close and Joanna and Annie walked with Pierré to the front of the hotel. Joanna gave Pierré a pleasant smile and an embrace.

"Your hospitality has been overwhelming. Pierré, you are such a dear person and I will treasure your friendship forever. I cannot thank you enough."

"Ah, Joanna, it was my pleasure," answered Pierré solemnly, "to quote Dante Rosetti, 'My name is Might Have Been; I am also called No More, Too Late, Farewell. You will always be my elusive dream….like a moonbeam or a rainbow…beauty that can never be possessed.'"

He smiled sadly, bowed and then turned into the mist.

Joanna sighed, "Annie, I have the oddest feeling that Pierré is in dreadful danger. I wanted to warn him, but I could not think of a reason."

"Perhaps it is the little French lady you are thinking of," answered Annie.

"No, this is a feeling of disaster. Oh, me, I am just tired and saddened to say adieu to Pierré. We have been so close for ever so long. I am exhausted, it is time to retire."

The next morning Joanna and Annie shouldered their way through the great doors of the hotel. Everyone was rushing. The doorman and the porters were busy with the hassle of arriving and departing guests and were bowing as they tried to open and close the portals. Once on the street, it was claustrophobic with surging humanity, Market Street was alive with noise…hoof beats and carriages, hawkers, newspaper boys and trolleys. Odors of horse manure intermingled with scents of cigars and wood smoke.

"Lord, Annie, the sidewalks are a river of people. I am tired of the city, I want to go home," said Joanna loudly over the din.

"You don't find this exciting, Miss?" answered Annie, turning her head to and fro.

"No! I miss the quiet, the mountains and the fresh air!"

"Lah, you are a bit homesick," laughed the little maid.

Joanna rented a carriage to take to Post Street noted for its many shops. She bought souvenirs and gifts for her uncle and others. She purchased teaching ensembles at the Emporium and cosmetics at The City of Paris. On her return to the hotel she ate a simple lunch.

"I believe I will take a lie down so I will be fresh for the opera this evening," yawned Joanna as she sat on the chaise removing her slippers.

"You do that. I will begin packing for our leave tomorrow," replied Annie and began removing lingerie from a dresser.

Late afternoon Annie woke her mistress and removed a gown from the armoire that Joanna was to wear that evening. She let her hand linger lovingly over the rose brocade with its raised embroidery of gold. She hung it and smoothed the skirt lightly then removed the petticoats flounced with Belgian lace.

Joanna sat at her dressing table leaning toward the mirror. She was sipping tea and studied her face critically. "I look so pallid," she commented as she applied a dusting of color to her cheeks. "I am not on exhibit, but I don't want to embarrass Frieda." She then picked a piece of kohl from a small casket and very discreetly lined her eyes.

"Miss Joanna, you are always pleasing to the eye, come let me dress you," answered Annie.

The gown fell gracefully over the corset and petticoats. Annie snapped the bodice. Joanna's small waist and plump bosom were handsomely displayed. Her hair was still damp from her bath so Annie dressed it high with a cascade of curls over one ear. Joanna placed her diamond star above her brow.

"What else are you wearing for adornment?"

"Nothing, this dress is enough." She sighed, "I cannot recall when I have been less enthused about going somewhere. It would have been terribly selfish of me to have denied Frieda the opportunity of attending the opera. She has dreamed of this since leaving Europe."

"You are a gentle soul, Miss, you have much compassion for others," said Annie as she handed gloves to Joanna.

Joanna grabbed Annie's hand. She thought of all the anguish Annie had undergone.

"You give me strength, Annie, how fortunate I am that you are a part of my life."

She rose and grabbed her wrap. As she entered the sitting area Frieda was also entering from another area. "Oh, how lovely you look," exclaimed Joanna.

Frieda was wearing an ivory gown with matching cape. Her blond hair was swept into a becoming pompadour and sparkled with diamond clips. She pivoted for approval as she breathlessly said, "I cannot believe my good fortune. Having found John and now being able to see an opera again!"

Joanna kissed her lightly on a cheek, "You look like a queen, my dear and you so deserve this evening."

Frieda's lovely face beamed with pleasure.

They bade Annie good evening and took a carriage to the Grand Opera House. They slowly walked up the steps to the entrance as Joanna stared in awe at the couples seeping past them. Never had she seen such a dazzling display of jewels and furs.

"Do you suppose they left anything in the closet?" murmured Joanna.

"One must look closely to find the gown under the display....quite vulgar to say the least," whispered Frieda, looking at one dowager with a crown of diamonds and rubies.

"Nouveau rich, I am told," answered Joanna.

Once inside the huge building, Joanna stared about in wonder. The floor was tiled marble and on either side of the foyer, circular staircases carpeted in red velvet wound to the balcony. Hanging low from the ceiling which was at least four stories high was a magnificent chandelier. Gilt mirrors fronted by velvet settees lined the walls.

A doorman directed them to the cloak room and an usher led them to their seats in the gigantic rotunda. Joanna studied the program of *Lohengrin* by Wagner after being seated. She then mused on Wagner's *Der Fliegende Hollander* and smiled remembering the tears she and Elyce had shed during that opera.

"Did you ever attend "The Flying Dutchman?" Joanna inquired of Frieda.

"Ja, when I was about twelve, I believe. It was tragic as this one is also," answered Frieda.

"But 'The Dutchman' is so romantic, Senta dying for her love."

"True, true, but most operas are grand tragedies, very few comedies. People come, weep and feel great relief that maybe their lives are happier, yes?"

"I believe you have a point," Joanna stared at the private boxes surrounding the theatre and recalled her family's private box and how happy they had been attending. A feeling of futility assailed her and for a moment she felt faint. She came back to her surroundings with a jolt as the theatre darkened, the stage curtains parted and the orchestra began.

During the intermission she and Frieda were sipping champagne when she looked into a pair of familiar eyes.

"Phillip!" She almost swooned had not strong arms grabbed her. She opened her eyes and it was he, tall and handsome! He was outfitted beautifully in black tails and immaculate linen. He stood frozen…like a man shot. With great effort he removed his arm, nodded and turned away.

"Phillip, please!" called Joanna.

He stopped dead, Joanna hurried to his side.

"What, Joanna?" he asked, staring straight ahead.

"Oh, please, I have tried to contact you since Christmas. I went to Snowflake to ask your forgiveness, Phillip—"

"Pray, don't apologize," interrupted Phillip coldly, "you made yourself perfectly clear. Haven't you humiliated me sufficiently?" At that moment a distinguished older gentleman appeared at Phillip's side. "Father, may I present Miss Joanna Holan….Miss Holan, my father, Don Luis De La Cruz," said Phillip through gritted teeth.

"My pleasure, I am indeed honored," said Don Luis, his eyes twinkling as he bent to kiss her hand.

"Oh, sir, it is I who is honored. I am delighted to meet a member of Phillip's family!"

Damn, how lovely she looks. That ethereal face and innocent violet eyes make me almost believe she is telling the truth but then again… thought Phillip.

Turning, Joanna introduced Don Luis to Frieda.

Phillip then pulled her aside. "What is it you want?" he asked low and tense.

"You, Phillip," she murmured gently.

He looked deep into her eyes and put his hands on either side of her face. She felt tears behind her eyes and stiffened. His hands dropped despairingly.

"Don't torment me, Joanna," he whispered and turned into the crowd.

Joanna returned to Frieda who assessed the look on her face. Frieda grabbed her arm as to steady her.

"Before I take my leave, may I ask a favor of you, Senorita Holan?" inquired Don Luis.

Joanna gazed up at Phillip's father, such a handsome man, given his age. His black hair sparked was with gray, high cheek bones, a slender straight nose and he stood proudly like the nobleman he was.

She answered, "Sir?"

Don Carlos stared at her marveling at her beauty. This tall, exquisitely shaped girl befitted Phillip's attentions. Tears of dismay glinted in her eyes.

"Do not despair, Senorita. If you love him, it will come to pass. I know my son and he possesses deep feeling for you."

"Oh, sir, I do love him," Joanna whispered in an anguished voice.

"Give him time, he has been hurt and he is very proud." Having said this, Don Carlos bowed deeply to her and Frieda and turned away.

Joanna followed Frieda back to her seat and listened to the opera in a daze. She resisted the urge to leap up and search the rotunda for him. To know he was this close was like a knife in her heart.

When the opera ended they collected their wraps and Joanna looked futilely around as Frieda pulled her toward the carriage. Joanna wept quietly into a handkerchief on the return to the hotel. She cursed fate, Phillip and herself.

"Come darling, you must compose yourself," said Frieda on arrival at the palace. "Oh, Frieda, I have lost him. I hate caring so deeply. This is destroying me."

Angel: [ME., a OF. *-ele*, repl. OE. *engel:* - **angil-*, Com. Teut. Loan, a. L. *angelus*, Gr. Messenger.] A ministering spirit or divine messenger; one of an order of spiritual beings superior to man in power and intelligence, who are the attendants and messengers of the Deity OE.; hence b. one of the fallen spirits, who rebelled against God OE.; c. a guardian or attendant spirit *(lit.* and *rhet.)* ME.; *Fig.* a person who resembles an angel in attributes or actions 1592. 2. Any messenger of God, as a prophet or preacher (a Hellenism) ME.; a pastor or minister of a Church ME; *poet.* A messenger ME.; *fig.* in *angel of death* 1574. 3. *transf.* A conventional figure with wings 1536.
–*The Shorter Oxford English Dictionary on Historical Principles*

BOOK TWO

CHAPTER ONE

The Casa de Flores Ranch, originally part of a Spanish Grant, was located in a vast green and gray valley. The New Mexico Territory was wild and the beautiful and the jagged mountain ranges surrounding the valley were lofty and peaked with snow. The Spanish mansion sat on an incline, its white magnificence framed by green pine and cottonwoods. Barns and sheds were scattered east of the mansion. The ranch buildings were surrounded by an adobe wall with large wooden gates set in arches. Flowering vines flowed along the walls. Beyond the main gate lay the forecourt and centering this was a huge tiered fountain with cascading water splashing into a tiled basin. Agaves and succulents lined walkways and flowers of all colors overflowed from glazed pottery. A planked porch ran the width of the structure supported by large hand hewn columns and the ceiling was made of aspen and willow latillas. Ristras of red chilies adorned the adobe walls either side of the main entrance.

Inside the stuccoed walls were warm comfortable rooms with soft sculpted fireplaces that burned away the chill of morning and night away. The Mexican paver floors were scattered with woven Indian rugs and soft sheepskins. The large living room had a huge arched adobe fireplace at the far end with chairs and settees positioned comfortably about it for comfort.

There, in the early morning, Don Luis and his wife, Mercedes sat before the fire. They were discussing their beloved Phillip over cups of cinnamon chocolate.

"I do hope the fiesta for Phillip's natal day will be a happy one," Mercedes said, blowing delicately on the steaming cup she held.

"Darling, your fete will go well. Phillip needs this diversion. The visit to San Francisco proved to be a sorry event. His encounter with the Senorita Holan was very unsettling for him," answered Don Luis.

"Describe her to me, dearest."

"Decidedly pretty, quite charming and enraptured by Phillip! Do you know, my dear, I actually felt sorry for her. Phillip behaved like a gentleman, but very aloof. His pride will not allow him to forgive her."

"Humph," snorted Mercedes and tossed her beautifully coiffed head. "He told me he handled the proposal abominably. I fear I would have reacted much the same way, why should we women be treated as property to be bargained over? Mark my words, someday men will be forced to treat women as equals!"

Luis sat quietly astounded. Never, he thought to himself, impossible! Finally he said, "This is absurd, try to think of more pleasant things. Let men take care of such trivials. Is it not enough to be worshiped and adored, my darling?"

She purred, "You can charm the whiskers off a cat, but then you have always been respectful of my womanhood."

"Ah, yes," he answered gently, "your womanhood makes me always feel like an old stallion wanting to rear and plunge."

"Luis! I wasn't referring to that, you misunderstood me," squeaked Mercedes, her face glowing pink. "You are a sly old man!"

"Sip your chocolate, darling or I just might ravish you here and now. I am not that old yet!"

"Behave yourself, Luis; we have business of an important nature to discuss. I swear you try my patience." Mercedes blushed prettily.

Over his cup, Luis eyed his wife. She was still a handsome woman, in fact lovely. He still was astounded at his good fortune in having won her, "So, you feel the trip was a debacle," Mercedes looked keenly at Luis. "You feel he won't forgive this poor broken girl although she apologized and still adores him?"

Don Luis frowned. "I don't know, Phillip is a challenge to understand anymore. I think he holds himself responsible for Leonora's death in some small way. As for the young lady...I only wish her well."

"Dieu!" Mercedes cried, "You men can be so heartless. She is most likely heartbroken. Phillip, our beautiful son, has broken many a heart."

"I do not believe it has always been intentional. Phillip attracts women like bees to a flower."

"Oh, I know, but he is not so young anymore. Oh, Luis, if only he can find happiness."

Luis slipped his arm around her shoulder. "Let us put aside Phillip for a bit. I missed you and I need to hold you."

She snuggled into him. "Are you tired, darling? I'm sorry the trip was dismal, you are home now, rest." It distressed her to see him so wan beneath his tan.

Luis rested his chin on her glossy head and sighed contentedly. His mind drifted. Indeed, he was home. His land old with history with its plateaus of juniper and pine, mountains of ponderosa, fir and spruce had known royalty and Franciscans and Spanish soldiers. This land had felt Spanish compassion and Spanish cruelty. The wars between the Spanish and the Indians had been fierce, but today they lived in peace. The Penitentes slumber in the high hills and the old missions look out into the desert like sentinels. Close by lay the Great River Trail which brought the Spaniards from Old Mexico to northern New Mexico. His father, Don Carlos, had been one of them. He had been appointed by the King as a diplomatic representative of the highest rank and was rewarded with an enormous land grant. He stayed in the New World and had workers fashion sun baked bricks of straw and clay covered by stucco into this impressive ranchero where visitors and travelers alike sought haven. Not long after Anglo Americans had ranches a few miles away and set up emporiums in the Spanish towns.

Indian women began working for the Los Americanos and the Senoras could then ensconce themselves on the cool verandas and complain of the heat. Indian men traded and began working for many of the Patrons of the large rancheros.

When Don Carlos returned to Spain for his wife and son he brought back Andalusian horses. They bred well in the new country and he soon had a flourishing herd. Following this he bought two Hereford Bulls and twelve shorthorn cows. He prospered as did Luis in their new home. But wife and mother, Carlotta, drooped like a wilted rose. She seemed to have left the brightness of her mind in Spain. She became subject to violent headaches and spells of depression. She went through long periods of withdrawal spent behind closed doors. Each time she emerged she was more confused. Don Carlos was beside himself and finally decided to take her to Spain hoping it might restore her mind. Carlotta's family placed her in a convent, but she did not improve and eventually died. On his return to America, Carlos and little Luis became very close. They rode under the azure skies, crossed fertile mesas, and rode high into the canyons of the Sangre de Crista Mountains. Don Carlos grieved for the loss of Carlotta, but lived for Luis. When Luis was in his late teens he and his father made a business trip to New Orleans. There Luis was presented to Mercedes Emily Fontaine and his life changed forever.

"What of your thoughts, Luis?" Mercedes inquired, jolting him back to the present.

"Of you, Dona Mercedes," murmured Luis inhaling the floral scent of her hair, "you always look and act like a queen even here in this desolation." Thinking of his mother he asked, "Do you ever regret marrying me?"

She drew back and looked at him lovingly. "Mon cher, never except birthing and that was short lived, for no one could have been more deliriously happy with such beautiful sons!"

Luis crushed her in his arms and kissed her deeply. They were unaware of the tall figure who watched them wistfully.

"Ahem," he said and they both sprang apart and rose to greet their son.

"Ah, Phillip, here you are!" Luis said, composing himself and shaking his son's hand.

"Darling," said Mercedes with great relief, "we thought you had gotten lost. Sit down by the fire and I'll get you some refreshment. Have you had breakfast?"

"I want nothing at the moment, Mama," said Phillip, leaning over to plant a kiss on his mother's cheek.

"Antonio and Margarita will be arriving tomorrow. Oh, I am so excited that my two boys will be together. What a grand occasion this will be to celebrate! What a solemn face, darling, please don't be difficult!"

"Mama, I am honored by your preparations, but I am in a funk. Please bear with me, I will overcome it. In fact, I am going for a ride to get some of the cobwebs out of my head."

"Have Juan saddle Pegasus for you. He is my latest purchase and has a good mouth and gait. You will like him, he is a great colt," suggested Don Luis.

"I appreciate that, Father. Until later."

"Vaya con dios."

Phillip walked to the stables. There was a lot of activity with hands feeding, watering, and grooming the horses. He asked for Juan and a worker pointed out a weathered nut of a man showing a lad how to throw a lasso.

"Buenas dias, Senor," said Phillip as he joined the two. "I am Phillip de La Cruz, are you Juan?"

"Si, I am Juan Dominguez," the old man answered. "Y este est mi nieto, Sancho."

"Habla English?"

"Oh, si, you are Don Luis's son?"

"Yes, you are new here?"

"Si, I lost my ranch to Americano bandidos. I drove my horses to Don Luis. He gave me shelter and a place for my familia here."

"How did you lose your ranch?"

The old man's face fell into itself and his eyes teared. He wrung his hands as he continued with a horrifying story. The Americanos wanted his ranch with its natural springs. When he refused to sell or move they came late in the night and burned him out. His wife and baby died in the fire. They took his cattle. He, his daughter and Sancho rounded up what was left of his horses and drove them to Casa de Flores.

"Senor Phillip, this is not a good land now for a Spaniard." Juan's speech was dull and almost incoherent.

"Que lastima! I am so sorry, Juan." Phillip's features were clouded and set.

"Juan, I want to ride. Father said you would help me with Pegasus. When I return we can talk more."

"Si, Senor Phillip, come I will fetch Pegasus."

The vaquero led him into the enormous low roofed structure. A wide lane ran from one end to the other. It contained twenty stalls on each side that held his father's prized Andalusian thoroughbreds. While Juan led the colt out to be saddled Phillip put on chaps and long Spanish spurs. Juan held the dancing young stallion as a groom saddled him. He was led out into the sunlight where he shone as silver as the moon. "He is magnificent!" exclaimed Phillip. He walked around the animal allowing the colt to get his scent and then patted the neck under Pegasus's wavy mane. "Ho, boy, you are a king." He continued to talk as the horse blew and shook his lofty neck. Phillip leaned into the horse and rubbed his forehead, nose and neck whispering to him softly. Pegasus became very quiet and his eyelids closed. The man and horse bonded and became as one. Phillip mounted and rode away from the ranch. The rocking canter of the stallion began to relax him as he took a trail into the foothills.

The spirited animal soon set a brisk trot as if eager to climb the first ridge. It was good to be alone. The beat of the horse's hoofs was like music to Phillip's ears. He inhaled the cool, fragrant breeze coming down from the majestic mountains. He loved this land; brutal but beautiful. They gained the top of the ridge and Phillip gave Pegasus a few minutes of rest. The wind whipped against his cheeks. He lifted his face inhaling the sage and pine. Here he could see over the pastures and the endless roll of land and the blue sky. Beneath him the horse blew and stamped, impatient to be on his way.

"Okay, boy, we will give it a go." They began an imperceptible climb and the changing altitude gave way from cedars and junipers to pine and fir. Stands of quaking aspen clung to canyon walls, their leaves dancing in the sun like new dollars. The only sounds that broke the silence were the chirps of birds and a clatter of stones under the stallion's hoofs.

Joanna came to him flooding his mind with her beauty and scents. A tender yearning swept through him. When he had kissed her and held her close he had felt supreme joy. It had been such a revelation realizing he was finding love again. For the first time since Leonora's death he had felt the layers of anger and bitterness peel away.

How could he have been do blind? How she had betrayed him! Hadn't they pledged their love in embraces and looks? He had told her he would return! He had loved her enough to go to Denver to get her shoes made. Suddenly a fierce anger rose inside him…damn this woman! He must put her out of his mind!

He started Pegasus down a canyon into a stand of aspen. He let the horse drink from a trickling creek then slowly headed back to the hacienda. Frustration boiled in him, he felt sick and empty. How could he have been so deceived by her? The other one, Winifred, had been a constant enticing shadow. She lusted, but Joanna seemed so different…pure, strong minded and incredibly lovely. He played it over in his mind, again and again. Blazes, put it to rest, Phillip. She, obviously, was not for him.

He returned Pegasus to his paddock, unsaddled and curried the animal. A groom offered to help, but Phillip insisted on taking care of the horse himself. This mighty colt had captured his heart and he stroked the beautiful head with love.

Two days later the guests for the fiesta began arriving at dawn. All morning they came until all the ranchos within miles were represented. Some came on horseback, some in carriages or carretas. By nightfall the big wooden gates were closed in the outside wall. A dozen carretas stood just inside the wall and the horses had been turned into corrals. Guitar music and laughter drifted from the big hacienda as Mercedes oversaw food and accommodations for the guests. Woman and girls were bustling to and fro from the large patio to the house. Gradually people bedded down and the rancho quieted.

Mercedes could not have asked for a more glorious day for her fiesta, morning greeted her with a blue sky and a soft breeze. As the family gathered for breakfast her joy over the party was somewhat dimmed as she saw the scowl Phillip was wearing.

"Darling, this is your day, please wipe away that horrid frown. Are you not pleased that Antonio is here?" she asked.

"Of course I am," Phillip answered as he lifted up a chubby little one-year-old.

"So, Carlos Luis Tomas, we meet at last! I am your Uncle Phillip."

The little boy squirmed in his arms and then laughed at the comical face Phillip was making. It was an instant love affair between the two. As the child snuggled in to Phillip he hugged him close and said over his head, "He looks like you, Antonio, same laugh and eyes."

Antonio was a man of medium height with a square jaw, raven hair, eyes the color of blue chalk, and the same sensuous mouth as Phillip's. He stood leaning against the buffet with an arm around his pregnant wife. He smiled a lazy smile and replied, "But of course, he had better!" His pretty dark haired wife snorted and twirled out from under his arm.

"Do I look like I have time for anyone else?" she said as she patted her stomach. Both men regarded her with amused eyes as she took the child from Phillip. Little Carlos began to weep. "Shhh, darling, you must eat and then you can play with Uncle Phillip." She turned to Antonio, "I am going to take him to the kitchen."

The family sat down at the table when two women came bearing trays groaning with food.

After Don Luis blessed the food, the maids fussed over them passing bacon, eggs, melon and hot piping biscuits.

Antonio sensed there was something terrible wrong with his brother. He watched him across the table for a few minutes and forked up some bacon. "Well, little brother, how are things with you? What is happening at the ranch up north?"

Phillip, who was stirring cream into his coffee, stopped and grouched, "I imagine okay, I haven't been back for over four months."

"Dieu, Phillip, I thought you were doing well. Papa said you were finishing your house and your letters indicated you were happy."

Phillip laughed bitterly. "I thought I had found a wife; pretty as all get out and smart, too. She is John Holan's niece from New York and teaching at Locket Springs."

Antonio raised an eyebrow in question, "So what happened? Did she return to New York or find another?"

"Neither," Phillip said shortly. "I asked her uncle for her hand in marriage and she refused, turned me down cold. She was furious because I had not asked her first."

"Judas Priest, can you beat that? Women are crazy at times." Antonio began to eat his eggs and then abruptly stopped. Holding his fork in mid-air he waved it at Phillip. "If you care for her get back up there and plead your cause. Damn it, man, you have women falling all over themselves just to look at you. It must have been your timing."

Phillip laughed without humor. "Well, I certainly did something wrong. I will go back in a while, but not to change anything. I will not beg anyone, you know that."

Don Luis then spoke. "I met her in San Francisco and I found her to be very charming. I feel she cares a great deal for Phillip."

Phillip was forced to smile. "Certainly, you didn't take her seriously, Papa! She just turned on her charm like she did to me when I first met her."

"You question me, Phillip? Humph, well, that is your prerogative! I felt nothing, but pity for a young lady that had made a mistake in her thinking."

Mercedes interrupted with a bright smile. "Enough talk, we are celebrating Phillip's natal day! We have much work to do. Luis, dear, will you take the boys and the male guests to the stables and a tour of the grounds?"

"I would be delighted. Nothing will make me happier than to show off my beautiful sons and horses!" he exclaimed, smiling broadly.

By evening lamps and colorful lanterns lit the patio. The drawing room was stripped of furniture and musicians were tuning their instruments. The evening festivities began when *El Tecalero* (the dance master) called for a fandango. It was a colorful scene with the senoras in elaborate gowns and the senoritas in costumes of bright colors. The Spanish gentlemen wore embroidered velvet suits with flared pants. The large room was decorated with colorful ribbons, flowers and elaborate wrought iron candelabra. Phillip danced with many senoritas, but, sadly, none with violet eyes or hair like burnished copper.

He eventually danced with his mother. She looked up at him with sad eyes and said, "Mon Cher, it does not please you, this celebration?"

"Dearest Mamam, it is wonderful. I just unwisely gave my heart to someone. It seems I cannot get her out of my system."

"Phillip, you want a wife who walks beside you, not behind you, n'est—ce pas?"

"I don't follow you, what do you mean?"

"This girl, Joanna, has…what you call—spunk! She wanted you to come to her first. Arranged marriages are sometimes very difficult, it demeans a woman. As you know, ladies are raised to accommodate men's desires. It is considered improper for a woman to show her intelligence or speak her mind, evidently this girl thinks otherwise."

"Mamam, didn't you and Father have an arrangement?"

"Hmm, well, he had to seek permission to court me and had to prove that he came from an aristocratic background with wealth. My father could have said no and I could have done nothing…even loving your father as I did, it would have mattered little. I was fortunate, the marriage bans were posted and Father's lawyers arranged the contract."

"I wanted to do everything right this time. When Leonora and I married in secrecy her family disowned her. She was devastated because we loved and forgot convention. I don't believe she ever recovered."

"Times are changing, Mon Cher. Some women need their independence to survive. I understand Miss Holan has no father and that must be a hardship."

"Possibly…"

"Oh, here is the Senator Hobart and his lovely daughter! I must go greet them. Have you met his daughter, Pansy, Phillip?"

"Yes, earlier this evening, she is most charming."

"They will be staying a few days longer as the Senator is interested in purchasing a mare from your father. Perhaps you might try to become better acquainted with Miss Hobart."

"Perhaps…"

Phillip was never off the floor. Then he found himself dancing with a petite blond with crystalline gray eyes, Pansy Hobart.

"Having a good time, Miss Hobart?" he asked.

"Just marvelous now that I am in your arms," she answered in a warm, husky voice. She exuded sensuality. Her look conveyed real interest, no simpering coyness. "And you, are you enjoying your birthday?"

"As a matter of fact, no. Soirees make me uncomfortable."

"Indeed? Who would have thought it? You appear to be wildly enjoying yourself."

"Ah, Miss Hobart," he answered gently, "looks can be very deceiving."

"Umm," she murmured throatily, "yes, I agree. I would much prefer riding on one of your magnificent steeds than flouncing around like a preening fowl."

He stopped in the midst of twirling her about. Hmmm, what was this exquisite little creature alluding to? "Perhaps, my dear, you would prefer I show you the stables?"

Her gray eyes sparkled and she drew herself taller. "I would like that, unfortunately, you are the honored guest and it would be a faux pas to whisk you away. I would consider it a privilege to ride with you. Perhaps at dawn the day after tomorrow?"

"But of course!" He began to realize the novelty of such a flirtation in the vastness of nowhere. It excited him. Her fresh young mind most likely wanted a few hours away from all the stuffy receptions she must endure with her father...those old men and prissy wives in the claws of political decorum. He added, "It will be my pleasure, Miss Hobart, we can meet at dawn."

"Pansy, please," she whispered, lips parted and eyes wide with desire.

He touched her soft cheek and a delicious thrill coursed through him.

"Until our morning rendezvous, then," he murmured as he pulled her close and then swept her back to her father.

"Daddy, um hmm, Phillip and I are going riding. Probably day after tomorrow. I know you have business with Senor de La Cruz and Philip has volunteered to show me some of the beauty of the ranch."

The rotund senator beamed and shook Phillip's hand. "Thank you, young man. Sugar here, gets so bored when I go horse trading. Just take good care of my precious."

"That I will, Senator," Phillip said with a broad grin.

"Thank you so much." Pansy fluttered her long lashes and pursed her luscious lips.

"I'm so looking forward to seeing the mountains and breathing the magnificent air."

At midnight a supper of many entrees was served followed by a huge cake wheeled in for Phillip. Before serving the cake, Don Luis announced his gift to Phillip, the magnificent colt, Pegasus. Phillip was so overcome he grabbed his father in a bear hug and all but wept. He would ride his wonderful steed with Pansy Hobart....life was good!

The summits blazed in the glory of the sunrise. Phillip and Pansy were following the groom to their mounts. He felt strangely embarrassed when Pansy announced she was riding unaccompanied. It was seldom young women rode without a duena. A defiant young Winifred had often ridden by herself in Wyoming. Phillip had always sent her home when she purposely stalked him, but Pansy Hobart was no child and she gloried in her independence. She wore a green velvet riding ensemble and looked good enough to eat. The groom helped her up to the side saddle. The horse was spirited, but she deftly handled the animal showing that she was an experienced horsewoman. Phillip had expressed his concern over her choice of steed.

"My dear," she sniffed. "I have jumped since childhood and been on numerous hunts....please, let us ride."

And they did, trotting out into the morning. Colts frolicked in the meadow and calves joined their mothers grazing in the pastures. They left the lowland and began climbing, skirting aspen and weaving through spruce and pine. The trail was a mire thread winding up through the canyons. They reached an opening where lay a high meadow scattered with wild flowers. Deer and several elk dotted the far slope. The peaks above were blue with patches of snow in shady places.

They rested their mounts by a stream of cloudy blue snow water. Phillip spread a tarmac down beside the stream in a lush grassy area then assisted Pansy down. He let the horses graze and opened a lunch that the sleepy eyed cook had packed for them. Pansy removed her large feathered velvet hat and undid the pins that were holding her blond tresses upon her head. Her hair fell in a golden shower about her shoulders. She dimpled at him.

"You are even more beautiful in the morning," he said as he opened a bottle of wine. "Fine thing in a lady!"

"Ah, you are so gallant, you flatter me," Pansy replied as he filled a glass for her.

The dappled sunlight fell across his face, mercy, he was such a handsome man!

They sipped their wine and slowly ate the lunch. Phillip made small talk and began to feel a bit uneasy as Pansy with slow deliberation moved closer to him. He began to pack up the left overs when she moved directly in front of him and ran her hands up his chest.

"That can wait, darling, I cannot," she purred. When she felt him stiffen, she laughed. His muscled body was like fire to her. She leaned into his face, her lips not far from his and gazed up at his lidded eyes. "Are you sleepy, darling?"

"How could a man be sleepy at a time like this?"

Her full soft lips curved into a smile. Her eyes locked with his and he could not look away. He saw the desire clearly reflected in the depths of her gray eyes.

"I have great affection for you, Phillip," she whispered in a throaty growl.

"You are bold, Pansy. You keep tantalizing me and I am going to seduce you here and now!" replied Phillip huskily.

He rolled away from her and sat up. When he turned back to her she was undoing her bodice. He groaned, "My God, woman, what are you doing?"

She pulled the jacket off and ripped her lacy chemise over her head. Her perky full breasts were glowing like pearls as she opened her arms to him.

With a sharp ache in his groin he sighed in resignation, "You won't be satisfied until you have your way, will you?"

He reached and grasped her by the shoulders then roughly pulled her into his arms. Deep hidden emotions came to life within Phillip. His hand drifted down to her waist and he pressed his lips to her throat and then kissed his way to her breasts.

She arched against him and her voice came out in a throaty whisper, "I want you now!"

In a flurry of wild abandonment, breeches, shirt, skirt, pantaloons plus other accessories were tossed in a pile.

There was no need for gentleness or patience. In unison they came together, naked body against naked body, touching, searching exploring. A moment in time to seek, to feel, to soar. It mattered little what was happening today or tomorrow; there was only now, only them! They rutted like animals and did the act again and again until exhaustion.

As the whirling passion cleared, Phillip was horrified at what had happened. He fought to gather his thoughts. "Pansy, I have comprised you and I apologize."

Pansy was stepping into her clothes and turned to him wide eyed, she laughed uproariously. "My heavens, Phillip, don't take on so! I have a great carnal need for satisfaction and I seek and find it. Did you not enjoy it?"

"Yes," he whispered in a husky voice, "it was most pleasurable and exhausting."

"Dear man, you must understand, most women have needs, too! It doesn't mean she must marry to fulfill her desires. I will marry when I find a great lover with a title and wealth. Until then, I will enjoy my pleasures as I find them."

Phillip's eyes widened in disbelief, the esteemed Senator Hobart's daughter had the morals of a hussy!

"Darling, we really must be getting back, Father might become concerned if we are gone too long," Pansy sniffed. She pulled her chemise over her rosy hued nipples and fastened her bodice. She carefully pinned up her hair and donned her hat. Phillip marveled; Pansy's swollen lips were the only give away she had been indiscrete.

Sheepishly, Phillip began pulling his clothes on and cursed himself for the fool he was. He would never understand women!

He handed her up on her mount and they made their return to Sweetwater. Once in the stables Pansy turned to him and whispered, "We will be in Santa Fe for at least a month. Wouldn't you like to come and feast again?"

He sighed as he looked down into face. Her eyes caressed him and a grin split his face. "Of course, you wicked little temptress. I will keep you busy. May I begin tonight?"

"Sugar, you know Daddy is planning to leave tomorrow. I must pack and I would never be able to get away," she pouted prettily.

"I cannot resist a challenge, we will see about that. "

His mouth descended on hers. A sigh escaped her and she whispered against his lips, "I will meet you here tonight."

In the following weeks Phillip roamed the country on Pegasus. He spent much of his time in Santa Fe calling on Pansy Hobart.

His mother became concerned as he spent more and more of his days and nights away. She said to Don Luis one evening, "Luis, whatever is to become of Phillip? He is like a ship without a rudder. I am so worried about him."

"Pshaw, Mercedes, he is just getting some wild oats sown. He never had time to be a young stud so now he is becoming more of a man."

"Luis! Don't be crude!" she exclaimed her eyes sparking. "He needs to begin facing his responsibilities. What about Snowflake, you have made excuses for him long enough!"

"Si, little mother, I will speak to him," answered Don Luis with a slight frown.

As it happened Phillip came to his senses on a hot afternoon in Santa Fe. He arrived unannounced at the home that Pansy and her father were occupying and found her in the arms of a wealthy easterner. She was infuriated and had him shown to the door.

Following this betrayal, despondency settled on him. He yearned to return to Snowflake and the solitude.

At dinner the next evening, Don Luis asked, "Phillip, you are so restless. Why don't you run some stock north? You should be overseeing your ranch. No crops, no tilling...what about your house?"

Phillip looked over at his father and thought, *What a splendid gentleman he is. I have been such a disappointment to him.* Because he was morose, he had no reason to make his parents suffer. They were concerned and had endured his day rides and night visits to Pansy Hobart for weeks.

"I owe you both an apology. I have wasted weeks that should have been put to better use. I realize I must make a decision about Snowflake. If I can be of help here I will stay, otherwise I will make plans to return north. Antonio being the heir apparent is making plans to soon bring his family here."

"Mon Cher, you know you can stay here indefinitely, this is also your home, eh, Luis?" His mother's lovely face expressed her love and concern.

Don Luis put down his wine glass and looked tenderly at his wife. "But of course, Mercedes, I am concerned that Phillip is wasting time and himself."

"Father is correct, Mamam, I am long overdue in returning to my responsibilities," said Phillip.

Don Luis then explained, "Some renegades are being paid to run out the ranchers in this valley. The Anglos are becoming greedy for land and power. Casa de Flores has much water, natural aquifers and many springs and water is as precious as gold in this land. Casa de Flores is at risk because of this and the fact I am Spanish. The Anglos don't like our large land grants and some want them taken away by adjudication."

"Can they do that to you?"

"Not at this time, but someday in the future it will happen."

Don Luis leaned back in his chair and pressed his palms together while looking intently at Phillip. "I want you to take Pegasus, two of our best stallions and some mares north with you. If something should happen here at least part of the herd will be protected."

"To move stallions and mares will be a challenge, Father," Phillip said with concern.

"It can be done if we run cattle and keep the stallions in front of the herd and the mares in the rear."

"This country is big enough for everyone; I shall stay and support you, Father!"

"Young man, I have an army here if I need it. I am trying to convey to you how valuable these animals are and, therefore, we need to protect them. You still do not fully appreciate the heritage of these horses. Have you forgotten the Iberian horse dates back 6000 years?" retorted Don Luis angrily. "Homer wrote of them in the "Iliad." In the 1500s mares and stallions were sent to Lipizza to the Archduke Charles and from these animals came the Imperial Stud followed by the Spanish Riding School of Vienna! Royals and aristocracy have always preferred Spanish mounts....."

"Father," Phillip interrupted with a grin, "you taught me well. You neglected to say they were the first horse on the American continent and the Andalusian forebearers were several thousand years prior to the Barb and the Barb forebearers were a thousand years prior to the Arabian!"

"Hmph!" Don Luis's frown gave way to a grin. "Well done, my son, it is good to know you have retained this knowledge. Sometimes the very young do not fully appreciate the teaching of the father."

Phillip quirked an eyebrow, "If the very young had a father like mine, it would indeed be an insult to dishonor him by not retaining his teachings."

Mercedes looked from the proud face of her husband to her son's...both full of adoration.

"Ah, Phillip, it will be a praiseworthy undertaking," she assured him. "Your father has been so concerned about these animals. The north will be a safe haven for them. It will be a great credit to you if you get them safely to Snowflake."

"We will start tomorrow making plans and getting provisions. Still I hesitate to leave you both," said Phillip in a tense voice.

"Bless you, darling," his mother said with a catch in her voice.

"Thank you, Phillip," Don Luis said quietly. "I appreciate your concern. We will survive, the horses will be a target long before we are. This will ensure their future. I have two fine Hereford bulls and a decent herd of short horns you can take, also. We can discuss all of this in the morning."

"Please ask Juan to bring his mandolin and play for us," said Mercedes, "we need to hear with our hearts tonight of love and land."

The next day Phillip and his father concentrated on the best trail to take north. It was decided that Phillip would pick up the old Goodnight Loving Trail into Colorado. The old Dawson Trail would be overrun and was full of hazards and bad terrain.

As Phillip and Don Luis put together the outfit and hired hands they both felt the need for closeness. This undertaking would be dangerous and with problems.

Don Luis said, "I should be going with you."

Phillip replied, "Father, let me do something of value for you. I do not need your assistance on the trail, but I do need your advice now."

Don Luis knew that his son was a man of the highest honor and character, willing to go to heroic efforts to account for every animal and for every man. He was sending his head herdsman, Nate Crook, with Phillip. Nate knew stock and how to manage herds in the worst of conditions. He, also, would ride ahead and scout for water and grazing sites while Phillip and the men broke the herd and horses to trailing condition.

Phillip had made drives with mixed herds in the past. It was to be expected that a few head would be lost. He prayed that all the animals would survive this trek. Generally a drive began in early spring. It was now June which meant he must push hard.

After a long and tedious inventory, Phillip and Don Luis set the following morning for the drive to begin.

As dawn broke and the sky began to pink, Phillip and the drovers made their farewells and began to move the stock. The stallions would follow about three miles behind. It was at best, very dangerous but Phillip, Nate, and Don Luis decided it would be too risky to have them near the mares. The stallions were on leads with ten vaqueros and two grooms to handle them. Four expert marksmen brought up the rear.

Phillip headed east to follow the Goodnight Loving Trail through Colorado to Wyoming. Long cattle drives these days were almost non existent. With railroad spur lines being built daily most herds were being shipped directly to market. Phillip was pleased that the cattle were fat and healthy. The two prize Hereford bulls were ambling quietly, their red hides glistening in the sun. His father had paid dearly for them and Phillip had a moment of panic…..nothing could replace so many of these blooded animals. He looked closely at the two bulls with horns curving around their white faces like royalty. One bull glared balefully at him and snorted air.

Phillip laughed, "Okay Your Majesty, just keep that arrogance and we will come through this together."

Phillip tied a kerchief over his nose and pulled his hat down over his smoked glasses. He thought on the men who had founded this historical trail and what a legend they had become. Oliver Loving knew cattle and could manage huge herds over the worst terrain. Col. Goodnight, a former Texas Ranger, raised cattle to make drives north to market. He knew the country and had fought Indians. Both men were of the highest honor and character. The two met and took many herds north together. On their last move Comanches were seen ahead. Loving and three others rode ahead to scout and were ambushed at the Pecos River. Loving was left for dead and when found by Mexican children, he had a gangrenous hand and was taken to Fort Sumner. The story, told over and over, tells of Loving's refusal to let the doctor amputate the arm until his partner, Goodnight, came. On Goodnight's arrival, the arm was amputated, but complications set in. Loving knew he was dying and made Goodnight promise to see that his wife and nine children were provided for. Loving's dying wish was that Goodnight take his body back to his ranch. The dramatic tale of Colonel Goodnight's heroic travel back to Texas with the body had made many authors rich.

These men had overcome insurmountable obstacles and Phillip knew their deeds of courage would be an inspiration to him and his men. The trail was well worn now and marked by estacados (a series of wooden stakes) in the desolate desert floors and canyons.

He stood in his stirrups shading his eyes as he looked to the north. They had been on the trail three weeks; twenty five men, forty horses and a herd of close to two hundred shorthorn cattle. It was a long drive that lay ahead and they must make Wyoming before winter began. For now it was wide open country and if they needed help there was no one to aid them; they were completely on their own. They made about nineteen miles a day while the country was flat and rolling. As they climbed into mountain passes they were slowed to maybe eight or ten miles a day depending on the terrain. The days followed one another clear and warm. The farther north they traveled the greener the land became. Phillip let the animals graze late afternoons to fatten while they could.

So far progress had been good, but he was very anxious to get the prized stock to Wyoming. It had devastated his father to send these animals on a trek to a possible nowhere; so much depended on making the journey safely.

Nate and Phillip would walk among the campfires at night to listen to any complaints. For the most part, the drovers were proud of their work. There was a buzz of talk and guffaws, even a guitar and singing, which was an indication the men were satisfied.

"Senor Phillip, the horses are doing well. They are strong good animals and I don't think they will spook easily," said Nate one evening.

"Nate, forget the Senor, you make me feel ancient," laughed Phillip. "You have been through the sweat and tears of raising these animals, I am fortunate to have you along. As you know I am carrying out my father's wishes to save and protect them. I pray we don't meet any overwhelming obstacles."

"We will make it and so will the animals, if it is God's wish. "

Phillip stretched out and leaned against his saddle enjoying a cup of strong coffee. His cigarillo glowed red in the darkness. The mournful howl of a wolf floated from the summits.

"Hope they have had plenty of kill," commented Nate.

"You've got that right," answered Phillip quietly. Finishing up his coffee, he pulled up his blanket. "Buenos noches, Nate."

"Yeh, Boss, sleep well."

The weather was intermittent, sultry and overcast the next two weeks. Rumbles of thunder came from the north and heat lightning jagged across the night sky. They were well into Colorado and climbing. There was good water and thick grass. The stallions and mares continued to be kept separated. The saddle horses were geldings except for Pegasus. Phillip kept a strong rein and kept well ahead so Pegasus had no chance to fight the other stallions or try to claim a mare.

One afternoon the sky darkened with nasty rolling clouds and Philip gave orders to slow the herd. Sizzling bolts of lightning began to streak from sky to ground followed by peals of thunder.

"Round up close to those small hills. Find a canyon if possible," called Nate to the drovers as he galloped back to the restless cattle. "Storm coming!"

"Muchachos, pronto!" Phillip yelled as he whirled back to help.

Rain came down with a vengeance and some cattle began to run. The vagueros herded them toward a canyon shouting and swinging lariats. Thunder rumbled and the streaks of lightning were blinding blue white.

"If the downpour doesn't let up shortly we will have to move out in case of a flash flood," yelled Phillip wheeling on Pegasus.

A mare lost her footing and lay screaming in pain, a foreleg obviously broken. Phillip rode to the mare, dismounted, and put a merciful end to her agony. Sadly, he recognized her to be one of his father's prized mares.

The rain suddenly stopped, the animals quieted down and a few of the men gathered by the mare.

"Were there other causalities?" Phillip asked, his face grim.

"No, boss, sorry about your loss. We had better get these animals out of this canyon. There could be flood water if it starts raining again," suggested Nate.

"Right, Nate, let's find level ground and set up camp," Phillip agreed, pulling his hat low over his eyes.

The following days continued without mishap. One morning Phillip called attention to the beauty of the surrounding area.

"This country has natural 'pleasure grounds.' The government passed laws that no 'injury or spoliation' can overtake some of these new set asides," commented Nate.

"Yes, I have been to Yellowstone Park, it is something. Jim Bridger wrote 'there's a river that flows so fast it gets hot on the bottom.' One can fish a trout out of an ice cold stream and cook it in a spring of boiling water. Geysers of steam spout everywhere, it is like another world!"

"Yep, mighty strange country," agreed Nate, "but this is my kind of heaven." Truly, the mountains, spruce and sparkling lakes were magnificent.

As they climbed higher the sun became more intense, but the air cooled at night, which made for perfect sleep. There were streams and grass in abundance. Phillip and the men were pleased with their progress, even Luke, the cook and his chuck wagon were holding up well.

As they ate around the campfire that evening Luke remarked, "Boss, if we keep this pace we should be in Wyoming by the middle of August. Are we gonna go near Denver?"

"Hadn't planned on it, we will be about fifteen miles away. Is there something you need there?" queried Phillip looking at Luke with one raised brow.

"Naw, I knew a fancy gal there once. She's probably high tailed outta there by now or maybe even dead," answered Luke simply.

"Rather keep away from the big cities, Luke. No time for women on this run."

"Yeh, I understand, boss. I just felt lucky haven't had to repair or replace a wheel on the wagon yet."

"You handle it well, Luke. Got a way with the reins…that is as important as the cornbread," Phillip chuckled.

"Wal, thank you boss, plumb appreciate that," the cook said with pleasure written all over his plump face.

"Yeh," Nate laughed, pouring a cup of coffee from a big agate coffee pot. "You have done well, but just remember the snow flies sometimes early September in the North Country. We can still face some danger especially with stallions and mares; they are hard to herd. We have been blessed that the mustang herds have been far away and spooked. I hope they stay that way. "

"I agree, that could be dangerous for all concerned," answered Phillip as he stood and stretched. "I think I'll turn in."

He walked over to his bedroll, stretched out and lay back to look at the stars in the dark heavens. He thought of Joanna and then quickly put her out of his mind. He would think on that later when he got to Snowflake!

The drive continued without incident. Phillip was especially careful while crossing streams and rivers. He and Nate scouted to find shallow water for the heavy supply wagons. They had to ford without danger, couldn't afford to lose provisions. Nate made the men loosen cinches on saddles before going into rivers as the horses would bloat when swimming.

Phillip took every precaution to ensure both the animals' and men's safety. They crossed the Arkansas River outside Pueblo City without incident.

When they entered Arapahoe Country they spotted a stagecoach swinging over a rough and heavy road. As the coach got within shouting distance, Phillip hailed the driver and rode to the stage as it came to a halt. Passengers were peering from windows.

A soldier on horseback sat with a Spencer rifle pointed at Phillip as he rode up. The soldier was obviously a guard for the US Postal Service and that meant there were road agents or desperadoes around.

"Hello, I am driving a herd to Wyoming from New Mexico. I would appreciate your taking some mail from me and my men," yelled Phillip.

"Who you be with?" yelled the driver.

"The Casa de Flores Ranch," Phillip yelled back.

"Luis de La Cruz's place, right? I used to drive from Santa Fe to Albuquerque. I delivered supplies to Don Luis, you work for him?"

"I am his son, Phillip. I have a spread in Wyoming and taking some stock north for my father."

"Ride on in, boy. I recognize his horses when I see them, fine animals."

The driver reached down from the boot for the letters and Phillip handed them up with a gold coin.

"Glad to make your acquaintance, son. Gotta stretch leather. You be on the lookout, we got some roughuns runnin' around out here. One of our stages was robbed a couple weeks ago," said the driver, putting his hand to the brim of his dust covered hat.

"Was ist das, wer ist da?" An agitated guttural voice called out from the coach.

"Sorry to disturb you, mein Herr," said Phillip loudly.

"Was in der Tuefel do you want?"

Phillip laughed and nodded good bye to the driver and guard then galloped to catch the herd.

The last week of August found the drive heading out of Rawlins. The nights were cooling considerably.

"I hope we don't have an early fall. We have at least three more weeks ahead of us," commented Nate as he looked at some high clouds.

Phillip nodded, "I have noticed the aspen in the high country, some looks to be turning already. We will just pray the weather holds." Pegasus tossed his head and whinnied as if to agree with Phillip.

Nate burst into laughter. "I swear that hoss understands everything we say!"

That evening Nate and Phillip walked the camp near twilight.

"We have been lucky so far. I don't want to lose any men or animals now that we are in Wyoming Territory. With any luck we should be home by the end of September." For many days Phillip had puzzled over a feeling of dread that he couldn't explain. "Pass the word, Nate. Have the men be certain their rifles and six shooters are loaded. I want the guards to be alert, this close to the end of a drive men get careless. These animals are too valuable to lose now."

Nate regarded Phillip for a moment and shook his head in agreement, "You are right, boss, I will tell the men now."

Phillip went to the chuck wagon to get his supper. After eating he drew his Spencer rifle from its scabbard and rechecked to make certain it was loaded. It usually was, but he was double checking tonight.

It was Jethro Wilkes turn to guard the remuda. Pablo Montero was strumming his guitar and serenading the cattle. The small crescent moon was gliding in and out of clouds which made for a dark night away from the fires of the camp.

Jethro was sitting with his back to a large rock, his rifle cradled in his arms. He could hear the guitar music and smiled to himself. He heard a loud thump and sat up...silence! He began to crawl through the tall grass to see if something had happened to Pablo. He squinted through the darkness, but saw nothing but the outline of cattle. Suddenly a bullet grazed his shoulder. With a cry of alarm Jethro raised his rifle at a dark outline.

"Pablo?" he hissed. Two flashes of gunfire answered him. He fired three times at the area where the flashes had come.

There was a strangled cry and silence.

Jethro rose and ran toward camp yelling..."Bushwhackers!"

Nate, Phillip and Juan ran in a crouch and knelt beside one of the wagons. More flashes of fire as the bushwhackers opened fire on the camp. Phillip and Nate fired repeatedly in the direction of the flashes of gunfire. Screams of pain announced that their bullets had reached their target.

The cattle were in full flight, running in every direction. The horses had been securely hobbled in two areas so Phillip hoped they were still close by. Two of the men were about to mount horses.

Phillip yelled..."Don't get on a horse. They will pick you off; we can round up the stock once this attack is over!"

There was another flash of fire. Juan shouldered his carbine and fired twice. There was a howl of agony and a call, "We're done, you bastards. Hold your fire!"

"Come out slow and easy, throw your weapons down by the fire, arms in the air!" snarled Phillip.

Two men came into the firelight. A short man was dragging a leg that streamed blood. A taller man followed behind and growled at the wounded man, "You stupid jackass…gettin' yourself shot!"

When they reached the fire, Juan tied their hands behind them. The wounded man fell forward.

"Pull him out of the fire and wrap a bandana around his leg for a tourniquet," said Phillip. He then nudged the taller man with his rifle and made him sit.

"Nate, have the men check the whole area. Take no chances, there may be more. Check the horses and then we will go after the cattle."

Phillip stood over his prisoner. "Who are you and what the hell are you doing here?"

The man who looked up at Phillip made him shudder. His face had a jagged scar that ran from his left ear to the corner of his mouth. The scar had puckered as it healed, pulling down his eye and cheek in a grotesque grimace.

"I'm called Diablo Jack. We was diggin' for gold in Colorado but never saw no color. We thought we could pick up a few strays cuz we're hungry. This here's Johnny Reb who's still fightin' the north. The other boys fell in with us."

"How many?" spat Phillip.

"Four."

Jethro and another vaquero carried Pablo over to a tree by the fire. "He's dead, Boss," said Jethro sadly.

The Johnny Rebs's head rose, his eyes glittered defiance and he fell back drawing his last breath.

Juan said, "He lost too much blood, Senor. He is also dead."

"It is just as well, Juan, if he is still so rabid with hate after all these years he would have just kept killing," answered Phillip, shaking his head.

Turning back to Diablo Jack he asked the given name of the dead man. "Dunno, we just called him Johnny Reb." The following morning they buried the dead. The vaqueros, led by Phillip and Nate, then rode out after the cattle. It took most of the day to round them up. By count there were five missing.

Phillip gave an extra day of needed rest to his men. The attack and round up had exhausted man and horse and Pablo's death was disheartening.

They broke camp at dawn the next day and continued north. The men were quiet, a pall had settled over them after the harrowing experience that had befallen the drive. Diablo Jack was securely tied to a horse being led by Nate.

"Beats me why this bunch of roughnecks came so far north. Someone must have been after them," Nate said in a quiet voice to Phillip.

"I agree, Nate. We will drop off this scum at Fort Wilson and let the army handle him," answered Phillip, his handsome face full of contempt.

As the day wore on Phillip's thoughts turned to Joanna. He face softened as he remembered her gentle heart shaped face, the lovely violet eyes and tumbling copper hair. He said to himself, *Joanna, if this drive is successful, I will swallow my pride and make you mine whatever I have to do. Although you are a stubborn lady, I will do my best to prove I love you.*

"Boss, hey boss, we've got a rider ahead!" yelled Jethro, bringing Phillip back to reality. He urged his horse to where Jethro and three other men waited. The rider rode upon a pinto pony and was dressed like an Indian, but had matted blond hair and blue eyes. His leggings were rawhide, his shirt of antelope skin and over this a frock of fringed buckskin fell to his knees. Necklaces of many colored beads and bones were draped about his shoulders. He had a muskrat skin cap on his head which partially covered an ugly wound. There was clotted black blood dried over one side of his face and forehead.

"Phillip de La Cruz? I'll be blessed, what are you doin' out here in the middle of nowhere?"

"Elijah Barnum?"

"Damn, it is you, Phillip! You are a sight for sore eyes. I thought I was having hallucinations when I saw your remuda. I have been so dizzy by spells I feared I was dying for certain."

Phillip leaned over to shake the big man's hand. "My God, Elijah, what happened to you? Where are your men?"

The older man drank deeply from a canteen one of the men handed him, wiped off his chin and spoke gravely, "I was on my way back from Cheyenne with my top hand, Skidmore Nelson...you remember him?"

"Yes..."

"Well, I had sold my herd and turned the help loose for the winter. Skidmore and I were put upon by bushwhackers. They shot Skidmore in the back and took the horses, left me for dead. I got a creased skull, bled mightily and fell still as death. Come daylight, there was my mare. Still had a tether, but somehow she came back to me." He patted his horse on the neck, tears in his eyes.

"How many men, Elijah?"

"Four. By damn...he's one!" He exclaimed, pointing to Diablo Jack as Nate rode up with his prisoner.

"Let me at him, Phillip!" Elijah dismounted unsteadily and Phillip immediately jumped off his horse restraining the newcomer.

Phillip reasoned with him, "Don't waste yourself on this piece of manure, let the law hang him!"

"He killed Skidmore!"

"They also killed one of my men, Elijah. We can't take the law into our hands or we become like animals. Ride with us to the Fort and we will make certain he pays for his crimes."

Elijah, his face white with anger and weak from his head wound and shock leaned over his saddle. "I am too weak to protest, but I would like to put a bullet through his black heart!"

Phillip nodded, "I know. Let's take a look at your head, Elijah."

Phillip led the wounded man over to a flat area. "Nate, bring me my canteen and some herbs out of my saddle bag."

Nate compared the two men as Phillip worked over Elijah. They both represented the best of the country. Phillip was wearing a sombrero and had taken off his kerchief to wash Elijah's wound. His legs were encased in leather chaps and his boots had sterling spurs. His handsome aquiline face had darkened from the sun and his blue eyes gleamed like turquoise. He spoke to Nate as he worked.

"Elijah has lived around the Shoshone Indians for as long as I have been in the Territory. He lives in Deer Lodge Valley in Montana Territory with a War Chiefs daughter from the Wind River Reservation. Her name is Flashing Water and she is right pretty and smart. For some time, Elijah has caught and broke mustangs for John to sell to the army."

Between grimaces Elijah added, "I have acquired a small spread with a herd of Hereford cattle. My four half breed sons and a daughter have helped me make a good living. I know these mountains like the back of my hand and I have trapped and hunted the Rockies from Colorado into Canada."

Phillip gave Elijah's shoulder a compassionate squeeze when he finished cleaning and bandaging the wound.

"Don't fret yourself, that tear will heal in a few days. Ride with us and then decide your way from there. We will help you in any way we can."

"You are a good man, Phillip, just like your father. Those are mighty fine animals you've got there. Don't tell me you've had them on lead from New Mexico?"

"That I have, Elijah. Father fears the migration west. Lots of spreads have been taken over by killing and burning owners out. Some by Anglos, some by renegades and some paid pistileros. Father hopes to insure the Andalusian line so they won't kill them off. That is one of the reasons we are doing this trek."

"Now, we must get you help and care. I'll not leave you behind, Elijah."

The man dressed in buckskin was considerably heartened by these words. He took a deep breath and pulled himself to his feet. Phillip helped him mount and the drive continued.

Four days later, moving slowly to let the horses and cattle graze in the deep buffalo grass, the outfit sighted Fort Darling.

A sentry rode out to greet them. Phillip shook hands with him and rode ahead with the sentry to make arrangements for camp. Colonel Nick Simons, in charge of the Fort, was a gracious older man and made Phillip welcome. Diablo Jack was put in the stockade until such time he could be taken to the Territorial Prison. Elijah was treated by the Fort Doctor who complemented Phillip on his nursing skills. The wound was healing cleanly.

The Colonel insisted that Phillip join him for supper. Phillip was taken to the enlisted men's quarters to bathe and shave. He was thankful he still had a clean shirt in his saddle bag, wrinkled but presentable.

The Colonel's home was a well kept house that looked to have been recently white washed. Perlina Simons was a small gently rounded woman many years younger than the Major. Her eyes shone with delight as she was introduced to Phillip.

The two men enjoyed a drink and Mrs. Simons proceeded to serve the three of them with great skill. She stared at Phillip over her tea cup, her eyes pleading insistence.

To what? Phillip thought with a bit of annoyance.

As they ate he had an opportunity to study her in detail as the Colonel seemed intent only on his food. Her pretty rounded face had large dark eyes, a dainty sculptured nose and her mouth was unusual in its ripeness. She wore a decorous dress of dark green bombazine. Her ample bosom rose and fell in small shuddering movements. Phillip had been on the trail a long time and he felt a slight stirring in his groin as she stared up at him hungrily.

After supper the men sipped brandy. The Colonel recounted the latest news to Phillip for the better part of an hour continually refilling Phillip's snifter. The excellent dinner and the brandy were making it difficult for Phillip to be a coherent guest.

Mrs. Simons joined them and smiled prettily at Phillip. Phillip said, "I find exhaustion overtaking me and must beg your leave, Colonel. My men will be expecting me."

"Oh, sir, not so soon! We don't get many visitors, you know," Mrs Simmons dimpled at him.

"I understand," he replied, "It must be very hard to maintain a social life in this vast area."

A warm flush suffused her cheeks and she lowered her eyes, "There are few wives here and they are intimidated by rank. It is difficult to make close friends when one is the commanding officer's wife."

The Colonel's face lit up and he boomed, "Stay the night, sir! We have a guest room and we can have an early breakfast. That will delight my Perlina!"

"Yes, indeed, darling," she eagerly concurred.

"I must decline for I am obligated to my outfit, but I appreciate your kind offer."

"Pshaw, I absolutely insist! You need a good night's rest and I will have sentries posted. I will send my corporal to notify your men. Early morning you will be free to leave and rested, eh, Pearl?"

"Yes, dear," answered the diminutive woman.

Phillip felt almost a prisoner in this situation and his head was spinning. He had no choice but to hope his men would be understanding...although he wasn't certain he understood the Colonel's insistence.

Later alone with his thoughts Phillip lay naked on top of a big bed while a lamp flickered beside him. He surmised the room; it was furnished in heavy walnut and marble...quite ornate for a guest room. Still pondering his eyelids became heavy and he was fast asleep on minutes.

He awakened to a feathery lingering kiss on his mouth. "What the!?...."

With a sob of delight, Perlina Simons locked her bare body around his and caressed him with a rare and unexpected pleasure. She was kissing him everywhere in a gentle persuasive way. Her tongue caressed and licked...making him thrill and quiver to her touch. "Mon Dieu, woman, your husband!" Phillip managed to exclaim.

"Shhh, it's alright, he knows!" She continued feverishly kissing and licking Phillip. He was trying to use force to push her away.

"Oh, no, no!" she pleaded in an anguished voice.

Phillip was turgid with desire and her soft full breasts were pushing in his face as she began to ease herself down and ride him. He rolled her over roughly. Their coming together was explosive as unleashed fury of pent up emotions long suppressed was unleashed.

When it was over, he lay beside her staring at the ceiling. "Why?" he asked.

"Oh, my dear," she breathed as she leaned over and cupped his face in her hands. "You must understand, I do love my husband. I was only fifteen when out of pity; he bought me from the owner of a house of ill repute. He married me and gave me a new life. He was trained at West Point and in the War of the States he was sent immediately into the fray. In the last week of the war he was wounded and lost his manhood. So, at rare times, when a young healthy young man such as you appears, he makes it convenient for me to try to become in the family way."

"Oh, my God!" Phillip snorted.

"I was an orphan born in a foundling home to an Irish immigrant. My father was from a rich influential family and abandoned my mother. On my twelfth birthday I was sold to a madam."

"How old are you now?"

"Twenty."

"Dios, what an existence!"

"It is not so bad. Nick loves me and I him. He will retire soon and return east. His family is in steel and the father is old and feeble. We would like a child to return with...an heir, so to speak."

She began to run her hands over his body. Phillip pushed her away, jumped out of bed and quickly began to dress.

"Please don't despise me, "she pleaded. "Life is full of unfortunate circumstances. We must survive in our own way."

"I am not a stud animal!" he all but shouted. "You have taken advantage of me, you are very skilled at what you do, Mrs. Simons."

"Don't go, please," she murmured sadly, wiping a tear from her eye. "Try to understand, life is cruel. What he did for me is beyond comprehension. To give him a child to love is my only desire in life. He has given so much for his country and saved me from a fate worse than hell. I won't ask forgiveness, that must be my maker's decision."

When Phillip returned to his outfit it was early in the am. He lay quietly down by Nate who was awake.

Nate whispered, "Boss, I am glad you are back. They said you were held over on business."

"Well, I am here. Don't ask for an explanation. I couldn't give you one because I don't understand what happened myself."

Nate looked at the stars and puzzled over Phillip's answer. He soon heard Phillip's deep breathing. He was certainly exhausted, must have been a lot of paperwork.

205

Shortly after daylight they began to break camp.

"Is Elijah coming with us?" Phillip asked Nate as they drank their coffee by the chuck wagon. Phillip felt as if his head was as big as a melon.

"He said the colonel and his wife wanted to keep an eye on him and were going to move him into the Colonel's house until Elijah's head was completely healed. I guess he'll head for home in a few days."

Phillip looked at Nate astounded and then began to guffaw. He laughed so hard he slapped the side of the wagon.

"Boss! Hey, Boss, you okay?" asked Nate incredulously, witnessing Phillip's hysterics.

"Oh, Nate, he is in for the ride of his life! Let's saddle up!" Phillip answered as he bent over to buckle his spurs still chuckling.

Nate raised the brim of his hat and scratched his head in puzzlement. Whatever had transpired the fore night had left the Boss in one hell of a mood!

The nip in the air kept Phillip awake as he was half dead with exhaustion. They were headed for a line camp he and John Holan had built for round ups. It was located in Little Dixie Valley and about a four day trip. He had decided to take it slow and easy and let the stock graze. The buffalo grass here was mixed with blue grama which made excellent feed.

They reached the line camp on the fifth day. There was a log cabin with a door and two windows. It sat among the trees facing the Little Dixie Creek There was a good sized corral made out of cedar posts close by. They unharnessed the wagon teams and turned them into the corral. There was an abundance of water and grass.

The cabin had an iron cooking range, a skillet and a few pots. There were bunks for five, a bench, two chairs and a table. Some cut firewood was piled in a corner. Miquel carried in chips and twigs, lifted a round lid on the stove and kindled a fire. "I'll have beans, biscuits and bacon started in a jiffy," he said.

Phillip, Nate and the vaqueros secured the animals for the night. Some of the horses were put in the corral while others were hobbled.

The vaqueros watching the cattle were fed first and then the rest of the remuda.

After supper Nate and Phillip walked the camp and returned to the cabin. They sat close to the stove; the evening air had a chill to it.

"Four more days and we should hit the pass to Snowflake," said Phillip. "God has been good to us. We encountered a couple of unfortunate incidents but, otherwise, we made good time and had good grazing for the most part."

"Yep, we've been lucky. We will have to watch for a grizzly that hasn't bedded in for the winter or a lazy lobo who might like a tethered horse or a heifer. There are many herds of antelope, deer and elk so the wolves should be well fed."

Phillip lit a cigarillo, propped his boots against a stove leg and tilted the chair back. He let his thoughts turn to Joanna. He wasn't harboring any illusions; she would be hostile as hell. He might also be too late. He had been gone over nine months, yet, she was still single when he had run into her in San Francisco.

Maybe, just maybe he could tame this wild swan!

For the next four days he was too busy to think of anyone. They began to drive the herd hard as the days became increasingly chilly and there was now frost in the mornings. It was early for snow, but in this country one could never be certain.

It was a happy day when they rode into the meadows of Snowflake. Phillip waved his hat as a rider came galloping toward him.

"Eddie?"

"Yeh, Mr. Phillip," he shouted. "Are we ever glad to see you!"

Phillip could hear the relief in his voice. As he came abreast Phillip leaned over and shook hands.

"We were getting worried what with the weather changin' and all. The animals look to be in good shape," said his foreman, twisting around in his saddle.

"I had fine help and we found good grazing and water. The weather held even though we got a late start."

"Well, I will ride ahead and have the missus start fixing some food and get the rest of the boys to help. We will put the cattle in the upper pasture.

As soon as all the stock was settled in Phillip walked to the log house.

Martha met him at the door. "Mr. Phillip, you are a sight for sore eyes. I've got supper started and I'll bet you could use a bath." Not waiting for an answer she turned and yelled, "Girls, get out here, now! Get Mr. Phillip's tub out and fill it with hot water from the reservoir."

Sarah and Bonnie came on the run, curtsied to Phillip and went outside. They came back in giggling and carrying an elongated metal tub. As they climbed the stairs Sarah said, "Isn't he just the handsomest man? So dark and tan with those fierce blue eyes and those shoulders....Oh, my!"

Bonnie shook her blond pig tails, "He is nice looking, but he is so old!"

Sarah sighed, "I will be thirteen next month! Mr. Goddard is nigh forty and he married Emmy Watts, she is fourteen!"

"Oh, pish, who wants to marry some old man and kiss them? That is icky!"

"You are such a child!"

"Girls, hurry up there, now!" bellowed Martha up the stairs.

"Yes, Mama," answered Sarah.

Phillip soaked his bone weary body and after supper went outside on the porch to smoke with Jonathan and Eddie. They brought him up to date on the ranch and he was pleased with both men. They worked well together and he was fortunate in having them and their families at Snowflake. After the two men retired he just relaxed. A moon hung low in the western sky and he inhaled deeply of the wonderful night. The smell of pines, the smoke of fresh cut wood and odor of animals from the corrals made it home. Sadly, It also brought a feeling of loneliness…of desire for that woman in the next valley.

He thought of his parents. Well, Father, we made it. The stock is in good shape and the gold is in the barn. Buenos noches, Padre y mia Madre, I love you.

Early next morning Phillip and Nate went to the stables. Frost was shimmering silver in the meadows. "We got home just in time, Nate. Look at those low clouds sitting on the mountains."

"Yep, and did you notice the hollows? The shrub maple are on fire and the quakies are dancing gold."

"It won't be long before we are covered with snow. I thank God again for our safe journey."

Everything was quiet at the stables. The horses had their noses buried in alfalfa and the grooms were currying Pegasus and Diablo in their respective stalls.

Phillip led Nate to the chuck wagon. "Have Miquel get all of this unpacked immediately. I want it stripped and then you harness a team and bring it around to the big house in back. I will be waiting there."

"Sure, Boss. You want everything out?" asked a puzzled Nate.

"Stripped, and bring a crowbar with you!" answered Phillip as he walked briskly away, leaving Nate scratching his head, perplexed as usual.

Phillip pushed open the beveled glass and mahogany entrance doors to the big house. The unfinished interior had an aroma of new wood. The hickory hardwood floors were burnished like satin. Martha had kept the interior spotless. The only furnished room was Phillip's library. A rich Brussels carpet had been laid and his collection of leather bound books lined the walls. An oak desk sat in the middle of the room, two large leather chairs faced the fireplace. Phillip kindled the fire and turned to the desk. Retrieving a key from a drawer he unlocked a panel on the east wall which opened out revealing a large iron engraved safe. He spun the lock and the massive door swung open. Once the fire was burning well he walked out to the veranda. He watched the team and chuck wagon climb the hill, motioned Nate to the back and walked through the house to the back entrance. Nate secured the brake and climbed down as Phillip tied the team to the hitching post. Phillip climbed inside the wagon and began prying up the bottom boards with the crowbar. Nate climbed in and watched him, eyes suddenly attentive.

"Give me a hand, Nate. I want all these boards ripped up!"

Nate was astonished to see another layer of floor being exposed about four inches deep. Even more astonishing were the small canvas bags that had been hidden and lay the length of the false bottom. Phillip pulled a bag open and dumped its contents. Gold coins and notes spilled from it.

Nate's eyes bulged. "Sweet Jesus, we carried all this with no guard!" He gulped and stared at the gold, "I feel sick, we could have lost this a dozen ways!"

"Nate, I couldn't tell anyone. Father and I decided it was too risky. If no one knew about the gold, then men would not be hurt or killed for it. It was a chance we had to take. Help me get it into the safe. Tonight I will pay the drovers and vaqueros off so they can return home. Tomorrow I will take part of it to the bank in Stirrup Crossing."

"It was a hell'va setup, Boss. No one suspected a thing, you even rode from camp...even spent a night away in the fort!"

"Ah, yes," Phillip replied lightly, "that was not exactly my doing, but 'all's well that ends well.'"

He then thought of Joanna. He must get to Locket Springs as soon as possible. He picked up some of the bags and carried them to the safe.

When the gold was secured in the vault he paid Nate his wages plus a hefty bonus for his loyalty. The grateful man assured him he would stay at Snowflake as long as needed.

Nate felt great sympathy for this man. Phillip del La Cruz had been well educated in foreign schools, but adapted himself to the rigors of the west. His wife and new born son died at Snowflake yet he came back to all these sad memories because of the love he had for his father. Nate admired him for his loyalty.

"Well, Boss, I hope this will be security for the stock of Casa de Flores. I hope your Papa will have no trouble."

Phillip leaned over the mantle staring into the flames. "I pray that he will not have to endure a range war. The ranch was founded after the land was assigned to my ancestors as a Private Grant for service. The Del La Cruz family has endured extraordinary hardships to keep and work their land. It is shameful that these hardy pioneers' legal claims are being called into question."

"It is only greed and politics. Some bloody fools want something for nothing and use force to take it! They find a band of immoral and ignorant men who have a chip on their shoulder to do their dirty work."

"It has been going on for centuries, Nate and it will continue. It is the nature of mankind, unfortunately," Phillip answered and turned from the fire. "I am honored to have you as a friend, Nate, and glad you are working with me. The drive was hard on everyone, but you kept up the morale of the men and I will be forever grateful. I never intend to take on a responsibility such as this past one, believe me. Father and I discussed the many ways of transporting the horses and the gold. We knew we could do part of it by rail, but then the gold would have been a problem. In the end we decided to make it a combination drive; throw in a couple of prize Hereford bulls with the cows and horses. Not easily done and most old ranchers would have scoffed at our thinking, but we can now say we accomplished, perhaps, the impossible."

"You can bet your spurs on that! Those outlaws may be stopped soon by the law. It isn't right that they continue to burn and run people off their land."

"Well, our Ancestoral Grant was signed by the King of Spain as well as the Alcalde Mayor. The map describes the grant boundaries, the visible features of the landscape such as the mountain ranges, the river, the arroyos and the hills. If it is ever adjudicated by the American government, it can never be declared invalid. It is the physical demonstrations by the paid renegades which I fear. I hope Antonio will hire extra men and locate his family there quickly."

"Don Luis has many friends in Santa Fe. Can they be of help?"

Phillip soberly nodded then poured a brandy for himself and Nate. "Yes, he had many friends, but these outlaws are like wolves. They run in packs, strike unexpectedly and do so much damage and killing; they are hard to identify. To be sure, they are being paid well by land developers or unscrupulous ranchers. It will be a struggle for Father and Antonio, but if they can keep the herds together and hire enough vaqueros they will keep the ranch."

Nate shook his head as he sipped his brandy. He stood looking out the study window.

"Good job on the new barn."

"Yes, it is more than adequate. Now this house must be finished and furnished."

"That is good news. This is a fine house and needs to be lived in!"

Phillip furrowed his brow thoughtfully. "I must get my life together. I may have waited too long to settle a couple of things." At dinner that evening he made inquiries about Locket Springs.

"No, Mr. Holan would not return until spring; he and the Missus were going to Europe."

"Yes, Mr. Alexander and his wife had arrived."

"Yes, Miss Holan still taught school at Locket Springs."

CHAPTER TWO

She stepped to her bedroom window and gazed out at the green fields…such a beautiful view and so serene. Joanna was happy to be back at Locket Springs. The simple easy reality of life found here made the sense of time vanish. The formality and rituals of high society peeled away following her return from San Francisco. Despondency clouded her for a moment, and then she smiled. Elyse and Timber were arriving at the end of the week! Try as she may, she couldn't remember Timber's face. But she would never forget the aqua blue eyes bright with expectation that dimmed and filled with cold fury last Christmas. Oh, dear God, I lost Phillip and I remember every part of that haughty aristocratic face!

She looked again at the letter she held in her hand and reread part of it.

> *Only a few more days and we will be on our way to you. I am so happy and excited I cannot concentrate on anything else. What a pleasure to find ourselves in such fortunate circumstances. Uncle John and Frieda will now be able to leave on their honeymoon after attending Winifred's debut.*
>
> *Mama is her usual glittering self…beside herself finalizing Winifred's gala and envisioning a smashing success.*
>
> *Social life has no charms for me since my disfigurement. I hate bother and publicity as does Timber so this journey will be a blessing for both of us. Timber cannot wait for me to see his Wind River Mountains.*
>
> *I have not approached this subject before, but I feel it is long overdue. I hope you bear me no malice because of my love for Timber. He has been my salvation. Both he and his dear mother nursed me back from the brink of despair with a devotion and care that knew no break. The intimacy between Timber and I developed daily as I grew well. I love*

*him with all my being, Joanna. He is such a dear, good man
and I am so blessed. I know you cared for him at one time and
I pray that this will not come between us.*

*Unfortunately, I still have horrible nightmares of
Marshall. What anguish he has caused. How right and
reasonable you were to oppose him. Reflecting back, I wish
I could have seen him through your eyes.*

*There is much happening around us. There is a great
drive for men to be subscripted into the army. It seems every
young man wants to go to Alaska to the Klondike Rush!
Parades with remarkable spirited marches composed by
John Phillip Sousa are attended by huge throngs of people.*

*We now have rural free delivery, pray tell, what next?
It has been something of a marvel this past year...electric
current with incandescent globes, and Timber purchased an
Edison phonograph. Such a delight, I have played the Maple
Leaf Rag over and over!*

*I have nothing else of importance. Grandmother is
well.*

*Until I see you in Wyoming, I am so excited. It has been
ever so long.*

*Your devoted sister,
Elyce Alexander (Mrs)*

Joanna folded the letter and carefully slid it into its envelope. She lovingly
pressed a finger over the sealing wax impressed with an elaborate A that still
clung to the flap. Joanna, too, was looking forward to her reunion with her
beloved sibling.

"What to do today?" Joanna asked herself.

"I want to ride into the mountains!"

Following a light breakfast she asked Annie to join her. They changed into
split skirts and boots. Grabbing a wide hat and her gloves Joanna ran
excitedly to the barn. She found Madison looking over harnesses.

Joanna asked, "Madison, how would you like to ride today? Can you be
spared to accompany us?"

Madison nodded, "Sure thing, but I need to tell Mr. Buck and Mr. Tony to
make certain I can leave. They has wanted someone to look for a stray steer.
You go see to the horses and I will be there shortly."

It was a brilliant June morning, buckwheat and sorrel was springing out of the warm earth. It made a quiet ride with only the creak of leather and rattle of reins as they began to climb into the high country. As they topped a ridge onto a meadow new born elk calves were opening their eyes to the sun. The mothers watched the riders warily, but made no move. Joanna inhaled the pure mountain air and marveled at the snow capped peaks with timbered ridges running along canyon walls. They continued on and into an immense aspen grove which formed a canopy of leaves over a green velvet floor. Joanna heard a great roar.

"Good Heavens, what is that?"

"Come, I will show you," answered Madison.

Joanna heard the rushing water before they topped the ridge. A sliver column of water was plunging down the mountainside into a pool. They dismounted and Joanna began walking closer to the water, the spray causing rainbows of color. The black mica and rose quartz lining the pool glistened like fine diamonds in the sunlight. A ledge spread away from the pool on one side and a stream bounced down the mountain side on the other.

"What a magical place," Joanna exclaimed.

"Over on the other side of that ledge is a trail that leads down to the Snowflake Ranch," said Madison. This is called Table Top Rock. You can see both spreads from up here."

Joanna and Annie walked over and peered over the rim. The view was breathtaking, but over the rim was a sheer drop many feet down.

"Take care, girls, it is a far piece down from this here ledge and mighty dangerous!" Madison called.

They mounted their horses and turned down a trail leading away from the falls.

"We must watch for El Oso, Miss Joanna," cautioned Madison.

"What is El Oso?" Joanna asked.

"He is the bear, this is his country," he replied. He also remonstrated about the danger of mountain lions. He stopped stock still beside a tall spruce. He pointed to long parallel indentations about eye level. "A bear marked his territory not too long ago, a big one." He dismounted and squatted at the base of the tree pointing out rounded prints of large paws. The horses were blowing and stepping nervously.

"They horses are a bit spooked, they can still smell Oso."

"By the living God, these prints scare me also," exclaimed Annie anxiously glancing about.

Madison's eyes twinkled with amusement and then he was all concern and reassurance. "That bear ain't here at the moment or your horses would be rearing to go and I mean, rearing! Just keep those carbines handy and watch the ridges and tree lines....most likely this time of day old Oso is huntin' grubs."

Joanna looked intently at the tall black man. He was very muscular with huge callused hands. His mahogany face had a look of great sadness.

"Tell me, Madison, how did you end up here so far north?"

"A long story, Miss Joanna. I am a Mandingo and we prized for our size. Massa Charles bought my father as a young'un for a field slave. As Pa grew, Massa took a liken' to him and trained him for a house servant. My Mammy was a sweet woman named Bess who worked in the big house, too. Massa Charles and his son, Massa Brent, joined the Reb army when the big war come. They left the plantation and before they got home the Yankees came with General Sherman. They burned the plantation to the ground and scorched the earth as black as my face. They took my mammy as a camp worker and she had a babe in arms! We never saw her again. Pa and me stayed at the plantation...what was left of it until Massa Brent came home. Massa Charles had been killed. Paw and Massa Brent worked the fields side by side until they had decent crops again. Later Massa Brent gave Paw a piece of land in appreciation. Paw died a few short years later. I think he grieved his'sef to death over my mammy. I worked that land and helped Massa Brent. I added a couple of rooms to the cabin and found a good woman by the name of Tansy. We had Lionel and we was happy. One morning Tansy got up with a fever and before nightfall she died.....just like that!" Madison snapped his fingers and his eyes misted.

"Oh, God in heaven, Madison, I am so sorry," breathed Joanna laying a hand on his shoulder.

Madison wiped a tear from his eyes and turned to the horses. Wiping a tear from her cheek also, Joanna jumped up and mounted her horse. "Let's ride," she yelled and urged her mount to jump an old rail fence.

"Ye Gods, Miss Joanna, you have nerve. I would never attempt that on a strange horse!" gasped Annie as she trotted up to her.

"Well, we made it," Joanna laughed. "Oh, look, what is that?" She pointed her quirt at a structure above them in the canyon amid big ivory boled quakies.

"That be a trapper's cabin," explained Madison.

They rode up and examined the cabin. Nasty looking traps hung along the walls. A rickety table, two chairs and an iron bedstead were its only furniture.

The cabin looked as if it had not been used in a long time. They found a root cellar with some jerky and an array of home canned vegetables and fruits in jars coated with dust.

"Hmmm, there must have been a woman involved at one time," said Joanna as they emerged out of the cellar.

Bluebonnets, paintbrush and genetians were dotting the hillside and the glistening peaks were beckoning.

"I would like to go higher, what do you think, Maddy?" Joanna asked.

"Not today, but one day soon," he answered. "We best start back, it's near noonday."

The sun was high in the sky now and Joanna adjusted her hat so the brim shaded her face. The horses picked their way carefully around polished granite boulders, remains of a long ago glacier. A stand of tall cottonwoods could be seen in the canyon below.

"Dash it all, I have I have no idea where we are, I have lost all sense of direction. Madison, I hope you know this country!" exploded Joanna who was suddenly seized with panic. The mountains looked unfamiliar as did the canyons.

Madison drew rein and a smile lit up his face. "Miss, after six years in this heah' country, I know it good. We can top that ridge over yonder and you will likely see Locket Springs to one side and Snowflake Ranch in the far valley. When you work on a spread as big as Massa John's, getting lost is not healthy. I know these mountains like the back of my hand. A man can't ride careless. You pick landmarks. You watch the sun and watch mountain tops. We bring Massa John's hunting parties up here in the fall. Hafta' keep your bearings and not lose camp."

"It is sad they kill these magnificent animals," said Joanna with a shiver.

"It is a man's thing. They hunts to eat. It is part survival and part sport. Hunting is about connecting to the wild, to the land and to other beings. The big Hunting Parties pay good, they eat good, tell good lies and jokes and ride good horses. They sip good whiskey. They connect with something ages old…"

Joanna broke in. "Man tries to dominate everything and his gun becomes part of his domination; he is then all powerful!"

"Yeh, but I know one thing, those city people learn. They watch sunrises and sunsets and moonlight on the peaks. They feels the cold of a camp and know the joy of a warm fire. They drinks from streams and learns to listen and wait….for the wapiti, the wolf, the deer, grouse…anything. They forgets that other life for a spell."

"That is an interesting viewpoint, but I still wish the animals could be spared," Joanna answered in a hushed voice.

"What is a wapiti?" asked Annie.

"That's the Indian name for elk," laughed Madison. He clicked to his horse and rode on ahead beginning to climb a ridge. When they topped the ridge Joanna and Annie both gasped at the view. Below lay Locket Springs, an emerald jewel covering the floor of the valley. Beyond in the next valley was Snowflake, certainly not as large, but it gleamed with shades of green, also.

"We are startin' down. We will water the horses at a small pond below. You will hear water in a quicken."

The horses wound down the canyons for close to an hour. Joanna listened for the rustle of a creek. Instead of a rustle, she began to hear a roar and breaking through a clump of trees she looked in amazement at another small but beautiful waterfall. They dismounted and let the horses drink. Joanna sat in the sun on a large boulder beside the pool. She was sensing something dream like, a powerful sensation of something spiritual, of being in tune with everything around her. She felt a passive force and looked about her, nothing tangible; wild roses grew along the banks as well as chokecherry and pussy willows. Small stands of quaking aspen and willows lined the gurgling stream flowing away from the pond.

The horses, satisfied at last, lifted their dripping muzzles from the water. They looked around, ears pricked.

Madison helped the women up. "We'd best be gettin' back, time is gettin' along fast."

Joanna followed Madison for a short distance, then suddenly turned her mount and walked him back to the pool. Annie and Madison waited for her return.

"I had to take one last look, it is so magical, what do they call this place?" she asked.

"Fairy Dell," stated Madison.

"What a lovely name, I must come back one day."

"Oh bother," she muttered as she pricked her finger. Joanna laid her hoop of embroidery down and held a handkerchief to the droplet of blood. "I seem to have trouble doing everything lately. I cannot concentrate." A deep sadness engulfed her. Her mother's latest letter indicated how scandalous twenty year old Joanna was…neither married nor had a suitor in mind.

"Ah, Mama, you and your gilded life! If you only knew I have lost my true love by committing the unforgivable. I contradicted and humiliated, not only Phillip, but Uncle John as well. I will not marry well if at all."

Joanna picked up the correspondence and walked through the vast room. The house smelled of lemon and beeswax, of fresh flowers and baked bread. The help had polished and cleaned everything to a high sheen. Elyce and Timber were arriving tomorrow with an entourage. Lady Adelaide and her maid, as well as Elyce's nurse and maid and another couple who were close friends of Timber's. Uncle John and Frieda were departing by the end of the month.

Peering out the large windows, Joanna saw large thunderheads building over the mountains. The wind had come up and it felt like rain.

"Oh, I do hope it will be nice tomorrow for their arrival," she said aloud to herself.

"It will be, these storms pass quickly and are really very refreshing," Frieda responded behind her.

Joanna started and turned, "Oh, I didn't know you were in the room."

"You are anxious to see your sister, yes?" smiled Frieda

"Oh, yes, it has been so long and so dreadful for her. I do hope she is happy now...but of course she is! Timber is a wonderful man," replied Joanna with feeling.

A brilliant flash of lightning lit up the room followed by a crash of thunder. "Here it comes," Frieda said.

Rain began pelting the windows and within minutes rivulets of water were running in the driveway.

Joanna got her wish. The morning of Elyce's arrival, the day dawned bright and sunny. Joanna paced nervously until she saw the dust clouds signaling the approaching carriages. Once in the driveway, Joanna rushed down to the leading carriage.

Timber handed Elyce down. She was dressed in blue from her bonnet to her toes and a heavy veil of netting covered her face.

The sisters fell into each other's arms and openly wept. John waited on the veranda to welcome the party to Locket Springs.

"Heavens, I was told to expect a log house, but, Uncle John, this is a splendid mansion! It is astonishingly huge and what a profusion of trees and shrubs and flowers! I shall love walking about and admiring all the beauty!" Elyce exclaimed mopping her eyes under her veil.

John introduced Frieda who was quietly waiting in the receiving hall.

"Welcome, welcome, would you like tea or would you rather be shown to your rooms?" she asked.

"Oh, I would like to freshen up a bit," answered Lady Adelaide and Elyce agreed that would be her wish, also.

Joanna led Elyce upstairs to her room. Timber and the help followed lugging trunks. Elyce's nurse hovered about her, removing glove, cloak and finally the bonnet and veiling. Her lovely blond hair was pulled back into a chignon and she turned to face Joanna. The left side of her face was the lovely Elyce, but the right side was puckered with faint pink and purple scars.

Joanna gasped involuntarily and her hand covered her mouth. "Oh, dearest sister, that vile monster!"

"Don't distress yourself so, Joanna. I have become accustomed to my disfigurement. I have hats and veiling in most colors so I do not shock the public. I am alive, I have my love and I am indeed fortunate. Now, you must be happy for me—no pity—promise?"

Joanna hugged her sister close and kissed her scarred cheek. "I will never mention it again, I promise." She then flopped on a settee and for over an hour the women exchanged news.

In the following days Joanna and Ella took Lady Adelaide and Elyce about the property. They oohed and aahed over the schoolhouse, the glorious views of the mountains and fell in love with the many animals.

Joanna found she had no misgivings over the relationship between Timber and her sister. It was obvious they adored each other and he doted on Elyce's every whim. Her beautiful eyes sparkled with happiness.

"I have such a wonderful feeling of freedom here. I think I can go about in this wilderness and not wear veiling. Am I being insensitive to other people's feelings around me, Joanna?"

"Fiddle, we out here in the west accept the person, not the looks and not the clothes. I have learned that much," snorted Joanna, "be yourself and forget the scars, I am hardly aware of them until you call attention to yourself."

Frieda gave a resplendent dinner two evenings before her and John's departure. Guests included Lord Durstan from the Thunder Valley Ranch and Lord and Lady Milhaven who owned a extensive spread upon which sat a massive stone castle. It was rumored Lord Milhaven fashioned the castle after one he had in England. It was also rumored he was losing money by the day because of poor management.

Joanna was seated next to the *picturesque* Lady Iris Milhaven. Before marrying Lord Milhaven she had been a wealthy widow named Iris Myrtle

Hobbs. It was obvious the Lord had been smitten with her multi millions and she was overdressed to the point of being garish. The sparkle of diamonds everywhere on her person failed to dim the mustache, moles and huge eyebrows that adorned her rounded face. Nevertheless, Joanna found herself enjoying Lady Iris's humor.

"My dear, you must shop around for a title, ready made American cash buys good Anglican blood. Many English aristocrats are down at the knees and if one has lots of tin, you can take your pick of the English marriage market."

"I think I shall bide my time," answered Joanna, recalling grimly her engagement to an Englishman.

"Don't wait too long, child, with your beauty you might just bag a prince!"

Joanna laughed and turned to the other diners. John sat at the head of the table and Elyce sat to his left. Her lovely right profile was exposed to the guests and the disfigured side to her uncle. Timber sat on John's right.

Formality and order ruled at this dinner. Frieda had made certain the dinner was ceremonial with rows of entree dishes filling the table. She was the perfect hostess in a dress of pink satin lavishly trimmed with Alencon lace.

Joanna mused to herself, *Shall I ever be as happy as those around me tonight? I doubt it, there always seems to be a heartbreak ahead for me.*

She heard Phillip's name mentioned and immediately came back to reality.

Timber was talking to John. She held her breathe as she listened to her uncle.

"No, Phillip decided not to sell Snowflake, he is bringing a remuda of his father's prized horses up north for safekeeping."

"Is Don Luis having problems?" Timber inquired.

"It is politics, Timber. Their vast land holdings are rich in water rights and newcomers, immigrants, and what have you want these large land grants. Supposedly our government is protecting owners, but the smaller land owners are being driven off their property under the guise of range wars. If the ranch owner doesn't have enough men to protect his spread, the law politely looks the other way, especially, if it pertains to Spanish Grants."

Timber frowned as he listened to John's explanation. "That's disgusting, people like Phillip's family have worked the land for years, clearing and cultivating plus adding their culture to our nation."

"Yes, it is sad and a grave situation, but America will always have problems because of the diversity of backgrounds. For the most part, we each possess a different heritage and want to copy the motherland. Our forefathers brought their prejudices and ideals with them and raised us to acknowledge them. Look at the fiasco of the Civil War. Granted, there should not be slavery, but the utter disregard for the South by the North after the war will be remembered forever. Possibly had President Lincoln lived it would have gone differently. There should have been help for the freed slaves, schools and jobs. The southern states should have adequate funds to begin rebuilding. They were left scarred earth that became the carpetbaggers. Banks should have made loans and some brotherhood should have prevailed. What happened...the South became more of a nation within than ever! It is part of this nation and we have only heaped more poverty and more disgrace to a shamed union. Sherman's outrageous acts left the South bitter and defiant. Who will feel the brunt of this? The black man and the white man...they will pay for freedom again and again for each must lay the blame on something, so...why not each other?"

"True, but does this mean as a nation we will never stand as one?"

"I doubt it. People suffer guilt just living...if too wealthy, if impoverished; if illiterate...being Irish, or Italian, or German...it goes on and on. The Americans will always envy Europe and therefore will never give up their heritage. How can cultures fuse if not willing to give up their racial background? Can you live in harmony with thirty countries in one city?"

"Yes, I believe so, if we can learn to respect our differences," answered Timber, toying with a glass. "That is what is so unique about this country, we are multifaceted."

"Then there is the question of the Irish, scorned beyond belief, refused in homes and public places. There are areas set aside for them befitting an animal not a human, what of that?" John inquired.

"Hmmm. yes, that is true, I have heard of Irish changing their surnames to survive, just to be hired in respectable jobs. Has this happened because of relations between England and Ireland or because of the Irish being tenants in the potato blight?"

Lord Milhaven, his beard twitching, spoke to this, "Unrest in Ireland has intensified. The Irish seem to have no strength left after the Parnell O'Shea scandal. Gladstone's replacement by Rosebery may help. Ireland is a sore and stricken country, the immigrants are truly impoverished and in a sad state. Many have moved to England as indentured servants. On a cultural level they are just about a rung above the freed slaves."

Frieda sensing tension building among her guests interrupted, "Really,

John, can this discourse continue after you gentlemen retire to the smoking room?"

"Of course, my dear, politics should be discussed over a good cigar and a fine cognac, say what?" John gestured to the men and they retired to the library.

"Ladies, would you care for more café or a cordial?" Frieda politely asked.

"Definitely a cordial," answered Lady Iris. "If the gentlemen want to solve world problems, what can we solve?"

Elyce grinned at her reply, "Not much, I'm afraid, we are only women and we know our place."

Frieda lifted her cordial and smiled, "To the manor born, child."

"Pardon…" Elyce said, an eyebrow quirked.

"My dear, you are from the manor bred and born into wealth and society. I was, also and we were taught a lady's place is to submit and never question a gentleman's decision. I used to think as you do, my family was wealthy and eccentric and never questioned a gentleman's word. One highly regarded gentleman brought down Prussia.

When I came to America I learned all men sat, sleep and drink accordingly. The gentlemen I had known in Europe, other than father, did not have to work. In America I have found gentle hard working men who understand themselves, my John is one of them. These men don't intimidate women; they actually listen and appreciate a woman's view. Your husband is also in that category. Dear Elyce, surely you realize how fortunate you are?"

Joanna empathized with Frieda. She felt righteous anger over the circumstances that had brought she, herself here. A wicked man under the guise of an aristocrat had raped and ruined her life. The same person had maimed Elyce and she was ostracized from society, not because of disfigurement but because of a divorce. Marshall had beaten her, caused her to miscarry, and had liaisons. Who ended up being punished…Elyce, because she was a woman!

Looking over at Elyce, she saw tears brimming in her eyes.

Elyce replied in a stricken voice, "I know how fortunate I am to have Timber, Frieda. You also know it is hard to undo one's upbringing. The hurtful way in which so many friends acted was almost more than I could bear. When Father died our family became outcasts. Marshall treated me with scorn and shame from that day on. I had prized my social standing and I was quite taken with my social status, after all, that was the way I had been raised!

It is still hard at times. I feel myself full of quilt at ruining Marshall's social standing." With that, Elyce released a shuddering sigh.

"Oh, Mein Gott! What have I done?" Frieda cried, rushing to Elyce. "Oh, my darling!" She sat beside Elyce and pulled her to her. "Forgive me, I did not mean to insult you, I just get so angry at men sometimes."

Joanna had also left her seat and laid a protective hand on her sister's back.

Lady Iris broke the tension. "Blessed Mother, let us forget the male animal. I want to discuss all the new and fashionable things. I purchased two bicycles; they are really all the cat's meow! Lillian Russell used one in her show; diamonds inlaid in the spokes...what a sight to behold!"

Joanna replied, "Both Elyce and I had bicycles and lovely biking costumes. We had wonderful times riding in the park, didn't we Elyce?"

"Oh, yes, it was such great fun! We even convinced Mama to try riding but the pantaloons were not to her taste. She never forbid us to go, but her body language certainly made it very apparent she was not in favor of it," smiled Elyce through her tears.

"I suppose one might try riding a bicycle here, but it would need to be a smooth path," laughed Joanna.

"I think I will leave these paths to the bovines, I would rather not meet one of them at any time. They do frighten me!" commented Lady Iris. Holding up her glass she said, "Frieda, I do believe this calls for another cordial!"

"Certainly, I will attend to it immediately. We will drink to this land and it's lovely women!"

The ladies joined Joanna around the Pianoforte. They sang the newest melodies and were later joined by the men who harmonized with them.

The evening ended on a happy note, if not a tipsy one!

CHAPTER THREE

It was early September and Joanna was getting the little school cleaned as lessons would begin within the month. For weeks she had been tutoring Willie in her spare time with the McGuffey's Eclectic Reader and he was beginning to show some progress. Willie tried so hard that Joanna was deeply moved. He was ecstatic when he learned a new word; his sweet voice full of happiness and blue eyes misty with unshed tears.

Elyce had come to the little schoolhouse and was seated at Joanna's desk, writing busily with papers spread about her. She filled a page, signed it with a flourish, blotted it and lay down her pen.

"I am done, Jo, I have finished all my correspondence! I always despair writing to Mama, she is so severe in her criticism," stated Elyce flatly.

Joanna was tutoring Willie and said softly, "Willie, we are finished for today and you did exceptionally well. Run along, dear, and we will read again tomorrow."

As soon as he exited the front door she remarked to Elyce, "Dear, Mama cannot help being Mama....you know, proper etiquette, socializing and being disagreeable."

Elyce began to laugh, "You are wicked Joanna, but it is indeed true. She makes everyone around her so uneasy. I always feel like a naughty child."

"Our saving grace is Gram. No one bests that dear soul. She always makes me feel special and pretty enough and good enough. What a blessing she was when Daddy died. Whenever we have needed support, who stepped in but Gram, always filled with comfort and tender assurances of help. In looking back, she had to have grieved terribly in private as Daddy was her son and so special to her."

"Yes, and Mother would have gone mad had it not been for her," mused Elyce. "I miss Gram dreadfully. I hope I shall see her once again in this lifetime." Joanna looked up quickly with a sad light in her eyes.

"My poor darling, how hard it has been for you so far from everyone and truly isolated here!" Elyce declared.

"Pooh, listen to yourself. You, who have walked through such adversity and pain! Oh, Elyce, you have been so strong and I admire you so. It is so wonderful to have you here!"

With that Elyce rose and came around the desk and hugged Joanna to her. She pulled back and looked at Joanna with great tenderness.

"I was so petted and cared for, I really felt guilt if I pitied myself. When I realized how loved I was by Timber and his mother, it made my shameful exile from friends easier."

"That is what is so wrong with society; men dictate our lives…possess women and children. Marshall was a dishonorable beast and betrayed you…yet you became the scourge of society. You were the model of an obedient wife and a loving and caring one. Where is the justice?"

Elyce wearily declared, "All that will change some day. Gram brought me a very special visitor one day. I was so impressed with her. A beautiful soft sweet soul with such intelligence. She began the Women's Suffrage Movement. She gave me her book called *Solitude of Self*, which I will give to you to read. Her name is Elizabeth Cady Stanton."

"But I thought Susan Brownell Anthony launched the suffrage movement."

"No, Mrs. Stanton began it. She and Susan Anthony were very good friends and have been working on the movement for some time. The last I heard Mrs. Stanton is going to devout her time now to work on a *National Woman's Bible* while Susan Anthony carries on the Suffrage Movement."

"It will take many strong souls to change society. Too late for your justice, though."

Putting her small hand across Joanna's mouth Elyce said, "Shhh, dear, now I have the love of a lifetime. Every hour I spend with Timber is beautiful. I am filled with genuine happiness and our souls are as one. I wish there had been no one before him and I do, at times, long to have my looks back for him. Otherwise, I am happy and content."

Joanna nodded without speaking. *Yes,* she thought to herself, *Timber never tired of looking at Eyce with adoring eyes. Both he and Elyce wore their love like shining mantles.*

"I pray I shall be as happy one day, but I seriously doubt it," said Joanna in a miserable voice. She had given her heart away and her soul grieved with endless longing.

"Someone has arrived, listen to the dogs baying!" Elyce cried as she hastily put on her straw and veiling.

A carriage was indeed pulling into the driveway. Joanna and Elyce began walking arm in arm up the long driveway.

"Do you recognize the buggy, Jo?" asked Elyce.

"No, but then I am no authority on carriages."

"Oh, My!" exclaimed Joanna suddenly, eyes wide as she saw the tall elegant figure step out of the buggy. Even at this distance she recognized Phillip!

"Jupiter, Elyce, it is Phillip de La Cruz from the Snowflake Ranch! I cannot go on!" She whispered in a frantic voice.

Elyce looked at Joanna in surprise, a smile beginning. "Who is this Phillip? Joanna?"

"Oh, dear, it is a long story, I will tell you later. He is merely a friend at present."

"Hmmm, well darling, you must not be rude, I insist you introduce me," said Elyce with a twinkle in her eye. She came to the conclusion quickly that this Phillip must be important for Joanna to be so flushed and rattled.

They entered through the back entrance, checked their appearances before a mirror and proceeded to the main room. Timber and Phillip stood as they entered.

Joanna behaved with exemplary propriety and called for tea. Her heart was hammering against her ribs and she feared she might faint. Trying to keep her composure Joanna seated herself and asked with a conciliatory air, "It has been ages, Phillip. How are things at Snowflake?"

To her delight Phillip answered her graciously, his blue eyes friendly. "We are busy, Joanna, preparing barns and laying in for winter."

Lady Adelaide joined them and Timber presented Phillip to his mother.

The tea cart arrived piled with watercress sandwiches and small cakes. While Joanna poured, Lady Adelaide filled and passed the china plates.

Timber spoke as he sipped his tea. "As soon as the hay is stacked here, we are going to assist Phillip. He has been on a long drive. We will all go for a few days to Snowflake. Perhaps, Joanna, you could postpone school for a few days and help Elyce prepare meals for the workers."

Elyce dimpled and answered before Joanna could get in a word. "Of course, darling, it will be fun to help. It will be educational to see what preparations you make for winter, right, Jo?"

"Well, I suppose…"

Joanna looked up to see Phillip quizzically arching an eyebrow. She shook out a napkin and covered her features as she smiled to herself. She would devote herself to gratifying him, anything to gain his respect back. She could hardly breathe she was so overcome with happiness. She also, could not take a bite of food; her stomach was misbehaving.

Timber suggested they take a stroll. Lady Adelaide declined; Joanna went for parasols and gloves.

Elyce stood looking up at the wide staircase as Joanna came bouncing down with hats and parasols.

"Well, here we are…" Joanna smiled; her color bright.

"Off we go then," said Elyce, carefully adjusting her veil and hat.

They pulled mantles about their shoulders and joined the men standing on the veranda.

Timber was pointing toward the Springs. "Lots of game this year, I have been watching with binoculars as they come down for water. The hunting parties will be pleased." Then as an after thought, "Phillip, if you are so inclined, I would appreciate your assisting me when the hunt begins."

"I would be glad to. I imagine the shooters, for the most part, are experienced."

"I would hope the two largest groups are. Elyce, you will have to put your social skills to good use."

As they began to walk, Elyce discretely asked, "Is dinner usually formal during the hunts?"

"On return, yes, we are in camp about five days. A few of the gents bring wives so you will entertain some."

"How lovely, we can have pheasant, partridge and beefsteak. Salmon and turbot can be shipped by rail as well as some vegetables. Then there also are saddles of mutton and venison, sirloins of beef and turkeys. Do we have Stilton and Camber cheeses? Uncle John's wine cellar is extensive so there will be sherry and liqueurs!" she answered excitedly.

"Whoa, darling, the meals do not have to be that formal! This is the country and they will be staying in the hunting lodge so perhaps nice suppers would be fine."

"Fine, then, Annie can help and Jo when she finishes classes. By the way, where is Annie, Jo?"

"She and Buck went to Stirrup Crossing to pick up material for her curtains. We must ride out soon and see what they need; they will marry in three weeks!"

Phillip tucked Joanna's arm through his and she felt her heart turn over. "Well, my swan, you haven't flown away."

"Most observant, sir."

"I had feared you might have gone. You are giving up all the social graces and the big city, then?"

Joanna withdrew her arm from his. Her voice was cool and composed. "I hate to be patronized, sir. I have already taken great advantage of my uncle's generosity. I would like to be independent and being indebted oppresses me."

"Your reasoning is very sound. So you wish to continue your teaching?"

"For now, yes."

"Hmmm, sounds as if the swan might become an old bird!" mocked Phillip with a smile.

"Oh, yes, that is a fate worse than death…to never marry, no children, to be an old maid…how socially unacceptable!" exploded Joanna twirling her parasol in anger.

"Joanna, how wicked you are!" scolded Elyce. "You are insulting our guest and being inhospitable!"

"I apologize. I fear I will never rule my tongue. Sometimes my actions seem misjudged if I defend myself! I wish I were as captivating and as sparkly as some people I know." Joanna glowered at Elyce and continued, "I shall be very guarded in my conversation in the future."

"As if that's likely," laughed Elyce.

Phillip was confounded by Joanna.

He looked down at this lovely woman with such a sharp tongue. He had intended waiting until a future date to see her but Timber and he had been close friends for years and he needed his advice. After losing his wife, Timber had Phillip work with him occasionally surveying. Timber had listened quietly to Phillip when he was entirely broken and the world had become an empty wilderness. One day Timber spoke of the Holan girls and the lovely sister who haunted his dreams. When she married, Phillip in turn had consoled him.

Timber had talked at length about both girls to Phillip and they became very real to Phillip long before he met Joanna. Of course, he was taken back at how she resembled her cousin but that was only momentarily. That was possibly why he felt comfortable in proposing. He now understood why she had felt rushed but still failed to understand her being so unreasonable. She was such a regal beauty, one could see it in the lines of her figure…the graceful hands, the glory of her hair and that lovely face resting on its swan neck. She was so unconscious of her looks it lent a certain charm to her. At present she looked very much like a chastened little girl. Her violet eyes were sparkling with unshed tears and her cheeks a blooming pink.

Phillip, from the beginning, had also noted a shadow of pain that touched her lovely face, a saddened expression that lay deep in her eyes. He attributed all this to the death of her father and the tragic accident of Elyce's. Now, he wondered if something had happened to Joanna, herself, personally...something that haunted her. She was terrified of being dependent, beholden to anyone, even family. He heard Elyce's tinkling laughter and saw that she and Timber were watching two squirrels and their antics. "They are making a last effort for food before settling in for the winter," Timber laughed.

Elyce had been shrouded in veiling but she now draped it back over her straw. She beamed up at her husband with love. "Isn't this the most heavenly place, darling?" she asked. The two were quite unconscious of anyone but each other.

"Well, Joanna, your sister seems happy. Timber, also. He has adored her for a long time," stated Phillip.

"Yes, I am so happy for both of them. They are both such deserving people."

With a desperate sort of patience Phillip said, "Joanna, sometimes people say no when they mean yes and drive a person out of their wits just for excitement. Have you done that?"

"No, Phillip, I never intended to hurt you or make you care; it just happened! I was in shock when you approached Uncle John. You don't know me. I am not good enough." There was a choke that could not be controlled.

Phillip stopped short, and caught both her hands, releasing the parasol.

"Now, let's be reasonable, we can begin this relationship over however you wish. You have only to name it, dear lady. I will try not to rush you or disappoint you. I care deeply for you."

"You must know this, then. I don't believe I shall ever marry. I treasure my liberty. I am very fond of you and if we can be friends I would like that." Joanna's heart stood still, if only she could tell him she had been disgraced, but she could not utter this dark secret to anyone.

Her answer was like flame to paper. Phillip face darkened, he looked at her as if he could not believe his ears, and then turned sharply away.

"There will come a time when you love someone enough to live and die for him...then you will marry. I shall not approach you again." Phillip straightened himself and walked stiffly ahead. Joanna drew a long breath and followed silently behind him. She felt as if she had been stabbed for she knew Phillip would never pursue the subject again.

It was difficult for Joanna to be gracious at dinner that evening. She did not want to provoke unpleasantness. She had to bite her tongue at times when Timber and Phillip began discussing women becoming secretaries and tellers. She felt Phillip was bringing up the subject of working women to antagonize her and to her despair both men felt women had no place in offices or banks. She felt the narrow, unchanging convictions of most males of the nineties acutely. Joanna stared at Phillip across the table, his handsome face was animated and he was deeply in his discussion with Timber. *Damn him,* thought Joanna, *why do I adore him so? Because...he is charming, well educated, speaks languages fluently, rides beautifully, dances gracefully and is the most beautiful man I have ever seen.....yet, he is insufferable.*

Phillip turned and his eyes met Joanna's, a dazzling smile was directed at her, her heart thudded and her breathe caught.

"My dear swan, you are so quiet tonight, and what can I do to bring a sparkle to those lovely violet eyes?" He grinned wickedly and his blue eyes twinkled.

Elyce sweetly said, "She asks nothing for herself but understanding. She never asks for favors and always thinks of others first. She is an absolute dear."

"Oh, please, Elyce! He is teasing and makes light of my considering some independence. We all know a well bred woman does not speak out or have opinions. I find that utterly shameful!"

Timber interjected, "We are hearing the phrase everywhere that 'women are winning the vote and losing the man.' Is this what God intended?"

"Not you, Timber? I certainly did not sense your demanding Elyce to obey your every whim!" retorted Joanna indignantly.

"I don't. Elyce and I have great respect for each other's opinions and ideas."

"Will you allow her to vote?"

"If she so desires."

Elyce pleaded with her. "Please Joanna; don't be so defensive, you take such offense to seemingly off hand remarks. Dearest, dear, you presume to feel some remarks are directed at you, it isn't true. That is why it is best gentlemen discuss matters privately over brandy and cigars."

"Oh, bother, I do not possess the marvelously gentle character you have, Elyce. I promise to try not to offer an opinion again."

Phillip looked at her over his goblet. Joanna lifted her eyes to him and smiled. They stared fixedly at each other with a desperate hunger.

•

Somehow, Phillip thought, *swarming in that jumbling brain was a hurt frightened girl longing to be loved, but afraid...afraid of who or what? Why pursue this, she can only mean more heartache and trouble. That beautiful face is masking emotions he had once seen and felt in his arms. She had been on fire with desire and love. Then the wall had gone up when he asked for her hand in marriage, why? She is always on the defensive and it was becoming boring.*

He shrugged the idea of trying to understand her and spoke, "It is touching to see one take such an interest in people and politics, but, lovely lady, you shouldn't concern your lovely head with such mundane matters. Tonight let us enjoy the excellent cuisine and company." His smile was indulgent as he looked at this confounding, exasperating woman!

Joanna's smile vanished. She looked at Phillip, incredulous. "I do not consider politics and people mundane, Phillip! I must learn and understand to teach my students!" Her lips parted in an expression of disdain and her eyes sparked like flames of violet.

"Oh, Jo, really!" snapped Elyce. "Phillip is our guest and I hardly think it is necessary to make him defend his beliefs at this table."

Joanna sprang from her seat, "If I may be excused." She threw down her napkin and ran from the room. Elyce also excused herself and followed Joanna up to her room.

"What on earth are you doing?" she demanded. "Every time this man utters a word, you insult him!"

"I honestly cannot help myself. He enrages me so, and I adore him which angers me even more!"

"You perfect little fool!" Elyce hissed, shaking her. "No man wants a woman wearing the pants in the family, why can't you understand that? With love and respect you can tame the wildest heart!"

Exasperated, Elyce turned to leave the room. At the door she stopped. "I am going to apologize and state that you are not feeling well. I don't understand your behavior. I know Daddy's death changed our lives and profoundly and you have not been the same since. We are here for you, Timber and me. We will help you in any way possible, but we mustn't be rude to guests, regardless."

Joanna was all apologies, "I promise I will not embarrass you again. I have much to involve myself with. School is about to begin and I have Annie to think about. I shall miss her dreadfully."

"Silly, Gram is sending you another maid. She wrote me of this, her name is Hannah."

"I don't want a maid!"

"By the loving God, Joanna, whatever! You are so contrary!" Elyce flounced out the door in a swirl of skirts.

Joanna flung herself across her bed, weeping and pounding the coverlet. "If you only knew, Elyce, I am deflowered and by your ex husband! He has ruined my life!"

CHAPTER FOUR

Summer danced into fall changing her colors from green to golden oranges and reds. The evening and morning skies were colored with rose, pearl and lavender tints, heralding the coming winter.

Annie and Buck were married in a quiet ceremony at Locket Springs. Annie's brother arrived from Chicago to give the bride away. Father Flavin of Stirrup Springs performed the Roman Catholic ceremony.

Joanna shed tears of happiness and sorrow. She and Annie were closer in many ways than sisters and parting was difficult. Annie would still be in the area as John had deeded twenty-five acres to Buck and Annie as a wedding present. The hands and Buck had built a two bedroom house on the property located in the southeastern corner of the ranch. Annie would continue to work three days a week at the big house while Buck kept busy with his overseer position. Joanna knew that Annie belonged to someone else now and her allegiance would be totally to her husband. Somehow, Joanna felt the odd one out now.

A letter arrived that changed everything. It was from Kate who wrote of Winifred's ball.

> *My dearest darlings;*
>
> *Your mother is too exhausted to write therefore I will. Winifred's coming out was a tremendous success. The creme de creme of society attended from here and New York City. It was held at the magnificent blue and gold Theatre Royale. Winnie was lovely in her white satin and John gave her a necklace of diamonds and pink pearls. John looked resplendent and Frieda was very well received. She was lovely in her silver and blue brocade.*
>
> *I confess I did not feel any great desire to attend, but once there I did enjoy the spectacle. The new fashionable*

decolletage was compensated for by a bounty of jewels. Never have I seen such an array of half covered breasts except on a plucked hen. And the jewels....tiaras, necklaces, rings and earrings, some with stones as large as pigeon eggs! Women were drowning in diamonds, sapphires and rubies. Many wore girdles of diamonds around their waists, even some gentlemen wore enormous collars of diamonds, imagine! I find the new fashions truly vulgar.

Dear Ella sat wide eyed with her vigilant chaperone. I like that girl, she reminds me of the two of you at that age.

I hope Winifred's popularity will not lead to over confidence. I realize she is spoilt and I keep reminding her of this much to her dismay.

Unfortunately, I must report a shocking circumstance. I was inclined early to retire from the ball and was about to pay my respects to Frieda and John when I spied Winifred dancing with, horrors, Marshall Davenport! Immediately I went to your mother to protest and make known my disapproval. She informed me he was again the darling of society and it would have been a breach of etiquette had she not included him. I was appalled, and certainly, you both know of my generalized animosity toward him. His despicable treatment of Elyce was that of a total cad. I am still venting my frustration over this and John has told me repeatedly that he, also, was shocked at seeing him in the receiving line, but could not ruin the evening for Winifred.

Even more disturbing, Marshall called on Winifred following the ball! John's reaction this time was one of horrified shock and anger and he forbade Winifred to ever receive him again.

She is such a flirtatious girl and loves defying authority. I pray she will heed her father's advice. That scoundrel has caused enough dark days in our family.

Dear little Hannah should be arriving shortly with Genevieve, Frieda's new housekeeper.

Darling Jo, I can well imagine how upsetting all of this is to you with Annie leaving, but you now have Elyce and Marshall with you. You are always welcome to return here.

Pray do not complicate your life if you find the west not to your liking.

My dear Elyce, I am so happy you are enjoying your stay at the ranch. It must be a delightful contrast from the city. I was much impressed by your descriptions of the picturesque mountains.

Please give my dearest regards to Lady Adelaide and Timber. I must end this note. I shall write more at a later time.

Ever,
Your adoring Grandmother Kate

Elyce, having read the letter aloud to Joanna folded it back into its envelope. She then stood up, her eyes narrowed and her hands clenched. Her scarred face was red with emotion. "Sweet Mary, how can she do this to me? After all that horrid man put me through, I will never understand Mama! Jo, whatever am I to do?" asked Elyce, tears spilling down her face.

Joanna stood and Elyce sobbed into her arms. "Shhh, you are here and he can never hurt you again. Timber and Uncle John would kill him first, to say nothing about what I would do," Joanna whispered in a consoling voice.

Elyce wiped her eyes and walked to a window. She crossed her arms in front of her and visibly trembled with emotion. "I will never treat a child as she has us. She uses people and then discards them if they cannot live up to her expectations. She is now putting all her wiles to work for Winifred."

"I wish I had some answers. I can only defend her in saying that the tragic progression of events in our family may have affected her thinking. Mama has always been one to run from reality and seems to embrace the unthinkable. With both of us gone she probably is living now through Winifred," Joanna surmised.

"Be that as it may, she is telling the world that I was at fault by sending an invitation to Marshall. I will never forgive her…my God, my own mother!"

"You have the love of a wonderful man and your future is ahead of you. You will have more happiness that you ever dreamed possible. You must come to terms with this and not allow it to take precedence over Timber."

"I know Jo, but it hurts so. I am blessed to have you and Timber."

At that moment Timber strode into the room carrying a bouquet of autumn mums and asters for Elyce.

Elyce gave him a sickly smile and he rushed to her, "What is it, darling? Are you ill?" His grey eyes were filled with concern as he turned to Joanna, "What has happened?"

Joanna handed him the letter and left the room. She hurried upstairs and began a letter,

> *Dear Mama,*
>
> *I am certain you must be aware of how deeply your actions have offended Elyce. I am at a loss to understand why you invited Marshall Davenport to Winifred's Ball. What you have done is dreadful and entirely unjustified I hope, in time, she will forgive you. I can only suggest that you write her a letter of explanation.*
>
> *Ever,*
> *Your obedient daughter, Joanna*

In the following weeks Elyce seemed close to a nervous collapse. Timber, Lady Adelaide and Joanna made certain one or the other was always at her side. Joanna worried continually while she was in the classroom and hurried home the minute the students were safely on their way. Finally Elyce rallied and gradually began to smile and take an interest in life again.

One day, at school, Joanna was pleasantly surprised by a visit from her sister who had just returned from town. They went inside the school leaving the outdoor players to whoop and holler in a game of Red Rover.

Elyce looked positively glowing and her blue eyes were glistening once again. Joanna could not remember when she had looked so radiant. "Whatever has happened to you?" asked Joanna, wide-eyed.

"As you know, Timber took me to Stirrup Springs for a few days. He shopped for provisions and then insisted I see Dr. Tuttle for a checkup. Well, my dearest sister, you are going to be an aunt!"

It took Joanna a minute to comprehend what Elyce was relating. "Oh, my goodness, you must sit down! I will make a cup of tea! Imagine…you a mother! Oh, my, this is just so exciting!" exclaimed Joanna.

"I am not staying; I just had to tell you, I could not wait a minute longer. The good Lord has answered my prayers; I was in such a state of despair and now I am delirious with happiness. Timber's child, oh, I will love him dearly!"

"So, already it is a boy?"

"Hopefully, but I do not care as long as it is healthy!"

"You are not afoot?"

"No, Timber is waiting with the buggy. I will see you later, dear."

The sisters embraced and Elyce left for the big house.

When Joanna closed the school later that afternoon she hurried up the lane anxious to see Elyce. She found her ensconced like a little old lady in front of a dancing fire sipping tea. Elyce motioned to a settee.

"You are not feeling well?"

"Oh, I am perfectly fine, inside and out." Elyce looked out the huge windows and sighed, "It is another world here, is it not? That other world seems like a dream, all that formal entertaining and the social events and belonging to the upper crust society." A shadow crossed Elyce face for an instant and then it was gone.

"You miss it, don't you? You loved to entertain and attend the opera and the balls?"

"Yes, I enjoyed the social whirl. I must be like Mama in that respect."

"I am sorry, El."

"Don't be, it can never be again. I am a divorcee and a marked woman. Country life suits me and Timber loves this land so. We will make our home eventually somewhere out here." She turned and looked at Joanna intently. "You should return east, your potential for fulfillment is so limited here."

"I should hate going back! You were always the self assured and confident daughter while I never enjoyed the soirees. I felt different and very uncomfortable. You and Mama were so regal and looked so comfortable in your skin. It made me feel incompetent, my confidence would seep away as events progressed and invariably I would make a social blunder. Being here I have become more outgoing and learned to welcome the world. My pupils demand attention. Forgetting myself has gotten me over a lot of anxiety and negative self talk."

"I am shocked. I always thought you were such a stately person. You conducted yourself with such a confident air!"

"It was a good act for I shook inside. I am rather like most of the transplants here. I have become attached to this beautiful country. There are too many grievous memories associated with the east. Gram I dearly love and miss and I must return to see her one day."

"Yes, she would like that. She worries about your happiness."

"I have been so fortunate in having Uncle John, well, actually we both have. How did Papa go so wrong and Uncle John be so well off?"

"Joanna, first of all, Uncle John is the eldest son of the eldest son. That is called primogeniture and, therefore, he inherited the family fortune. He made wise investments in trade, railroads, banking, gold, silver, shipping, real estate...."

"Papa invested, too!"

"Yes, but Papa gambled and he did not invest wisely. He loved the horses, gambled at the races and gambled with stock. It was a game to him. Usually if he lost stock he bought again and was lucky, but he lost too much over that last year. I believe he tried to come back as he had in the past. His pride was his downfall. He borrowed against everything when he should have gone to Gram or Uncle John. I suppose destiny had decreed that Papa would end it the way he did."

"Don't you miss him? I do terribly."

"Of course. I will never forgive the act, but I loved him. He obviously was a self indulgent person or he would have considered what he was doing to us as a family."

"Dear, you must quit living in the past. You have to accept what happened with Papa and put it in God's hands to judge. You must let go and get on with living. We all can live with could have beens or should have beens, but that is the part of life that is a mystery."

Joanna could not help bursting into tears, for Elyce's candor had entirely undid her. She felt an icy barrier beginning to dissolve within her that had been erected at her terror of being hurt. Her need for love poured through her.

She felt Phillip's tenderness and love and knew she needed him as a soul mate as well as physically. Warmth surged through her body. I am through with mourning and pity, I will seek my love! She smiled through her tears at Elyce and then hugged her tenderly.

"I am fine. I am going to my room to meditate."

That weekend Phillip brought a beautiful mare at Timber's request. He had told Phillip of his desire to purchase a horse for Elyce. Timber, Elyce, Phillip and Joanna stood at the doorway of the horse barn and watched the animal being led about the yard. She was a beautiful white mare, bridled and carrying a velvet blue side saddle.

Phillip stated, "Her mother was bred in New Mexico from the purest Andalusian stock. She was raised at Casa de Flores. She is well schooled, will move to a whisper and her mouth is as soft as silk. I know you wished to make a purchase for Elyce. I would like to make a gift of her to you, my good friends."

Timber replied, "You are most generous, my friend. Elyce will not be riding for some time. We have learned she is in the family way so we will have to postpone an animal for the time being."

"My heartiest congratulations to both of you!" replied Phillip, delighted.

While the niceties were being exchanged Joanna went to the mare. She caressed the curved neck and stroked her muzzle; the mare reacted with a gentle blowing. Joanna crooned low love talk and ran her hand gently under her mane. The mare tossed her head and neighed softly, it was love at first sight for the two of them.

"You are magnificent, splendid....oh, how I wish you were mine."

Joanna leaned against the mare's neck and could feel her pulse and strength. Joanna's throat constricted and her eyes teared with emotion. She reluctantly turned and walked for the barn. The mare neighed and tried to follow, the groom had difficulty in holding her.

Phillip soberly observed the reaction of the woman and the horse When Joanna joined them she turned back to watch the mare.

"Do you like her, Joanna?" Phillip asked with a knowing look.

She whirled about, "Oh, Phillip she is a wonder!"

"Why don't you take her out for a short ride and accustom yourself to her?"

"No," she shook her head, "it would break my heart to give her up."

The mare pulled away from the groom and trotted to Joanna then nudged her. Joanna soothed the noble creature by running her hand over the gleaming neck. "What is her name, Phillip?"

"Venus. Father likes his mythology."

"It fits her, such a regal lady."

"I have a feeling that she has adopted you, my swan. You now belong to her...she is yours."

Joanna shook her head in dismay, "Don't make fun of me. I have fallen in love with this animal!"

"I realize that, Joanna. I am giving her to you!"

As she saw the look of love in his eyes tears began to well in her eyes. "But I could never accept such a gift!"

Phillip shrugged sympathetically and shook his head. "Poor girl, she needs an owner and I have no time to pamper and pet her. Father made her a pet and she needs someone that will love her and care for her."

Her head spun. Ladies did not accept gifts unless they were affianced or the gift was from a relative. "Oh, Phillip," she murmured as she continued to stroke the mare, "I thank you, but, as I said before, I cannot accept so costly a gift." Her violet eyes were wide with emotion.

Phillip gazed down at her with intensity. Their eyes locked and in one stride he took her in his arms. She drew back, but he drew her back in his arms.

"Joanna, dearest," he said in a husky whisper, "I want you to have Venus as a token of my love."

She went weak with a surging joy. He did love her!

"Joanna," he whispered against her lips, "must I spend the rest of my life atoning for that misunderstanding? We belong together, even the horse knows it!

She pushed back her head. He gazed at her bleakly.

The world around her returned. She was aware of Timber and Elyce who were watching and smiling.

"Glory be to God!" she gasped, "I accept your gift, I want her desperately. I shall probably be struck dead for flaunting convention!"

"Oh, Joanna," laughed Elyce, "she is just magnificent. When I am able, you must promise me I can ride her!"

Phillip had the groom lead Venus to a stall, and turning to Joanna he said softly, "I must talk to you tonight."

"Yes, Phillip…tonight after dinner. I must be excused, I have some urgent things I must attend to," she said in dismissal with a lovely smile.

Her heart was thumping in her ears as she hitched her skirts and ran for the house. Stars in heaven! What had she done! In one fell swoop she had obligated herself to Phillip by taking the mare. She couldn't belief what had happened. First, to be transfixed by that magical animal and then overtaken by such powerful emotions. Of course, Phillip was quite a handsome animal and she would wager a divine lover! Her heart stopped a beat. *What a child I am! I have forgotten who I am and what I am. I must turn him away once and for all. And he must take Venus back!*

Dinner that evening had a celebratory air to it. Joanna and Elyce were both breathtaking in the glow of candlelight.

Timber continuously raised his crystal goblet toasting his wife and the forthcoming heir.

On occasion Willie came to supper and tonight he had joined them. He was very excited over the new mare. Phillip genuinely liked the handicapped young man. He carefully explained the blood lines and the history of the mare. It was a jovial meal although Joanna was dreading the meeting with Phillip.

Later in the evening they excused themselves and went outside to sit on the porch swing. A dull moon silvered the night and a cool breeze played among the trees. Side by side they sat as stiff as the wood that held them. Joanna pulled her mantle close and Phillip turned to her making the swing move gently. The moonshine played about her face and her eyes were like pearlized opals. Moonbeams glistened off the long sweep of her burnished hair and Phillip thought she had never looked so lovely...like carved marble. She looked at him with uncertainty.

Taking her hand he kissed the palm and murmured, "What is wrong, Joanna?"

She forced herself to look directly into the elegant face of her beloved. His eyes, even in the moonlight, were gazing at her with an intensity that took her breath away.

"There is something you hide from me, Joanna, something dark between us...you hold me at bay." He continued to gaze at her waiting for an answer.

She could feel the aching pressure of words unspoken. She sat very still for a moment. "I love you!" It broke from her involuntarily, "but I can never marry you!"

"Why? I demand an answer, you owe me at least that!"

"It is too difficult to give you an explanation, it is too humiliating," she answered as a tear rolled down her cheek.

"My dearest dear," he said tenderly, "there is nothing between two people who love each other that cannot be explained. Please, Darling will you tell me?"

"Yes," it was only a shuddered whisper and he had to lean to catch her words. She explained the horrifying night of the rape and felt as if a knife was cutting her in two. Phillip's face became white and he clenched his hands together.

When she ended her story she waited for the impact of his contempt. Instead he took her in his arms. "Darling, my darling," his lips met hers in a soft kiss, and then he drew her closer yet and buried his face in her hair. "I will make it up to you. Never again will any soul hurt you as long as I live."

He gently pushed the hair from her face. He raised her chin to look into her tearful eyes.

"My love," he murmured, "I would give you heaven if it was mine to give, but all I can do is promise to make you happy. I have lived just to find you for you are my destiny."

"You don't find me unworthy, unclean..." she said with a sob against his shoulder.

"Hush, I never want to hear you speak of it again, understood? You are as dear to me as the day I found you, nothing has changed."

His lips again met hers and her aching heart began to soar within her. The kiss stopped her reminiscences and doubts. She felt her love for Phillip spread through her body, flaming up to drive the killing cold from her heart. Pure exquisite pleasure drummed through her veins.

Phillip felt her passion and knew if he didn't stop he would be beyond caution. He pushed her gently away. Her eyes were half lidded with desire and her swollen lips were open like nectar laden flower. He crushed her to him once more and then gently shook her and stood up turning himself from her until he knew he was under control.

"Joanna, will you marry me?" he huskily asked.

"Yes, oh, yes," she cried happily. "But first I must get the school in order and request a replacement, someone should be able to be here by spring."

"Spring!" he thundered, "Hell's gates, that is months away!"

Joanna rose, smoothed her skirts and stood beside him. He turned and put his arm around her.

"I have waited so long; I suppose a few more months can be tolerated. I have a house to finish at Snowflake and other things to finalize." He drew a finger down her face and over her lips. "No doubt we will be well chaperoned. It will be good as you have no idea how much I want you."

"You also, dear. I will love you beyond reason," she avowed in a low, tremulous whisper.

They embraced once again and entered the front portal to impart their news.

CHAPTER FIVE

Fall continued in all its glory. A rich tapestry of color shimmered against an evergreen background.

There was a medley of activities at Locket Springs. Hunting parties arrived and part of the hired hands set up camp and riding with the shooters. Other help secured the ranch for winter. Everyone was busy. Elyce was a gracious hostess seeing to exceptional dining for the hunting parties and wives. She took great delight in all the visitors, many from Europe.

Joanna rode her splendorous white mare on Saturdays accompanied by a groom. High on a ridge overlooking the ranches, she would meet Phillip and share a lunch. The ritual had to end when snow began to fly in the high country and whitened the passes. This was followed by frosty starlit nights in the valley.

School progressed and Joanna was rewarded with her pupil's progress. To watch the students' delight as they solved a math problem or mastered reading a primer was to Joanna a thrill that brought joy to her heart. Dear Willie was now able to read short sentences and his face beamed with happiness.

At the start of school the marble season had begun for the boys. Each day they drew a ring on smooth ground three feet across. The boys anted up marbles which were placed in a line in the center of the ring. The players *lagged* to determine who shot first, the object being to use a favorite marble called the *tow* or shooters marble. They then would knock as many marbles out of the ring as possible to claim them as their own. There were rigid rules…players had to keep knuckles flat to the ground and no knees or wrists inside ring. The marbles became prize possessions and everyone marveled at the unusual and colorful little balls of glass. The boys carried them in small drawstring bags. A favorite call at recess was always, "Let me see your 'aggies.'"

The girls, in the meantime, played Tag, ally ally Oxen Free or Farmer in The Dell. Often they watched the boys play and hooted for their favorite.

Joanna was truly content and thanked God often for her happiness. She had written to her family of her proposal. Uncle John and Frieda sent a wire of congratulation from Europe. They also related they had located relatives of Frieda's and would spend the winter there.

At the end of the hunting season Timber left with a land developer to look at property in Montana. A large holding owned by an English Lord was for sale. Timber had been told it was well kept property; the house was large and richly furnished and had two large barns.

On his return he presented Elyce with the deed to the property. He had made drawings of the house and surroundings. She was elated. They decided to take possession after the babe arrived in the spring.

One gray snowy afternoon when Joanna saw Phillip coming up the driveway unexpectedly. She ran to the foyer and threw open the doors.

"Oh, Phillip, you are half frozen, take off your dripping garments," she cried with concern.

Phillip shivered, removing his snow crusted hat and Macintosh. "It is turning into a bad one, Joanna; I cannot believe how fast this set in. When I left Snowflake it was breaking dawn, clear and cold."

She called down the hallway seeing one of the maids, "bring some towels and set up tea."

After drying his hair, Phillip joined Elyce and Joanna in the big room. He grabbed Joanna by the waist, lifted her up and whirled her about as she protested laughing, "I declare, Phillip, you are in a mood!"

He set her gently down and kissed the end of her nose. He turned to Elyce and kissed her hand, "How are you, little mother?"

"Never better, I am sorry that Timber cannot welcome you, he is securing stock."

"I talked with him while I rubbed down Diablo."

"Please sit down, Phillip, tea will be here shortly," said Joanna.

Taking a seat beside her, Phillip drew a fold of papers from his vest. "Your Uncle John has consented to the marriage and the contract, Joanna. You can now plan your wedding date."

Joanna looked through the papers with misty eyes and said softly, "I cannot believe it is a reality. To have been fortunate enough to have found you in this life and to marry you is indeed a miracle."

"Nonsense, darling, I am the fortunate one," said Phillip, kissing her on her forehead.

"Oh, my, I have so many things to do. Elyce, you will advise me?"

"But of course, dear, it will be such great fun! We can begin at once!" answered Elyce eagerly.

"Whoa, ladies, first I have something very pleasurable that I wish to do."

Phillip stood before Joanna his blue eyes twinkling, then kneeled on one knee and placed a ring on her left hand. She was astounded for it was a huge blood red ruby surrounded by diamonds.

"Oh, Phillip," she cried, "I have never seen anything so beautiful! Please, my beloved, get off your knees, I am going to weep and I need your shoulder to cry on." She had not dreamed it could be like this. She was delirious with happiness.

Phillip stood and pulled her to her feet. "Excuse me, dear sister," he said to Elyce and kissed Joanna breathless.

"I wanted to give you your ring with a romantic candlelit dinner, but I just couldn't contain myself. I have to claim you for my own so I will never worry about you denying me again."

"Never, Phillip, I fell in love with you the first day I saw you on the mountain...and you were such a rogue!" she laughed.

"You were quite compliant as I remember. Though I mistook you for Winifred, I soon knew this was not Winifred with the sparks you gave off! What a vixen you were!"

"Pray tell, how could you compare me without having kissed my dear wicked cousin?" Joanna asked with a worried look.

"Do I detect a little jealousy, Joanna? Come now, dearest, I never kissed her although she dearly wanted me to. She was a child, and John's daughter to boot!" Phillip's eyes were dancing.

Elyce retorted, "For shame, you just became engaged and having a difference of opinion already?"

Joanna whirled to the window and stood with a small pout on her face. Phillip crossed to her and enclosed his arms about her. He whispered in her ear, "You are my beautiful swan and I love you beyond all reason. Your cousin was like a wild untamed animal and never was I interested in trying to tame her. You, my sweet, are a different story. I shall love taming you and pampering you. You are my reason to live in this crazy, frenzied world."

Joanna turned in his arms and lifted her face to his. "I love you," she whispered.

"It goes without saying," he murmured against her lips.

The two of them in their own ardent happiness were oblivious to the weather which was becoming steadily worse. For the next two days the storm raged with howling winds and swirling snow. The wind stopped, but for another two days the snow fell steadily. The silence was deafening. It was a cruel snow turning mean and biting. When it stopped, the drifts were huge. It took all the help plus Timber and Phillip to dig out.

Phillip was worried about the Wrights and hoped his hands had had no problems securing the stock at Snowflake.

Joanna knew his worry and comforted him.

"I must go as soon as possible," he told her.

"I shall go with you, I will ride Venus," she retorted, her eyes wide with concern.

"No darling. I realize you have become a superb horsewoman, but I would never expose you to these elements. I will take a couple of John's hands with Timber's permission."

She gave a sigh. "I will be sick with worry."

"Querida mujer, I am the master of Snowflake, I belong there and soon you will be the mistress. You think for one moment, after all we have been through, I would take a chance on your becoming someone else's wife! Never—you are my woman. Nothing is going to happen to me."

She walked to one of the large windows and pulled the drapes aside. The snow glittered like millions of jewels. A draft plow was clearing the road.

Phillip stood leaning against the mantle. The fire blazed invitingly and the fragrance of pine floated in the air.

"Please tell me you are not going to attempt the pass, Phillip?"

"Actually; I might use snowshoes. Don't you think that would be wise, love?"

"Nonsense," Joanna protested. "You are teasing me!"

There was a great thumping in the foyer and Timber soon joined them.

"We have cleared paths to the front door. One can sink knee deep in this heavy snow!" He came to stand in front of the fire rubbing his cold hands. Pouring a cup of tea from the tea cart Elyce carried it to Timber. He thanked her and sipped it slowly staring into the fire.

"Phillip, if you must go, leave Diablo here and take the sledge. It is the only wise thing to do. The draft team is hardy and will pull well."

"First light tomorrow I leave. I will borrow a hand from you."

Elyce sat by the fire. It reflected off the softness of her face and made a halo of her hair. "Listening to your conversation worries me, Phillip. I cannot believe that your trusted help would let anything happen in your absence. Most certainly another day would be to your advantage and you are most welcome here."

Joanna crossed her arms shivering from the cold as she looked out her bedroom window. Frost was etching its delicate designs along the bottom of the panes. Lanterns glow made the snow and ice sparkle and she was awed by the still beauty of it. An ice covered branch rattled against the window and she started. She walked across the room and smothered a brace of candles beside her bed. Shivering she undressed quickly. A north wind began to wail and despite the fire blazing in the hearth the room was icy cold. Her bed had been warmed and she snuggled down under the comforters. She lay watching the fire cast shadows on the silk patterned walls. Phillip had stayed the night and was sleeping in another wing. She was so relieved that he had not attempted to leave. She could not bear to think of anything happening to him. In this country only the strong survived and one could take no chances. Western winters swallowed the weak and crushed the foolish.

Phillip left early morning by sledge. Joanna watched him go with a heavy heart. She had pleaded that he should stay longer.

"Nothing would please me more, Joanna, but I have my responsibilities and I dare not risk another storm. If luck is with us the pass will be crusted and we will sock the horses' hooves.

She had reached up a hand to touch his face and pressed her lips to his. His hands had grasped her shoulders almost urgently. He whispered, "I will be back, weather or no. Now, don't fret so."

"Oh, Phillip, you cannot play God!" she exasperatedly burst out. "You must be practical, this is horrific weather and it will break my heart if anything happens to you."

"Joanna," he soberly replied, "I must take my leave of you." He bowed and strode out of the room.

She in turn ran after him to the front portal where he blew her a kiss and opened the door. She slammed the heavy door after him and cursed, "May the devil take you!" Horrified at what she had said, she leaned against the door and covered her mouth with her hand, "Oh, God, I did not mean that! Please, I pray you watch over him!"

It would be a week before favorable news of Phillip reached Joanna. The students from Snowflake were able to return to school and the weather stayed clear and cold.

Timber left to meet the train at Stirrup Springs. His mother, Lady Adelaide, was arriving. Both Timber and Elyce had sent wires advising her of the danger of traveling in the winter. She had wired back her arrival time and said no amount of discouragement would keep her away.

He arrived late afternoon by sleigh with Lady Adelaide. Her happy countenance upon arrival boasted everyone's spirits. She kissed and hugged Elyce to her.

"Oh, my darlings, I just had to be with our precious Elyce until confinement.

Imagine, my first grandchild and about time, I might add!" she bubbled as she was helped out of her furs.

"Sakes alive," she exclaimed as she entered the huge drawing room, "this place is huge, truly not what I expected at all!" Then she collapsed prettily on a settee.

Joanna poured tea and handed her a cup.

"We meet again, my dear. You have grown into a beautiful woman. Your mother told me you had been asked for. My congratulations."

"Yes, thank you. You will meet Phillip, he is quite remarkable. I feel very fortunate, indeed," answered Joanna with a smile.

"Excellent, dear. Oh, I almost forgot. Your mother sent a letter addressed to the both of you. Joanna, she had your dress form shipped."

"Oh, you jest!"

"No, dear, it is with the luggage."

Joanna looked at Elyce whose eyes were wide with astonishment and then a huge grin split her face. Both sisters burst into laughter and Joanna had to be excused as she could not stop giggling.

When she returned she apologized profusely. "I am sorry. I did not mean to be rude, but Mother is so very unpredictable."

Lady Adelaide, a gracious and still handsome woman, also had a wonderful sense of humor. "Whiskers, dear, she meant well. I am certain she felt you would need it for your dressmaker. Most every woman needs a dress form. Heavens, if nothing else, you can always dance with it when bored!"

Whereupon all laughed heartily. Timber had joined them and was pleased his mother was making herself at home.

Later in the afternoon Joanna and Elyce opened their mother's letter.

My Dears,

Lady Hungersford has graciously offered to carry this to you.

First I must tell you I was grievously offended by your letter, Joanna. I do not deny that the social situation with

Marshall Davenport is to my liking. You both must realize that I can do nothing socially to cause Winifred or John to lose social status.

It has been so dreadful since your father's demise; to all my friends in New York City, I have ceased to exist. Nothing could ever have prepared me for the humiliation or the scandal. When I went with your Grandmother to the bank, acquaintances stared through me. When I shopped for bereavement garments, those I knew shunned me and former friends would leave the establishments. Anyone I knew directly would cross the street to avoid me. No invitations were extended, even for tea. No sympathy was given; I shall never forget or forgive them.

Your Grandmother and Uncle John kept us from the streets. I must, therefore, be very guarded in what I dare say for I have no place assured in this world.

Elyce, your divorce was scandalous. As you are aware, the notice was in every paper. The damage was irreparable.

Elyce snorted, "Of course, the cur accused me of having relations with every male in his employment!"

"Shhh, do not become upset, for it is over," Joanna said quietly.

"They made a fool of me, Joanna, and now she is trying to do it all over again!" Elyce cried in a stricken voice.

"It was fodder for the gossips until another happening. You are no longer there; never will you be humiliated again."

"Pray continue; best we get this done so I can retire."

Joanna continued to read:

I hope you will not dispute with me on this matter: I know I have made mistakes and I can ill afford to make more. Winifred is attending many functions that require me as a chaperone. On many of these occasions Marshall is in attendance. He does not slight me nor I him.

Winifred is certainly a handful. She has not done anything seriously naughty, but given an opportunity she is likely to.

I am saddened you would not return East, Joanna, even for a short time. I cannot understand your high opinion of a

*man with a background such as this Philip. The Spanish are
known to be very impulsive and generally over rated...*

"Over rated in what exactly, Jo?" teased Elyee, her blue eyes dancing.

Embarrassed, Joanna blushed deeply and defiantly answered, "Really, he is a perfect gentleman and he has the blood of royalty...what does she require?"

"Fiddle, Jo, I am only teasing...carry on."

Dark are these days, I am so alone. Your father should be here to advise us! Your Grandmother is writing to you concerning the engagement. Maybe one of her suggestions will be to your fancy.

My question is unanswered as to whether you and the young man can be, after such short acquaintance, sufficiently aware of the enormous step you both are taking. This will bind you forever to each other. I wish you would wait for a period of time. Have you made any plans? Where will you marry and when? You are so indefinite. What worry and bother you are subjecting me to!

My dear Elyce, I am told you are enceinte. I hope you will write me of the details.

"Oh, if only Mama could see how I am increasing! She has made me feel great pity for her. Truly, life has been unkind to her. Papa was an unfaithful husband and did many scandalous things she was aware of and must have suffered dreadfully."

"Indeed, but he did give her everything she desired. Mama is still very attractive, perhaps she will remarry someday and find peace of mind."

Elyce shrugged, "She enjoys the Rochester social life and Winifred's outings. I have been a great disappointment to her."

"Dash it, Elyce, you were everything a daughter should be. We were both proper darlings! You became enamored with a despicable person. Let us be candid, Mama thought him a plum and it would have destroyed her had you not married him. I never saw her happier!"

For a second Elyce's blue eyes blazed with hatred and she said, "Do finish this letter, it is making me edgy and discomforted."

"Really nothing more than a bitter-sweet closing, I will go fetch the cards." Joanna realized how agitated her sister was becoming. She placed the letter atop a chest in the hallway. She would read the rest at a later time.

That evening Joanna walked slowly along the driveway. Moonlight glistened on the crusted snow and silence ruled over the wintry land only to be broken by the crunch of Joanna's boots. Lifting her eyes to the heavens, she stopped, astounded to see flickering ribbons of color in the northern sky. She held her breathe as she watched the bands of color extend across the heavens.

"The Aurora Borealis!" she exclaimed out loud; clapping her mittened hands together in excitement, "Oh, the splendor of this mighty wilderness!"

She was filled with a wonderful sense of serenity. God was truly in his mighty Heaven. She felt as if she were experiencing a waking dream. The beauty of the night sky made her feel His presence in a way she had never felt before. She stood in awe for a period of time until she became aware of stinging cold feet. Her nose was also beginning to burn from the extreme cold. She began walking back to the house. "Oh, Papa, where are you? Why did you leave us?" she cried into the night as her breath blew fog.

From afar a soulful howl of a wolf came in answer.

She hurried on and into the warmth of the great house "There you are, Joanna. We were becoming worried; thought you had wandered a bit too far. Timber was just getting on his Macintosh to go for you," scolded Elyce.

"Oh, I just impulsively wanted to walk. It is dreadfully cold out, but I was spellbound by the Northern Lights. I have never witnessed them before and they are breathtaking!"

Lady Adelaide stood up, "Timber dear, would you fetch my wraps I would like to see them."

"Oh, I would also like to!" added Elyce excitedly.

"Just sit and I will fetch your furs. Your both must promise not to stay out too long it is freezing. Look at Joanna's poor face!" answered Timber as he went into the hall.

"It is my feet that are hurting; I did not realize how numb they had become." Joanna made a face as she stood before the hearth. They were burning as the blood began to circulate through them.

She stood looking into the fire and felt a jolt of happiness. Now that ground and snow had frozen; her pupils would return to school.

They came by sled. Joanna was kept busy with her school while Lady Adelaide and Elyce prepared for the upcoming holidays.

A heavy snow made Thanksgiving a snowbound holiday, but it was enjoyed by everyone at Locket Springs. There was a bounty of food for the workers. The inhabitants of the main house sat down to a candlelit dinner with the best linen, crystal and silver.

The weather held for Christmas and overflowing sleds and sleighs left for Stirrup Springs. The town house proved to be the center of a festive holiday. Sleighs went to early morning services at the Episcopal and Roman Catholic Churches. Phillip came to town as did Annie and Buck. Joanna was deliriously happy and she could not help, but compare this holiday to the dreadful one of the previous year.

After the return to Locket Springs another roaring storm began for the New Year. This was followed by a hard deep freeze. Fires blazed in the stoves and on the hearths of the big house. Even so, there was still a chill in the air and the woman wore shawls and half mittens. They drew close to the fires and sipped hot tea or chocolate.

Timber, Buck and the hired help exhaustedly hauled hay by sled to the cattle. They cracked ice covering the drinking water and broke ice away from the animals' nostrils. It was an unending job. There seemed to be no let up to the extreme freezing temperatures. Joanna helped as she could to exercise the horses.

Timber had insisted that Buck and Annie stay at the big house until the freeze passed.

Joanna was concerned as Annie was very pale with dark purple shadows under her eyes and extremely thin. Joanna approached her about her health.

"Oh, Joanna, I am in the family way and I cannot keep a thing down."

"Hmmm, I am no doctor and ignorant of morning vapours, but I will ask Lady Adelaide's advice. She is so knowledgeable about healing and medicine."

A few minutes later Lady Adelaide came into the morning room bundled in a heavy coat. "Good morning, girls, oh, that coffee smells like heaven! I must have a cup to ward off the chill."

"Ah, just the lady we were speaking of," Joanna brightened and continued, "we need your medical expertise."

Lady Adelaide poured her coffee while Joanna explained Annie's complaint.

"I know just the cure," Lady Adelaide said with an emphatic nod to Annie. "I will make you flaxseed tea and have cook make consommé from my recipe. The consommé will be done within the hour. In the mean time I will bring you the tea and you can sip it with salted toast. You do look a bit under the weather, go lie down, dear. I will be up shortly."

When Annie had departed the room, Lady Adelaide sipped her cup of coffee "Poor child, if the tea and consummé doesn't help I will make her a boiled brew of chicken gizzard lining. I am certain I have some dried in my remedy bag."

"How ghastly that sounds, but then most remedies are," shuddered Joanna making a face.

"Yes, but most do work and that is what is important. I realize some cures have a terrible stench like my asafetida bags!"

"Oh, yes. I had the grippe at my grandmother's and she gave me an asafetida bag to wear, I smelled of turpentine and onion for weeks after."

"But darling, you got better, did you not?"

"Well, yes," Joanna agreed with a slight frown.

"I must call cook to prepare the tea and take it up to our poor wan girl, she does look frightful."

Annie did improve with Lady Adelaides's remedies and within a few days ate nourishing food. It was a great relief to everyone especially Buck who had been beside himself with worry.

At last the hard freeze broke and the temperature eventually warmed above zero. Joanna and Elyce bundled warmly and ventured out doors.

"Oh, I thought we would never be warm again!" laughed Elyce pulling the fur collar around her neck.

"The West is a country of severe winters! I have been reading to the pupils of John Fremont's expeditions and of his climbing the Sierra Nevada Mountains in the dead of winter. What determination those mighty men had!" said Joanna.

"Some say it was a great folly. I think of the poor Donner party! Do you imagine they attempted it because Fremont made it?"

"Oh, Elyce, I really don't think so. John Fremont and Kit Carson were legends in themselves. Your husband will tell you how much their mapping of the West opened up the trails to the pioneers, the surveyors, and the railroads. There are so many courageous tales of the mountain men and those that followed."

"Yes, I can imagine."

The aromatic scent of burning wood floated in the air. Hundreds of crystal icicles, glistening in the morning light; clung to branches and hung from the eaves. The snow was winter blue and the walkways carved into it were lined with piled snow three to six feet deep. Both women were mesmerized by the beauty of the winter landscape.

"It is breathtaking, but rather frightening: It makes me feel smothered by isolation," chattered Elyce nervously.

"Ah, but keep in mind, when this all melts there follows a glorious spring, a flower on every bush. It is nature at her very best. The deer, elk, moose, bear…every animal imaginable begins to appear and soon follow the babies; it is so wondrous," exclaimed Joanna, her face animated.

Elyce smilingly nodded her head, "Now that, I am looking forward to. I cannot imagine anything living through these winters!"

"But they do and so will you!"

"I know; I am just suffering a 'pity me' mood. As long as I am with Timber I can be happy anywhere. I suppose I have fears like any mother to be, but I do so want this child and it must be perfect for Timber."

Before Joanna could reply Willie came bounding towards them.

"Good morning! I just exercised Venus, Joanna. She..she was refusing to mind, had had to kick and buck!"

"Be careful Dear, horses are very frisky after being confined for a time," admonished Joanna.

"Yeh ugh yep; she's a m-m-mess, the corral was drug, but it is near mud. T-t-the grooms are laying straw." He bowed and then hurried by.

"Willie, there will be school as soon as the path is cleared," called Joanna over her shoulder.

"Shucks, then it will be M-M-Miss Holan again for you!" he laughed as he hastened toward the house.

Wonderingly, Elyce watched Willie's retreating back and then turned back to her sister. "I must say, his handicap, in no way, hampers him. He does not look or act like frail little Willie, anymore. It is truly a miracle."

"That's it exactly. The miracle being, first, he no longer has Winifred around to abuse him and second, he has found himself. Buck and the men adopted him and he loves ranching and the animals. He hasn't a mean bone in his body. Wish I could say the same for his sister."

"He is so changed, not the boy I once knew."

"You must remember, he was surrounded by dominate women, Grandmother, Winifred, and his pitiful demanding sick mother. Here he has been with his father and has lots of male role models. He wants to learn, he will be a boy mentally forever, but he can function."

Elyce looked at Joanna, her eyes tender, her voice soft. "You have been ever so patient with him and he adores you. You are a fine teacher and I admire that so much in you. You must take some credit for his change, also."

"Truly, it has been a joy to work with him," Joanna said with a smile. "The day he knew absolutely he could read a sentence he cried and I cried with him. God blessed us both. I am sure you have noticed he hardly stammers unless he is frightened or angry."

"Yes, how could I not? One could hardly understand him months ago." Elyce pulled the fur parka close around her face. "I am cold; I believe I have had enough fresh air." The two sisters walked slowly back to the house holding hands, each in deep thought.

The mail was delivered shortly after their return. As always, during winter it was a joyous occasion.

Joanna received a letter from her beloved Grandmother and a parcel of books. She made Elyce and herself cocoa, and then sat by the fire to read her letter.

> *My darling Granddaughter,*
>
> *Such happy tidings I have received in your wonderfully brilliant letter.*
>
> *Your Phillip sounds delightful. I am ecstatic over your engagement, Joanna. I am looking forward to meeting your young man and your wedding.*
>
> *Have you made any plans? Queensgate is at your disposal if you wish to be married in the East. If the ceremony will be in Wyoming I shall plan to come. I have always wanted to see the west so let us know when your plans are finalized.*
>
> *I am enclosing a draft for you.*
>
> *Uncle John has made arrangements for your dowry. You are to use my draft for your trousseau and wedding ensemble. I shall be most distressed if you do not have a fashionable wedding. I owe that to your father and do this in his stead.*
>
> *Your mother is fine and busy trying to shepherd Winifred.*
>
> *Winifred...her ups and downs are more trying and distressful than anything one can imagine. She seems to encourage impiety. The tongues are beginning to clack. She defies us and has left unseen with her maid in the late*

evening. She is obviously meeting someone. Dr. Grayson's wife made an issue of telling us that the good doctor had seen Winifred embracing a man in public. I have wired her father about her impudence and defiance. Perhaps he can send for her and put her in a finishing school in Europe. Your mother and I are in a state of continual apprehension never knowing what to expect from one moment to another. Ah, well, enough of Winifred although I have my suspicions as to whom she is seeing. I hope they are unfounded, but I have cause to believe it is that sartorial Marshall Davenport. John will horsewhip him if they are having a dalliance.

What exciting news about our dear Elyce. I will be a great grandmother! Sakes, alive, I feel as old as Queen Victoria and she just celebrated her Diamond Jubilee!

Timber must be elated and I know Lady Adelaide is. Give her my regards and I will write to her shortly.

I have been reading about the Gold Rush in the Klondike. It seems whole towns are being emptied by men and women rushing to San Francisco or Seattle to sail north to Alaska. You may recall John Chandler, the son of my banker. He left in May, crossed the country to Seattle to sail on the S.S. Portland. His parents are very concerned as they have not received any news of him in seven months. Mr. Chandler has hired a private investigator to search for him. Such stories of hardship and disappointment are coming down from the gold fields.

I could go on and on, but I must close. Somehow, speaking on paper makes me feel closer to you. I think of the many discussions we have had over the course of time and I miss them. If you ever need any ideas on the problems of life gathered from experience, hasten to me.

Lest I forget, one of the books I have forwarded to you is "Quo Vadis," excellent reading by Henry Sienkiewicz, a new Polish author.

Do write of your plans, darling girl. I am most anxious to hear from you of the upcoming nuptials. I trust you to use your own discretion in all of the particulars. I have utmost confidence in you.

I hope your winter is not too severe. Ours has been decidedly nasty. Furs and hot water bottles are the norm. God Bless you, dear.

Your loving and devoted grandmother,
Katherine Holan

Joanna was astounded at the amount of the draft. She would need Elyce's expertise and advice on the wedding...but first, she must consult Phillip. His wishes would be her first priority. She stood and hugged herself with happiness.

"Uh, huh, what is making you glow so, smug one?" queried Elyce behind her.

"My goodness! I didn't hear you!" gasped Joanna as she turned around. "Oh, Elyce, I am going to need all your help!"

"Oh?" Elyce's eyebrows quizzically arched. "How so?"

"Gram wrote and wants me to begin my wedding plans. She sent me an exorbitant draft for my trousseau and the wedding. She is going to come! You know I am no good at social arrangements. I must confer with Phillip also," sighed Joanna. "Oh, dear, I feel like a witless ninny!"

She looked beseechingly at Elyce who clapped her hands with joy. "Oh, dearest, it will be wonderful to help you with your plans. You must speak to Phillip as soon as the weather permits. We must send for catalogues. Oh, how exciting...a wedding and a baby to plan for!"

CHAPTER SIX

Joanna prayed for an early spring, but it was not to be. Everyone had become edgy and short tempered. The sight of gray skies and bleak fields was oppressive. Then the past week a beautiful winter weather phenomenon had occurred in the valleys. The Indians called it the *white death* while the hands at Locket Springs referred to it as Cheyenne Fog or Sea Smoke. It delicately frosted the landscape with fantastic crystalline shapes that emerged from an eerie fog. Once the fog cleared minute ice crystals sparkled in the clear sunlight. It was believed that exposure to this chill fog caused a fatal coughing sickness and, for the most part, people judged it safest to stay indoors until it passed.

At breakfast one morning Timber explained to Elyce and Joanna what he knew about it. "The Indians call it pogonip; there are two forms, hoarfrost and rime. One is seen suspended in clear air, and the other precipitates out of cold fogs. Airborne pogonip is hoarfrost drifting about on gentle breezes. One can see it as ice crystals sparkling in cold sunshine or it will dance in rainbow halos at night around lamps or carriage lights. Hoarfrost forms when water vapor changes directly into ice in the air. The frozen crystals grow when more cooled water droplets evaporate and then that vapor freezes into ice particles. Then one can actually see the *white death* like tiny diamonas scintillating in the air. Are you following me?"

"Do continue, Timber, this is fascinating," answered Elyce, shaking her head in approval.

"The other form of pogonip is rime ice. It differs from hoarfrost in that it forms on cold surfaces exposed to the super cold fog. Unlike other frost it forms only when fog is present. Rime crystals grow into featherlike shapes composed of hollow little needles. You have seen the delicate structures that build up to two or three inches in the wind. A magnifying glass will reveal intricate patterns. The past few days rime has changed the landscape into a delicate fairyland. The willows drip ribbons of diamonds; the tumbleweeds become lacy snowballs and the barbed and hog wire fences look like white spider webs. Have you noticed how ghostly the big trees look as they emerge from the fog with their frost encrusted limbs raised to the sky?"

"Oh, it is really an experience to be out in it although it gives me a great sense of isolation," Joanna said, then added, "but I never tire of the artistry of this phenomenon."

"I advise you to wrap your nose and mouth when out exploring. People who have been exposed to this fog for lengths of time have developed pneumonia like symptoms."

"Oh, we shall take great care, but it is so very beautiful!" answered Elyce.

"Be careful when walking under branches as the rime can cause them to break with a build up," Timber cautioned and excused himself to help with the stock.

Joanna settled down with her needlework while Elyce and Lady Adelaide played whisk.

Willie came for Joanna the following week to take her to school in the little cutter. The roadway was well packed and a dirty brown from use. The pupils were tired of stomping through snow and had trouble concentrating on the lessons.

Joanna had written Phillip a detailed letter and gave it to Sarah to take to Snowflake.

One morning after the pupils from Snowflake arrived; Sarah drew out a letter addressed to Joanna.

"Miss Holan," she said, her eyes sparkling with mischief, "Mr. Phillip said to tell you he would rather deliver it in person. As soon as possible he will high tail it here."

Joanna responded, "He did not exactly say 'high tail it', now did he?"

Sarah giggled, "Not really, but he said to me and Mama he would come soon. He also said when you become his wife; it will be the luckiest day of his life."

Joanna lowered her eyes and blushed. "Thank you for delivering the letter to me; now, we must proceed with our lessons."

Joanna rose from her desk and tucked the letter into a pocket of her smock. She then tapped her standard and had the children pledge allegiance to the flag, her lovely face composed and serious.

At lunch she opened her letter. Phillip assured her that September would make a fine wedding date; he felt that would give them time to make arrangements for their families to attend. He also stated that he would approve of any arrangements she made as long as he was the bridegroom. She was dizzy with happiness.

Joanna awoke to the sound of dripping water; at long last the spring thaw had begun! She arose, hurriedly donned a wrapper and lit the fire. Pulling aside the drapes she peered out the windows. The icicles were dripping and one cracked away from the eaves above as she watched.

She excitedly bathed face and body parts then donned her clothes and dressed her hair.

Hannah brought a tray of hot tea and toast. Joanna looked at her lapel watch. "Heavens, it is almost seven, Willy must be waiting and I will never get the school warm before the children arrive!"

Then she laughed aloud, "Stars, today is Saturday and I am going to visit Annie...no school!"

She hadn't seen her dear friend for a month, but Buck kept her informed of Annie's condition. On her last visit Annie had shown her the layette she was sewing.

Kate had shipped two cradles, one for Elyce and one for Annie. Joanna was to take the cradle with her today. Maddy was to accompany her.

Packages from Frieda and John had come sporadically from Europe for Elyce. Boxes of lovely baby garments trimmed in Brussels lace were unpacked and one was marked for Annie.

"How like Frieda and Uncle John, always thinking about the less fortunate. Annie will be so appreciative to have such fine things," said Joanna as she and Elyce unwrapped the latest arrivals.

"That is so very sweet of them and I am overwhelmed by the things they have sent me," added Elyce softly blinking away a tear.

"I know darling, I really must go," Joanna answered and kissed Elyse's cheek. "It is such a bright morning and I am anxious to see Annie."

Annie stood framed in her front door her hands extended in welcome. "You are a sight for sore eyes, Miss Joanna, come in, come in!"

Then seeing Maddy carrying the cradle, she exclaimed, "Heavens, is that for me?"

"Yes, dear, from Grandmother for you and the babe, as well as a package from Frieda and Uncle John," chortled Joanna happily.

Annie hugged Maddy and showed him a space for the cradle. Joanna followed her into the small neat kitchen.

"God's teeth, Annie, you are almost as wide as you are tall. Do you feel well?" asked Joanna, seating herself at the round table.

"Never better, just slow and ungainly; the baby is so active I feel like I have a litter in here," she laughed as she patted her stomach.

Joanna smiled, "I envy you. I want a baby boy who will look just like Phillip!"

"Lah, Miss, you will get your wish, Mr. Phillip looks to be a good stud!"

"Annie, I cannot believe you said that! You have been around the hands too long!" exclaimed a flushed Joanna her eyes wide with surprise.

Annie pulled up her smock over her mouth, shaking with laughter. "I am sorry, me tongue ran away!"

Joanna began to laugh as she mimicked Annie's brogue, "And I'm supposin' I'll be a great breeder, also?"

Still giggling, Annie replied, "You'll be a wonderful mother. No one ever loved or cared for me like you. I was supposed to care for you, but you have given me more than I can ever repay."

"Oh, fiddle, you are most deserving and you will always be a part of my life. Don't forget, you saved my life!"

"That was something, wasn't it? That scum, someday he will pay for his sins."

"Hmmm, I wonder if wretched people like him ever atone. I doubt that he even has a conscience; he is so wicked."

"Ah, it will happen," the young Irish woman avowed, "it will be in God's time, but you'll see; Mr. Marshall will be punished some day!"

Annie rose and called out to Maddy to come join them for tea and sandwiches. He carried in her box from Frieda and John.

"I declare," Annie shook her head in disbelief as she lifted the baby garments from the tissue, "I have never seen anything so fine. Everyone's been so very good to me and Buck…"

"My dear, you are family and we all love you dearly."

"Oh, I cannot wait to put the wee one in these and rock him in that lovely cradle!"

Maddy added, "I am making a clothes hamper for you and it is almost finished. I can see you will need it."

"You are showering me with all this attention, I will be truly spoiled by the time the wee one gets here." Annie bowed her head and pressed a hand against her heart. "I am so truly blessed, it frightens me at times."

"I understand." Joanna rose and placed her hand on Annie's shoulder. "Just accept it all and be happy. What a good thing we did in coming west."

"I believe that it's the luck, you know," said Annie, lifting her head and smiling. "We Irish believe you are either born with it or you suffer all your days."

"What do you think, Maddy? Is it luck or fate?" asked Joanna.

"Ah, Miss, I don't rightly know. I cain't say I have had much luck, but if Lionel can have a better life and make somethin' of hissef, then I'll say God was good. It ain't easy to be black in a white man's world."

"It won't always be this way, Maddy. God made us all in His image and I believe souls have no gender or color. I just do not know why humans cannot respect and appreciate each other. Is it fear or is it just that one must feel a race is inferior to feel superior?"

Maddy shifted uncomfortably in his seat and murmured, "I know my place, Miss. I doan want to start trouble no how. Lionel is gettin' an education and that is really something."

Joanna straightened, then took her seat and said, "Maddy, I will help you if you would like to learn. I am certain Uncle John would have no objections if we did some work in your spare time."

"Maybe sometime, Missy. It would be something to be able to write my name." Madison thoughtfully stared at the tablecloth. "Some of the men might not take to it, tho. Just like if they saw me sittin' here, one or two would take offense."

Joanna smiled, "We can work something out so they are not involved. Let me think about it."

The next two weeks saw signs of spring everywhere. Birds had returned and trees were in bud. Joanna was pleased at how diligent her pupils were. She was happy that she hadn't had to chastise anyone for not having their lessons ready, after all, spring was such a beautiful season and it was hard to be indoors.

One morning during recess she found Lionel sitting on a log with his head down on his arms. "Lionel, are you tired or unwell?"

He lifted his head slowly and a sheen of perspiration covered his face. "Ah don' feel good, ma'am, my head is hurting, something fierce."

Joanna put her hand against Lionel's forehead; he was burning hot.

Sarah walked by and added, disdainfully, "Miss Holan, Angela is sick, too. She is coughing and she has spots!"

"What? Oh, my God!" Joanna said breathlessly, afraid to dare think she had a crisis on her hands.

She whirled and ran to the door, her face grim. Howard, Sarah's brother, was leaning against the outside wall.

Joanna called to him, "Quick, Howard, round up all the pupils and bring them indoors. I must speak to them at once!"

The students came in hurriedly. Angela appeared strained and pale and Joanna motioned for her to come forward. About the little girl's forehead and neck were distinct slightly raised spots. Her skin felt hot and dry, her lips swollen.

"Dear, how long have you been ill?" asked Joanna.

"A couple of days. I had a runny nose; Mama thought I might have a cold."

"Oh, heavens! Go back to your seat, darling. I will get help."

Joanna rose and hurriedly went to Willie; he followed her to the door. "Willy, please go for Maddy and Tony. Tell them we have an emergency. Please do not go near the main house and hurry back. Now, I repeat, do not go near the main house, understood?"

"Okay, ma'am, I'll hurry!"

As she went back to her desk as the children watched her with wide eyes. Once seated she addressed them in a quiet composed voice. "Now, we mustn't be frightened, but I believe Lionel and Angela have a contagion. We will send for Dr. Taylor so we can treat the illness. I want you to think hard and tell me what illnesses you have had such as measles, chicken pox and scarlet fever."

"Howard and I have had mumps and the chicken pox. I had red measles, but I don't know if Howard did, Maw would know," Sarah stated.

Jacob Clarke shook his head, "I know we was sick twice, but it wasn't chicken pox or measles."

Despair washed over Joanna for it seemed she had a problem.

"My God," she cried aloud, "Maddy and I were at Annie's Saturday!" She panicked for a moment, "I must wait for Dr. Taylor and seek his advice."

Willie arrived shortly with Tony and Maddy. Joanna explained through the door the situation. Tony agreed to go for the doctor. Maddy was to call at the main house and tell Lady Adelaide. She, in turn, could send word to Timber and Elyce to stay at the hunting lodge until it was determined what the children had. Willie would get cots, blankets and water immediately.

Within the hour, Joanna, Sarah, and Maddy had pushed and cleared the school house and lined cots on either side. Sarah bathed Lionel and Angela's foreheads with cold well water. Joanna gave the other children books to read and asked them to lie down. She sympathized with their fright as best she could.

"Yoo hoo, Joanna!" called a voice outside. It was Lady Adelaide.

"Yes," Joanna yelled back, "please don't come in, you will expose yourself!"

Lady Adelaide swished through the door. "Child, I have had everything imaginable and I am a great nurse. You are going to need me!" Her arms were piled with quilts and Willie followed her with more bedding. They laid the bedding on Joanna's desk and Lady Adelaide went over to Angela and covered her with a quilt. "Lah, looks like measles to me, but again, could be scarlet fever. We will let the doctor make the diagnosis."

She opened a large satchel that Willie had deposited at her feet. "I have sweet spirits of nitre and acetate of ammonium which will help with the fevers." She looked around and said, "We must cover the windows…we want as little light as possible for measles can injure the eyes."

The books were retrieved from the children and the school house darkened. "Maddy, will you go fetch me some chloride of lime? I can use that as a disinfectant for utensils and dishes."

"Be right back," said the big colored man who was whispering encouragement to his son.

"What about Elyce?" Joanna anxiously asked. "Nothing must happen to her!"

"Hush, dear. Word has been sent and my son is very resourceful, he will procure whatever they need for however long they must stay. Timber has had most childhood diseases. Has Elyce had measles or scarlet fever?"

"I believe we both had measles at Grandmother's one summer. I will have Tony send a wire to Gram to be certain."

Lady Adelaide turned to Willie and asked, "If you are not too worn, would you run to the house and tell cook to put out a teapot, mugs, tea and sugar? On second thought, take a wagon so you can also get loaves of bread, a bread knife and butter. Do not go in, stand a good distance away until cook puts all the things out. I will give you a list for things she can make up for the coming days."

Both women were heartened when Tony and the doctor arrived near sunset. Dr. Taylor examined the two sick children and confirmed they had measles. "It looks as if we may have an epidemic here. I am sorry Joanna, but I must quarantine your school."

Joanna nodded and despair swelled in her heart for a moment. She set her fears aside and joined Lady Adelaide in tearing cloths for compresses.

Dr. Taylor remarked, "I cannot stay the night as Sarah Brighthouse is about to deliver and she has edema. The coughs can be relieved by flaxseed tea with sugar and lemon juice. For the older children I will leave a bottle of elixir of terpen hydrate and heroin; ½ teaspoon every three hours for fever and cough." He then took packets and bottles from a medicine box. He held up two bottles; one with red liquid in it and the other with amber liquid. "This is syrup of wild cherry and chloride of ammonium which can be given to the younger children. This is cod liver oil and should be given once a day to all the children."

Joanna wanted to throw herself upon him, to beg him to stay and take care of the children. She looked about the darkened room with its two small candles flickering on her desk, at the pathetic little patients and calm took hold of her. These were her pupils, they trusted her and she would see them well! Resolution settled within her and the panic subsided. Moreover, she had Lady Adelaide and other help.

The following week became a nightmare. Joanna emptied chamber pots; changed bed linens sponged and fed the fevered children. All the children became sick except Sarah. Joanna was exhausted beyond endurance, but kept going.

A tent had been set up outside for two of the mothers, Lady Adelaide and Joanna. They spelled each other, sleeping in shifts. Cook made kettles of broth and Lady Adelaide made herbed teas. Joanna was amazed at how this titled sweet woman gave endlessly of herself.

Joanna lost count of the days. She awoke at dawn one morning and realized she had a stench. How long had it been since she had bathed? Washed her hair? She poured water from a bucket into a ewer and stripped off her clothes. There were clean garments at the foot of her bed, they had been sent from the main house. She washed her hair and then poured more water and bathed as best she could. As she toweled off she realized no corset! She refused to put the corset back on she had been wearing; it was stained with perspiration and smelled. She pulled a camisole over her head, stepped into slips and skirt and slipped her arms into a mutton sleeved blouse. As she buttoned up the high necked waist she felt quite naked without her iron maiden. Her breasts were firm and her waist was narrow so the effect was hardly noticeable. She brushed her hair up and pinned it into a roll.

Lady Adelaide came in with a cup of tea for her. "I think the worst is over. No more fevers and the rashes are beginning to disappear. Dr. Taylor is due today; praise God, the babies are getting well."

Joanna felt as if a huge weight was lifting from her shoulders.

When Dr. Taylor arrived he confirmed Lady Adelaide's predictions. "The children should be able to return home within the week, Joanna. I must look in on Buck's wife; it seems she has contracted the fever."

"Oh, not Annie!" The blood drained from her face. An icy fist of dread circled her heart.

"What about the baby, Doctor?"

"I haven't seen her yet. Buck just met me at the pass," he answered gravely.

Terror shot through her. She nearly stumbled as she ran for a wrap. "I must go to her!"

Lady Adelaide grabbed her by an arm. "Darling, wait until the doctor sees her. If it is not the measles, you don't want to expose her! Sit, you are as white as a sheet."

In fact, Joanna felt so weak she could hardly stand and she sat down hard on a cot.

"I went to see her. If anything happens to her it is my entire fault!" cried Joanna.

"I will look in on her and send word about her condition. If she has the contagion then you can go to her. Buck indicated she had care, but I can understand your concern, Joanna," the doctor said in a low voice.

"You have no idea, I may have carried this to her. I am so frightened for her!" The doctor took his leave and Joanna kept busy hoping to hear the news that Annie was not infected.

At dusk one of the hands called and Willy ran to within shouting distance. He came back with a note for Joanna. The doctor wrote Annie indeed had the measles and he would be attending her throughout the night.

"I must go to her, Willie, please have a carriage brought round for me," whispered Joanna, horrified.

"Y-y-yes, Joanna, r-right away," Willie called as he ran to get a carriage.

Joanna's worst fears were confirmed when she entered Annie's house. Buck was sitting with his head in his hands beside a tossing feverish Annie. Maude Shaw, a neighbor, and Dr. Taylor were attempting to put cool cloths on her fevered brow.

The doctor turned to Joanna and told her in hushed tones that Annie's condition was grave. "We must break the fever or we will lose her."

"What can I do?" she whispered.

Buck raised his head and stared at her in shock. "Miss Joanna? What are you doing here?"

"Oh, my dear, to help in any way I can."

He blinked uncomprehending, "My darling Annie is so sick, so sick...," and tears began to stream down his cheeks.

With that, Joanna began to weep also as she bent over her beloved friend. Annie was flushed from the fever and panting.

Dr. Taylor told Buck to soak blankets in cold well water.

"Strip the bed clothes, we must cool her down quickly!" the doctor ordered Joanna and Maude.

They followed the doctor's orders by bathing Annie with cold cloths and changing the bedding as needed through the night. When dawn broke, so did Annie's fever. Her respiration was ragged.

The exhausted doctor listened to her heart and said, "It is in God's hands now, I have done all I can for her." He gave them packets of medicine before leaving to attend other patients.

Maude and Buck insisted that Joanna lie down in the other bedroom. She protested weakly, but gave in when Maude said she would wake her if there was any change.

She stumbled away and fell face down on the bed; when she awoke it was dark. She faintly heard the sound of voices and couldn't remember where she was. Then her memory snapped…"Annie!"

She threw a blanket around her and walked to the kitchen doorway. Maude was pouring coffee for Phillip—Phillip!

She croaked, "Phillip?" and he hurried to her immediately. "My poor darling," he said and enfolded her in his arms.

"Oh, Phillip, how is Annie?"

"She is sleeping, she is going make it."

Joanna let out a deep sigh. "Thank God!"

"I am taking you home, not to the schoolhouse, but home. Everything is under control and I have help coming for Buck." Pushing her hair away from her pale face he said, "Come, it is time to go." Phillip bent close to her, his blue eyes stormy, his strong and sensual mouth set in a firm line.

"Let me look in on Annie and we will go then," she whispered looking deep into his eyes.

He kissed her lips lightly and her body jerked with response. She was exhausted, but it had been so long since she had seen his beloved face. She felt his arms tighten around her and she remembered she was bereft of corset and pushed him away. He lifted one of his handsome brows and didn't trouble to hide his amusement. Her face reddened in embarrassment. She turned and went to Annie.

Buck was asleep in the rocking chair by the bed; Annie was breathing normally, but mottled with the contagion.

Joanna put her fist to her mouth to keep from crying. *Oh, poor little dear, and what of her babe? Please God, let her be well.*

She stumbled from the room; Phillip covered her with a coat and led her to out to the buggy. She was fast asleep before they had left the Buck's ranch. Within the hour she was huddled in her bed under a thick quilt with a plate of sandwiches and a pot of tea nearby. She fell asleep, the sandwiches and tea untouched.

In the morning she awoke to birdsong. How glorious, she was in her own bed! Oh, to have a bath and wash her hair! She rang for Hannah. In short order she was in her claw footed tub drenched in fragrant bath oils and salts. The tension within gradually gave way to a sense of well being. Hannah told her some of the students were going home today and the others tomorrow. The quarantine was over!

She lifted herself from the tub and wrapped in a bath towel. She looked at her image in the cheval mirror and, yes, she looked as bad as she feared! Her wet hair curled about a pale, pinched face. Her lavender eyes were shadowed with dark purple making her appear ghoulish. She opened her towel and was again shocked to see how thin she had become. Her ample breasts had shrunk from firm globes to small apples. Her hip bones jutted below a wasp waist.

"Oh, I look emaciated, what must Phillip have thought?" she said aloud.

Hannah entered with a large tray. "Breakfast, miss, orders from the Lady and she says to tell you to eat every bite. She will be in the drawing room when you come down."

Joanna donned a wrapper and sat down before the fire to eat. She devoured her food like a hungry wolf. She thought of dear Annie. *Shame on me, stuffing myself like an owl while my dearest friend may be a death's door! I will dress and see to her condition.*

She began to pull lingerie from a draw and then a dress from her armoire. "Curses, I can't wear this corset, it's enormous. Well, a camisole will have to do."

Hannah helped her into her garments, the dress hung on her like a shroud. "Fetch me that sash off my wrapper, Hannah, and a fringed shawl from the closet. It is the best I can do for now," Joanna made a wry face. "If Mama could see me now, she would never acknowledge me as her daughter."

"Miss, now don't despair, you will soon gain your flesh back. The pink will return to your cheeks, and you will be your pretty self again."

"Oh, Hannah, you are a dear and I thank you for your help. I will go down to see Lady Adelaide; I imagine she is delighted to be back."

Joanna slipped her hand lightly along the balustrade as she descended the staircase. She found she was still a bit shaky after her long ordeal.

Lady Adelaide was reclining on one of the overstuffed sofas in front of the enormous fireplace. Joanna eased into a chair quietly. Lady Adelaide opened her eyes with a start.

"Well, child, how are you?" she asked, sitting up. "It seems the worst is over."

"I do hope so, but Annie is still very ill."

"Phillip has seen to all the care she and Buck need at present. She is in good hands, Joanna. You are quite exhausted, and you must look to yourself now. Dr. Taylor, by rights, should have quarantined you again so you dare not go back."

A maid pushed a tea cart to Lady Adelaide.

Joanna watched her pour and commented, "You look as if you had never left this house. You worked tirelessly and yet you look remarkable."

"I am blessed with incredible stamina and try to ensure I do not push myself over the edge," Adelaide answered, handing Joanna a bone china cup and saucer. "By the by, your Phillip will see you this evening. He went into town to purchase blankets and goods for the Indians at Standing Water Reservation. The poor Red People have the contagion and are dying like flies. He is sending supplies to help."

"Oh, he is not going there?" She forced the words out as her throat tightened in terror.

"No, dear, I said he would be here tonight, most likely for dinner."

Joanna lifted her cup just as a loud hammering started somewhere behind them. This was followed by a loud crash and Joanna jolted spilling tea on her napkin. "Goodness, what is that all about? Shall go investigate?"

"That won't be necessary. Your Uncle is having a mechanical lift installed. It seems Frieda injured her ankle and he would like it finished before they return. It looks like an elegant bird cage with gold leaf gilding."

"Gracious, how extravagant! I hope her injury is not permanent," exclaimed Joanna.

"No, just requires time to heal. I think it is wonderful! I, myself, find it rather painful, at times, climbing the stairs. In fact, it quite takes my breath away."

"Of course, it will be a great help. We had one in our home in New York," answered Joanna, a bit mollified.

"Dear, there is quite a bit of correspondence for you. I took the liberty of putting it in the study for you. I read some of mine earlier; I will be days getting caught up."

"I do not know what we would have done without your help. My nursing abilities are so pathetic."

"Stuff and. nonsense, you did admirably. It is the learning that comes from experience that counts. For a sheltered young woman raised in a city, you did very well nursing the children. Sadly, you almost starved yourself, though! I should have watched you more closely to see that you ate."

The noise continued in the background and was giving Joanna a frightful headache. She asked to be excused and went to find her mail.

Joanna clutched up the mail and headed to her room still fraught from exhaustion. She sat by her fire and read a short letter from her mother with no acknowledgment of the epidemic that had swept her little school. Her Grandmother's letter, however, shocked her so it constricted her heart. It read;

> *What a sad day it was to learn of Winifred's elopement with Marshall Davenport. I wired John immediately and he has hired a detective to locate them; she and Marshall sailed for Europe. I have washed my hands of her; she has always been a naughty, capricious girl. John and Frieda are on their way back from Switzerland.*

Joanna flung the letter from her as tears blinded her. "Oh, dear God, will we never be rid of that devil?" she cried in an anguished voice, "I will have to tell dear Elyce. Winifred, I am afraid, will suffer a bleak future with that cad."

Late afternoon Joanna huddled under a down quilt. She was still in a state of shock after having read her Grandmother's letter. How could anything ever be right with that sinister Marshall a part of the family again? No one was safe, he was evil incarnate.

Joanna struggled to get up as she knew she must tell Lady Adelaide and also it was time to dress for dinner.

With slow painstaking movements she stood and rang for Hannah. Joanna surveyed the room through a state of frustration. Earlier she had piled lacy under garments, masses of petticoats and dresses in a heap trying to find something suitable to wear that fit. She had on her camisole and held an outdated lace-up corset. Hannah entered the room and her eyes widened at the clutter.

"Are you all right, Miss Joanna?" she asked.

"Oh, Hannah, I need your help. Please lace up this god awful corset and help me find something that fits. Everything is too big!" wailed Joanna.

"Now there, Miss, we will find something," answered Hannah as she began picking up articles of clothing.

Joanna finally stepped into a grey silk gown, her lacy bloomers disappearing beneath layered petticoats. She pushed her feet into leather kid slippers as Hannah overlapped her bodice with a huge silk bow.

"Oh, Hannah, I look a sight, I am so scrawny," sighed Joanna sadly.

"Here Miss, use your rouge pot, you need some color," answered Hannah, handing her a small jar. "You look very svelte, not at all unbecoming."

"Svelte," snorted Joanna. "I look like a crane!" She patted some rouge on her cheeks and grabbed a shawl.

"I am sorry I made such a mess, Hannah," she said over her shoulder as she left the room.

The gas lights cast globes of yellow haze in the hallway as she walked to staircase and descended in a fog of indifference.

Her sense of indifference was shattered when Phillip appeared at the foot of the stairs. He looked magnificent. He wore a *chaqueta*, a jacket embroidered in silver cord and *calzoneras*, pants pleated from hip to ankle. The whole was trimmed in tinsel lace and Phillip looked every bit his aristocratic heritage. His blue eyes shimmered beneath his beautifully arched eyebrows.

As he watched her descend his heart did a little dance. How slender and graceful she was. Her face was a bit gaunt with shadows under her cheek bones which made her amethyst eyes huge, yes, there was a distinct fragility to her that hadn't been there before.

"Welcome home, my swan," he said, taking her hands in his. "I have missed you dreadfully."

"Oh, my dearest, I have missed you. It has been a nightmare, all those dear children so ill!"

"It's over, Joanna," he said, pulling her close. He bent over her and their lips touched. She closed her eyes and lost herself in the warmth and strength of his body. He kissed her deeply and her response was abandoned and uninhibited as she let her body fold into his. Abruptly he lifted his lips from hers and gently pushed her away.

"Ah, I find a damnable steel maiden," he grinned wickedly, referring of course, to her corset, "I liked the au naturel."

"You found me in an embarrassing situation, I rather had no choice," Joanna said, tossing her head. She wanted to rage at him, but his good natured smile stopped any further comment. He kissed the tip of her nose and each cheek.

They pulled apart as a maid entered the foyer.

"Best we join Her Ladyship for dinner," said Phillip as he tucked Joanna's arm through his. They entered the dining room as the butler was holding out a chair for Lady Adelaide. She eased her voluminous skirts to accommodate her seat and Joanna noted how regal she looked this evening.

Two huge vermeil candelabra cast a golden glow over the table. A gold Limoges service complemented the sterling flat wear and Baccarat crystal. Joanna sat opposite Phillip and as they consumed a dinner of Filet de Bouef; Phillip complemented Lady Adelaide on the cuisine.

"Ah, my Chef trained with Escoffier and I paid a mint for him to come west with me. He is an absolute delight and we shall dine like Parisians often. I hear grumbling from the kitchen at times, either he is having a 'to do' or else Cook is. They grate on each other, but that is understandable."

As they were enjoying dessert and champagne Phillip handed Joanna a black velvet box. Inside was a rope of pearls glistening like small opalescent moons.

"Oh, Phillip, you are too extravagant, they are beautiful!" exclaimed Joanna, her eyes sparkling with joy.

"They were my mother's, they have been in the family for ages and she wants you to have them."

"I will cherish them always. I must write and thank her for such a lovely gift."

"You will like each other. You both have much in common…me!" Phillip laughed mischievously.

"Oh, you…but I know I shall love her for she gave you life. I can well imagine what a lovely lady she is," dimpled Joanna as she caressed the pearls.

Phillip rose and fastened the necklace about Joanna's throat He gazed down at her with longing. Angling her head to one side, Joanna looked up at him through her long lashes. She took his breathe away. He kissed her neck and whispered, "It is tempting to just run away with you. Do we really need a large wedding?"

"Yes, Darling, I would be disowned if I eloped."

CHAPTER SEVEN

Joanna walked slowly through a golden sun washed morning. She loved the early morn with its bird song. The air was soft as a kiss and smelled of moist new growth. The apple trees were a blaze of white and pink and rose buds were opening along the brambles on the stone wall. Her body was alive and tingling with anticipation, aching to bloom like nature around her.

Annie had given birth two weeks ago to a beautiful boy and they named him Benjamin. It had been a hard labor, but the baby was flourishing and seemed to have suffered no ill effects from the measles. Elyce was due any day and the big house was bursting with activity. John and Frieda arrived home and had announced joyously that Frieda was pregnant! And amid all this excitement the details for Joanna's wedding were being finalized. It was almost more than one could bear. She wished she and Phillip had just run away and been married. It was definitely not a possibility now.

John laughed that Lady Adelaide and Frieda would put drill sergeants to shame. The garden was a sight; trellises and arbors had been built and sweet peas and other climbing vines had been planted. Frieda had *tubs of bulbs,* as she referred to them, strewn along the walks and the verandas.

"Heavens," Joanna had remarked, "there is so much natural beauty, you really don't need to go to all this work."

"Oh, bother, my dear…you only marry once and it should be as beautiful as one can make it. We must have baskets of flowers inside as well as outside," answered Lady Adelaide, "and we must have enough flowers and tulle to wrap the railings and balusters."

"Oh, I agree," Frieda had answered, "a perfect setting for our beautiful bride."

Joanna was relieved to be able to get away from the entire bustle to her school house. She loved teaching and her students. It gave her such a sense of fulfillment when she saw a child's face light up with acknowledgment. The written word was the source of all knowledge and when a pupil learned to read…the world was his for the taking. She had ordered books as parting gifts for her students as most could not afford them. The new teacher would arrive by September and Joanna would be a new bride by then.

She clasped her arms about her and hummed with happiness. Phillip had come for her on two weekends to seek her opinions of furnishing the house at Snowflake. It was much smaller and not as opulent as the big house at Locket Springs. Joanna convinced Phillip that details mattered little to her as long as it was comfortable. She would live in a tent if he were with her!

So much was happening, for an instance she felt a sense of panic. Her mother and grandmother were arriving the later part of June. Her feelings were mixed; joy at being with her beloved *Gram* again, but her feelings for her mother still bordered on disgust.

A sudden fury welled up inside her. Cousin Winifred was back in the States and pleading with John to give her permission to bring Marshall Davenport West for his blessing. Uncle John, so far, had refused to receive them. Joanna was concerned that someday they would arrive unannounced to once again cause heartache. Elyce and Timber would be moving to Montana after the wedding so, hopefully, her sister would not be subjected to this despicable pair should they come.

She stopped to look over the green fields rolling toward the lofty blue mountains. A mare and her colt were gamboling and the pure joy of being part of this brought a tear to Joanna's eye. She felt at home here, not a stranger in the world as she had before. She could understand the siren song of this wild country and why it had called the restless, the searchers, and dreamers like herself.

CHAPTER EIGHT

Joanna was waiting expectantly with Phillip as the carriages arrived at Locket Springs. As two women were helped down from the lead carriage, Joanna began to trip down the stairs toward them. Phillip followed while Joanna threw her arms around a striking woman in a large plumed hat.

"Gram, is it really you! I have prayed for this day!" cried Joanna with tears of joy sparkling in her eyes. Then she turned and holding a lace handkerchief to her eyes, introduced Phillip.

"I am honored, dear lady," said Phillip as he kissed Kate's hand.

Kate beamed at him as she adjusted her hat. "So, you are my dear Joanna's beau. I am delighted to meet you."

Then another voice echoed from the background. "Don't I even merit a greeting?" sniffed Caroline.

Joanna's smile vanished. "Oh, Mama, of course, welcome to Locket Springs."

Caroline turned her cheek for a kiss and then turned questionably to Phillip.

"Mama, may I present my fiancé, Phillip De LaCruz; Phillip, my mother, Caroline Holan."

Phillip responded, "Delighted to meet..." as Caroline disdainfully swept by him and proceeded up the stairs.

Phillip had been raised to have great respect for ceremony and ritual, especially when it came to elders. He was enraged with Caroline Holan's behavior and now understood Joanna's dislike of her mother.

Kate put her hand on his arm and smiled, "Young man, I would be honored if you help this stiff old woman up the stairs."

Phillip melted; what a magnificent lady. She had an enduring beauty and her bearing was almost regal.

Joanna grinned, "You see, Phillip? Gram is the Lady in our family!"

"Well, darling, luckily you have inherited her fine qualities," he answered as the three climbed the steps.

John was waiting at the portal. "Welcome, Mother," he said, embracing Kate. "Oh my dear, it is good to be here. Your house is beautiful."

He ushered them through the double doors into the foyer. Elyce was standing quietly as Caroline was helped with her wraps. Elyce joyfully turned to greet her grandmother with enthusiasm and love.

"Look at you! You are blooming like a rose, child. How lovely you are!" Kate exclaimed as she embraced Elyce.

"John, I am exhausted, may I be shown to my room?" grumbled Caroline.

"Of course, Hannah will show you to your rooms. You may take a bath, have a nap and if you feel refreshed enough you can join us for dinner. If not we plan a celebratory dinner tomorrow evening. Your luggage will be up promptly."

Dinner was a quiet affair with only John, Timber, Phillip, Lady Adelaide and Joanna. Frieda was nauseous, Elyce suffering back pain and Kate and Caroline had dinner in their rooms.

Phillip was seated next to Joanna.

"I do not understand your mother being so distant with you," he stated thoughtfully.

Joanna shrugged and took a sip of wine, "I appreciate your concern, darling, but she has always been this way. Mama will be Mama."

His eyes narrowed thoughtfully, "There must be a way to win her over. I can't imagine not having a close relationship with my mother. She disliked me immediately, is it because of our engagement or my heritage?"

Joanna curled her fingers over his arm. "Please do not be offended. Mama has been pampered all her life. She has yet to forgive Elyce her divorce."

"But my God, the circumstances!" His throat went dry. "I don't want you hurt, Joanna."

"A long as I have you, nothing can hurt me again." Her eyes were sparkling with unshed tears. "You make me cry, I love you so," she whispered softly.

John harrumped. "The family will be united tomorrow night. Mother will be excited to see the progress that Wilfred has made."

That brought a smile to Joanna's face. She was so proud of Willie and happy that she had been able to help him master reading and some writing.

"Uncle John, he was a gentle, sensitive young man trapped in a shell. You let go of him so he could find his way in a frightening world. He is a product of that love," stated Joanna.

"And yours, my dear niece. I will always be indebted to you for the many hours you spend with him," John answered as he toasted her with his glass.

"It was a learning experience for both Willie and me. I am glad to help and overjoyed at the progress he has made. Goodness, you have been so kind to me and my family; it was the least I can do."

John beamed at her. "Joanna, you have been a great source of pride to me. Knowing you will continue to be a part of our great valley gives me great happiness."

Phillip chuckled, "Not half as much happiness as it gives me."

Joanna blushed as he grabbed her hand and put it to her lips. He looked deep into her eyes; his voice warm and rich with emotion, "I have waited a lifetime for you. You are a vision I had as a lad, the woman of my young dreams and to think we almost lost each other..." He let out a long breath.

"Ah, sweet love! You wear it beautifully, children. Never have I seen two people more deserving than the two of you," Lady Adelaide said in her cultured warm voice. "Actually, I feel much the same about my dear son and Elyce. What romance, just like a story...two city bred, upper class girls finding their hearts in the West."

"Although Elyce misses the theaters and fancy restaurants, once that baby is born and she is settled in her new home; I think she will have all the contentment and happiness she can handle," added Timber smiling tenderly at his mother.

"Without a doubt," chuckled John pushing away from the table. "Brandy, gentlemen?"

Later in the evening Phillip and Joanna climbed the circular stairs to retire. When they reached the landing Joanna turned to Phillip, "It was a relaxing evening and I am so happy. Soon we will never have to part and say good night like this."

Phillip pulled her close, "I need a parting kiss to keep me warm, love."

His mouth captured hers and her body jolted with arousal. Her arms encircled his neck and she kissed him in return.

Phillip pulled back, stunned by the passion of her sweet mouth. Her uplifted face was flushed with desire. "Darling," he murmured and his lips brushed over hers. She moaned and he pulled her to him in a deep penetrating kiss. She moved her body into his and swooned in surrender.

Not now, not yet, he ordered himself. He pushed her gently back.

Dreamily she opened her eyes. "Phillip...?" Then the blur began to clear. A faint flush pinked her cheeks. "I must retire, good night, darling."

"Good idea as I have a mighty yen for you, lady," he replied, lifting an eyebrow in humor as she continued to blush and back away. "I can wait a bit longer, but it's not to my liking...best you scoot before I change my mind."

Relieved, she beamed with a mischievous grin, "I am glad you are such a gentleman as I was a bit forward tonight."

"My dear, you have no idea what forward means," he murmured then grabbed her and kissed her soundly. Leaving her head spinning he turned down the long corridor.

Holding fingers to her tingling lips, Joanna watched him stride away. She sighed as she watched the muscles ripple in his hard lean body. How magnificent he is…

Joanna woke to bright sunlight and stretched luxuriously. Phillip…what a, glorious name for such a handsome man! And to think she was to spend the rest of her life with him!

She ran her hands down her supple body and wiggled with delight thinking of all the wonders to come! Then…she remembered—Gram and Mama are here!

Joanna sat up and drew her wrapper around her. "Ahh., Mama., why can I not break through to you? Why can you not be happy for me, why are you so horrid to Phillip? Mama, I am marrying him with or without your blessing!"

Hannah helped her with her toilette. She brushed her lush radiant hair around a rat. The stylish roll framed her face and the soft tendrils fell about her ears in the "Gibson Girl" girl look. Joanna peered intently at her image in the silvered mirror. A large lace collar accentuated her black silk dress, certainly, her mother would approve. She pinned a cameo pin at her throat.

"Hannah, do I look as prim as I feel?' she giggled.

"Miss, you could dress in a coal sack and still be pretty," smiled Hannah.

Joanna stood, gave Hannah a hug and twirled out of the room.

The dining room sideboard was lined with silver serving dishes. The delectable odors emanating made Joanna's stomach growl. She poured a cup of coffee from an urn as the butler came forward. "May I serve you, senorita?"

"Gracias, Jose, but I will just help myself to whatever strikes me this morning. Have any of the family been down yet?"

"Si, senorita, Senor John and Senor Timber were here and gone long ago. The Lady Adelaide is in the Morning Room."

Warm teasing lips nuzzled her ear and she jolted and almost spilled her coffee. She turned and looked up into Phillip's eyes.

"Morning, love, you are up early!"

"Phillip! How you startled me; I never heard a thing!" She pouted prettily.

"Well, my dear, I cannot wear my spurs on an Aubusson carpet, now can I? That would really add to my disfavorable image."

Joanna giggled and continued along the sideboard. The green baize doors to the kitchen opened and Caroline came in with a swish of skirts.

"Good heavens! This place is so vast, I lost my way and ended up in the servant's quarters," she sniffed.

"Good morning to you, too, Mama," Joanna said as she took a tentative sip of coffee.

"Oh, but of course, it is a good morning...Joanna...Phillip," responded Caroline.

Phillip smiled as he pulled out a chair for Joanna then turning to Caroline he gestured, "May I?"

She swept by him and motioned to the butler.

Joanna felt her mouth drop. Phillip stood behind her, his smile gone. Joanna recovered herself, extended her hand to Phillip, but he excused himself and withdrew from the room.

Joanna sipped her coffee thoughtfully then addressed Caroline. "Mama, I need to have your opinion on a couple of issues."

Caroline arched an eyebrow. "With all due respect, Joanna, I cannot imagine your wanting my opinion on anything. You came west against my better judgment; you have become engaged without my meeting your fiancé, and you have made your wedding arrangements without consulting me. Frankly, what can there be left to discuss?"

"The fact remains that we are mother and daughter. I should hope that we can resolve some of this misunderstanding and be some what closer."

Caroline pursed her mouth which made small lines appear about it.

Although Caroline was still a stunning woman, Joanna sadly noted she wore a bit too much kohl and rice powder. There were definite lines around her mouth and the corners of her eyes. *Why, Mama has aged tremendously*, thought Joanna.

Caroline then scowled and it made her look even harsher. She changed the subject by saying, "I do give John credit. I am much impressed by this huge 'whatever' in the middle of nowhere. It must cost a fortune to maintain and run."

"It is quite self supporting, Mama. Much of the food comes from the gardens, orchards and animals. Uncle John has a vast herd of cattle and a good market for them. He also raises and trains horses. He runs a very smooth operation."

"Well," frowned Caroline, "he is ancestral rich; also railroad, bank and stock rich should one care to take note? Remember…because your father had no sense with money, we are now beholden to this family and I have lost my daughters!"

To this Joanna merely shook her head. "Regardless, Gram and Uncle John have been wonderful and gracious about the circumstances. I have never been made to feel intrusive and always accepted as family."

"Be that as it may, you are still a poor relation as I am, Joanna," stated Caroline.

"Oh, really Mama, quit feeling sorry for yourself and be thankful you have this family!"

"Someday you will realize what independence is when you have your own home and you are the mistress of it!" Caroline snorted and continued, "I came to your father with a large endowment, but I had no say in how or where it was spent. I was such a fritter-head about the necessities of life and it is too late for me now."

"Mama, you are still young and attractive. Possibly you will meet someone yet in life that you can care for. I wish you could be happy for me, and Mama, please do not be so rude to Phillip."

"Rude?" answered Caroline blankly. "I have hardly said a word to him."

Elyce came in quietly and was seated.

Joanna nodded to her with a smile and continued the conversation with her mother. "Don't pretend your behavior has been exemplary. Phillip is a wonderful person and I will not have you treating him like a barnyard fowl!"

"Heavens, Joanna, you jest! You push this part Red man in my face and expect me to welcome him with open arms…oh, I think not!"

"Mama!" exclaimed Elyce with disgust.

Joanna pushed away from the table and threw her napkin down. "Phillip is of royal heritage; he is half French and half Spanish. He is not an Indian…but it would not matter to me, I love him! And a little advice, Mother, while here I would not be too critical of the Indians. Many work for Uncle John and he would take great exception to that!"

"Yes, Mama, we would hate to see you scalped for they are a very proud people!" laughed Elyce.

"Oh, bother, you have both lost your senses! I do not understand how both of you with your background and raising have become so wanton!" wailed Caroline.

Elyce scolded, "Come now, Mama, we are going to get mired in awful quicksand here if you do not stop this sarcasm. Neither Joanna nor I have done anything immoral. Furthermore, your disdainful treatment of Phillip is disgraceful. Your prissy airs will do you in one of these days!"

Turning to Joanna, Elyce stated, "I am going to have my coffee in the Morning Room."

As Elyce rose and started toward the door, Joanna saw rage flame in her mother's eyes. "So...you both think I am a bigot and prissy, do you? I will tell you this; you have both pained me beyond endurance! I have no control over anything. Your father destroyed me and neither of you have any respect for me. I have lost any meaning to my life!"

Joanna bit her lip and then softly said, "We all suffered, Mama. Elyce is now happier than I have ever known her to be. Look at the horrors she suffered with that heathen that Winifred ran away with. He will do the same to her. Be happy for Elyce."

Caroline sniffed, "He adores Winifred; he has lavished boundless gifts on her. Granted, I regret that they eloped; it could have been the wedding of the season!"

Joanna stared at her mother in disbelief. She was truly frightened by her reasoning.

Caroline, in turn, studied her daughter. She had to admit Joanna had matured into a beautiful woman. Her violet eyes had always been outstanding and there was a definite glow now that had never been there before. Strange how Winifred and Joanna resembled each other, almost twin images. Winifred was more garish, true, but she enjoyed being seen and socializing; Joanna never had. Winifred, in many ways, was more like her than her own daughters. Ah, well, there was a wedding to prepare for even if it wasn't to her liking. Then, there was that baby coming. Caroline Holan, a grandmother...still quite unthinkable!

"Mama, did you hear a thing I said?" Joanna asked.

"Oh, I was a world away..."

"Please, I should like to go over my wedding plans with you. Elyce has been a great help, but she tires easily now. You are so accomplished at organizing functions and I really need your help. Phillip's parents will be arriving in a matter of weeks and I must plan for their comforts as well. They have an enormous ranchero in New Mexico and are close friends of the Governor. He has been invited and may attend, also. I would like to have a dinner in their honor before the wedding."

Caroline brightened at this information.

"Hmmm, Phillip's family must be in the proper social circles if they are friends of the Governor! Yes, helping to plan the festivities will keep me from being bored out of my mind."

Relieved that her mother was warming up to her appeals, Joanna continued, "It would be such a great relief and would mean so much to Phillip and I if you would help with the preparations, Mama."

"I must admit it sounds promising. I would like to see your gown; Lady Adelaide assured me it was stunning."

"Whenever you wish, Mama."

Kate entered on the arm of John with Lady Adelaide following.

"Good morning! Oh, Gram, it is so good to have you here!" exclaimed Joanna, rising to kiss Kate's cheek. "Are you exhausted?"

"My darling girl, I feel wonderful. I was out early taking the morning air when this handsome rogue spotted me and escorted me in for breakfast. Lady Adelaide joined us and we have had the best visit. I am going to retire for awhile."

"And I must go find Phillip, we still have many details to finalize," Joanna stated. She turned to her uncle and inquired, "Is Frieda feeling better, Uncle John?"

"Indeed, she is budding like a rose!" John retorted, his face beaming. "Am I not fortunate, Locket Springs will have its own wee one at last?"

Phillip was leaning against a wall in the stable watching the horses being groomed, his mind on Joanna. He was thinking intensely about her relationship with her mother. *My sweet love is strong willed, but so innocent and vulnerable. I will wager her mother has never given her an ounce of direction except to look exquisite and learn the social graces. She seems to have no knowledge what so ever of sexual matters. She has been hurt and frightened, which seems to make her keep her distance...but there is an underlying passion beginning to bubble. Her response to my kisses is about to undo me and I struggle to keep myself in control. She is so sensuous in her lady-like innocence. Ah, what a marriage this will be, to feel that satin skin against mine and those long, slender legs wrapped around me! Slow down, Phillip...you are getting wicked thoughts.*

He felt her presence before he saw her. She was coming toward him with rapid small steps. Taking a deep, steadying breath, he stood tall and watched her approach with a roguish grin.

Joanna's heart began to do a little dance as she took in every magnificent inch of him. His eyes locked on hers, the look was definitely smoldering. In two strides he had her in his arms.

"Phillip, the grooms!" she whispered against his lips.

"S-h-h-h, come with me," he whispered back and led her away from the grooms and horses to an empty stall beyond.

"I came to find you so I could apologize for my mother's insolence," she said softly.

He pushed her up against the wall and began to kiss her. The kiss was sweet and hot and Joanna lost herself in the sheer ecstasy of it. She felt his fingers move down her throat and his hand cover her breast. Jolts of liquid fire turned her knees weak.

As he kissed her eyes, her cheek, her throat…he soon felt her arch into him. His nobility took hold and he pushed himself from her.

Joanna, none to pleased by the interruption, blushed prettily and smoothed her dress and hair. She then smiled impishly, happy to be back in control of her emotions although she found Phillip's aggressive behavior intoxicating. She knew she was acting improperly, but it was thrilling to have the power to make Phillip desire her so. She was dizzy with love and she wanted him, she felt very naughty. This was so delicious!

Willing her heart to slow, she purred, "I like these discussions. I hope we can have many prolonged ones in the future, darling."

"You are becoming a venturesome vixen. Now I understand why tantalizing little girls like you need chaperones!" Phillip said, breathing hard.

"Oh, to protect little girls from lusty big boys like you?" she teased.

"No, imp, to protect boys like me from ravishing delectable girls like you!"

With that he nibbled her lips, then thrust his tongue in her mouth and kissed her deeply until she swooned in his arms. He released her, grabbed her hand and pulled her along behind him. "Time to find a chaperone," he snarled.

"Ah, you are so noble," she squeaked, trying to keep up with his long strides.

"Careful, pet, I will tell your mother, she will be appalled at your behavior!"

"Most assuredly! Oh, no joking about Mama; she gives me a frightful headache," pleaded Joanna.

"Sorry, shall we go to the house and discuss whatever? I believe it wise as I cannot keep my hands off you."

"I suppose I should be grateful for your concern, Phillip," then blushing again, she said, "It is just that I am experiencing so many new emotions!"

"Wait until you are mine, dear one. I will make you unfold like a rose, each experience more delightful than the last."

"You promise?"

"I do."

"This school marm of no shame can hardly wait. We really must be wise and cause no raised eyebrows meanwhile. I shall not give my mother any reason to frown on our behavior."

"I should say not," said Phillip as they stepped up to the veranda. "Therefore, I will not stay in your presence without someone present."

"And I will be a model of virtuous behavior!" dimpled Joanna and batted her long lashes at him.

"Stop that, you have no idea the effect you have on me."

Laughing together, they entered the vast hall. Phillip kissed her cheek and left her for John's study. Joanna went into the morning room where Frieda, Caroline and Lady Adelaide were chatting.

Frieda was indeed blooming in looks and circumference. "You've never looked more beautiful, Frieda," stated Joanna.

"Pshaw, can you believe this foolish old woman in this condition?" answered Frieda with a twinkle.

"It becomes you and Uncle John is about to pop all his vest buttons," laughed Joanna.

"Really, Joanna, don't be vulgar," admonished Caroline.

Lady Adelaide raised her eyebrows mocking Caroline and then winked at Joanna. "Perhaps we might show your mother your gown. I am certain she will approve."

"Of course, if she is of the mind…Mama?"

"Yes, I would like to see her choice," said Caroline and accompanied Joanna and Lady Adelaide out of the room. As they walked the hallway to the sewing room, Kate exited her room.

"Come join us, Kate, we are going to look at Joanna's gown," said Caroline.

The richly textured gown on the dress from brought gasps of appreciation from both Kate and Caroline. The oyster white satin had floral appliques of pearls, silvery beads and golden embroidery cascading down the front skirt of the gown. Exotic beadwork enhanced the bodice and rear back. The slight bustle was overcast with a removable train. The headpiece was attached to the top of the dress form and a long white lace veil swirled from it to the floor.

"How dramatic! Imagine finding something this elegant in such God forsaken country!" Caroline exclaimed wide eyed.

"Oh, Mama, honestly…you give me a dreadful headache! This land is inhabited by intelligent civilized people. You tend to think only the east coast is America."

"Humph," snorted Caroline, "what advantages have you here? There is no society, no balls, no theatre and you are marrying an unknown. Remember, daughter, there is more than the business of a trousseau in a marriage! Your husband owns you, everything you have is his…even your correspondence…and he can demand an accounting day or night. Now that I have learned that your husband to be is from an ancient aristocracy, I hope you are aware they give no privileges to their women."

"Goodness, Mama, Phillip knows I am of an independent nature; he would never humble or mistreat me!" Joanna answered, greatly agitated.

"The Spanish have an inflexible code of honor, Joanna. They are reputed to be hot blooded, full of temper and marry only for begetting heirs."

Phillip is half French. He was born in America and his father married for love as Phillip and I are."

Kate interrupted the heated conversation by inquiring as to where she could find the writing room. She hugged Joanna, complimented her on the gown and hustled Caroline out of the room.

A great sense of despair came over Joanna and she sank to the floor in a billow of skirts. She began to sob like a child. Why did Mama always find fault? She continually took away the joy of the moment.

"Oh, my poor darling!" exclaimed Lady Adelaide sinking to the floor beside her.

"She surely isn't as shallow as she sounds, love. She loves you girls."

Joanna answered between sobs. "She is somehow incapable of loving me. I continue to hope that someday I will meet with her approval. She can, in a word or a look, make me feel so incompetent and insignificant." She blew her nose in a lace hankie and continued, "Poor Mama will never understand as Papa never loved her as Phillip does me."

Lady Adelaide cooed, "Then you are indeed blessed and remember that always, child. Someday, perhaps, she will understand seeing your happiness. Now, please help this old woman up; I should never get in such a position!"

Joanna laughed through her tears and rose to help Lady Adelaide by clasping hands and pulling. Once on her feet Lady Adelaide hugged Joanna fiercely and said, "Be strong, dear."

CHAPTER NINE

The very day Phillip's parents arrived by train at Stirrup Cup, Elyce went into labor at Locket Springs. A lusty little boy was born shortly after midnight. The relieved family members were ecstatic. Both mother and baby were fine.

The doctor assured everyone that Elyce had been further along in her pregnancy than he had thought. "Nor unusual for a first child," he commented as he enjoyed a brandy with Timber and John.

Timber toasted his wife, "To my beautiful wife; am I not the most blessed of men? She has given me a miracle…was there ever such a child?"

"But of course, my friend, we all marvel at the miracle of birth. It brings us closer to our Maker…imagine the joy He experienced with the birth of His son," John said with gusto.

Joanna slipped into the room where Elyce lay. In the soft light she looked radiant. Her hair was in disarray and faint violet shadows were apparent under her eyes. When she saw Joanna she smiled with a joy so intense her eyes beamed like sun on blue topaz.

"Oh, Jo, I am exhausted, but so happy. Isn't he beautiful?"

The baby was wrapped in a cocoon of lace and blankets and cuddled in the curve of his mother's arm. A crown of pale gold fuzz framed a perfect little face with a rosebud for a mouth.

"Indeed he is, dearest, and now you must rest. Timber insists on staying with you so I will look in on you later."

Joanna kissed Elyce lightly on her forehead and quietly left the room, tears sparkling in her eyes.

Joanna slept fitfully, pursued by dreams. She awoke cold although coals glowed in the fireplace and she was buried under her goose down quilt. Still exhausted from the few restless hours of sleep, she found it impossible to stay in bed a moment longer. There were dozens of things to attend to and Phillip's parents were to be honored at a dinner two nights hence.

She would be forever grateful to Frieda, Lady Adelaide and Mama who seemed to be in their glory making arrangements. They must be exhausted over the birthing, but it would indeed add to the festivities!

Annie had agreed to oversee the new hires and as Joanna came downstairs it became obvious the whole manor was alive with decorating. Flowers were arriving in long waxed boxes by wagon. Frieda had the kitchen help baking and preparing menus for the following days. Everything looked to be going well so Joanna decided to go upstairs and visit Elyce and the baby.

Kate and the nurse were in attendance.

"Joanna, dear, would you like to hold your nephew?" asked a beaming Kate.

"Oh, Gram, I would love to." Gingerly Joanna shifted the baby into her arms. He felt so fragile and small. She touched his cheek with her finger and a tiny fist gripped it. She fell instantly in love.

"Oh, my, is there anything more perfect than a baby? He even smells heavenly!"

"Oh, Jo," laughed Elyce from her bed, "you are smitten, too. I never thought I could love anything as I do this baby. My heart is bursting, he is such a miracle. I have never felt closer to God." Elyce wiped a tear from her eye and continued, "And Timber, he is beside himself..." and she began to cry, "Oh, I hope nothing happens..."

Joanna handed the baby to the nurse who smiled and said, "That's the way of it, new mothers all happy one minute and weepy the next."

Joanna knelt beside her sister. "Elyce, darling, you are the dearest, sweetest sister anyone could ever want. You deserve this happiness. You have been blessed with a wonderful husband and this cherub. You will soon be in your new home and never will you want for anything again...emotionally or materially. Shhh, no more tears."

"I know, Jo. It's just that I am so happy it frightens me."

"I feel the same way," answered Joanna simply. "Sometimes when I awake I fear I have only been dreaming. I also feel guilty that I have such joy while Mama is so sad."

"Ah, Mama revels in her state. She can be a great actress and knows when to manipulate us all. I honestly don't believe she realizes she drives us a bit looney."

The bedroom door opened and the fragrance of roses engulfed the room. Annie came in carrying two baskets of white and pink roses. Timber followed with more flowers.

"My stars, how lovely!" exclaimed Elyce holding out her arms to her husband. Timber sat the flowers beside the bed and crushed his wife to him. Joanna discreetly left the room with Annie.

"Curses, everything happens at once," Joanna muttered as she pined her diamond star in her hair. She still had a headache that had been dulled by powders Lady Adelaide had given her and now the word arrived that the musical trio had canceled because of illness. This would make it necessary for her to play the piano following dinner.

Heavens, she was nervous enough having just met Phillip's mother. The Snowflake entourage had arrived early afternoon. Senora Mercedes De La Cruz was lovely and had charmed everyone including Mama. Joanna smiled as she knew her mother had been most impressed with Don Carlos. *Mama will never admit it, but I could sense it. I believe Don Carlos swept her quite off her feet with his manners and Senora Mercedes can match Mama's flair for flamboyance; won't that be interesting?*

What an understatement ! When Don Carlos, Mercedes and Phillip were announced that evening, Mercedes wore a simple satin gown, but on her head she displayed a diamond and pearl diadem. A diamond and pearl choke collar sparkled around her throat and bracelets of diamonds glittered over elbow length gloves. Don Carlos looked his aristocratic best in immaculate black and white. Phillip, as always, was breathtakingly handsome.

Joanna watched the three of them descend into the Great Room and she was overcome by pride and emotion. She felt fleeting regret that her father could not he here. He would have thoroughly enjoyed Don Carlos.

Dinner was a happy occasion. The men discussed America's future of trade, banking and the great influx of foreigners. The women, when possible, described the latest fashions to one another and the plans for the upcoming wedding.

Mercedes poise and knowledge were most impressive and when she addressed her audience, she spoke in glowing terms of her love of family and of the Casa de Flores Rancho. She added that everyone was welcome to come as guests at their earliest convenience.

An astonishing change came over Caroline in the following days. She had been so impressed and charmed by Phillip's parents that her disapproval of Phillip evaporated. Joanna could not believe at what a turn around her mother made and was very relieved.

"Maybe I misjudged Mama too harshly," she said to Elyce as they discussed the turn of events.

Elyce reminded Joanna with firmness, "Never forget, for the most part, Mama is acting in a dream world. She is far too involved with herself to actually give a hoot about anyone."

These words were spoken with such a coldness Joanna was taken back. "But, dear, she was there for you during your difficulties and healing," sputtered Joanna.

"Only because Gram shamed her into being there. Lady Adelaide was also insistent that she be with me!" Elyce cooed to her newborn and said, "Now that I am a mother, I find it even harder to relate to Mama."

Joanna, loving and sensitive to other's feelings was bereft for her sister. Perhaps, in time, Elyce could let go of some of the bitterness she felt towards Mama; especially now that she had such a devoted husband and her beautiful baby to love.

"And you, Joanna, how did you react to her allowing Winifred to see Marshall? All of this is too disgusting for me to deal with," continued Elyce.

"Oh, I agree," Joanna said defensively, "I feel a dangerous and evil force at work in that relationship. I believe that Mama thought that Marshall was a plum for social affairs. I do not think she realized how much Winifred would do to get her way. I cannot say I ever understood or liked Winifred. Her childhood circumstances were never the best with her mother so ill and Willie was such a great embarrassment to her. Thank Heavens for Gram; what would have become of any of us?"

Joanna looked pensively out the window. "We both know how ruthless Marshall was. He may have changed, I doubt it, but possibly Winifred has his complete devotion and abiding love. I truly pray he has changed and he is not as perverse; he was so very cruel in his irrationalities."

"Yes, like a snake!" spat Elyce.

Joanna turned and walked over to Elyce and the baby, "Let us forget Winnie, let me hold my adorable nephew."

Elyce handed the baby to Joanna as they continued to talk, each consoling the other as best they could about their mother.

"Have you and Timber decided on a name for this angel?" Joanna asked.

"Yes, he will be christened Charles Andrew after his grandfathers," replied Elyce.

"That is so special, our little Charlie."

"Never, it must be Charles. Timber and I are in agreement on that," Elyce solemnly avowed.

"Then Charles it will be, little darling," said Joanna as she kissed the infant on his forehead.

CHAPTER TEN

Joanna awakened filled with an unfamiliar sense of euphoria. It was the day before the nuptials and the anxiety and sadness she lived with daily was replaced with relief and joy.

She arose quickly and pulled on her dressing gown as she hugged herself and laughed out loud. Tomorrow was her wedding day! Her Phillip was everything she could ever want or desire in another human being! He would be hers and she would be his forever.

So much had been taken from her; Papa…her home…the loss of her sister to the devil…then losing her first love to her sister…her maidenhood…the loss of security and the anguish of little or no self esteem. The awful knowledge that Mama seemed incapable of loving her; the enormous expectations Mama had that could not be met under any circumstances once Papa had died had only added to her unhappiness. Now, she happily, will be a part of a new family, an intimate close knit one. Phillip's brother, Antonio and his wife had arrived last evening. Joanna was anxious to meet them, but, in all likelihood, would not until tomorrow.

After dressing she tripped down the stairs and was greeted by female voices and sounds of workmen coming through the terrace doors. She immediately went out to the terrace where a vision of loveliness greeted her. Tables covered in linen were being set up centered with candelabra surrounded by pink roses and baby's breath. Large vases were being arranged from huge tubs of lilacs interspersed with Blue Mist Spirea, Lily of the Valley, Virgin's Bower and purple cornflowers. Baskets of pink and white roses banked the arbor. The arbor itself had been interwoven with white ribbon, wild asters, pink roses, evergreens and baby's breath. Lady Adelaide was spritzing it with water. White and gold Chinese lanterns were being strung from branches while potted palms lined the aisle to the arbor. The effect was magical. Two long buffet tables were set up on either side of the aisle. Caroline said one was for the bride's and groom's cakes and the other for the buffet. Caroline was placing name cards and putting small pebbles on them so they wouldn't blow away. She was humming to herself. Joanna smiled inwardly; Mama was always happy when entertaining.

Meanwhile at Snowflake, Phillip and Don Carlos were in the study going over books. "Well done, son, you have made this old man very proud. You have not only turned this spread around, but it is now running in the black. The stallions are healthy and the mares have thrown some promising colts."

Phillip poured brandy into two snifters and handed one to his father. "To Snowflake and the future," he said as he touched his crystal rim to his father's.

Don Carlos inhaled deeply of the snifter and then savored a sip. "Does Joanna favor riding?"

"She is very at home in the saddle. She enjoys riding into the mountains and loves the solitude and scenery. Although she is a crack shot, it is still wilderness and I insist she never ride alone."

"That is a wise precaution, especially for a woman. Lots of cats and bears to say nothing of the wolves out there."

Finishing his brandy, Don Carlos went to the window. He clasped his hands behind his back and took a slow sweep of the panorama. The jagged mountains rose purple and blue; green fields dotted with livestock fell away to the river sparkling in the distance.

"Beautiful country, my son, I forget how magnificent it is. I wonder how long it will be before it becomes overrun? What of our Indian brothers? The Americanos drove them deep into Mexico or put them on reservation. I love America, but my ancestors in their search for oro did more harm than good."

"Ah, Father, if it had not been the Spanish, it would have been the French or English. It was just a matter of time: pointed out Philip. "And you have forgotten the slaves, are you going to add that to the discredit of Spain, also?"

Turning away from the window Don. Carlos's face was a picture of disgust. "Yes, they had slave ships, also. Believe me, Phillip, greed made the white men heartless when it came to Negroes and the Red Man."

Phillip retorted swiftly, "But, Father, the Negro tribes sold their own people...never forget that! Then there were the Europeans who sold indentured humans as slaves...most of them debtors...and not black! How about the Irish, talk about heartless...Annie is a good example. Because of a potato blight, the English landowners starved the Irish almost into extinction. Annie's family managed to get her to America and if it had not been for Joanna's grandmother, Annie would never have had a chance. Joanna taught her to read and write; she is bright young woman. And lest we forget...the child labor! America runs on it!"

"The white man again!" retorted Don Carlos.

Phillip pushed back his chair and stood up. "Apparently, there are no quick solutions. England is shipping her prisoners to Australia. What will the future of that country be? I still believe that democracy works, not perfectly, but maybe in time."

Don Carlos studied his handsome son for a minute. "I hope so for the sake of my grandchildren and those yet to be. America is like many little countries trying to be one. There can never be a true American until the country is totally interbred which may never happen."

"The true American is the Red Man, Father."

"Amazing, Phillip, after all your education, you assume this?"

Phillip nodded. "They have been here for centuries."

"Si, but what does history say? They came across the continent from Asia then down from the Aleutians."

"Granted, but that is an assumption, also."

"No…"

A firm knock on the door halted the discussion.

"My dears, are you noting the time? We must leave shortly for Locket Springs, I would hate to be tardy," came the sweet familiar voice of Mercedes outside the door.

"Enter, my darling, we are receiving today." laughed Don Carlos opening the door and bowing from the waist.

"Oh, M'sieur, how gracious of you," twinkled Mercedes as she swept by him.

"Seriously, loves, I am most anxious to be on our way."

"Madre de Dios, the wedding is tomorrow. Rest your worries, we will get your son there well before evening," chuckled Don Carlos putting an arm around his wife.

"I will have Sanchez get the carriage ready," said Phillip as he left the study.

Pulling open the massive oak door, Phillip headed for the stables. His thoughts turned to tomorrow. He pictured his violet eyed Joanna coming to him, her hair cascading about her shoulders like liquid copper. His breath caught at the image. Tomorrow she would be his! What a rocky relationship so full of misunderstandings it had been. The one thing they had in common was the love they had for each other. Well, maybe two things in common, their love of the savage beauty of this country.

She was so dependent on her show of independence! He laughed to himself; she had fire, his Joanna! He had hardened himself to ever feeling anything after the death of his wife and yet, in the twinkling of an eye, this minx had ridden into his life, turned his insides to mush and changed his life forever.

"Hey Senor Phillip, you need your carriage?" Sanchez fell in along side.

"Yep, amigo, it is time. You will take care of my parents while they oversee the ranch until my return from the honeymoon?"

Sanchez slapped him on the shoulder. "Don't worry, señor, you take care of that pretty girl and I will guard Madre y Padre with my life."

The wedding dawn was gold and rose. Joanna sat in her wrapper sipping coffee while buffing her nails. Her teeth were actually chattering from nervousness! Her night had been fitful and full of sad dreams. She loved Phillip more than life itself and yet, the fear was beginning to creep in. True, she was *soiled*...not a virgin physically, but virginal in every other sense of the word. The horrifying experience of her rape by Marshall had made her weep in despair for months. Now she had surrendered her heart, but would she willingly be able to surrender her body? She felt stricken, could she be responsive to Phillip, or would she repel his love making? Would she do something rash to disappoint him? Would she make him happy?

A rap came at her door, she all but jumped out of her skin. "It is Gram," called Kate.

"Oh, come," sniffed Joanna.

Kate entered and her weepy granddaughter threw her arms about her. "Why, child, whatever is wrong?"

"Oh, Gram, I am so frightened...absolutely unhinged! I cannot marry Phillip!"

Kate led Joanna over to the settee and sat down beside her. "I think everyone soon to take their vows feels something akin to panic. We can only touch hearts through God and have the faith He brought you together."

Kate looked into space for a minute, smiled and then said, "It seems only yesterday that I felt the fluttering of my heart when I married your Grandfather. My legs were like water as I walked the aisle in Trinity Church." She laughed, "I kept saying to myself, 'Lucky groom, there he stands with his fellows while I am on display like a prize heifer...one turn of the ankle and 300 guests will be in titters!' My anger keep me upright on Father's arm as I made that ghastly walk. Then, a wonderful thing happened; the minute I looked up at your Grandfather standing there so tall and victorious, he looked down at me and winked! My butterflies subsided, the anger forgotten and my heart soared. I never had a doubt after that moment."

Kate rocked Joanna as she had as a girl. Joanna felt her panic lessen as she inhaled the sweet scent of lemon verbena that Kate wore; it comforted her just as it had when she was a child.

"Thank you, Gram. At times I feel God brought us together but then, I am so conscious of the inequity I bring to this marriage. I have no assets, so to speak, I am not a good cook, I have no experience in handling a household and…" again Joanna began to weep. "You and Uncle John have been so supportive and caring, what will I do without you both?"

"Heavens, John will be just over the hill from you. You will always be in my heart as I am in yours. God watches over us both You created a school out of nothing, studied and became a teacher. That is a hard thing for today's woman! Becoming a housekeeper on a ranch will also be a challenge, but I know you will do the task well. You will make a splendid wife and mother, Joanna."

Drawing apart Kate continued, "Dry your eyes and I will have a breakfast tray brought to you. Do you want Elyce or your mother with you?"

"Neither. Elyce will be feeding Charles and Mama would just make me more crazy. Hannah will help me dress and Annie will dress my hair. I will be fine now."

"Good," said Kate. She pressed Joanna's hand and stood. "Just remember God is with you both."

Joanna's eyes now sparkled not from tears, but determination and a bit of thoughtful bliss. She rose and went to a drawer and removed a tissue wrapped bundle. She removed the beautiful pair of pumps Phillip had given her that long ago Christmas when he had first proposed.

Late afternoon Hannah and Annie carefully lower the satin gown over her head. Joanna looks at the amazing creature that gazes back at her from the cheval mirror. A woman with dreamy long lashed eyes, a woman with dramatic decolletage and graceful arms and shoulders melting into oyster satin…this is an illusion! I look beautiful…I would imagine all brides must feel this way. Annie pins her veil onto a pearl comb and hands her a bouquet of rose buds and lilies-of-the-valley.

"Are we ready, then?" asked Elyce from behind her. Elyce was a vision in aqua French Crepe. Her hat of aqua plumes curled over the left side of her face concealing the puckered scar. She flashed a smile that bespoke of her happiness for Joanna. "You look divine, darling."

Annie and Frieda, her bridesmaids, were gowned in watered champagne silk.

"So unconventional," Caroline had complained

"We are very common folk here, Mama…and they are my best friends!" Joanna had replied, ending that discussion.

The sound of music could be heard faintly and the four women hurried to the lift. Once the stuttering cage stopped they began the walk to the garden.

A hush of expectation fell over the seated guests. Following the procession of relatives, matron of honor and bridesmaids, Lohenegrin's Wedding March began.

Joanna comes into view on the arm of her uncle, there is a gasp from the crowd; she looks beautiful. The flickering candles caress her glittering image as she moves slowly toward the arbor where Phillip awaits. A whispered murmur of appreciation follows.

Philip, immaculate in tails, is overwhelmed by the vision coming to him. Truly, this memory will linger forever and his eyes dim with tears. No bride was ever more breathtaking. Joanna's veil covered her from head to toe both revealing and concealing exquisitely. When Phillip took her hand from John, his heart turned over. They clung to each other in happiness as they pledge their lives to each other.

"The ring, Phillip, the ring," nudged Antonio holding the platinum band.

Phillip shakily placed the band on Joanna's finger as the priest intoned the blessings. Elyce lifted the veil over Joanna's head. Her eyes were sparkling with tears. Phillip leaned and kissed his bride. She felt like heaven and looked like an angel! He touched her cheek and whispered, "My dearest wife."

"Oh, I am so happy, Phillip, I now belong to you." She smiled through her tears.

"Indeed you do, darling."

The magical evening began as they greeted their guests and became surrounded by family and friends.

Joanna was standing quietly watching Phillip as he danced with his mother when she felt a tap on her shoulder.

"Jo-o-o, m-m-may I have the pleasure?" Willie stammered with happiness.

"Indeed you can, dear," smiled Joanna. Her beautiful pumps were beginning to pinch after being swirled about for ever so long, but she would never refuse Willie a dance.

"You know, I c-c-could never have l-l-earned to dance if you h-h-had not taught me," he commented as he led her in a waltz. "You have been so g-g-good I love you."

"Oh, my dear, I was just a small part of it. You feel secure here with your father. Buck and the rest of the men have given you self confidence. You are wonderful with the animals."

"Yep, I love animals. I asked Aunt Caroline to dance. She said I s-s-smelled like a h-h-horse!"

"Well, we live in horse country and I would wager we all smell a bit of horses!"

Willie snorted and laughed heartily. "When I grow up, I am g-g-going to f-f-find me a gal just like you...you make me feel okay."

"You make me feel okay, too, Willie," she said, and to herself she prayed, *Lord, take care of this child in a man's body. He is a good boy!*

Phillip was waiting as she came off the dance partition. "Come, darling, grab your bouquet and kiss the relatives. It is time for us to be on our way."

Kate was the last person Joanna embraced and tears streamed down both faces. "Gram, you will be gone upon our return and I shall miss you so!" wept Joanna.

"Stop that infernal sniffling, child!" said Kate, wiping her eyes. "Phillip has promised to bring you to Queensgate before returning to the ranch."

"Oh, dearest Phillip, I so love you!" she smiled as she kissed her groom on his cheek.

"Please, darling," urged Phillip, "we must discard our wedding clothes and be on our way. John's railway car is to be switched in the morning. We shall miss the east bound if we dally any longer."

The Pullman Palace car was indeed elegant with thick Brussels carpet and velvet drapes. Walnut woodwork, plate mirrors and chandeliers all added to the ambience. Joanna collapsed on a velvet ottoman and looked about her in wonder. True her father had had his private car, but it had been ages ago or so it seemed. Joanna had forgotten how luxurious they were. In the early dawn a bed would be heaven, she thought. She was exhausted and her eyes were heavy.

"How thoughtful of John," said Phillip as he lifted a magnum of champagne from ice. With a flourish he uncorked the bottle. The pop of the cork quite jolted Joanna awake and she watched a Phillip poured two flutes and came to her.

Holding a glass out to her, he smiled. "I know love, you are about done in, but let us toast our wedding night or rather, morning. You can then undress and nap."

Joanna drank deep of the champagne; it was cold and delicious. "More please," she said, holding the faceted crystal goblet up. The warmth of the golden liquid coursed through her body.

Phillip pulled her to her feet and led her to the bed compartment. Joanna saw her peignoir lying across the bed. She picked it up with a nervous laugh and closed the door to the lavatory. She scrubbed away the dust from the carriage ride, undid her hair and slipped into the lacy gown. She blushed as she looked into the beveled mirror....my heavens, she was practically nude! She reached for the wrapper and tied the bow; the high lace collar scratched her chin.

Phillip was sitting on the edge of the bed in a velvet smoking robe when she emerged from the lavatory. He gave her a charming smile lifting an eyebrow in appreciation.

Just then a hard jolt was felt and Joanna fell into Phillip's arms.

"They are coupling the cars, darling and perhaps, that is what we should be thinking about." He kissed her deeply and began to untie the bows of her peignoir. The slow motion of the train began.

"Are you really too exhausted to let me love you?" Phillip whispered as he kissed her face and nuzzled her neck.

"I don't know..." she forced out; her heart leaping into her throat...

His fingers brushed like feathers over her taut nipples. He kissed her lightly with small kisses all over her face then drew back and looked at her. Her eyes stayed on his, trusting, as he peeled back the peignoir and rolled with her onto the bed. He nuzzled her breasts through the silk then eased her back and took off his robe. He again kissed her until she felt herself teetering on the brink of wanting...wanting. His mouth left hers and wandered down...down. He peeled the gown down and removed it. Her skin was the color of cream; her full breasts tipped with pale pink nipples were utter perfection...the small waist and then the lovely curve of her full hips and those incredible long legs. A low moan of appreciation escaped from Phillip. Joanna watched him cautiously now very aware of her nudity.

"You are spell binding, Joanna, so very lovely," he murmured. Then his mouth was on hers and he growled deep in his throat. She arched into him and her hands began to move over him as urgently as his mouth was over her. Her body was singing with desire. In an exhalation of surrender she continued to run her hands over him shyly, feeling his contours; this magnificent male body banded with muscle...and yet the velvet hard shape of him!

Phillip caressed her body until she felt faint with wanting him. He gently forced her legs apart and his hand cupped and stroked. She went blind with sensation and he then moved gently on top of her.

The horror of Marshall came back; the reaction was instinctive. She tried to roll away and pushed against him. "No, no!"

"Hush, my darling, it is me….just try to relax. There is nothing to fear from me. I promise I will never force or hurt you," whispered Phillip into her quivering mouth. He carefully, tenderly once again kissed and loved away all the inhibitions and apprehension. Slowly she opened up, then erupted and gave him her body with love. It was more than could be imagined, she wept with joy and thanked God for him. They consummated their marriage again…and again as the train moved eastward.

CHAPTER ELEVEN

What days and nights of bliss. All about were the sounds of Parisian French, a language like a verbal message of love. Joanna and Phillip spent hours strolling down the streets of Paris built long before America was born. They went to the Sorbonne and walked the high ceilinged halls. The crossed the Pont au Double Bridge to He de la Cite and entered the quiet of Notre Dame. They oohed and awed at the Chapelle Haute with its expanse of stained glass windows. One early morn they hiked to Montmartre and ascended the long flight of stairs to stand at the rail outside Sacre Coeur. They were in awe of the view of tout de Paris.

Phillip took Joanna shopping on Avenue Montaigne where the shops were elegant and costly. They entered a perfume shop where decanters of golden fragrance lined the walls. In glass cases elaborately decorated containers were holding vari-colored bath salts. The perfumer created a scent for Joanna.

"It is you, dear!" Phillip whispered as he inhaled her scented wrist.

"Hmm, I thought it was a bit heavy, but if you like it then that is what matters," laughed Joanna.

They spent a day at the Louvre and its world of art. "Oh, one could spend a lifetime here and never see it all. It is overwhelming!" Joanna said in a hushed voice after hours of wandering past paintings of renowned masters. "My second visit and worlds to go."

Though both Joanna and Phillip had been in Paris before, it was all new through love's eyes. Images, sensations and memories were burned into their beings never to be forgotten. The French fare savored with French wine in candlelit cafés were followed by nights of exquisite pleasure.

There were evening strolls over bridges with moonlight dancing on the rippling Seine. They sat among sparkling fountains, reflecting pools, stone angels and masses of flowers. This achingly beautiful city of light became a honeymoon dream.

The week before they were to return to America, Phillip took Joanna to the opulent Opera Garnier. The last tour was to the Les Jardin des Tuileries once the playground of prince and princesses.

As they sat in the beauty of the gardens, Joanna wiped a tear from her eye and remarked, "We should return each year for our anniversary. It is our city now."

"Perhaps, we can. Not every year, but maybe every five. It does make me rather proud of my French heritage," smiled Phillip.

"Oh, I like your French, too, darling. To be French makes one a great lover, I have been told."

"You have been told? Hmph, I would assume Madame, that you would know by now!" answered Phillip, arching a brow at her.

"But, dearest, I have no one to compare you to!" smiled Joanna coyly, dimpling.

"Why, you little minx, I have a mind to…"

"Yes, dear?"

"Come, Madame," said Phillip, offering his arm, "it is time to return to our room where I will once again make you aware of my French prowess! In fact, I will throw in a few hot Spanish caresses…we will have a love feast."

"Darling, I am in a state of anticipation…can we walk a bit faster!"

It was late August when Phillip and Joanna returned to America. A stiff wind whipped the trees as their carriage entered the driveway at Queensgate. Joanna peered out the oval window of the barouche taking in all the old familiar sights.

Standing on the portico talking to a groom was Kate. Joanna gave a gasp of joy, "It is Gram, Phillip!"

Kate turned and watched as the carriage pulled up. Her face suddenly bloomed with a smile of recognition. She stood with open arms as Joanna hitched her skirts and climbed the steps. Joanna was soon encircled in the familiar embrace that had meant love and security most of her life.

"Dearest Gram, we are finally here!"

Her grandmother pulled away, her hands cradling Joanna's face. "I have been waiting impatiently. Just look at you, you shine like the sun!"

Phillip stood quietly smiling. Kate turned to him and kissed him on the cheek, "My dear Phillip, welcome to Queensgate!"

"Thank you, Kate. It is really an honor to be here. Joanna has told me so much of her wonderful childhood spent here.

"Come, children, we must let Caroline know you have arrived. She has been most anxious."

Phillip reacted to Queensgate much as Joanna hoped he would. He was impressed with its comfortable, but elegant atmosphere. As they walked down the foyer they saw Caroline standing as stiff as a stuffed owl and with eyes as large. She was predictably dressed in a fashionable gown.

"Good heavens, it is you, Joanna!" Caroline smiled a cordial welcome at Philip and kissed Joanna on the cheek. "My eyes are becoming a bit on the dim side so forgive my rudeness. Until one is practically on top on me I have trouble with recognition."

"Mama, you must see about glasses, it would be a great help," remarked Joanna.

"Possibly in time, I am still vain about having spectacles," she frowned and then continued, "Let us have tea and you will have to tell me about your trip aboard."

"That would be lovely, Mama. It is good to be back although I was very pampered. You would have loved the shopping, the boutiques were unbelievable as was the cuisine."

"Yes," answered Caroline, taking Phillip's arm as they entered they entered the drawing room, "no one can make specialty dishes like the French. Oh, I love the escargots, pate de foie gras and pattes de grenouilles!"

"Forgive an old lady's ignorance, but what are pattes de grenouilles?" asked Kate, who was seated and beginning to prepare to pour.

"Frog's legs, Gram, not particularly one of my favorites," answered Joanna, wrinkling her nose.

"Ah, reminds me, supposedly one of the reasons they call the French 'frogs' as they export so many of them."

"Really, how interesting," remarked Caroline.

"You have a lovely home," said Phillip as he took in the view from a tall window.

"I do love it, especially when we have our autumn. The maples are such a show of color…all red, orange and gold. I hope you can be here to see it."

"A pity we cannot stay, but the snow flies early at home and I want Joanna comfortable and settled in before the harsh winter arrives," answered Phillip.

Joanna felt a flicker of disappointment, but it was quickly replaced by the thought she had a home to decorate and would be very busy.

The following days were filled with reminiscing and discussions of current events. Kate made them comfortable and Caroline oversaw entertaining them. She invited some of the local couples for dinner and they attended the opera.

One evening over a particular lavish dinner, Caroline mentioned Marshall and Winifred. It would seem they were now the élan of society in New York City.

"Marshall is insisting that they visit John in the spring. He wants to become better acquainted and would also like to see the West," trilled Caroline.

Joanna felt every nerve tense and her heart fell to the floor. With a shaking hand she set her goblet down.

Phillip noted her ashen face and immediately leaned over her whispering, "It is nothing to worry about, dearest. You have me and he will never harm you ever! I will kill him first!"

"How dare they?" she sputtered, glaring at her mother.

Turning to Phillip she whispered in a despairing voice, "Oh, Phillip, it will ruin everything!"

"Sweetheart, be reasonable; Winifred is John's daughter. She will not stay long, we all know she despised Locket Springs. Judging from what I gathered about Monsieur Davenport, one dust storm and he will be off. He definitely will not linger long. I, personally will see to that."

Joanna hoped that Phillip was correct, but she shivered with dread. She never wanted to lay eyes on that monstrous man again!

The dawn of the morning of departure was a purple gray and a fine cold drizzle had set in. Joanna felt as bleak as the weather. She wept in her grandmother's arms. To her surprise she wept, also, when she hugged her mother farewell.

"I know I haven't been the mother I should have been," wept Caroline. "I realize it now and should have focused more on the gifts God gave me...you and Elyce. I hope someday I can make it up to you somehow."

"Oh, Mama, just love me and love Phillip," sniffed Joanna. "That is all that is important, the past is gone, but we have tomorrow."

"Be happy," smiled Caroline through her tears.

"God speed your journey," called Kate as they began to pull away from Queensgate.

Once settled in their compartment on the Pullman, Joanna fell into Phillip's arms. "I am looking westward, darling. It is time to go home."

"Yes, I am also. We have much work to do. Setting in will take time and I pray you will not be disillusioned with ranch life, Joanna. I feel putting you in the wilderness is like placing a rare gem on a shelf without a proper setting."

"Phillip, as long as I can spend my life with you, I am properly set! We will have a family shortly and it will all be so perfect," she sighed. "I so want a little boy that looks just like you."

A shadow crossed Phillip's face and he felt a chill around his heart. The thought of Joanna bearing a child made his blood run clod. He could never bear to lose her as he had Leonora.

CHAPTER TWELVE

They were hardly isolated; Snowflake was really a small community. The big house on the hill stood only a few hundred feet from considerable other buildings. The closest was the log house the Smith family lived in and the Clarks were further over the hill in the small house. The bunkhouse lay to the north behind a garden plot. Below the hill and to the far south, horse and cattle barns were adjoined.

Joanna loved her house although it was certainly not on the grand scale as Uncle John's. Actually, it was probably a third of the size. It was comfortable and large enough for guests. It had four bedrooms on the second story and two on the third plus an attic. Hannah and the new hire stayed on the third story.

She and Phillip had been home two months when the place began to take on the appearance of a lived in home. Hannah and Martha had helped her unpack her wedding gifts. The silver and crystal sparkled in her china cabinets. The Spode china gleamed in dining room recesses. The spacious kitchen was Mrs. Smith's pride and joy. Phillip had recently hired a woman in Stirrup Crossing to assist her.

Joanna decorated the drawing room in flocked beige and cream wallpaper which complimented her thick Brussels carpet. Her piano, a gift from Kate, was the curiosity of everyone living on the ranch. The children lovingly ran their hands over the ivory keys and carved panels of mahogany. The piano stool was the center of attention with its fancy turned legs and its claw feet holding crystal balls. The adjustable seat was spun by each child and adult as they took a turn seated on it. Joanna would play in the evenings and quite often a sing along was a treat for all.

Joanna did not touch Phillip's study except to dust as she knew he needed a place all to himself. She did order two leather chairs for comfort and filled the shelves with more books.

One evening as they relaxed before a crackling fire in the drawing room, Joanna curled up in Phillip's lap and gestured around the room. "I asked your mother's opinion about the colors I have used. She helped me with ordering the furniture. She and I looked at the rolls of wall paper you had stored in one of the rooms upstairs. Some were water stained and she absolutely forbade me to use the red flocked paper anywhere. She said it looked as if it belonged in a bordello."

Phillip snorted, "How would my mother know anything about the inside of a bordello?"

"Really, Phillip, women discuss these places among themselves. Wives have a natural curiosity about the houses and the 'ladies of the evening.' For instance, perhaps a doctor attended a 'soiled dove' in one of the bordellos and his wife questioned him about it…"

"If he told her…"

Joanna laughed and shook her head. "Well, I would think he would tell her where he makes calls, you know, in case she needs him."

"Are you suggesting that Mrs. Tuttle asked her husband to describe the bordello?"

"Hmmm, perhaps, like I said…wives feel threatened by these houses."

"Only if the wives close their bedroom doors or their legs to their husbands, darling," replied Phillip, blowing a smoke ring.

"Oh, you!"

Joanna jumped up and Phillip grabbed her arm pulling her down again into his lap. He held her face and kissed her eyes, her nose and then her lips. He whispered against her lips, "You never have to worry about this man wandering; you are all I need and all I can take care of, understood?"

"Yes, dear," answered Joanna as she kissed him back. "I gave the red paper to Mrs. Smith, she was delighted. I will have the upstairs done by the holidays and I believe you will like the color."

"Whatever you want, Joanna. Ah, another thing, we must think about our horses. We should ride in the mornings. The snow level is beginning to drop and it will be in the valleys before long."

"I would like that. Shall we begin tomorrow?"

"Fine, but tonight let us concentrate on the finer points of marriage," smiled Phillip as he began to kiss Joanna deeply.

The helper Phillip had hired for Martha was English, young and had perfect diction. Her name was Maude and her husband had been killed in Colorado in a mine cave in. She had been sitting in the telegraph office when John had entered to send a wire. He saw the poor woman in tears and the station agent explained she was destitute and had had only enough money to make it as far as Stirrup Crossing. She had wired friends to no avail. John approached her to ask if he might help. She said she needed employment and that she could cook or be a nanny. John took her to a hotel and then sent for Phillip.

Maude had proved to be more than accomplished and she taught Joanna many new things. She took over the dairy workings and was delighted to see the grinder windmill. She immediately began to grind wheat for fresh bread. Joanna was a bit stunned; she knew the windmills were used to pump water, but had no idea how versatile they were. The two windmills at Snowflake were used for sawing wood, grinding and cutting feed.

The handsome oak refrigerator became Maude's prize possession with its large chest. She soon had it filled to the brim.

Joanna had learned to use her brand new *Western Star* washing machine and she was a bit smug in showing Maude and Martha how to use it and make washing fluid. She demonstrated how to place the clothes in a tub filled with rain water to soak overnight. In the morning she would fill a wash boiler three fourths full and bring the water to a boil then cut into it one half bar of soap and washing fluid.

Following this she said, "Get some writing materials and I will give you my recipe for the washer fluid."

Martha and Maude sat on a wash bench and wrote as Joanna read the recipe. "Take one pound of potash, found here," she pointed to a large container, "one ounce of salts of tartar and one ounce of ammonia," and then pointed to the shelves where located. "Place the potash into this large crock and pour a gallon of hot water slowly into it. Let this cool and then add the tartar and ammonia. When dissolved, I bottle it. I have one bottle left so you will have enough for two weeks. All right, after adding the washing fluid and the water is boiling…put in your clothes and boil them ten to fifteen minutes. Wring them out, place in the machine and work them ten minutes; take them to the wringer bench, rinse in clear water then wring into blue water, rinse again and hang. It will take you both to do wash day. It takes about three to four hours. Frieda and I frequently did this before I left for school. Oh, do not put over five shirts or three sheets at a time in the machine. Any questions?"

"It certainly beats a wash board for certain…and the time saved!" exclaimed Martha.

"True, but I still use one for my under skirts, waists and cambric drawers," stated Joanna.

"Any unmentionables should not be boiled, then?" Maude asks.

"Well, nothing delicate like silk or lace."

Joanna would have been overwhelmed had it not been for Maude. The English woman had a great sense of organization and soon had the house running smoothly. The upper rooms were hung with paper and Joanna's bedroom was elegant with a solid brass bed with handsome ornamentation. An armoire and dresser added to the ambience. A large bathroom adjoined the master bedroom and Joanna's.

Phillip's walnut suite had been given to him years before by his parents. It was a massive hand carved six foot head board with a four foot carved foot board. It was a marvel; even the sideboards were fancily hand-carved. A matching walnut dresser and armoire completed the set.

The other bedrooms had iron or brass beds, chiffoniers and night stands. Both Joanna's and Phillip's rooms had small fireplaces. In the hallway a Duke Cannon Stove that burned either hard or soft coal heated the rest of the second floor. On the third story a small box stove with cooking lids was used for heating and boiling water for Maude and Hannah.

By the time the snow began to darken the sky, Joanna and Phillip had secured Snowflake for the long winter ahead. The large pantry was filled as were the cellars. Storage sheds and the barns were overflowing with feed and grain. Large hay stacks were covered and weighted with canvas.

Joanna hated the shrieking wind that began accompanying the storms. She then sewed making the shuttle fly to drown out the wind or played the piano. On quieter days she would lose herself in Holmes, Brontë or Dumas. Lady Adelaide had sent Joanna fifteen of Bertha M. Clay's novels and if Joanna wanted a bit of light reading, she would lose herself in one of the popular tear jerking novels. Phillip had an original Edinburgh edition of the Encyclopedia Britannica and Joanna very much enjoyed the maps and illustrations, to say nothing of the knowledge contained within.

John and Phillip had agreed at an earlier time to put in a private line for a telegraph between the two ranches. They had strung lines with pony glass insulators and installed iron and gravity batteries. The Pony Sounder Tubulars were hooked up and steel lever keys mounted on brass. Phillip had shown Joanna the battery jar, the zinc and copper for each battery and the Blue Vitrol. It was too advanced for Joanna, but Phillip insisted she at least learn the Morse Alphabet so she could transmit in an emergency. She did as he wanted, but did not like the upkeep of the batteries nor the telegraph.

"Someday, dear, we will use the line for a long distance battery telephone," he stated, "but for now we will at least have a way to communicate to the outside world."

"Things are moving so fast today it is mind rattling…horseless carriages, electric lamps, and telephones….what next?" Joanna asked, shaking her head.

It was a cold cloudless morning when John's carriage pulled up. The rubber side curtains were drawn and the buggy aprons up so at first glance Joanna spied only her uncle and Buck. Then they were out and helping someone out of the backseat who was covered in fur.

"Frieda," shrieked Joanna and she dashed for a wrap. Throwing open the front door she hurried down the steps. Hugging the three of them, she bubbled, "Come in, come in, it is cold out here!"

Over tea she and Frieda chatted while the men went to the barn to find Phillip. Frieda said that Ella would be home for Christmas and would stay on for the birth of the baby. She also relayed that Annie's baby was growing like a weed, but seemed to be having a hearing problem. Dr. Tuttle had found no outward signs of damage, but said sadly that measles were known to cause sight or hearing problems. Annie and Buck were very saddened, but hoped that the hearing might eventually improve.

Frieda took a big breath and put her teacup down. "Winifred wrote she and Marshall have made plans to come to the Springs in April."

"Oh, Frieda," gasped Joanna, her heart twisting, "I had hoped for all our sakes, she would not come west again."

"Joanna, I do not know what will happen," Frieda answered, her eyes moist with tears. "She despises me so and with a new baby, a half brother or sister, how will she handle this?"

"Shhh, dear, you mustn't think of this now. Spring is months away and Winifred, in all likelihood, will have made other plans by then."

"Ach, I hope you are correct; she has been so malicious. I have never forgotten her insolent reference to me as 'soiled goods' at your grandmother's."

Joanna's eyebrows raised in shock and she asked, "Have you ever disclosed this to Uncle John?"

"No, I wanted to avoid further heartbreak. I knew she was most upset when John married me, but I hoped she would change her opinion of me. I still do."

"Perish the thought! Winnie has always been disturbed, jealous and often irrational. Just remember we are here and will do all we can to help. Philip knows her faults, also. She constantly pestered him…many times riding alone to find him. Thank Heavens, my Phillip is a gentleman and a very moral man," sighed Joanna.

"Gott in Himmel, she was just a child!"

"She was never a child, more a little demon. Everyone made excuses for her because her mother was ill. Uncle John spoiled her horribly and she was beastly to poor Willie. I can make excuses for some of her actions, but never for marrying Marshall Davenport. He is sin on the hoof!" Joanna spat.

With an anguished sigh, Frieda said, "I pray she does not try to come between John and me. He is such a good man and he loves his children."

"You are a brave woman, Frieda, and also a strong person. You must remember you are having Uncle John's baby and he will now have a new family. He may pamper Winnie, but if she hurts you or the babe, I know he will not tolerate it. He loves you and don't you ever doubt it."

Before Frieda could respond they could hear the men laughing and talking as they came into the house.

Maud announced dinner shortly.

Joanna casually mentioned during dinner she would like to have the Christmas holiday at Snowflake.

"It will help Frieda to stay off her feet. Ella will be here and we shall take such good care of you, Frieda," said Joanna, reaching for her hand.

"But John likes to have Christmas dinner for the help and I have always been in the kitchen," retorted Frieda.

"That is exactly why I am suggesting you come here. The help can make dinner for themselves and we can make you stay quiet as the doctor has suggested," countered Joanna.

"It is settled then," boomed Phillip, "John and I can attend to our needs with the stock and bring Frieda the week before Christmas. We will take her back for the remaining weeks before the birthing."

Joanna's lips curved at Phillip and she laughed, "Yes! That will be just what the doctor ordered."

"Ella will be over the moon; she dislikes working in the kitchen," smiled Frieda, "such good friends you are."

"And Uncle John, please bring Willie," said Joanna gently.

"Indeed I will. Joanna, stubborn you are, and always were. I think that is a good thing...eh, Phillip?"

"At times, John. She is a hard one to let go of anything once her mind is made up. Remember what a devil of a time I had convincing her that she should marry me!"

"Love won out, it has a way of overcoming most obstacles," answered John as he smiled at Frieda.

CHAPTER THIRTEEN

Meanwhile in his palatial home in New York, Marshall Davenport was indulging himself to a sensual evening at home. He had been staying at the Racetrack for better than a week. His losses had been high so he was in a nasty mood.

Wearing only a burgundy dressing gown, Marshall was smoking a Havana cigar as he leaned against the headboard of his massive bed. He had just finished a bath of scented oil and perfumed rosewater. He lazily looked over at his wife dressed only in a black silk shift hiked about dimpled knees. Her copper hair was spread about her face as she lay inhaling a panatela. She blew the smoke out in rings as she popped her cheek. The black provocatively set off the milky pallor of her skin. Her full breasts rose and fell under the silk whispering delight.

"Got to give you Holan women credit, you are beauties. You really set off a swell like me," he praised her. "I don't know why I married you, Winifred,, but you do please me mightily at times. Sadly, you have lost a lot of fire and there is only one left among you with real spunk!"

"Oh, to be sure, her Highness Joanna," snarled Winifred sitting up. "You don't know why you married me...can't you now? Because I look like her, you are obsessed with her and because you can't have her...I became your game of prey."

"Hmmm, well, maybe so, maybe not. She is a wildcat to be sure," he said in a husky voice. Just thinking about Joanna made him throb with desire. He grabbed Winnie by the arm and put out her cigarillo.

"Come, dear, do what Daddy likes best!" He pushed her to the floor and opened his dressing gown as he sat on the edge of the bed.

Winifred sat a bit stunned, her eyes filling with tears.

"Well, are you going to pleasure me or shall I get my riding crop?"

"No, Marshall, I will do as you ask..." Obediently, Winifred hunched forward on her knees, her hands spreading apart the robe and began to caress him.

"Put me in your mouth, dear," his voice hoarsened in anticipation. As she worked him her shift fell forward revealing her lush breasts with pink succulent nipples. He leaned down and grabbed a breast and then fell back with a shuddering cry, his mustache twitching. He pulled her up beside him, tore the shift off and lapped at each breast. He squeezed hard and made Winifred moan; then he bit her severely.

"Hurts," Winifred whimpered, "please, Marshall."

He leaned over and opened a drawer in his night stand. With a sadistic chuckle he drew out a slim, flexible riding crop. "Come my little filly, you have been a very bad girl, time for your punishment."

With a stifled sob, Winifred rolled onto her stomach. Her buttocks were covered with fading yellow bruises.

"You are too saucy, ma petite. You must be a good wife; you belong to me and must please me. I can do anything I wish with you, do you understand?"

"Yes," sobbed Winifred into a pillow.

Because of Marshall's foul mood he whipped her until his face became flushed and he then screamed explicit and lascivious words. He rolled her over and plunged into her like a rutting bull. When finished he bent his knees and pushed her off the bed with his feet. He snarled, "Go away, I need my rest!"

Winifred grabbed her shift and wrapper and ran to her room. She cried as she refreshed herself in a tepid bath. She reflected on this evening as she had so many others and wished she had never become involved with Marshall. She despised the decadent, pleaded with Marshall to let her return to Queensgate for a visit. He had threatened her and carefully instructed to take her anywhere without his permission. He escorted her to dinners, the opera and to balls always debonair and handsomely dressed. He demanded that she dress in the latest mode. He accompanied her shopping buying her gowns that set off her magnificent hair and the pale milky skin of a true redhead. Her sparkling jewels complimented her outfits, but the sparkle in her eyes was unshed tears.

She was becoming more and more distressed as she realized she had married a very sadistic man on the brink of insanity. She now could understand the grief and torment Elyce endured while married to him. She prayed, in time, she would be able to somehow escape the beatings that were becoming more severe. If she survived until spring, certainly she would find help at Locket Springs. She must use all her wiles to placate Marshall and stay alive until then.

"Oh, Daddy," she sobbed to herself, "how could I have been so foolish? I am doomed, I fear."

CHAPTER FOURTEEN

Joanna studied herself in the mirror. She was wearing a new seven-gore skirt made of lizard cloth. It was black wool with a grey rustle taffeta stripe. It was faced with canvas for stiffening and had a walking train. Her shirtwaist was grey sateen with a white linen collar and the new fashionable "mousquetaire" sleeves. She felt quite elegant after wearing her ranch clothing…plain percale dresses.

It was almost six on Christmas evening; she had been preparing all week with Maude and Hannah for her first entertaining on a holiday.

Uncle John, Frieda and Ella had arrived by sleigh earlier in the week. Frieda had been a sight, bundled in fur from top to bottom with warm bricks to keep her legs and feet warm.

The weather had stayed clear and cold so the snow was crusted and hard; perfect for the sleighs. A grocery sled had followed them filled with provisions and gifts.

Two arms encircled her and she smelled Phillip's shaving lotion. He whispered in her ear, "You look lovely, dearest."

She turned in his arms and saw the adoration in his eyes. "Oh, dear Phillip, you have made me so happy. I, at times, feel guilty that I don't deserve you!"

He kissed her gently. "Marriage becomes you, you grow more precious to me each day." He handed her a velvet jewelry box. "I want you to have an early gift this evening to wear."

Joanna opened the box to reveal an exquisite carved cameo brooch encircled with diamonds and sapphires. "Oh, how very lovely!" she exclaimed as she removed it and pined it at her throat. "You are too good to me, I am becoming quite spoiled."

"Indeed," smiled Phillip, "perhaps this will make up for the Christmas pumps that I gave you so long ago."

Joanna blushed, "I was so young and full of myself. I shudder when I think I almost lost you."

"I think you needed love to grow, but it almost broke my heart," commented Phillip sadly.

"Oh, my sweet darling, I promise I will never hurt you again," whispered Joanna putting her arms about his neck.

Phillip kissed her deeply then gave her his arm as they went to join their guests. The drawing room glowed in the lamp and firelight. The tree glittered and sparkled with spangles and tinsel; the smell of pine filled the air.

Frieda, in flowing black velvet, was ensconced in an armchair by the fireside. John stood behind her while Willie and Ella were deep in conversation seated on the mohair settee.

Conversation ceased when they entered and Phillip apologized for their lateness. "Time flies by when attending to details," he said.

"Think nothing of it. We were discussing what a pleasant visit this has been," answered Frieda with a smile. "It has been good for John to relax a bit."

"To say nothing of keeping you out of the kitchen!" John laughed.

"True," laughed Frieda, "and I am ample enough without the rich food. Baby will be healthy, that is certain."

Joanna studied Ella after seating herself. Ella was becoming a lovely young lady. Her blonde hair was done in a bouffant roll and worn in the latest fashion. She was wearing the new Henrietta skirt and a handsome Alaster choke collar.

"You look smashing, Ella, Europe agrees with you," complimented Joanna.

"I loved every minute there, but I want to be with Mummy now until the little one comes," dimpled Ella.

"You are making your mother very happy. I know your being here is greatly appreciated." Joanna asked Willie if he were enjoying himself.

He smiled broadly and stammered, "It this is so good. I-I-I like it here and it has been fun!"

"Then you must come to visit us more often, Willie, I miss you!" Joanna answered as she leaned forward and grasped his hand.

"I miss you, t-t-too, Joanna."

Maude announced dinner. The festive table was centered with the new candelabra and springs of pine and holly surrounded it. The crystal and flat wear sparkled in the candlelight. Grace was given and the conversation rose and fell as the dinner courses were served. Following dessert, crackers were pulled and the gifts and riddles contained within enjoyed.

The women withdrew to the drawing room while the men enjoyed cigars and brandy. Later they all sang carols around the piano until exhausted and then heartily wished each other a Happy Christmas and retired.

Once in her room Joanna let out an involuntary sigh of relief. She was very pleased that everything had gone well.

"Did you say something, dear?" asked Phillip, leaning against the doorway.

"No, I just sighed, I believe I indulged just a bit more than I should have." Stifling a yawn she smiled. "I am not so tired that I cannot join you, though!"

He smiled, "That is a wise decision and I will kiss you awake…just for a bit."

Joanna lie in bed and felt the comfort of the house about her. Their home…her refuge and joy! She looked over at her sleeping husband. The morning sun slanted over him. Tousled hair curled over his forehead like a boy's. His face was relaxed and his sensuous mouth soft. High sharp cheekbones fell into hollows of his cheeks. The bedding was twisted around his waist. His gorgeous torso, still tan from outdoor work, was muscled as if carved from marble. She leaned over and barely touched her lips to his.

He opened one eye and smiled lazily. He tugged her down and whispered into her mouth, "You want more, Madame? I thought you were satisfied last eve."

She feather kissed him and murmured, "You are addictive, dearest."

With that he rolled her over and began to pull her gown up.

"It is daylight," she squeaked, "it is naughty. What will the others think?"

Phillip guffawed, "Oh, my precious, do you really believe they know or care? John is probably pleasuring Frieda at this very moment."

Joanna's eyes went wide with shock, "Really…honestly? She is with child."

"Darling, how naive you are! People make love well into the carrying months."

"Oh, I am truly stupid about such things…it is embarrassing!" she pouted prettily.

"Ah, love, you are perfect just as you are. You forget I was married before and I have had doctor's advice."

"You will have to teach me…"

He stifled her as his mouth covered hers.

She writhed for a moment beneath him until his hot hands and warm mouth sent jolts of sensation throughout her body. She began to arch into him and then mindless pleasure poured over them both.

Phillip leaned over her on his elbows. "Now, that is a lovely way to begin the day. We must do it more often as winter can get mighty boring!"

"But it is very naughty. Ladies don't make love in the daylight and do not disrobe at night," she yawned stretching long like a cat. Her magnificent hair spread over her up thrust breasts.

"It is cold," she shivered. The down quilt had slipped off the bed and as she reached for it, Phillip leaned down and kissed a nipple that peeked through her hair. He then hopped over to the fireplace. "Stay under the covers. The fire will be blazing in no time." With that he climbed back in beside her and began to kiss her once again.

Frieda, John and Willie left late morning. Many hugs and kisses saw them on their way. Phillip had chores to attend to and Joanna went to the kitchen to have coffee with Martha and Hannah. It seemed so quiet. She missed Frieda already; she enjoyed and loved her like an older sister.

Joanna opened a letter from Elyce, written late January. Elyce implied they were still overrun with guests and Mother Adelaide was entertaining in her usual lavish style. She also said Timber had gifted her with a diamond brooch for Christmas and had a cape and hood fashioned for her out of sable.

> *I really have no excuse for not venturing out and I must say my cape keeps me cozy warm in the bitter outdoors. Montana certainly feels much colder to me than Wyoming although Timber says the temperatures are much the same. Of course, the further north one goes it becomes colder.*
>
> *Baby Bruce is growing and is absolutely the most beautiful child ever born! Of course some would say we are prejudiced, but I don't think so. My wonderful caring mother-in-law is having the time of her life with her grandson. Oh, Jo, I am so happy.*
>
> *Have you seen the new arrival? I can imagine Uncle John is just so proud.*
>
> *Please write for I have not heard from you in ever so long. Of course, being a newly wed I can understand!*

Joanna knew she must answer the letter while she had a minute or it would be a week before she might have time again.

> *Dearest Elyce,*
>
> *So happy to hear from you and know that all is well with you and the family. We had a nice holiday with Uncle John,*

Frieda and Ella. Willie came also and it was enjoyable. Frieda is such good company, so dear and undemanding.

It is bitter out, but I try to stay occupied. In his spare time Phillip has been teaching me a bit of bookkeeping so I now can help with the registry and brands. I find this very interesting.

Phillip and the hands keep very busy seeing to all the stock. He is so tired at night my heart aches for him. We have about four feet of new snow at ground level and drifts over eight feet. The last fall was day before yesterday. At the beginning of winter I thought it so beautiful, but now that I see how long this winter is lasting and how hard it is on the stock, I pray for an early spring.

Phillip has horses that he must deliver in the later part of May. I miss him already and it is still four months away. Isn't it odd, we live our younger lives without any knowledge of this very special person and then we meet and fall in love and cannot imagine ever not being with them! I do not think I could survive without Phillip!

When he is not dreadfully exhausted we play cards or read in the evening. Phillip ordered a stereoscope from the Sears, Roebuck catalog and it is so entertaining. The slides are of cities of America, picturesque points of Europe and Africa, sporting scenes and the new parks...Yellowstone land, Alaska and Niagara Falls. It is all thrilling, one can almost walk into the pictures they are so realistic to me. Do get one.

We have visited the new baby once since his birth. He looks like Uncle John. He is such a chubby; laughs and coos and simply adores his Mama and Poppa. I have never seen Uncle John so ecstatic; his feet haven't touched the ground since the baby was born. Frieda looks like a Madonna, she simply radiates. To find such happiness after all the heartache they both have endured is close to miraculous. I must close..I promise to be more diligent in writing.

Ever your devoted sister,
Joanna

A second letter followed in a month.

> *Dearest Elyce,*
>
> *I love my house; it is cozy and comfortable. I enjoy going for runs in the sleigh with Phillip when we have clear days. One day we saw two wolves running along the timber line. One was grey and the other a solid black. They were magnificent animals. Phillip said that he would do nothing to them if they kept their distance and did not bother the stock. He said one kill and he and the men would go on a hunting party. Then, El, one late evening I awoke to the sound of howling. I quietly went to the window and peered out. There sitting on their haunches with moonlight pouring over them were the same pair of wolves. The dogs began a real chorus and I watched until the two of them ran off into the night. It was eerie and chilling. It is amazing what is "out there!" Do you have wolves?*
> *I wish I were closer to play and hold little Bruce. What a joy he must be for all of you.*
> *We paid a visit to Annie (long overdue). Little Benjamin is an adorable child; unfortunately, he is deaf and this has been devastating to both Annie and Buck. It is a hardship for Annie as she must be so vigilant. Uncle John spoke to Buck of a school for the deaf in Denver and said he would look into all the particulars for them. I have ordered books for Annie so she can learn to do sign (language). She is such a dear person and has such patience with Benjamin.*
> *I must close and get busy.*
>
> *Good Health and many blessings,*
> *Your devoted Jo*

The next few weeks remained bitter cold then one morning a Chinook wind began blowing and by evening the eaves were dripping. The next morning much of the frost had melted from the window panes and Joanna was ecstatic; spring was on its way. Within the next two weeks the snow had all disappeared from the lower valleys. The ponds were brimming with water from mountain run off. Planks were laid around the ranch to walk on as the mud was ankle deep.

Soon the soft green of new grass began appearing in the meadows. Wild geese began flying overhead signaling their return. Joanna loved to listen to the honking calls drifting down. In the early morning the chirping of birds began and all about the ranch there was signs and sounds of spring. Soft rains fell intermitted with days of warm sunshine.

One bright moonlight night Phillip asked Joanna to don a riding habit. "I have something astounding I must show you."

"Really, darling, at night?" questioned Joanna.

"Trust me, you will never see anything quite like this again," Phillip answered with a smile.

She dressed quickly, shaking with excitement. His eyes were twinkling with impatience.

"I am hurrying, Phillip," she said, opening a drawer. "Oh, where are my gloves?"

"Put on mittens, they will do as well."

As they ran to the barn Joanna was amazed to find the horses saddled and waiting. They rode into the night and she inhaled deeply of the fresh fragrance of spring. There was still a chill in the air, but it was exhilarating. The land was silvered in moonlight, every detail outlined in velvet shadow. Phillip headed Pegasus down to the valley flats.

"What a breathtaking night, Phillip," Joanna said. "One could almost expect to see fairies dancing in such bright moonlight!"

"I suspect there just might be a few," laughed Phillip. "There is a mesa just ahead. Before we top it we will dismount and on foot climb to the top. You will see dancing as you have never seen before…but we must be quiet."

"Oh, is it Indians, will this be dangerous?" Joanna whispered, a bit apprehensive.

"No, not at all. I would never put you in harms way, darling. Just trust me."

"Oh, I do, but I am so curious."

They rode in silence to the bottom of the mesa and dismounted. Phillip tethered the horses and put a finger to his lips for silence. They climbed the short distance to the top. Phillip then held Joanna in front of him and whispered, "Ahh, they are here." He handed binoculars to her and pointed. At first glance she saw nothing, but a small herd of bison then to her utter astonishment she saw some bulls jumping stiff legged into the air! They seemed as if on springs. Making a slow sweep with the glasses she was further mystified to see a herd of antelope with many jumping in a like pattern. The animals backs were arched and all four legs stiff with hooves pointing downward.

"It is astounding, Phillip; whatever is wrong with them? I have never witnessed such a sight!"

"It is called 'totting' or 'pronking.' They are doing it tonight to play in the moonlight. If they feel especially threatened they will do it in the daytime. I have seen deer also do it."

They watched this unusual sight for sometime. Joanna began to shiver and Phillip motioned her down to the horses. Once mounted, he told her, "It is a fairly common sight in the spring and summer when the moon is full."

"That must be what they mean by moon madness," laughed Joanna. "The wonders of nature never cease. I know you like to hunt. It supplies us with meat, but when I think of the hunters that come to Uncle John's hunting lodge just for the sport, it makes me ill. If they continue these large hunts they will wipe out the remaining bison and other animals."

"Yes, I agree. The men who head hunt and leave the land strewn with rotting carcasses are despicable. They will likely decimate the small herds that are left."

"God must surely shake his head in disgust at such waste and cruelty," sighed Joanna. "Those dancing creatures tonight were a sight to behold. Thank you for taking me. How did you know they would be there?"

"I prayed they would be. I have watched them evenings in the past. Fortune smiled on us tonight. I couldn't really explain it to you so I had to have you witness it firsthand."

"What an intriguing land. Nature and all her mysteries teach us so much."

On their return they tended to the horses and began walking with arms about each other to the house. Joanna leaned her head on Phillip's shoulder. Imagine, a man considerate enough to steal her away to watch antelope play! Poor Mama...she missed so much cinched in her silk and satin. Joanna knew she could never again fit into her former eastern life.

The moon hung luminous and lower to the mountains since their return. Joanna looked up at Phillip and he smiled down at her. "Let's go pronk," he wickedly said.

CHAPTER FIFTEEN

April's sunshine was golden and spring came in all its glory. Wild violets began carpeting the grassland and wild roses were beginning to bud. Joanna potted geraniums in the windows. Phillip and the help were getting the harrows and plows ready to work the land. They would sow wheat and oats. Alfalfa was beginning to sprout by the end of the month. The first week in May the trees began to blossom in the small orchard.

One morning as Phillip and the grooms were working the horses to be sold the dogs began to announce someone's arrival. Joanna had been intent on watching Phillip through the cedar post fence. She hitched her skirts and began to run to the house.

A buggy had pulled into the driveway; it was Frieda and John. John waved and smiled as he hopped down from the buggy. Frieda sat very stiff and silent until John helped her down.

Joanna hugged them both and they entered the house.

John excused himself as he had some business to discuss. Joanna asked Hannah to bring tea. Frieda was muttering to herself as she sat down. "I just don't know if I can handle all this chaos."

"Whatever is wrong, Frieda? I know Winifred and Marshall are at the 'Springs', but I had hoped it would be a good time for all."

"When they arrived I was shocked and saddened to see how poorly Winifred looked. She told her father she was being treated for a disorder and was taking Laudlum for the pain."

"My heavens, it is an opiate!" Joanna said with dismay. "Why would she be on a narcotic such as opium?"

"That was my first thought, also. That man is such a weird person, Joanna. I think she has had the spirit whipped out of her."

"May God have mercy on her if this is true, but, surely, she would have said something to Uncle John?"

"He questioned her and she told him Marshall was a devoted husband."

"Never!" snorted Joanna. "That demon will never change. Sometimes I wonder at men. Uncle John knew the condition Elyce was in when Marshall left her."

"Granted, but Winifred eloped and he cannot interfere unless Winifred will agree to it."

"Winifred had such spunk and fire. I am indeed sorry she is ill, but I will not come to see her as long as that man is with her." Joanna poured tea and sipped it quietly. She was concerned over Frieda's agitation. "Frieda, has he bothered you in any way?"

"Not in a way that I can complain over. He stares sometimes so boldly at Ella it upsets me."

"Never let her be alone with him at any time. He is not to be trusted. I know from past experience that he lusts over any innocent."

"Annie is with her and the baby today. He supposedly is out riding. He seems to enjoy early morning rides by himself."

"I wish a lion would get him. Oh my, I shouldn't have said that, but I do despise him," said Joanna, making a move. "Excuse me for a moment; I want to see to dinner. I am certain my girls are already busy preparing it, but I want to make certain."

Meanwhile on a ridge overlooking the ranch Marshall Davenport watched the house with a pair of binoculars. His eyes squinted against the morning sun and he pulled the brim of his Stetson low over his eyes. He sat on his horse absorbed in thought. He had watched Joanna as she ran to the buggy to greet John. She was still lovely. Her magnificent hair cascaded like a fire fall down her back. Her heart shaped face was animated as she reached to hug Frieda and John. He caught a glimpse of her violet eyes before she turned away. When he first met Winifred he was astounded at the strong resemblance she had to Joanna. He had been drawn to her immediately and had possessed her as he had never been able to do Joanna. Winifred was so disgusting now; looks like a skeleton and so wasted. Poor spoiled child without a brain in her head. Ah, well, she would be an heiress to a fortune. There was Wilfred, no worry there, but that baby, John! The child could fall prey to a terrible mishap with his mother in the future; he would see to that! How Winifred loved her laudanum! What a brainchild it had been to procure a Chinese girl from a close friend as a personal maid for Winifred. As per Marshall's instructions, Mei Ling began giving Winifred laudanum as a sleeping aid. That had worked perfectly and she was now so hooked she would do anything to have it. He knew eventually he had to bring her to see her father or John would have come to her.

Frieda had been a little suspect of something at first, but he played the caring husband at all times. Frieda was a good looking woman, but pale as moonlight, like Elyce. Ella was a pretty thing, but he would take care of her later. He wanted Joanna who was full of fire. She had radiated like a brilliant sunset until that stupid maid had interfered. His crotch began to pulsate thinking of her. Lewd images began to flash through his head. *By damn, I will have her somehow. Her husband leaves soon so I can make plans then.* With a zest and eagerness he had not felt since arrival he turned his horse and loped towards Locket Springs. He made plans as he rode of his conquest of Joanna De La Cruz...she owed him!

The last week of May, Phillip told Joanna the news that he would be leaving soon. She knew the drive was one that had to be made, but her heart sank.

"I asked John if Willie could be here with you while I am away. He will be coming tomorrow."

"How thoughtful of you, Phillip, I will enjoy being his being here," answered Joanna.

"I thought of Annie, but it is too busy at the Springs for her to be gone now."

"I will do just fine, dear. It isn't as if I am alone here. It is like a small community, actually. It is you I worry about. You will wire Uncle John the minute you get there, promise?"

"Of course, darling. Someday in the near future a railroad spur will be built to Smokecreek and then I can ship the horses by rail."

All too soon the dreaded day arrived and Phillip bade farewell to Joanna. He emerged from the house and walked to the white gelding that Ramon had saddled for him. He turned his horse to where Joanna was standing and leaned over to her and softly said, "You are my life, mi corazon. Be with me in thought and be waiting here for me on my return."

"Dearest one, be careful. Come home safely to me," Joanna answered as she stood on tip toe and kissed him. He rode to his waiting men and the horses. Joanna watched tearfully until they rode out of sight then turned and ran into the house.

That afternoon Willie listened attentively as Joanna instructed him about Pegasus and Venus. "You are a hard worker while at the Springs, but here I want you only to groom these two animals. Pegasus can be exercised on a lead in the large corral. When I ride Venus you can ride Barnum with me. Someday soon I will have Maude pack us a lunch and we will ride to Table Top."

"Okay, Jo. I forgot, is t-t-that far?"

"Not really, about an hour's ride and it is beautiful. You must have been up there at one time or another. It is in the high country and there is a broad shelf that overlooks the valley. It has a wonderful view of the far mountains, in fact; you will be able to see part of the Springs. I caution you to keep away from the ledge, there is a sheer drop hundreds of feet straight down. Phillip and I picnic up there; it is one of our favorite places. Would you like to go one day?"

"Deed I do! H-h-how soon?"

"We will do it before Phillip's return. I am so happy you are here, Willie. I miss Phillip dreadfully!"

"Y-y-you could g-g-go see Winnie if you are lonesome," responded Willie.

"Ah, well, that may be a nice thought, but she and I were never comfortable with each other so I believe I shall keep busy here. Mind you, you are welcome to visit her whenever you wish, dear," Joanna responded with a sad smile.

"Naw, I-I-I am in her way and M-M-Marshall despises me."

"What makes you think that?" Joanna questioned.

"When h-h-he came, Papa introduced me and M-M-Marshall would not s-s-shake m-m-my hand. Winnie hugged me, though!"

"I am glad she did that. Mr. Davenport does not have a nice attitude, Willie, so don't you fret," responded Joanna with a slight frown. "Come, let's go into the kitchen and find something delicious to eat!"

With each passing day Joanna grew more restless. She had never missed anyone as she did Phillip. Nevertheless, she kept her feelings to herself and worked with determination. She helped in the garden, churned butter, mended and applied herself to her needlework. She could not concentrate on reading and she found her knitting frustrating. She had to force herself to eat as she had lost her appetite when Phillip had gone. She and Willie rode often in the mornings which brought her joy. The beauty of the area always amazed and comforted her. Willie was fascinated with rocks and would often dismount to pick up unusual pieces of quartz; on occasion he would find obsidian or flint that had been pieces of arrowheads. He was still a child at heart whooping with glee at capturing a horned toad lizard or a gopher to take back to the ranch. Many times they found whole arrowheads. Joanna marveled at their beauty and would turn them over in her palm and wonder what warrior had used them and who had made them.

Phillip's absence gave Joanna the opportunity to visit Annie when she was not working at the Springs.

One morning Joanna packed pies and homemade bread and then had Willie drive her to Annie's. It was a heartwarming diversion of exchanging confidences and hospitality over coffee. Joanna adored little Benjamin who happily entertained himself.

"Have you been visited by the Davenports? I sometimes see them riding at a distance. I cringe, but he never comes this far over," asked Annie.

"No, and I pray I won't ever have to come face to face with that beast again. Winifred never liked me so I feel confident they will not visit Snowflake," answered Joanna grimly.

Mid-afternoon Joanna kissed Annie and Benjamin warmly good bye and departed for Snowflake.

Marshall Davenport watched through his binoculars as the buggy rolled way from Annie's. Joanna's sailor shaded her face until a strong gust of wind carried it to the back of her neck where it hung by streamers. Her lovely face was animated as she reached back for the hat. She turned towards him as she secured it back on her head and Marshall felt the impulse to wave, but knew she could not see him.

My dear Joanna, it will not be long before I make a visit. While the cat's away the birds will play and I have a week before the cat will return. He chuckled as he put away the glasses.

Joanna was experiencing strange mood swings and she felt queasy at the smell of food. *Maybe I am in the family way...oh, perish the thought....but then, I might be. Let me think, how long has it been?* She began counting and her eyes became very wide. *Hmmm, I must take closer note and watch for other symptoms!*

Marshall Davenport walked slowly deep in thought, disgruntled and bored beyond belief. He missed the city, the excitement and his social set. The mountains and stillness made him restless. He was sick of listening to Winifred babble, weary of pretending to be her concerned devoted husband. The only thing that gave him pleasure was thinking about Joanna and how ripe a beauty she was. He decided to ride to Snowflake on the morrow; he would pretend he was delivering a telegram from her husband. If he got lucky she might take pity on him, Winifred being sick and all. With her husband gone he could give her a tryst she would never forget. Ah, yes, tomorrow would be perfect. John and Frieda were going to Stirrup Cup. Grinning at his own cleverness he rubbed his crotch enjoying the sensation and the thought of putting his member inside Joanna. He strode back to the house, his demented mind in a state of high excitement.

The next morning Marshall mounted his horse. He was tall and straight in the saddle, wearing a riding jacket, new boots and breeches. He wore a confident smile. The groom stood attentively. Marshall waved nonchalantly as he nudged the horse into a canter and rode off. The eastern sky was a mass of flame.

Meanwhile at Snowflake Joanna had awakened and uttered a contented sigh. She stretched long like a cat. Her thoughts were of Phillip who was due home in just a couple of days. She must get up and get dressed. She had promised Willie a picnic and he would probably be waiting anxiously with the horses.

She hurriedly bathed, washed and dressed her hair. She donned a riding habit and went to the kitchen. Maud set before her oatmeal, biscuits and coffee. She fidgeted nervously in her chair; she looked at the oatmeal and felt ill.

"Maud, I am too nervous to eat; it is the excitement of knowing Phillip will be here just any day now," she said and pushed her chair away from the table.

She grabbed the picnic basket that had been prepared and then her hat and jacket. As she had surmised Willie was waiting anxiously at the barn with horses saddled and waiting.

"Good morning Willie, I apologize for my tardiness. It looks to be a perfect day," Joanna said as she hurried to the tethered horses. She handed the basket to Willie and mounted her horse.

With a giggle, Willie said, "I am s-s-so happy to be g-g-going to the mountain I would have waited all day."

The sun was warm and golden and dew sparkled like diamonds in the meadows. Joanna felt her restlessness fade as they rode toward the foothills. She loved the solitude of the morning broken only by the creaking of saddles and hoofbeats.

They began to climb and saw the hint of blue, pink and white as wild flowers were beginning to bud. Some Indian paintbrushes were nodding in the breeze.

"Ah...my very favorite wildflower," Joanna remarked upon seeing them.

"I-I-I like the wood violets," stammered Willy looking about for a glimpse of one.

"It is just a bit early. About the second week of June they will be a carpet of blue," was her answer as she inhaled deeply of the pure air. "I found my heart in this country and I know this is my home...so magical and wonderful."

"T-t-this is my home, too," answered Willy happily. "It feels good in here," and he placed a hand over his heart. Joanna nodded and smiled.

Their docile and obedient mounts continued the along the mountain trail flicking ears now and then at strange sounds. Topping a ridge they looked down on upon a lake. A flock of ducks and two trumpeter swans were sparking the surface with ripples as they swam.

"Bet there is trout and walleye in there, Jo. Look at the watercress in the far stream."

"You must make plans with Phillip to come and fish. I will bring a lunch and read," she said happily, thinking of Phillip's return. Straightening in her saddle she urged her horse on.

They continued to climb and Joanna was lulled into a half dream state. She thought back on her life—what had shaped it, her heredity and environment? But what had been the element, that process within her that had beckoned her so strongly to the west? Was it a primitive throwback to migration or was it God? Man had migrated from the beginning of existence. The westward pioneer movement had caused a magical dream to people—a destination to freedom of a sort—beyond the shimmering horizon...what? Many of the pioneers had been businessmen, artisans, professionals—why did some come and others stay? She knew from study the pioneer movement was like unlike anything before in history. Many died, of thirst, hunger, cold. The Indians killed them, but still they came, fighting elements...dust storms, snowstorms and themselves. The courage, oh yes, it took great courage and those who survived had to make great compromises! They were of every faith, of every state, of every country and every tongue. What a great understanding had to have taken place. Survival meant compromise and adjustment. Men can never think alike; past wars have proven that. Education can open the mind to other's ideas and experiences by the written word...but to experience what has been read becomes the greatest education! Joanna knew her books of the west had begun the dream but borne within her was the force to go. In finding Phillip her dream had come full circle. This land was home—she felt as if she had lived here in some past life. Perhaps a cell of memory had filtered down from a primitive ancestor, one who had walked this land.

"Whoa," Willy's voice stopped her train of thought. The horses halted by a stream at the foot of a cliff.

"We s-s-should let the horses rest," Willy suggested.

"Yes, of course," answered Joanna as she dismounted. She sat on a deadfall log and took in the scenery. Clumps of quaking aspen, hawthorn, spruce and alder were fluttering in the breeze. The air was fresh and cool. A bird swooped toward a bush, then spotting her veered upward and away. The horses were contentedly grazing flicking their tails at an occasional fly.

After a period of time that she felt sufficient for the horses she rose and brushed off her split skirt. Willy helped her mount and they continued their climb.

They spotted tracks of elk as they skirted a canyon wall. Following the well marked trail, Joanna was the first to spy the herd. The elk were slowly moving across a clearing several yards ahead. They halted and watched the herd enter into the timber on the far side. Joanna clicked her horse onward; the wind was toward her so the elk would not pick up their scent. If they did not spook the herd, it would go under brush to rest and wait out the day.

The mountains towered above them, craggy and steep. Snow lay in purple shadowed canyons.

"Oh, my, Willy," exclaimed Joanna, "these are fresh!"

They pulled up, looking at a tree. There were fresh claw tracks of a bear. Phillip had explained on an earlier outing of how a bear marks his territory by standing upright as high as possible and clawing a tree.

"Best to keep moving, Joanna," said Willy, pulling his carbine from his sheath.

The trail followed close by a stream. They took caution, spotted no movement, only an eagle from above. Continuing they wove a precarious trail through the timber and large boulders.

They were almost at their destination…ahead was the large gateway of stone.

Within a few minutes they were riding through the archway and a wondrous sight awaited them. A waterfall sparkled and cascaded from ledges high above. It fell into a basin causing a mist of color in the sun; from it a stream trickled and bubbled. A meadow lay before them circling the top of a large flat ledge. Sheer walls fell into a steep slide hundreds of feet below. The view was breathtaking; the valley below spread out in squares of green and gold. The buildings at Snowflake looked like matchboxes.

On earlier visits she and Phillip had pushed dead logs together under the pines to sit upon. Today she and Willy ground tethered the horses here. Willy emptied the saddlebags of the picnic contents. They munched fried chicken, watercress sandwiches and oatmeal cookies.

"I'm stuffed," said Joanna, cleaning up the refuse. "I will keep my apple for the return home."

Willie wandered over to the stream edge and began scooping up fragments of quartz and sand. "Jo, t-t-there is quartz here. There must be a vein of t-t-this quartz here and some of these pieces have specks of g-g-gold!"

Joanna walked over to the stream and took a piece of the quartz that Willy held out to her. She turned it in her palm. "Phillip told me he that these pieces had broken off years ago and fallen into the pool. He found some tiny flakes and nuggets further down the stream. Rather exciting, isn't it?"

"G-g-golly, I am going to walk the stream. J-just for a short ways," he excitedly said.

"Please do not go far. Have you your revolver?"

"Yep."

"Be careful, Willy," admonished Joanna, "watch your back and listen."

"I will, just holler if you need me!"

Joanna sat on her jacket and unlaced her velvet vest. She leaned back against a log and opened a book. The sun was warm and she tended to doze.

CHAPTER SIXTEEN

Within an hour after Joanna and Willy had departed Snowflake Marshall rode up the lane. Judging the large house on the rise to be the main residence he reined up to the hitching post in front. For a moment he panicked. She would likely slam the door in his face, on the other hand, that might call attention that she might have problem. He knew he was taking a great risk, but he was so damn bored. He had to see her and besides, he had a score to settle! He would stick his foot in the door…yes, then there would not be a problem!

A comely young woman opened the door. "And who might you be, sir?" she asked. Marshall handed Martha his card and bowed.

"Marshall Davenport at your service, ma'am. Is Mrs. De La Cruz at home?" he asked with just a hint of a smile. "I am her cousin by marriage and have an important telegraph for her."

"Oh, my," answered Martha, looking at his card. "Mr. Davenport, you just missed her. Her cousin, Willy and her went riding; they went up to Table Rock."

"Where is this Table Rock, dear lady?" asked Marshall as he eyed Martha's young, ripe body.

"It is a spot in the mountains behind us where we go to picnic. It's not far about an hours ride." She gave him a quick and sincere smile.

That sent a slow tingle through Marshall's body. He eyed her up and down with a discernible leer. She blushed furiously. Too bad, he thought, she would have been amusing under different circumstances. Gallantly, he reached for her hand and put it to his lips. "I will need a fresh horse to carry the message to your mistress. Can you be of help?"

"Oh, indeed I can. Meet me at the red barn and I will have my Daddy get you one. Of course, we have men who could ride and bring the Mrs. down."

"No, my dear, this is too important. I will deliver it in person."

He was soon on his way with a fresh mount. They had given him good directions. He was about an hour behind them. Negotiating the mountain trail was easy. Marshall kept his eyes glued to the imprints of the horses' hooves.

It was early afternoon when he reached the irregular terrain outside the stone arch.

He reined his horse to a halt as he spied Willy bent over in the middle of a stream. He rode to a thicket and quickly dismounted. Creeping quietly with his revolver drawn he bore down on the unsuspecting young man. The gurgling stream drowned out any slight noise he made. With a bound he forcefully hit Willy with the gun. Willy fell face down in the stream with blood staining the water crimson. Marshall waded into the water and leaned over Willy. He nudged him with his foot...waited...nothing. He reached down and with some effort turned the body over. Blood was seeping from Willy's nose and mouth.

"Damn," he said out loud, "I have killed him. I will tend to this later." He backed out of the stream and hiked quietly through the stone arch.

She was lounging against a log dressed in a dark green riding costume. Above the split skirt was a pointed basque with a tightly nipped waist. A bodice lay beside her and she had unbuttoned her jabot leaving her sheer cotton guimpe showing. Her bosom gleamed like ivory through the fabric. The sun shining through the trees made an aurora of her fiery hair. She was intent on her book smiling over something she was reading.

Marshall stood transfixed. She was so very lovely he had to have her. He began edging toward her quietly. He stopped when he saw the carbine beside her, then slipped behind a tree. "Now," he said to himself, "Don't hurry this. Have to get the gun, no sense in getting my brains blown away over a woman!" If she didn't submit to him, he would kill her without hesitation. After all, her Irish maid had almost killed him! But first, the gun! Stealthily he crept closer, his heart began to pound. Now!! He rushed her, kicked the rifle away and grabbed it.

"You!" she snarled, then screamed, "Oh, God, no!"

Her eyes went wide with shock. She grabbed for her bodice jacket.

He snapped the rifle. "No, Joanna, not this time!"

Joanna closed her eyes and tears welled on her lashes. Willy...he would come, she must remain calm.

As if reading her thoughts, he said, "Willy can't help you. He's dead...purely accidental."

"You crazed beast, not poor Willy!" She shrieked and struggled to stand.

"Shut up! There is no one to help you. You are going to pleasure me this time until I get my fill of you. Do you understand?"

Joanna's face was crimsoned with anger and shame, her eyes narrowed with hate.

"Now my dear, begin by taking your clothes off…everything," he ordered, his mustache twitching.

"I would rather die!" she snarled.

He back handed her hard and she fell to the ground. Blood ebbed from a split lip.

"I meant what I said, if you don't obey me…you die!" he growled pointing his revolver at her head.

Joanna knew he would kill her, if she acted carefully perhaps she could find a rock, something to stop him.

Very slowly she unlaced her basque, unbuttoned her skirt and eased it over her hips. Then, her eyes filling with tears, her head bowed, she pulled the jabot and guimpe off. He gestured for her to stand. She stood tall in her French drawers, woolen stocking and boots. She was shivering from fear and cold, the awareness of what was coming made her teeth chatter. She crossed her arms trying to hide her nipples; purpled and puckered from the cold wind.

"The rest, love," said Marshall as he lustily licked his lips. She began to unbutton her boots, her lips moving in silent prayer to save her from this crazed devil. She trembled so hard that she shook. She pulled her garters and stockings down. Marshall grabbed her and pushed her down, his eyes glazed with lust. He ripped off her drawers and opened his breeches. Closing her eyes, her body rigid, she felt her ravisher cover her; his male member prodding her thigh. She gave a whimper of revulsion and despair.

He pushed the gun against her throat. "We are just beginning, sweetheart, so relax and open those legs!"

Suddenly there came a snarling, whirling red dervish thing that smashed into Marshall, clawing and tearing. It rolled with Marshall on the ground. Marshall managed to stand and kicked at the red creature.

Joanna uttered a cry of horror as she recognized Willy who was covered in blood. Marshall began stomping Willie; Joanna crouched and flung herself forward butting Marshall in the abdomen and sending him sprawling. He picked himself up and came at Joanna grabbing her by the throat. She tried to break his grasp, but began to lose consciousness.

Willy jumped on Marshall's back and gouged his eyes. Howling like a mad dog, Marshall dropped Joanna and ran in a crouch circling closer and closer to the edge of the crumbling cliff. He continued to try to shake Willy off, but lost his footing and both went over the ledge.

Joanna became aware of someone screaming. The screams were harsh and guttural. She pulled herself to a sitting position.

"My God, it is me!"she said aloud. "Stop, stop!" Then began sobbing uncontrollably. She realized she must get home.

"I must go for help," she repeated over and over. Trembling still she dressed herself hurriedly, blinded by tears. She went to the horses, tied the reins of Willy's horse to her saddle, mounted and left Table Rock. Coming down the trail she saw the horse Marshall had ridden and untethered it.

The horse followed as she had hoped it would. She shook from nerves and cold and by the time she reached Snowflake she was babbling incoherently.

Martha and Maud bathed her and sent for Dr. Tuttle and the Sheriff.

Two days later an exhausted Phillip returned. When told of Joanna's ordeal and salvation Phillip wept. The doctor had kept her sedated because of shock. The doctor and Phillip discussed her condition at length. Phillip was assured she would be her old self in a few days, especially now that he was back.

"She is a strong girl both emotionally and physically and will be up and about soon. Bring her in to see me in a couple of weeks," were the good doctor's parting words.

Buck and hands from both ranches located the bodies of the two men. They brought them out in canvas bags on pack saddle. A weeping John Holan took his son home for the last time.

Phillip stayed at Joanna's side day and night. One evening Joanna awakened to find her beloved husband beside the bed with his head on folded arms asleep.

"Phillip," she whispered, "Is it really you?" She weakly put a hand on his arm, afraid she was dreaming.

He immediately awoke. "Darling," he said, his face radiant with joy. "It is I, just rest and let me talk."

"I thought I was dreaming, but I am so happy I'm not," she whispered, touching his dear face. "Oh Phillip, it was so horrible! Did they save Willy?"

He sat on the edge of the bed and cradled her in his arms. "No, dearest, he died as he lived, a warrior."

"He gave his life for me," she wept against his heart. "Dear Willy, it is all my fault. I should never have gone up there."

"Shhh, it is over. Willy is in a far better place; he is whole and happy," soothed Phillip.

"I sincerely hope so. If there are angels, he is one of them," she tearfully replied.

Phillip encouraged her to eat the tea and toast that Martha brought. When she had finished he put a shawl around her and lifted her into a rocker facing the fireplace. The fire crackled and danced and Phillip knelt beside her. Taking her hand in his he told her quietly that Dr. Tuttle had confirmed she was going to have his child.

A look of awe transfixed her face and tears once again welled in her eyes.

"That is why I have been acting so strangely; all those sick spells and no appetite. Oh, Phillip dearest, is it pleasing to you?" she asked, her violet eyes misting.

"Absolutely," he laughed, "I feel so blessed."

With a wondrous smile he kissed her ever so gently.

EPILOGUE

Long fingers of rose and gold gently stroked the amethyst sky with color. Joanna clasped her arms in awe as she watched the sunrise. She always felt heaven near at the dawning or ending of a day. One could not watch the Heavenly Artist without being inspired. She turned from the window and was careful not to awaken Philip's slumber, although she knew little Will's crying would soon waken the household. She put on her wrapper and once again stood at the window gazing at the beauty of the rose tipped mountains.

Joanna had never known such peace and contentment. She often wept with joy at the beauty of her baby and loved to hear him cooing and chortling. The wondrous sight of Phillip cradling their child in the rocker; his smiling face looking down into a small miniature of him made her heart turn over.

She thought back on the past year and its many changes. Everyone had been amazed and gratified at the change in Winifred after Marshall's death. She had become infinitely older and wiser after recovering her health. At Uncle John's insistence she went with Caroline and Ella to Europe. Ella returned to school and Caroline and Winifred shared an apartment in Paris. Winnie was studying art and was becoming quite accomplished.

Uncle John and Frieda were happily expecting another child.

Don Carlos and Mercedes were arriving for an extended stay to get acquainted with their new grandchild. High time as Will would soon be six months old!

Lady Adelaide, Elyce, and Timber had spent a month at Snowflake. Bruce was a beautiful little blue eyed boy. Timber was selling their ranch and moving the family to San Francisco. Elyce loved the Bay and the fast growing city. Lady Adelaide was *thrilled beyond words*, as she put it, to be able to once again entertain in a grand style.

As for Joanna all the jewels and fancy clothes and mansions could never compare to the riches she now possessed. Her handsome, caring husband and her beautiful child was truly a gift from heaven.

She thanked God and the blessed winged child...her baby's namesake, Willie. Tears glistened in her eyes as she whispered a prayer of thanks to him as she so often did for saving her life. She also knew he heard her.